HAPPY FAMILIES

CARLOS FUENTES, Mexico's leading novelist, was born in Panama City in 1928 and educated in Mexico, the United States, Geneva, and various cities in South America. He has been his country's ambassador to France and is the author of more than ten novels, including *The Eagle's Throne*, *The Death of Artemio Cruz*, *Terra Nostra*, *The Old Gringo*, *The Years with Laura Diaz*, *Diana: The Goddess Who Hunts Alone*, and *Inez*. His nonfiction includes *The Crystal Frontier* and *This I Believe: An A to Z of a Life*. He has received many awards for his accomplishments, among them the Mexican National Award for Literature in 1984, the Cervantes Prize in 1987, and the Légion d'Honneur in 1992.

EDITH GROSSMAN, the winner of a number of translating awards, most notably the 2006 PEN Ralph Manheim Medal, is the distinguished translator of works by major Spanish-language authors, including Gabriel García Márquez, Mario Vargas Llosa, Mayra Montero, and Álvaro Mutis, as well as Carlos Fuentes. Her translation of Miguel de Cervantes's *Don Quixote* was published to great acclaim in 2003.

BY THE SAME AUTHOR

Aura
The Buried Mirror
Burnt Water
The Campaign
A Change of Skin
Christopher Unborn
Constancia and Other Stories for Virgins
The Crystal Frontier
The Death of Artemio Cruz
Diana: The Goddess Who Hunts Alone
Distant Relations
The Eagle's Throne
The Good Conscience
The Hydra Head
Inez
Myself with Others
A New Time for Mexico
The Old Gringo
The Orange Tree
Terra Nostra
This I Believe: An A to Z of a Life
Where the Air Is Clear
The Years with Laura Diaz

HAPPY FAMILIES

CARLOS FUENTES

TRANSLATED BY
EDITH GROSSMAN

B L O O M S B U R Y
LONDON · BERLIN · NEW YORK

First published in Great Britain 2008
This paperback edition published 2009

This work was originally published in Spanish as *Todas las familias felices* by Alfaguara, Mexico City, Mexico, in 2006.

Bloomsbury Publishing Plc
36 Soho Square
London W1D 3QY

www.bloomsbury.com

Bloomsbury Publishing, London, New York and Berlin

A CIP catalogue record for this book is available from the British Library

ISBN 978 0 7475 9617 2

10 9 8 7 6 5 4 3 2 1

Printed in Great Britain by Clays Ltd, St Ives plc

Happy families are all alike;
every unhappy family is
unhappy in its own way.

LEO TOLSTOY,
Anna Karenina

Contents

HAPPY FAMILIES

A Family Like Any Other

THE FATHER. Pastor Pagán knows how to wink. He's a professional at winking. For him, winking an eye—just one—is a way to be courteous. All the people he deals with conclude their business with a wink. The bank manager when he approves a loan. The teller when he cashes a check. The administrator when he hands it to him. The cashier when he plays the fool and doesn't inspect it. The chief's assistant when he tells him to go to the bank. The porter. The chauffeur. The gardener. The maid. Everybody winks at him. Headlights on cars wink, traffic lights, lightning in the sky, grass in the ground, eagles in the air, not to mention the planes that fly over the house of Pastor Pagán and his family the whole blessed day. The feline purr of the engines is interrupted only by the winking of the traffic on Avenida Revolución. Pastor responds to them with his own wink, moved by the certainty that this is dictated by good manners. Now that he's on a pension, he thinks of himself as a professional winker who never opened both eyes at the same time, and when he did, it was already too late. One wink too many, he thinks in self-recrimination, one wink too many. He didn't retire. He was retired at the age of fifty-two. What could he complain about? Instead of punishing him, they gave him nice compensation. Along with early retirement came the gift of this house, not a great mansion but a decent place to live. A relic of the distant "Aztec" period in Mexico City, when the nationalistic architects of the 1930s decided to build houses that looked like Indian pyramids. In other words, the house tapered between the ground floor and the third floor, which was so narrow it was uninhabitable. But his daughter, Alma, found it ideal for her equally narrow life, devoted to surfing on the Internet and finding in its virtual world a necessary—or sufficient—amount of life so she did not have to leave the house but felt herself part of a vast invisible tribe connected to her, as she was connected to and stimulated by a universe that she thought the only one worthy to take possession of "culture." The ground floor, really the basement, is occupied now by his son, Abel, who rejoined the family at the age of thirty-two after a failed attempt at leading an independent life. He came back proudly in order not to show that he was coming back contrite. Pastor received him without saying a word. As if nothing had happened. But Elvira, Pastor's wife, reclaimed her son with signs of jubilation. No one remarked that Abel, by coming home, was admitting that at his age, the only way he could live was free of charge in the bosom of his family. Like a child. Except that the child accepts his situation with no problems. With joy.

THE MOTHER. Elvira Morales sang boleros. That was where Pastor Pagán met her, in a second-rate club near the Monumento a la Madre, on Avenida Villalongín. From the time she was very young, Elvira sang boleros at home, when she took a bath or helped to clean, and before she went to sleep. Songs were her prayers. They helped her endure the sad life of a daughter without a father and with a grieving mother. Nobody helped her. She made herself on her own, on her own she asked for a job at a club in Rosales, was taken on, liked it, then went to a better neighborhood and began to believe everything she was singing. The bolero isn't good to women. It calls the female a "hypocrite, simply a hypocrite," and adds: "perverse one, you deceived me." Elvira Morales, to give conviction to her songs, took on the guilt in the lyrics, wondered if her fatal sap really poisoned men and if her sex was the ivy of evil. She took the lyrics of boleros very seriously. Which was why she inspired enthusiasm, convinced her audience, and provoked applause night after night in the white spotlights that fortunately obscured the patrons' faces. The public was the dark side of the moon, and Elvira Morales could give herself blindly to the passions she sang about, convinced they were true and that, since in song she was an "adventuress on earth," she would not be one in real life. On the contrary, she let it be known that the price of her love was high, very high, and whoever wanted the honey of her mouth would pay for the sin in diamonds. Elvira Morales could sing melodically about the abjectness of her fate, but offstage she jealously preserved the "springtime of her worth" (it rhymed with "adventuress on earth"). After the show, she never mixed with the audience. She would return to her dressing room, change, and go home, where her unfortunate mother was waiting for her. The patrons' invitations—a drink, a dance, a little love—were turned down, the flowers tossed into the trash, the small gifts returned. And the fact is that Elvira Morales, in every sense, took what she sang seriously. She knew through the bolero the dangers of life: lies, weariness, misery. But the lyrics authorized her to believe, to really believe, that "*true affection, with no lies, no wickedness,*" can be found when "*love is sincere.*"

THE DAUGHTER. Alma Pagán made an effort to find a place in the world. Let no one say she did not try. At eighteen, she realized she could not have a career. There was no time and no money. Secondary school was the most she could hope for, especially if the family's resources (so limited) would go to help her brother, Abel, at the university. Alma was a very attractive girl. Tall, slim, with long legs and a narrow waist, black hair in a helmet cut, a bust ample but not exaggerated, a matte complexion and veiled eyes, a partially open mouth, and a small, nervous nose, Alma seemed made to order for the recent occupation of aide at official ceremonies. Alma dressed just like the other three or six or twelve girls selected for business shows, international conferences, official ceremonies, in a white blouse and navy blue jacket and skirt, dark stockings, and high heels; her function was to stand quietly behind the speaker, refill glasses of water for panels, and never smile, much less disapprove of anything. Expel her emotions and be the perfect mannequin. One day she joined five colleagues at a charity event, and she saw herself as identical to them, all of them exactly the same, all differences erased. They were clones of one another. They had no other destiny but to be identical among themselves without ever being identical to themselves, to resemble one another in immobility and then disappear, retired because of their age, their weight, or a run in a black stocking. This idea horrified Alma Pagán. She quit, and since she was young and pretty, she found a job as a flight attendant on an airline that served the interior of the country. She didn't want to be far from her family and therefore didn't look for work on international flights. Perhaps she guessed her own destiny. That happens. And it also happens that on night flights the male passengers, as soon as the lights were lowered, took advantage of the situation and caressed her legs as she passed, or stared hungrily at her neckline, or simply pinched a buttock as she served drinks and Cokes. The drop that filled her glass—of alcohol, of Coca-Cola—to overflowing was the attack of a fat Yucatecan when she was coming out of the lavatory. He pushed her inside, closed the door, and began to paw at her and call her "good-looking beauty." With a knee to his belly, Alma left the peninsular resident sitting on the toilet, pawing not Alma's breasts but the paunch of his guayabera. Alma did not file a complaint. It was useless. The passenger was always right. They wouldn't do anything to the pigheaded Yucatecan. They would accuse her of being overly familiar with the passengers, and if she weren't fired, she'd be fined. This was why

Alma withdrew from all activity in the world and settled into the top floor of her parents' house with all the audiovisual equipment that from then on would constitute her secure, comfortable, and satisfactory universe. She had saved money and paid for the equipment herself.

THE SON. Abel Pagán did not finish his studies in economics at the Autonomous University of Mexico because he thought he was smarter than his instructors. The boy's agile, curious mind searched for and found the obscure fact that would leave his professors astounded. He spoke with self-assurance of the "harmonies" of Bastiat and the GDP in the Republic of Congo, but if they asked him to locate that country on the map or to make the leap from the forgotten Bastiat to the very well-remembered Adam Smith, Abel was lost. He had learned the superfluous at the expense of the necessary. This made him feel at once superior to his professors and misunderstood by them. He left school and returned home, but his father told him he could stay only if he found work, this house wasn't for slackers, and he, Pastor Pagán, hadn't been lucky enough to go to college. Abel responded that it was true, one bum was enough. His father slapped him, his mother cried, and Abel sailed away on the ship of his dignity. He went out to find a job. He longed for freedom. He wanted to return home in triumph. The prodigal son. He confused freedom with revenge. He applied to the firm where his father worked. The office of Leonardo Barroso. Abel told himself he would show that he, the son, could handle the position that had destroyed his father. "Do I care about Barrosos? Little authoritarian bosses? Tin-hat desk dictators? Let them act tough with me!" He didn't have to wink. They received him with smiles, which he returned. He didn't realize that fangs lie halfway between smiles and grimaces. Big fangs. They took him on without further negotiations. Not even how easy it was perked up his antennae. They needled him, as if they were afraid that Abel was spying for his father, which meant he had to prove he was his father's enemy, and this led him to rail against Pastor Pagán, his weakness and his laziness, his lack of gratitude toward the Barrosos, who had given him work for over twenty years. The son's attitude seemed to please the company. The fact is they gave him a job as assistant floorwalker in one of the firm's stores, where his occupation consisted of walking among possible buyers and impossible sellers, watching them all to make sure that one didn't steal the merchandise and the other didn't take little breaks. Abel was the elegant civilian gendarme of the store. He became bored. He began to long for his university days, the protection of the family, their savings destined for his education. He felt uncomfortable, unappreciated. His own filial insolence, his own love of easy living, his ingratitude, appeared to him like habitual, ungraspable ghosts. He felt that the carpets in the store were clearly wearing out under his useless walking back and forth. He made friends. The best salespeople received commissions and appeared in the weekly celebratory bulletin. Abel Pagán never appeared in the bulletin. His bad reputation spread. "Be more accommodating with people, Abel." "I can't help it, Señor. I've always been rude to stupid people." "Listen, Abel, you saw that Pepe was in the bulletin this week." "How little intelligence you need to succeed." "Why don't you try to get into the bulletin?" "Because I don't care." "Don't be so difficult, kid." "I'm not difficult. I'm just taking on the disgust all of you ought to feel, a bunch of brownnosers." "Why don't you accept things the way they are and try to improve them every day, Abel?" "Because everything is the way it is, and it's not my style." "I wish I understood you, pal." Life was turning into a very long walk between the shoe department and the shirt department. Then the unforeseeable happened.

THE FATHER. Looking back at the past, Pastor Pagán asked himself, Why wasn't I dishonest when I had the chance? Weren't they all thieves? Except me? Why did I have to speak to Señor Barroso himself and tell him that everybody had gotten rich but me, Señor? Why did I settle for the pittance—a check for five thousand dollars—that they gave me as a consolation prize? Why, from that time on, did they stop winking at me? What crime did I commit by talking to the big fish, to the boss? He soon found out. When he presented himself as the only honest employee, he implied that the others were not. For Barroso, this meant he was belittling his fellow workers. A real lack of solidarity. And without internal solidarity, the company didn't work. When he set himself up as the one employee above suspicion, Pastor aroused Barroso's perverse intelligence. As far as the boss was concerned, they were all corruptible. This was the central premise at all levels in Mexico, from the government to the company and from the grocery store to the communal pasture. How could Pastor Pagán presume to be the exception? Barroso the boss must have laughed to himself. Pastor did not commit the crime of asking for a taste, he committed the crime of calling himself honest. He did not understand that it wasn't enough for a powerful man like Leonardo Barroso to give an improper commission to a minor employee. Pastor offered up his naked breast so his boss would try to really corrupt him. Now, forced into retirement with a pension for life, Pastor had time to reflect on the motives that drive each person to destroy others. Sometimes it's necessity, when the enemy is dangerous. Sometimes vanity, when he is stronger than you. Sometimes the simple indifference with which you squash a fly. But on occasion it's also to eliminate the threat of the weak man when the weak man knows a secret that the powerful one wants to keep hidden. Pastor Pagán lived in retirement, shuffling the possibilities of his destiny, which, after all, had already been fulfilled. The truth was they exchanged the whip for the cudgel. When he asked his employer to let him be another militant in the gigantic army of corruption, he committed the crime of accusing others while excusing himself. From that moment on, he was in the hands of the boss, which is to say, power. After that, Pastor would lack moral authority. He would be just another crook. The rule, not the exception he had been before. What would he have gained by not asking his employer for anything? Would he be freer, more respected, still employed? The bitterest day of Pastor Pagán's life was the one on which he realized that whatever he did, and without even knowing it, he was now part of the web of bribery in the small country of his own job. For years he had served corruption, carrying checks back and forth, accepting false accounts, winking, being winked at, morally captured at that photographic moment when a single eye closes in complicity and the other stays open in shame. But he had remained pure until now. He looked at himself in the mirror, searching for a halo, and all he found was a circle of thinning hair. He proposed a martyr's reflection, and the response was gray skin, a face with defeated cheeks, evasive eyes, and nervous eyebrows. He straightened his torso, and his chest caved in.

THE MOTHER. The bolero proposes lovers to us. Some are fatal. They live waiting for their luck to change or for death to come like a blessing. Others are nostalgic: We will live like the wandering bird, longing for love. There are those who are devotion's beggars: The woman he loved took everything and left him alone. There are boleros bursting with passion: They want to drink the honey in the woman's mouth and, in passing, be enthralled by her skin. There are dominating boleros that impose the heat of their passion. Elvira Morales sang all these feelings but kept them in her bosom, which was why she communicated them with so much power. She avoided looking at the people who, night after night, listened to her sing in Aladdin's Cave. She made one fortunate exception. Something magical, mysterious, must have guided her eyes as she sang "Two Souls" and stopped them at the man who looked back at her with eyes different from all the others. Accustomed to denying the correspondence between the words of the boleros and the presence of the men who listened to her, she felt this time that the song and the person magically coincided. "Two souls that God had joined in the world, two souls that loved, that's what you and I were." A tender man: That's what the eyes of the spectator said as he was isolated in the nocturnal darkness of the cabaret by a spot just like the light that emphasized Elvira Morales's moon face and bare round shoulders, and paused at the low neckline of the red sequined dress, leaving everything else in the penumbra of mystery. Why were just two faces illuminated that night, Elvira's and the unknown man's? Who but God, or an archangel on a divine mission, was operating the spotlights that night? The fact is that Elvira, for the first time since she left home and began to sing, felt that a man deserved her voice, understood her lyrics, incarnated her music. This lasted only an instant. When the song was over and the lights went on, Elvira Morales looked in vain for the man she had glimpsed as she sang. Could it have been an illusion, a strange projection of the bolero into reality? No. The place was there, but the seat was empty, and when the table was occupied by a couple who had just come in, she knew that the man who had captured her attention had been there before, and even if he had left, she would still be there, and he would know where to find her. If he really wanted to see her again.

THE DAUGHTER. From the moment she decided to seclude herself on the third floor of her father's house, Alma Pagán had also decided on her new—and permanent—lifestyle. She felt revulsion when she remembered being as cold as a statue at conferences and charity benefits, or when she remembered being pawed, pinched, insulted on the Mexico City–Mexicali or Mexico City–Mérida flights. She didn't blame anyone but herself. Her body was the offender. Good-looking, desirable, corruptible. She alone was responsible for inciting macho lust. She punished herself. She abandoned her flight uniform and adopted the style appropriate to internal exile. Keds, jeans, flip-flops, and sometimes sweatshirts from Indiana University Kokomo. A perpetual baseball cap from the ancient Jaibos of Tampico. Appearance wasn't the important thing, though it was enough just to see her not to desire her. The important thing was that by isolating herself from a hostile, unpleasant world, Alma could enter completely into a world of action and excitement, of vicarious emotion, of endless accident, and all of it without physical consequences for her. The world of the reality show. She bought a subscription to receive periodically the best programs about these real-life situations in which young, vigorous men and women participate in daring adventures, constant competitions, select prizes. . . . Right now, in the middle of the story, Alma follows with almost strabismic attention the beginning of the adventure of a group of four couples who must compete for the first three places in a journey filled with obstacles. The odyssey begins in Ciudad Juárez and ends in Tapachula. That is to say, it starts at the border with the U.S.A. and ends at the border with Guatemala. The contestants have to compete, overcoming deterrents to reach the objective in first, second, or third place. The couple who comes in last is eliminated. The winning couple receives a week on the luxury cruise ship *Sirens of the Sea*. Those in second and third place receive thanks and a DVD on mountain climbing. Now Alma observes the departure of the four couples on the international bridge between El Paso and Ciudad Juárez. It turns out that four of the contestants are gringos and the other four are Mexican. The first gringo couple consists of two young men, Jake and Mike, slim and handsome, as if born for reality stardom. The second is two women, one black (Sophonisbe) and the other white (Sally). On the other hand, the Mexican couples consist of a man and a woman, as if avoiding suspicions of homosexuality. There are two short, skinny young people, Juan and Soledad, and two thin, weather-beaten old people, Jehová and Pepita. The North Americans wear T-shirts and shorts. The young Mexicans are attired like Tarahumara Indians from Chihuahua, that is, with bare legs, embroidered shirts, and red bandanas tied around their heads. The old people are dressed just like Alma Pagán. It shocks her that the most decrepit have appropriated the dress of the youngest. Is there no longer a difference in ages? Perhaps not. But the most interesting thing is that the race from frontier to frontier begins on the one between Mexico and the United States, that is, the contestants run from the border that millions of Mexicans would like to cross to find work in the prosperous north. And they end up on the border between Mexico and Guatemala, that is, the dividing line between two miseries that poor Central Americans sneak across to get to the United States. This paradox is not lost on Alma. It is part of her education. She begins to feel that the reality show is the university she never attended. Vicarious reality. Emotion without a value-added tax. Movement without danger. Alma finds her reality. She no longer has a reason to put herself at risk and go out into the hostile, degrading world. Thanks to the Net, the world was within reach; she felt that now she was becoming part of an instant tribe, connected by virtual Nets, stimulated by the audiovisual universe, and overstimulated by the temptation to make contact with other seafarers like herself. But she still didn't have the courage to chat.

THE SON. Leonardo Barroso was a powerful man because he did not ignore details. His eagle eye swooped down from trading stocks on the Hong Kong exchange to the life story of his humblest employee. Abel Pagán was situated midway between a billion-dollar investment and a porter's salary. Barroso had paid attention to him ever since the young man asked for a job and stupidly announced that he had come to degrade his father. Abel was intentionally sent to walk department-store floors. Just to soften him up and show him who was in charge of the company. Who was "top man." Which was why the call to come to the office of the boss, Don Leonardo, and then the peremptory offer, were so surprising. The son would do what his father had done for twenty-five years. Receive checks from the accounting office, take checks to the bank. Ask no questions. It was a position of trust. Don Leonardo winked: Abel ought to learn to wink. Wink at the bank manager. Wink at the teller. Wink at the driver. Wink at everybody. "They'll all understand, because that's what your father did. You just say: 'My name's Pagán, and Don Leonardo sent me.' They'll all understand. But don't forget to wink. It's the sign of assent. If they don't return the wink, you'd better be suspicious and leave." Abel was torn between satisfaction and doubt. Barroso trusted him. But he was manipulating him, too. More than anything else, he was placing Abel in a sequence of unknown actions in which the son's work was the continuation of the father's. Blindly, the young man decided to try his luck. After all, he had moved up from the counter to management in the wink of an eye. The boss trusted him. They gave him a raise. He rented a very small apartment over a bridal shop on Insurgentes. In no time he was living beyond his salary, given the demands of his status. Broads began to pursue him, and he couldn't receive them in an apartment damaged by earthquakes. He moved to the Hotel Génova in the Rosa district, and his screwing was regular but lacked the pleasure of conquest. Tasty. Girls offered themselves to him insinuatingly (suspicion) and fucked as if obeying orders. Whose? Abel began to be even more suspicious. Expenses increased. So did his work. And, in the end, his frustrations. Abel lived like an automaton. The table was set for him. He didn't have to make any effort. The measure of his ambition was constantly frustrated by the abundance of his success. They called him Don Abel at the hotel. A table was permanently reserved for him at the Bellinghausen restaurant. They gave him a clothing account at Armani. They presented him with a red BMW, "Don Leonardo's orders." The broads, every single one of them, pretended to have torrential orgasms. In the bathroom, he was supplied with cologne, soap, toothpaste, and shampoo without having to ask. They even put pink condoms with little painted elephants on them in his bureau. Faithful to his origins and temperament, Abel felt that he had higher aspirations—call them independence, personal expression, free will, who knows—and that his position at Barroso Brothers didn't completely satisfy them. He also realized that his work was illusory. Without the nod from Barroso, his world would collapse. He owed everything to the boss, nothing to his own efforts. Abel Pagán wasn't a fool. Understanding embittered him. He began to feel an urgent need to prove himself. Not to depend on Barroso. Not to be anybody's servant. Did anyone think that he, the young man, didn't know more than the adults (Barrosos or parents)? Did anyone think he couldn't fill his own position, an independent position in the marketplace? He looked at everything around him—hotel suite, plenty of women, expensive restaurants, luxury cars, Armani clothes—and told himself that he, without anybody's help, deserved all this and had the brains and the guts and the balls to get it on his own. He began to long for a freedom that his job denied him. What did he have that would allow him to enter the job market with autonomy? He counted up his marbles. Very few and pretty faded. All of them said: "Property of L. Barroso." He wanted desperately to assert himself. He let his hair grow and tied it back in a ponytail. He couldn't go any further. He wanted to live a different reality, not his parents'. And he didn't want the reality of his contemporaries, either. It made him sick to his stomach when someone in the office said to him, "You've arrived, Abel," and the more vulgar ones, "Broads, bread, the boss's protection, you fucking have it made, what else could you want, do you want anything else?" Yes, he wanted something else. Then everything began to change. Little by little. That's how it was. Abel had a secure job in an insecure world. He was smart and realized that the company was growing and diversifying production while work was being reduced. The fact was, you could produce more and work less, Abel told himself. He thought about all this and felt protected, privileged. And still he wanted more. Then everything began to change. They canceled his credit card. The little sluts didn't visit him anymore. The office didn't pass him checks anymore. There were no winks anymore. They put him in a dark tiny office without light or air, almost a prophecy of prison. Finally, they fired him. Disconcerted, not to mention stunned, overnight Abel Pagán found himself out on the street. Wasn't this what he had wanted? To be independent, first of his family, then of his boss? Sure, it was just that he wanted to do it on his own terms, not anybody else's. Barroso had given him a destiny and now was snatching it away from him. Abel imagined the boss licking his lips with pleasure. Barroso had humiliated the father; now it was time to humiliate the son. Abel felt like the sacrificial lamb, ready to have his throat cut. Abel asked himself what Barroso was up to. Testing the father's fidelity by testing the son's honesty? Abel looked at his hands, dirtied by more checks than the legs in a colony of spiders. "It's not fair," he murmured. He felt adrift, vulnerable, without direction. He felt dispensable and humiliated. He felt that his efforts had not been compensated. Didn't he deserve, on the merits, a better job because he had more education? Why were things just the opposite? Something was wrong, very wrong. Now what was he going to do? Where would he begin again? What had he done wrong? He screwed up his courage and asked for an appointment with Don Leonardo Barroso. He was turned down. But the boss's secretary handed him an envelope. Inside was a check for five thousand pesos and a phrase in Latin: *Delicta maiorum immeritus lues.* A professor at the university was kind enough to translate it for him. "Even though you are not responsible, you must expiate the sins of your father."

THE FATHER. Pastor Pagán was a good man, and he welcomed the prodigal son with dignity. He was moved by Abel's wounded vanity, and to avoid any hint of anger, he turned a blind but tearless eye when opening his arms to Abel. It was better to proceed as if nothing had happened. Look ahead. Never behind. He realized that the son, like the father, did not have many resources for confronting anything. Abel's return made them equal. The thought worried the father a good deal. Should he ask Abel directly: What's going on? Did not saying anything imply that he could imagine what had happened? Did saying something open the door to a confession in which the past would infect the present forever? Abel gave him the key. A month after his return home, after thirty days of pretending that nothing out of the ordinary had happened because the ordinary was fatal, Abel thought that if he was going to live with his parents and sister forever, the best thing was to say, "The truth is, I wasn't ready for that position." Which was his father's old position. These words of his son's confused the father and hurt him deeply. Pastor Pagán didn't say anything. He took refuge in the ruins of his pride only to confirm that Abel's return meant that neither father nor son controlled his own life. Pastor lacked energy. Abel had no will, either. When the father realized this, he began to bring up topics indirectly to see if he could finally tell his son the truth. One night they got drunk in a cantina out toward La Piedad, and in the heat of the drinks, Pastor thought the ice was breaking—the iceberg that the years had built between father and son—and he dared to sigh: "The goddess success is a whore." To which Abel, for the first time in a long time, responded, "Sure." "To be successful, you need losers. If not, how do you know you did well?" "Sure, for each success you have, it has to go badly for somebody else. It's the way the game is played." "And what happens when first things go badly and you move up and then things go badly and you fall?" "You become a philosopher, my boy." "Or you sing songs in cantinas, Pop." Which, being pretty tight, they proceeded to do. "The one who left." Not a woman. Luck is the one who left. Fortune is the one who got away. They embraced, though they were thinking different thoughts. The father was afraid Abel would sink into rancor and not know how to get out. The son put together alcoholic lists of the mistakes he had made and was still making. "How many mistakes did I make today?" he asked Pastor with a thick tongue. "Whew, don't count mistakes, son, because that's a count that never ends." "What do you regret, Pop?" Pastor answered, laughing: "Not having bought a painting by Frida Kahlo for two thousand pesos when I was young. And you?" "Getting things that I flat out didn't deserve." "Go on, don't get depressed on me. You had everything given to you." "That's the bad thing." "You didn't have to save as a young man just to lose it all with inflation and currency devaluations." "Is that why you sold yourself to Barroso, Pop?" "Don't fuck with me, son, show some respect, I worked a quarter of a century to put a roof over my children's heads and educate them. Don't try to find out how I did it. More respect. More gratitude." "But the only thing I want to know is if he treated you as badly as he did me." "Worse, son, worse." "Tell me about it." "Look, Abel, don't look back, let's look ahead." "The problem is, I'm seeing double." "What?" "I'm seeing you double, as if you were two people." "You're tight." "Who knows. Suddenly, I'm as sober as I ever was." "Go on, finish up your tequila and let's go home. Our girls are waiting for us. They must be worried."

THE MOTHER. Elvira Morales decided not to lose her joy. She proposed a daily celebration of their meeting, thirty-three years ago, in Aladdin's Cave. She was singing. He knew where to find her. She wouldn't go away. And he came back. They married and were happy. Elvira wanted to sum up her existence in this sentence: Let arguments always remain embryonic, their differences hidden, and all the rest resolved romantically by dancing together again at the cabaret whenever there were clouds on the horizon. The cabaret had been the cradle of their love, and in it Elvira felt that the juices of their love were renewed. Pastor Pagán once again became the lover of her dreams. The incarnation of a bolero with no tears or complaints, though certainly filled with sighs, Elvira stopped being a martyr to her husband's destiny. When she felt trapped, she would return to the bolero, and then her marriage reeled. The entire sense of her life consisted in leaving song lyrics behind, nullifying them with a reality in which her portion of happiness was larger than her share of misfortunes, and therefore, when something clouded the happy marriage that was Elvira's sacrament, the altar of her spirit, she would invite her husband to dance, to return to the cabaret, to what were now called "caves," and dance, holding each other very tight, very close, feeling how the sap of illusion began to flow again. When he was younger, Abel would laugh at these nostalgic excursions. "And in its caves let the earth tremble," he would say in a parody of his favorite author, Gonzalo Celorio. But in the end the children were grateful for these ceremonies of renewed fidelity because they brought peace into the home and gave some leeway to questions about the children's position in the world: at home or not at home. Elvira realized that more and more children were remaining at home beyond the age of thirty or returned home at the age of Christ, like her son, Abel, or were prepared to grow old at home, like Alma, locked away in her garret. All of this only reinforced Elvira Morales's conviction: If the children were tightrope walkers in the circus of life, their parents would be the safety net that broke the fall and kept them from crashing to their deaths. Was this the real reason for Elvira's behavior, why she forgave mistakes, why she fed the sacred flame of love with her husband, why she forgot everything dangerous or disagreeable, why she kept secrets so well? Because life isn't a bolero? Because life ought to be a sentimental ballad that soothes, a secret idyll, a pot of flowers that wither if we don't water them? That was why she and her husband would go together to the old bars and dance in cabarets. To remember what isn't forgotten by endlessly identifying happiness. Elvira's aged mother died while her daughter was singing boleros in Aladdin's Cave, on the night she identified Pastor Pagán without knowing that her ailing mama had passed. That's how destiny deals the cards. And destiny is reversible, like a coat that keeps out the cold on one side and protects against the rain on the other. That was why Elvira Morales never said, "But that was then." That was why she always said, "Now. Right now. Right this very minute."

THE DAUGHTER. The two American women (Sophonisbe and Sally) didn't get past Ciudad Juárez. On the first day of the race, they disappeared and then were found dead in a ditch near the Rio Grande. Two residents of El Paso, Texas, had to be called very quickly to satisfy the rules of the competition. No gringo couple had the courage to cross the river. The organizers resigned themselves to recruiting a couple of Mexicans prepared to do anything in order to win a trip to the Caribbean. In their eyes, the palm trees drunk on the sun were already before them, behind them the deserts of huisache cactus and rattlesnakes. The aridity of northern Mexico was part of the test for winning. The competitors in the reality show were receiving written instructions in manila envelopes. Now stop to pick prickly pears or pack serapes. You're free. Choose. What's faster? It doesn't matter. Now they have to cross the desert riding unruly burros. Now they have to take a train up to Zacatecas, and the ones who miss it will have to wait for the next one and fall behind. They have to make up for lost time—how? Getting on a rattletrap bus that drives along a mountain road. The gringos shout with glee on every deadly curve. The Mexicans maintain a stoic silence. They lose it when they have to let themselves be pulled by a team of oxen through a muddy swamp. They survive. The desire to win moves them. Each couple is pursued by the one behind. Each is treading on the tail of the one in front and prefiguring the panting of the one that follows. They have to go into a bullring with a red handkerchief (courtesy of the house) and fight a bull calf disoriented because it ate cornflakes for breakfast. Once again, the two gringos are jubilant as they fight, giving Apache war whoops. The Mexican women abstain. The men—old Jehová, skinny Juan—make passes more worthy than the frightened, confused calf. Now they're traveling through the middle of the country. There are posters, there are colors, there are instructions. Stop here. Sleep wherever you please. Outdoors. On a bench. However you can. The next day everyone has to shovel up the manure on a local cattle farm. They complain, it smells bad. Pepita falls down. She eats shit. A gringo falls down. He eats shit. He declares that this is very sexy. The women caress their breasts as if to confirm that they're still intact. They all get into a bus heading for Oaxaca. Another bus appears, going in the opposite direction. Will they all die? Alma Pagán turns off the television set. She doesn't want to know what happens. She doesn't want the violence to interrupt, perhaps forever, not her second but her authentic life, the existence that offers her, free of charge, with no danger to her person, the reality show. She turns on the set in order to enter into the danger on the street. Though seeing it clearly, the small screen saves her from danger by giving it to her right here, where it doesn't touch her, in her house. She feels alive, stimulated. She no longer knows she is vulnerable. In her way, she has entered paradise.

THE SON. Why did he go back like a miserable pain in the ass, to ask for another job with Barroso? Is this the effect of the moral hangover from the night with his father in the cantina in La Piedad? Did he see his father for the first time? Or did he see himself for the last time? Why did he know more than his parent but not have a secure position in the marketplace? Did mockery defeat him, the irresistible temptation to laugh at his parents? She sang boleros. She thought living contrary to the lyrics was enough to be happy. She hadn't realized she was living in a false world of illusion. She believed in the lyrics. Why had she stopped singing? Didn't she realize that the sacrifice wasn't worth it? She had traded the gold of an independent career for the small change of conjugal life. She was a sentimental slave to the bolero and became the martyr of the family. She never had escaped from the bolero. How ridiculous. She had sung in Aladdin's Cave. Aladdin didn't have a cave. He had a lamp. The one with the cave was Ali Baba. His folks are so ignorant. What a fucked-up life. A school for the children. A home for the old folks. What a choice! Still, there are times when he is overcome by emotion, especially when his vanity is catered to by the perpetual cooing of his mother as she caresses his forehead and describes him, how handsome my boy is you're my boy your broad forehead your black curly hair your silky skin the color of dark mamey your profile like the king of clubs, like a Roman emperor, that's what they say, a nose with no bridge your small but full mouth, that face you make my boy as if defying a world you don't like, that cock-of-the-walk tension in every last inch of your sweet body, you were that way when you were little, you're that way now that you're big, tell me, who admires you more than I do? And his sister gets on his nerves. How easy to lock yourself up with a laptop in a safe imaginary uncontaminated universe with no stardust, no offensive smells. And his father the worst of all, the high priest of deception, a man trapped in lies. And he himself, Abel Pagán, did he still have aspirations? And if he did, would he realize them one day? And where would he "fulfill" himself best? In the shelter of his family, at the age of thirty-two, or unprotected out on the great street, knowing that his vanity, no matter how small, was going to demand more and more effort? With what conviction would he arm himself to leave the no-cost comfort of home and go back out into the world? Was he going to tell himself: Stop brooding, Abel Pagán, the future's here, it's called the present? Or better yet, am I going to accept everything we were and improve it every day? How do you reject the past without negating the future? What would be the cost of his two rebellions, the insurrection against his family and the revolt against his office? Would he be capable of denying reality in order to bring it up to his desire? Could he forget completely what it was that opposed the ideal life of Abel Pagán, fortune's darling? Or should he submit to everything that denied him a happy—that is to say, an autonomous—free life without any obligation to subject himself to the family or the office? He had to choose. Secretly, he wrote desperate phrases in order to obtain some light. We are destroying ourselves to reach the unrealizable. To be a son, it's not enough to be against your parents. To be free, it's not enough to be against your boss. I need to change. I can't separate myself from my life. My family doesn't care about oblivion. They don't care that by midcentury no one will remember them. But I do. I do. What am I doing? Who will remember me? How do I make my mark on the wall?

THE FATHER. It wasn't that the drinks in the cantina went to his head. It was that for the first time, he felt like a friend to his son. They were buddies. Maybe it was that they hadn't had the chance to chat before. It was that they might not have the chance to talk frankly again. It was that the time had come to prepare the balance sheet of one's life, one's history, the time one had lived. We are children of an ill-starred revolution, Pastor had said to his son, who looked at him with uncertainty and suspicion and a kind of distant forgetfulness close to indifference. What revolution? What was his father talking about? The technological revolution? Pastor continues. He thinks we did a lot of things badly because we lost our illusions. The country slipped from our hands, Abel. And so the ties that bound us together were broken. In the long run, it's a question of surviving, that's all. When you have ideals, you don't care if you survive or not. You take the risk. Now there are no more connections. They were broken by forgetting, corruption, deceit, winking. The wink instead of thought, instead of the word, the damn dirty wink, Abel, the sign of complicity for everybody and between everybody and for everything. Look at me and contemplate the sadness of a survivor. I worked very hard to feel like a moral man. Even realizing that in Mexico the only morality is making a fortune without working. Not me, son. I swear, for my whole life, I did nothing but take care of the work they gave me. Cutting through red tape. Negotiating licenses. Lowering fees. Going back and forth with checks, funds, bank deposits. What did I expect in return? A little respect, Abel. Not condescension. Not the wink of a crook. I showed I was a decent man. Courteous to my superiors. Not obsequious. How could I not notice that the thieves, the asskissers, the grabby ones moved up very quickly, and I didn't? I seemed fated to always do the same thing until I retired. It cost me twenty-five years of honesty to reach an instant of lying. Because a five-thousand-dollar concession on a contract isn't a crime, son. It's a weakness. Or charity. In other words, what they call an existential stupidity. Then Barroso found out I had my price, too. I noticed the cynical, knowing gleam in his eyes. I was just like all the rest. I had just taken a little longer to fall. I was no longer his honest, trustworthy employee. I could be bribed. I was like everybody else. What to do with a brand-new thief, hey? In that exchange of glances, I knew that my destiny and my boss's were joined only to put an official seal on a pact of complicity in which he gave the orders and I kept quiet. He didn't have to say, "You disappointed me, Pagán." He knows how to speak with a movement of his eyelids. That's all that moves. Not his eyebrows or his mouth or his hands. He moves his eyelids and condemns you to complicity. I didn't have to do anything to feel that my poor triumph—five thousand dollars in charity—was my great failure, son. A mess of pottage, that's what it was. At that moment I felt obliged to really want what I once said I despised. I was disgusted with myself. I tell you that openly. I also knew I had to hide what had happened. That made me even more ashamed. And I knew that sooner or later I'd pay for my weakness in the face of power. "Don't worry, Pagán," Barroso said in a voice that was metallic and syrupy at the same time. "To be good, it has to be convenient." That wasn't true. I could confront life only because I didn't tolerate cheating. I didn't resign myself to being guilty. That was my mistake. If I wasn't innocent, I'd at least be as perverse as they were. A game of cat and mouse. Except that the cat was a tiger and the mouse a meek little lamb. I didn't have to threaten anybody. I didn't have to say a word. I had to put up with the consequences of actions that I thought were honorable, but they weren't. I didn't understand the value of a wink. I didn't understand the cost of a bribe. But as soon as he realized I was vulnerable, Barroso decided to destroy me so my weakness wouldn't become a danger for him. Each of us—Barroso and I—thought his own thoughts. I understood what was happening to me. Barroso always knew, and that's why he outstripped me. "Look, Pagán. There's a crime called fraudulent management. It consists of carrying out operations prejudicial to the owner's wealth for the benefit of oneself or other parties. It consists of making a profit as a direct consequence of issuing documents made out to an individual, on demand or to the bearer, against an assumed person. For example, selling the same thing to two different people. Altering accounts or contractual terms. Declaring nonexistent expenses." He sat looking at me, I'm telling you, like a tiger you suddenly run into in the jungle, a wild animal hidden until that moment, though predictable. You knew it was there, that it always was there, but you thought it wouldn't attack you, that it would look at you in that sweet and at the same time threatening way typical of felines, thought it would disappear again into the underbrush. Not this time. "In other words," the boss continued, "you're guilty of fraud against this company for your own benefit." I could stammer that it wasn't true, that I had only followed instructions. That there could be no doubt about my good faith. Barroso shook his head in compassion. "Pagán, my friend. Accept the offer I'm making you for your sake and for mine. Your secret is safe with me. I'm not going to investigate where you got the five thousand dollars in your bank account." "But Señor, you gave them to me." "Prove it, Pagán. Where's the receipt?" He paused and added: "I'm going to give you a pension. A pension for life. You're fifty-two years old. Prepared to live quietly, with a secure envelope each month. A receipt isn't necessary. A contract isn't necessary, what an idea. Ten thousand pesos adjusted to inflation. Accept and the matter dies here." He made a melodramatic pause, very typical of him. "Refuse and what dies is you." He smiled and held out his hand. "What do you prefer? To be free and happy or in prison for twenty years? Because you should know that your crime carries a sentence of five to ten years in jail. Ten more on top of that will be because of me and the influence I have." He smiled, and his smile disappeared instantly. Look at my hand, son. That's what we've lived on since then. With the necessary adjustments for inflation.

THE MOTHER. He knew where Elvira Morales sang, and he could always find her. In the eleven o'clock show at the cabaret Aladdin's Cave. Would he come back? Or wouldn't she see him again? Looking at the past calmly, Elvira Morales always calculated that the anonymous spectator who had shared the white lights with her one night would come back to hear her and have the courage to talk to her. She kept the image of a tall, robust man, his incipient baldness compensated for by long sideburns and a well-groomed mustache. Though it was also possible he'd never come back, and it was all a mirage in the great gray desert of the Cuauhtémoc district. The fact is, he did come back, their eyes met as she sang "Two Souls," and in what was an unusual move for her, she came down from the small stage surrounded by applause and went over to the man waiting for her at table 12A. Pastor Pagán. "Shall we dance?" In her heart of hearts, she had made a bet. This man seems arrogant because he's shy. Which was why now, thirty-three years later, when Elvira felt that a second desert was growing, the desert of married life, she continued the song knowing that Pastor, when he heard her, would ask her to dance that same night. There were no working-class cabarets like the ones they used to have. The life of the city had broken through the old borders. Nobody dared to go into dangerous neighborhoods. Young people went far away, to the edge of the city. Old people were more secure, frequenting the salsa dance halls in the Roma district, where everything was so dependable you could even go up onstage and show your skill as a dancer. This was where they went, though Elvira and Pastor got up to dance only to the slowest, most melancholy boleros. Listen. I'll tell you in secret that I really love you. And I follow your steps even if you don't want me to. Then, in each other's arms, on the floor, dancing the way they did when they met, she could close her eyes and admit that when she gave up her career and agreed to marry, it was to become indispensable at home. If she didn't, it wasn't worth it. To be indispensable, she soon discovered (not now, now she's dancing cheek-to-cheek with her husband) that once out of her profession, she was free to bring the song lyrics into her private life. She realized, with bitter surprise, that the bolero was the truth. In the cabaret, she had sung what she hadn't lived: the temptation of evil. Now, in her home, the lyrics returned almost like something imposed, a law. Say it isn't true, Elvira. Say I didn't fall in love with you because of a secret despair, that I didn't transform the ringing of wedding bells into a prelude to an emptiness so profound that only a poor tyranny over the house can fill it. Giving orders. Being obeyed. Never being dominated. Hiding her probable melancholy. Burying her unwanted restlessness. Devising matrimonial strategies so he would never say what she feared most: "We're not the way we used to be." He never said it. They went to bars with the illusion that there was never any "used to" but always nothing except "right now." She always sang, and he knew where to find her. Always. She wouldn't leave. "You have an exciting voice." Mustache. Sideburns. Incipient baldness. Attributes of a macho. "Thank you, Señor." She did have an exciting voice as a singer, that's true. As a woman and mother, she felt her sentimental voice gradually turning into something else difficult to describe aloud. In her heart, she perhaps could tell herself—dancing very close to her past, present, for always lover, her man, Pastor Pagán—that instead of the woman's martyrdom typical of the bolero, she now felt tempted to identify with the wife and mother who gives orders, however small they may be. And who is obeyed. This causes melancholy and agitation in Elvira Morales. She cannot understand why she doesn't accept the simple tranquility of her home or rather, even if she does accept it, why she feels attracted to the misfortune at the heart of the song, though when you sing it, there's no need to live it, and when you stop singing it, you fall into the trap of giving it life. "I don't recognize myself," Elvira whispers in Pastor's ear when they dance together in the club. She doesn't go on. She suspects he wouldn't understand, and neither would anyone else. She would never say: "I regret it. I should have continued with my singing career." And neither would she say something as melodramatic as: "A mother and wife needs to be worshiped." She would never say a thing like that. She preferred, now and then, to declare her love. To her husband, her children, Alma and Abel. Her children didn't return the favor. In the shrug of their shoulders, in their cold eyes, she recognized that all of a mother's sentimental baggage seemed despicable to her children. For them, the bolero was ridiculous. But for Pastor, the music was just what it should be. The key to happiness. The prologue to the feeling, if not the feeling itself. Something overly sweet. Strange but overly sweet. Dancing in the half-light of romantic dance halls (there were still a few left), Elvira realized that what her children rejected in her was exactly what she rejected in her husband. The dreadful mawkishness of a world that decks itself out in colored spheres, as brittle and hollow as the balls on a Christmas tree. Was it necessary to elevate like a profane Eucharist one's cheap and overly sentimental innermost feelings in order to disguise the lack of emotion in daily life, the absence of seriousness in the eternal disorder that affirms us in the face of the void, that distances us from everyone—from other people and from ourselves? Elvira Morales dances with her arms around her husband, and Pastor Pagán says into her ear, "How long are we going to pretend we're still young? How long are we going to admit that our children threaten us? That they annihilate us little by little." When she married, she thought: I can turn him down. But only now. Later, I won't have that freedom. And before returning to the everyday schedule, the customary obligations, the degrees of indifference, the thermometer of real or imaginary debts, he would say into her ear as they danced to boleros, holding each other very tight: "Once, there was magic here."

THE DAUGHTER. The four couples, fatigued, are approaching the final goal. The border with Guatemala. The Mexicans, Jehová and Pepita, have taken the train that goes to the Suchiate River, and the two North American boys, Jake and Mike, have opted for motorcycles. The Chihuahans, Juan and Soledad, prefer to run with a marathon highland rhythm. Only the Mexicans from Ciudad Juárez, the last-minute contestants, have lost their way in Oaxaca, where they finally were found in an inn sick with indigestion from a black *mole*. Half an hour from the goal, in the Chiapas forest, the train is halted by trees blocking the track, and out of the forest come ten, twelve young devils. Heads shaved, naked from the waist up, tears tattooed on their chests. The announcer on the reality show does not omit these details. He thinks it's one more obstacle anticipated for the race. Part of the show. It's not. Five or six boys get into the train with machine guns and begin to shoot the passengers. Jehová and Pepita die instantly. The gringos, Jake and Mike, arrive like the cavalry in a cowboy movie, realize what is happening, get off their motorcycles, attack the devils of the murdering gang with their fists. They can't subdue them. Four boys with shaved heads shoot the young North Americans. They fall down dead. The forest is inundated with blood. The Chihuahans smell the blood from a distance. They have an ear for violence. They have suffered it for centuries at the hands of whites and mestizos. It is their inheritance to be suspicious. They don't approach the train. They take another road to the border. They win the competition. In Indian dress, they are right in style to take a Caribbean cruise. "We've never been to the ocean," they declare when they are awarded the prize. Alma Pagán turns off the television. She doesn't know when she'll turn it on again. In any case, she feels better informed than her parents. They are very ignorant. And without information, what authority can they have over her and her brother, Abel? She thought this and didn't understand why she felt more vulnerable than ever.

THE SON. Abel Pagán walks along the avenue, its walls heavily painted with graffiti. On wall after wall, the Mara Salvatrucha gang announces that it will bring the war to the city. They are young Central Americans displaced by the wars in El Salvador and Honduras. Abel feels sad looking at this graphic violence that makes the city so ugly. Though making Mexico City ugly is a tautology. And graffiti are universal. Abel saw and felt the immense desolation of the broad gray street. There was nothing to be done. He reached the metro station. He decided to jump the gate and board the train without paying for a ticket. Nobody saw him. He felt free. The train, filled with people, pulled out.

THE BOSS. Leonardo Barroso shows no emotion at all when he reads these lines. Or rather, his lack of emotion is the most eloquent statement of his disdain. "Look, Abel. There are no indispensable employees here. Wise up, boy. With modern technology, production increases, and the worker goes down. If I ever offer you something, consider yourself privileged. Here you have a secure, steady job. What I don't tolerate are stupid whims. Personal rebellions in exchange for the privilege of working with me. With Leonardo Barroso. Understand? It's up to you. You're either in or you're out. I don't need you. The business will grow with or without you. If you want the truth, it'll do better without you. You should always feel that a job is a privilege, because you, Abel, are turning out to be superfluous."

THE FATHER AND MOTHER. I don't describe Elvira because in my eyes she's always the same girl I met one day singing the bolero "Two Souls."

Chorus of the Street Gossips

Exita gave birth in the street
Half the girls on the street are pregnant
They're between twelve and fifteen years old
Their babies are newborns up to six years old
A lot of them are lucky and miscarry because they're given a beating
And the fetus comes out screeching with fear
Is it better to be inside or outside?
I don't want to be here mamacita
Toss me in the garbage instead mother
I don't want to be born and grow dumber each day
With no bath mamacita with no food mother
With no nourishment except alcohol mother marijuana mother
Paint thinner mother glue mother cement mother cocaine mother
Gasoline mother
Your tits overflowing with gasoline mother
I spit flames from the mouth I nursed with mother
A few cents mother
On the crossroads mother
My mouth full of the gasoline I nursed mother
My mouth burning burned
My lips turned to ash at the age of ten
How do you want me to love me mother?
I don't hate you
I hate me
I'm not worth dog shit mother
I'm only worth what my fists deliver
Fists for fighting fists for stealing fists for stabbing mother
If you're still alive mother

If you still love me just a little
Order me please to love me just a little
I swear I hate me
I'm less than a dog's vomit a mule's shit a hair on your ass an
abandoned
Huarache a rotten peach a black banana peel
Less than a drunkard's belch
Less than a policeman's fart
Less than a headless chicken
Less than a bum's old prick
Less than the skinny ass of a Campeche whore
less than a drug dealer's spittle
less than the shaved ass of a baboon in the zoo
less than less mamacita
don't let me kill myself all alone
tell me something to make me feel like a real fucker
a real bad motherfucker mother
jes gimme a hand to get out of this mother
damned to this forever mother?
look at my nails black to the quick
look at my eyes glued shut by rheum
look at my lips chapped raw
look at the black slime on my tongue
look at the yellow slime in my ears
look at my green thick navel
mother gemme outta here
what did I do to end up here?
Digging gnawing scratching crying
what did I do to end up here?
xxxxxita

The Disobedient Son

1. Sometimes my father drank and sang Cristero songs.

2. He liked to recall the deeds of his father, our grandfather, in the War of Christ the King, when the Catholics of Jalisco rose up in arms against the "atheistic" laws of the Mexican Revolution. First he would drink and sing. Right after that he would remember and, finally, admonish. "May the sacrifice of your grandfather Abraham Buenaventura not have been in vain."

Because it seems that Grandfather Abraham was captured by federal troops in 1928 and shot in the Sierra de Arandas, a place, they say, that was fairly desolate and desolating.

"The fact is that it was his time to die. I don't know how many times he saved himself during the Cristero crusade."

Our father, Isaac, recounts that at times Grandfather Abraham showed too much compassion and at other times too much cruelty. Though all wars were like that. Many government soldiers fell at the battle of Rincón de Romos. Grandfather Abraham walked among the corpses, pistol in hand, counting them one by one by order of his superior, General Trinidad de Anda.

They were all good and dead. Except for one, lying in the dust, who moved his eyes and pleaded with my grandfather, Have pity on me, I'm a Christian, too. Grandfather Abraham continued on his way but hadn't taken two steps before the general stopped him cold. "Buenaventura, go back and finish off that soldier."

"But General, sir—"

"Because if you don't kill him, I'll kill you."

In our family, these stories were told over and over again. It was the way to make them present. Otherwise, they would have been forgotten. My father, Isaac, would not tolerate that. The Buenaventura family, all of it, had to be a living temple to the memory of those who fell in the Crusade of Christ the King. So long ago now because it began in 1925 and ended in 1929. But as current as the news on the radio in this remote ranch in Los Camilos, where there are no newspapers and even the radio played with intermissions of silence, thunder, cackling, and stuttering. The Sunday sermons (and every day's remembering) supplied the missing information.

The priest's homily invariably evoked the exploits of Christ the King and lashed out at Masons (where were they?), Communists (what were they?), and all impious people, especially the teachers sent from the capital: the men, sons of Lucifer, the women, socialist harlots.

"As if you needed to know how to read in order to pray," the good father intoned. "As if you needed to know how to write in order to herd cattle."

He would make a dramatic pause before exclaiming: "The good Christian needs only a rosary around his neck and a pistol in his hand."

My father drank and sang. He felt guilty that the war hadn't touched him. On the other hand, he had times of peace and prosperity here in Los Altos de Jalisco. The war was bloody and cruel. The government emptied the Christian villages and sent the people to concentration camps from which they trooped back in emaciated ranks. They say half of them turned into ghosts. They came back in long starving columns howling like dogs—says my father. The merchants barred their stores with chains. So great was the fury of those who came back that they destroyed the harvests so the shopkeepers would have nothing to sell.

"And they mutilated the animals," Isaac said, lowering his voice behind his wet, scaly mustache.

He sat at the head of the refectory with five keys—very large ones—in his hand and his chair set on the metal plate that leads to the mysterious basement where no one else but he can go because it has five padlocks and he is master of the keys.

He looks at us, his four sons, Lucas, Juan, Mateo, and me, Marcos, so named, my father said, to move from the Old to the New Testament once and for all. Otherwise, he advised our mother, Angelines, he would have had to call us Esaú, Jacobo, and right there the problems began, since Jacobo had thirteen sons and my father only four. His decision to change Testaments saved me and my three brothers from being named Isacar, Zebelún, or Zilpa.

Long live the New Testament, I said to myself and wondered from the time I was a boy why there was no Third Testament. What happens next, what's the Present-day Testament?

After the war, the agrarian laws of the Revolution were gradually set aside or punched as full of holes as a colander. There were no more haciendas. Now they were called ranchos. And all you had to do was put together small properties with names of various owners to have, at the very least, a mini-estate. And sometimes re-create a real old-fashioned land holding.

My father was in an intermediate position with his property, Los Camilos, thanks to the benevolence of successive municipal presidents, governors, and dignitaries of the official party, the PRI, the great political umbrella for all ideological postures, from ultraconservative

Catholics to simulated Marxists. The latter were radishes—red on the outside, white on the inside. The former, from holy cross-bearing families, had an obscene popular appeal.

Perhaps, for my father, the legacy of the bloody religious war was the obligation to restore the lands of Los Altos and wipe out all vestiges of faces and walls equally marred by disease and machine guns.

And that was what he did. The honor fell to my father of recovering his wealth without renouncing his faith. From the time we were children, he would take his four sons to visit the lands of the Los Camilos ranch, named in honor of the congregation founded in Rome in 1586 to care for the dying. "Because this land was dying, and only with reborn faith was the land reborn."

Herds of cattle. Extensive cornfields. Land without tenant farmers, all of it belonging to Isaac Buenaventura and his four sons. From the Sierra del Laurel to the border with Aguascalientes, there was no ranch more productive, better run, and with more certain boundaries than this property of Los Camilos, land that only the sons of Isaac and the grandsons of Abraham would share one day.

My father had us—Juan, Lucas, Mateo, and Marcos—learn about every corner of Los Camilos, the herders and the cornfields, how to tend to the mares about to give birth and how to count acres, but finding out as well that here the hail was severe, and there were snakes and huisache cactus, and the great organs of nopal were like the sentinels of our land.

For this was our land, and its miracle, to my young eyes, was that nothing had killed it, neither war nor peace, since both can suffocate life that isn't the extreme of violence or of tranquility but the object of constant attention, a state of alert to avoid falling into destruction or abstinence. It was enough to see and love this land to re-create in the soul a vigorous equilibrium typical of complete men, conscious of possible mistakes and reluctant to accept premature glory. Nature in Los Altos de Jalisco is frugal, parsimonious, sober, like the appearance and speech of the inhabitants.

And still there was a latent power in the herds and cornfields, in the clouds of slow urgency, in the wind trapped in the caves that didn't allow me to live absently, without ambition and even without rebelliousness. When the mountain approaches and the wheat rises, the brambles retract and the beeches grow until they reach their dense green coronation, a man is transformed along with nature and the senses are nourished by the smells and tastes of the countryside, smoke and tar and stables and sometimes the flashing passage of half-seen butterflies, more fragile than a rainbow, that blinded me with their rapid flight, as if saying, Follow us, Marcos, come with us, let yourself go . . .

But my father was anchored to this land and even more so to his place at the head of the refectory, sitting there with the keys to the basement in his hand and looking at us with severity when he said that if our Cristero grandfather died for religion, it was up to his son and grandsons to pay homage to Abraham's sacrifice by dedicating ourselves to God.

"That is why I have determined that each one of you, when you turn eighteen, will go to Guadalajara to begin your studies at the Seminario del Eterno Enfermo in order to enter the priesthood and dedicate your lives to the service of Our Lord."

His patriarchal glance cut off any response, protest, or personal opinion.

"The first to go will be you, Marcos, because you're the oldest. I've noticed you have a vocation because you fast so often."

I didn't disillusion him. If I fasted, it was not because I had a priest's vocation but because I was fat and wanted to diet to attract the girls in the settlement. But I didn't say anything. I bowed my head in acceptance and allowed my father to continue his heroic evocations.

"Grandfather Abraham's final wish was that they not give him anything to drink for an entire day before they shot him and allow him to piss before he stood against the wall."

He looked at us with a singular, terrible meaning. "You, Marcos, and then Juan and Mateo and Lucas, are going to the seminary the same way, without pissing your pants."

He made a Jupiter-like pause. "Grandfather Abraham died for religion. You must pay tribute to his sacrifice by dedicating yourselves to God."

If one of the four of us was tempted to yawn at the table upon hearing the same old song for the thousandth time, our astute father immediately brought into play the memory of our sainted mother, Doña Angelines, who died giving birth to Mateo and on whom, to assure her going to heaven, our father—he recounts it brutally—painted a cross on her breast with blood from the birth.

"Remember it, boys. Remember it, Mateo, when it's your turn to go to the seminary. You were born under the sign of the bloody cross, and only your dedication to the Lord Our God and His Holy Apostolic Roman Catholic Church will save you from the sin of having caused the death of the one who gave you life."

I dared to look at my little brother, barely twelve years old and terrified, mortified, disoriented by my father's words. I listened with my head held high. I looked at Mateo, lifting it even higher, encouraging him in silence, Mateo, don't bow your head, up, Mateo, up.

Right after that my father skewered us: "If all of you don't become priests, the ghost of Grandfather Abraham will haunt you."

That was why at night, all of us lying in the same large bedroom in accordance with another of my father's maxims ("This way you'll keep an eye on one another"), we spoke of our fear that the ghost of our grandfather, Abraham Buenaventura, would appear to us if we disobeyed our father, Isaac. We were frightened by the movement of the trees, the creaking of the grate, and the terror that into our room would come the Cristero parade of starving children clutching at their mothers' skirts, the marred faces of the soldiers, the corpses wrapped in sleeping mats, the dogs barking at the moon.

To say goodbye to me, my father ordered a funeral Mass, since it wasn't a matter of wishing me luck but of reminding me of our dead mother and in this way burdening me with the responsibility to honor her memory with my future priesthood. The Fiftieth Psalm was recited, intercession for the departed soul was prayed for, the mother of the forsaken was invoked, and then there was a huge ranch fiesta where everybody raised their lemonades and I was sent off with a variety of popular exclamations.

"Don't bump into any tarts, Marcos."

"Don't let your asshole pucker up in the city."

"Listen, Marcos, before you become a priest, break the cherries of a couple of girls."

My father gave me a snakeskin belt lined with silver pesos and newly coined morelianos. "So you don't ask me for more. Manage it carefully. There's no need to write to me. Don't think about me. Think about God and your dead mother."

And so I left behind my home village with a sound of barren rock and abandoned tools (which pursued me).

3. When I came back for a visit three years later to celebrate my twenty-first birthday at home, my father, filled with pride, ordered the church bells rung and boasted that now it was Juan's turn to go to the seminary, too, because he was almost eighteen, and then Lucas, seventeen, would follow in his footsteps and little—or not so little anymore—Mateo, who was fifteen.

I arrived dressed in black—suit, tie, shoes—and a white shirt but without a high collar, in order not to attract too much attention.

With a certain pleasure I recognized the herds and the cornfields, the roads and tools of my childhood, and prepared to hear again the exploits of the Cristero War during supper with my three brothers, my father presiding as always with the key in his hand and the patriarchal chair set over the metal door and the forbidden basement.

"Well, well," my father murmured. "Look, boys, at how they've sent your brother back to us so correct. You can really see his correctness, don't you think?" He laughed out loud. "As they used to say in my day, politicians and lawyers are big-assed creatures. You can really see"—he gave me an apocalyptic look—"that Marcos has grown wings and that the discipline of seclusion and frugal meals has made his spirit thin and enlarged his soul."

I imagined that my father would take these virtues for granted, without too much inquiry and almost as the work of the Holy Spirit.

"Well, Christian, what do you have to tell me?" my father, Isaac Buenaventura, said familiarly.

"Nothing," I replied very seriously. "I study a great deal and never go out."

"Learn something, boys," he said to my brothers. "And get ready, it's Juan's turn now to go to Guadalajara to become a priest, and then you, Lucas, and you, Mateo, will follow."

I dared to interrupt the old man, more wrinkled than a glove. "Tell me, Father, when the four of us are priests and you find yourself at the side of God, who will take care of the ranch?"

It was clear he wasn't expecting this clairvoyant question. It was evident he was perturbed: He squeezed the keys to the basement more furiously than ever and, something unheard of in him, stammered and didn't know what to say. It took him some time to find the words.

"What God gives us, God takes away. Think of your sainted mother."

"Which means?" I insisted.

"That the lands will be for Holy Mother Church."

"Why?" I asked with absolute relevance, I think.

"That's what I promised my sainted wife. 'Don't worry. The lands will belong to the Church. Die in peace, Angelines.' "

"And what about us?" I asked, this time with audacity.

Now the old man didn't hide his anger. "There are provisions in the will. Do you think I'm going to leave all of you out on the street?" He choked. "Insolent," he concluded and, for the first time, stood and left the dining room.

Then Lucas stirred the fire in the living room, and the four of us sat down, certain the old man was already in his room.

"Do you really want to be a priest, Juan?" I asked the brother who was next to me in age and destiny.

Juan said no.

"What, then?"

"I want to be an agronomist. That way I'll manage the ranch and make it prosper."

"I think it's dumb to go into the Church," said Lucas. "It's like going back to the rule of—what do you call it—"

"Mortmain," I said mildly. "And you, Mateo?"

The impetuous fifteen-year-old didn't restrain himself. "I want to get married. No priest, no nothing. I'd rather be an idiot in an asylum than a priest. I like skirts, not cassocks. I'm a man now. But damn it, if I tell Papa, he'll tan my hide."

I looked at the three of them slowly.

Juan with his face like a turkey egg, saved by large eyes as green as a volcanic lake and red hair very carefully groomed, as if he were afraid of himself in front of the mirror.

Lucas with his face of a psychic reader of tea leaves, very wise with his short brown hair and the tremulous ears of an amiable bat.

And poor little Mateo with pimples on a skin that promised to clear up as soon as he gave the green light to his recent appetite for women.

And in the three of them, the poorly disguised frustration of having to follow in my footsteps and go to the seminary.

"How well you look," Lucas said to me. "You've lost weight and gained some polish at the same time."

"It's obvious the seminary has agreed with you," added Juan.

I looked at them with amused eyes. "No seminary. I'm studying law. I'm going to be an attorney."

There was a stupefied and at the same time joyful silence.

"But Marcos!" Lucas exclaimed.

"Forget it. Brothers. Listen to me. I'm offering you a way out." One by one I observed them. "You, Juan, come this year to Guadalajara, enroll in engineering at U.G., and then you, Lucas, say nothing until it's your turn and follow me to Guadalajara because I have a feeling your field is economics and not mortmain. And you, little brother, don't give away the game with your impatience. Make love to the girls in the village; here, I'm giving you my supply of condoms, and you go have yourself a time in the brothels here in Los Altos. Then tell me where you want to study, and I'll arrange it for you."

I looked at them very seriously. "But it's our secret, agreed?"

And the four of us, on that unforgettable night of brothers, swore like panthers promising one another not to press the law and to let everything happen without wearing out our luck.

4. Years later, Don Isaac Buenaventura opened the padlock on his trapdoor and went down to the basement. There he knelt in front of the perpetual lights that illuminated each portrait. That of Angelines, his wife. And that of his father, the Cristero Abraham Buenaventura.

And then he said to them, "Don't blame me as if I were guilty of something. The fires have gone out, and the dogs no longer are barking. Well, before you eat the taco, you have to measure the tortilla. Am I remembering a past that never was? You are my witnesses. That past did exist. The good Christian does have a rosary around his neck and a pistol in his hand. Death to the impious, the sons of Lucifer, the teachers who are tarts. Now who will defend us, mother of the forsaken, father of all battles? And against whom do I defend myself? Are there any Masons left out there, or Communists? My life has been in vain? Ah, no, it hasn't, I deny it, now I realize that thanks to Marcos and Mateo, Juan and Lucas, I, Isaac Buenaventura, became a rebel again like my father because I prepared the rebellion of my sons, I told them, 'Let's see who has the balls to rebel!' And the four of them were rebels, the four of them were better and more independent than me, the four of them deceived me and left me like Policarpo in the song, who doesn't roll over even in his sleep . . . .
A crucifix of steel. Dogs that bark at the moon. Fires that have gone out. The Church a great corpse. And I, Isaac Buenaventura, with the scaly mustache and a face more wrinkled than a glove and the pride that my sons turned out rebellious, exactly the way I wanted them to be . . . . Long live Christ the King who performs these miracles for me, for the ways of the Lord

are mysterious, and not in vain, Angelines, did I make the sign of the cross on your breasts with the blood of your newborn son Mateo. And not in vain, Father Abraham, did you refuse to drink water before you were shot . . . . And let the grates creak, the dogs bark, the bells in the village ring in alarm, and the mares in heat and the mares giving birth all moan, because I'm still here guarding the earth, proud of my sons who didn't allow themselves to be manipulated by their father and took charge of forging their own destiny, dissident in the face of life . . . . Now I'm going to have a drink and sing a song."

Chorus of Rival Buddies

Don Pedro was fifty-two years old
His compadre Don Félix fifty-four
The baptismal font joined them
Pedro was godfather to Félix's son
Félix was godfather to Pedro's daughter
They got together on Sundays for a family barbecue
They were both supporters of the PRI they felt nostalgic for the PRI because with the PRI there was order progress security for people like
Don Pedro and Don Félix
Not now without the PRI
They became annoyed with each other only once
In the line to vote for the PRI
"I got up first"
"You're wrong I was here before anybody"
"What difference does it make Félix if in the end we're both voting for the PRI"
"Are you sure Pedro? Suppose I change my vote?"
"But the vote is secret"
"Then don't get in front of me Félix I got here first get in line compadre asshole"
And the second time was on the highway to Cuernavaca
They were going to celebrate the fifteenth birthday of the daughter of their boss
The undersecretary
But on the curves Félix passed Pedro and Pedro got mad and decided to speed past Félix
And the races began

We'll see who's more of a fucker
Félix or Pedro
Who's more macho
The cars ran side by side
Pedro gives Félix the finger
Félix comes back at Pedro with five insulting blasts on the horn
Shave and a haircut, dum-dum
Pedro pulls his car alongside Félix's
Félix accelerates
Pedro spits on the steering wheel
Félix feels his macho hormone-amen rising up
Pedro reflects hormones are idiots
The dog lifts his leg and urinates
The dog behind him tries to urinate more than the first one
In the sacred space where men piss
Félix jumps the median
Pedro goes over the cliff
The dogs urinate
They're served with parsley at the undersecretary's barbecue.

A Cousin Without Charm

1. We didn't talk about "That Woman" in this house. Even her name was forgotten. She was simply "That Woman." Some crossed themselves when she was mentioned; some sneered; some took offense. It was very difficult to convince the matriarch, Doña Piedad Quiroz de Sorolla, that "That Woman" was no longer here, and Doña Piedita could get out of bed and move around the desolate house in El Desierto de los Leones with no danger of running into the wicked "That Woman."

"There's no reason anymore to fulfill your vow, Doña Piedita. You can get up and walk. You can even change your dress."

Because the "vow" that Widow de Sorolla had imposed on herself consisted of two decisions. First, to take to her bed, and second, to take to her bed dressed without getting up or changing her "clothes" until "That Woman" had left.

The truth is that life was better before, or at least bearable. The big old house in El Desierto, submerged in mourning since the death of the patriarch, Don Fermín Sorolla, revived when the daughter of the family, Ana Fernanda Sorolla, contracted matrimony with a young accountant, Jesús Aníbal de Lillo. The wedding caused a great stir, and everyone remarked on what a good-looking couple they were: Ana Fernanda—tall, very white-skinned, with luxuriant black hair and a suggestive mixture of willfulness and affection in her eyes, lips always partially open to show off her teeth, her Indian cheekbones, high and hard under skin that was so Spanish, and her walk, also intriguing, tiptoeing and stepping hard at the same time—all of which seemed to support as well as complement the serious, dry personality of the bridegroom, as if the severe manner and amiable but distant smile of CPA Jesús Aníbal de Lillo served to toughen the barely "virile" physical beauty of a twenty-seven-year-old man who had kept the look of a beardless adolescent: impeccable skin and pale cheeks on which the long blond mustache could not erase the impression that Jesús Aníbal was a young Asturian Apollo with curly blond hair and a bearing not at all athletic, almost *consumed* in his refined, patrician physical essence, of ordinary height and only apparent fragility, for in the nakedness of their bedroom—Ana Fernanda discovered it that very night—the young certified public accountant possessed extreme virile potency, proclaiming in words, over and over again, his sexual satisfaction when he fell back naked beside a modest Ana Fernanda rapidly covered by the sheet while her husband declaimed with actions his instantaneous, incessantly renewed sexual hunger.

Ever since he met Ana Fernanda at the celebrated Christmas party of the poet Carlos Pellicer, Jesús Aníbal had felt attracted to her and stifled the ugly thought that the girl was rich, the daughter of a newly rich millionaire who was protected by powerful politicians, recipient of a thousand contracts, and married to a Quiroz of provincial lineage who had been impoverished by the same thing that had enriched her husband: the political changes that invariably translated into favor or disfavor in Mexico. But this time Jesús Aníbal was the pauper allied by marriage to a wealthy family. Wealthy but severely eccentric.

After the wedding, Jesús Aníbal de Lillo would have preferred to leave the ancestral home of the Sorollas in the solitary and perpetually démodé Desierto de los Leones in the far southwest of Mexico City: a steep forest of twisting paths, fragrant pines, and views of Mount Ajusco that startled the spirit with an intrusion so close, gigantic, and uninhabited in plain sight of twenty million residents. He would have preferred to join the modern, secure, and comfortable advance of the city, the urban development in Santa Fe and its tall condominiums on the road to Toluca, with all the amenities nearby: movies, stores, restaurants.

This was impeded by Ana Fernanda's will. The house in El Desierto de los Leones was where the Sorollas had always lived, her father had died here, her mother would not move from a house identical to her life: old, long, and empty. And Jesús Aníbal shouldn't even think, *not even think,* said the young bride, covering his mouth with a perfumed hand viscous and sticky with masculine love, about moving from here, but above all, he absolutely should not think about the death of Doña Piedad since Ana Fernanda would exclude her husband from the nuptial bedroom because that would certainly kill the matriarch, and she, Ana Fernanda, would not allow herself to be touched again by the young bridegroom if he insisted on moving from El Desierto to Santa Fe.

CPA De Lillo, however, not only was very much in love with Ana Fernanda Sorolla but also respected her for that charming mixture of inexperience and will that kept Jesús Aníbal in a state of delectable expectation. What would his wife ask of him this time?

Nothing. This is what the first five years of marriage brought. Nothing. The habit that becomes nothing. From the happy contrasts of their wedding night, the couple was moving to the never-spoken conviction that to love each other, there was no need to talk about love.

"Don't be so insistent."

That was the extent of Ana Fernanda's rejection, when she was fearful of physical contact with Jesús Aníbal after the birth of their daughter, Luisa Fernanda, and the mother had to spend three weeks in bed, grow maddeningly fat, suffer even more to recover her vaunted slenderness, and refuse to have another child, but was obliged by her religious conscience to forbid her husband to use condoms and limit their sexual contact to her safe days according to the rhythm method.

Jesús Aníbal didn't know whether to laugh or be angry when he found Ana Fernanda lying on the bed, scissors in hand, cutting off the tips of the collection of condoms that the misguided young husband had brought to the house in order to combine safety and pleasure.

"The Church forbids these nasty things."

The husband loved his wife. He did not want to find defects in her. He had no reason to be surprised. He had always known that Ana Fernanda was a devout Catholic. He had accepted this, and if he thought he could "cut it away" one day, it did not take him long to realize that in his wife's spirit, her love of God had precedence over her love of Jesús, no matter how ironic or crude that might sound, to the point where, on fixed days, when she accepted his favors, Ana Fernanda stopped exclaiming "Jesús Jesús" and began to say "Aníbal Aníbal" or simply "my love."

"At least call me Chucho," the genial husband said with a smile one night.

"You're blasphemous. That's a dog's name," Ana Fernanda said before turning her back to say the rosary, then facing Jesús Aníbal again only to conclude with precision: "Don't be stupid. Loving means not talking about love."

Jesús Aníbal didn't mind the daily trek from El Desierto to his office at Insurgentes and Medellín. There was no distance in Mexico City that did not require at least an hour of patience. If anything tested national stoicism, it was urban traffic. He listened to music. He bought cassettes of poetry in Spanish and felt the birth in his spirit of something that was his own but latent. He thought. Sometimes, thanks to Garcilaso or Cernuda, he even dreamed possible dreams: that Ana

Fernanda would finally give in before the evidence of her husband's affection and accept the normality of matrimony but not separate it from physical pleasure. Impossible dreams: that Ana Fernanda would agree to leave the decrepit, uncomfortable, gloomy old house in El Desierto. Forbidden dream: that the acerbic, closed Doña Piedita would pass from this life to a better one.

Ana Fernanda was not entirely unaware of Jesús Aníbal's unspoken aspirations. As the years went by, the house in El Desierto was growing not only older but more unrepairable, a leak here announced a damp wall there, a creaking floor in one place foretold a collapsed roof in another, and the old woman kept a fierce hold on life, though Jesús Aníbal began to think that once his mother-in-law was dead, his wife would inherit her manias, and just as the memory of the deceased patriarch, Don Fermín, kept them tied to El Desierto, Doña Piedita would pass on to a better life but not Ana Fernanda and Jesús Aníbal: The big family house tied them to the past and to the future.

Jesús Aníbal would come home from work and enter the desolation of an enormous living room, empty except for a piano that no one played and a good number of chairs placed along the walls. No pictures were hung, and the glass doors opened on a damp, untamable courtyard that seemed to grow according to its own desires and in opposition to all the efforts of the gardener.

Then the husband thought of something that would banish solitude and authorize repairs.

"To what end?" his old mother-in-law said with a sigh. "Houses should be like people, they grow old and die . . . This is an old, lived-in house. Let people see that."

"Ana Fernanda, don't we have friends, the people who came to the wedding, relatives? Wouldn't you like to invite them here once in a while?"

"Ay, Jesús Aníbal, you know that taking care of Mama uses up not only my time but my desire for parties."

"The people who came to the wedding. They seemed nice. Friends."

"They weren't friends. They were *acquaintances.*"

"Relatives?"

Ana Fernanda seemed surprised that her husband, for once, had an acceptable idea. Of course they had kin, but they were very scattered. Puebla and Veracruz, Sonora and Sinaloa, Monterrey and Guadalajara, every family who came to the capital came from somewhere else but put down roots in the city, the systoles and diastoles of the internal migration in the nation determined by wars, revolutions armed, agrarian, and industrial, the long nomadic border in the north, the muddy, wild border to the south, the poles of development, ambition, and resignation, love and hate, unkept promises and persistent vices, yearnings for security and challenges to insecurity.

This was how, Jesús Aníbal thought on his daily *viacrucis* along the Periférico Highway, the country had been made, and inviting distant family members was upright, it was entertaining, it was instructive, since all of them had gone through experiences that satisfied the lively curiosity of the young, unsatisfied husband who was eager as well to dilute to the maximum his own Basque inheritance and not think again about *gachupín* or *indiano,* the words for Spaniard in America. Take a bath in Mexicanism.

He had the reception rooms repaired, and the relatives began to arrive, with the cooperative enthusiasm of Ana Fernanda, who hadn't thought of a pretext, as she said, to "show off a little bit," fix up the house, and, in passing, free herself from the enslaving excuse of her mother.

And so the old Jaliscan uncle was constructing a family tree before the last Quiroz, that is to say, himself, disappeared. And the young nephew from Monterrey had created a center for technological development in the north. And the enterprising niece who was an executive in Sonora had joined a conglomerate of businesses in California. And Aunt Chonita from Puebla had arthritis, and it was hard for her to go every afternoon to say the rosary in the beautiful Soledad Church with its no less beautiful tiled dome, as she had been in the habit of doing for the past forty years. And her sister, Purificación, had died of indigestion from an orgy of marzipan, ham, candied sweet potatoes, and other delicacies of Pueblan pastry-making—and who told her to do that?—after a ten-day ecclesiastical fast in honor of the Holy Infant of Atocha. And (distant) Cousin Elzevir was on the run from Matamoros because of who knew what trouble with skirts or drugs or contraband, who can tell with somebody as disreputable as him. And the Sorolla twins from Sinaloa were looking for a singer to form a trio in Mazatlán. And Cousin Valentina Sorolla came from Morelia Michoacán to visit them, which was very unusual since she was known to be a reclusive spinster who did not even go to Mass though she did go to the bank punctually for the monthly allowance left to her by her miserly father, Don Amílcar.

"I'll bet she prays to Saint Anthony to get married. She must be over forty by now," said the Sonoran niece.

"Cousin Valentina was supposed to become a nun, but she didn't have the vocation," remarked the cousin from Monterrey.

Jesús Aníbal thought he had found in this lengthy parade of scattered clans the way to enliven the spirit of the big old house in El Desierto, learning in passing the peculiarities of related families and creating a pedigree for himself that saved him from an incestuous relationship between the Asturians and his beloved Basque country.

And so they call Aunt Teófila from Guadalajara 09 because she complains all day on the telephone. And the Quiroz family from Veracruz spends the entire day listening to boleros on a jukebox, all of them together as if they were at the Metropolitan Opera in New York, imagine. And Aunt Gudula from San Luis Potosí swears her house is a *bijou*, she's so vulgar. And Uncle Parménides from Mérida is such a kid that at night he runs past barracks so the soldiers will shout "Halt! Halt!" at him.

These anecdotes were accompanied by a chorus of laughter from the family visitors on duty.

Was this the happiness that was possible, the warmth of families, severe at times, affable at others? Was this clan passive and happy or active and unhappy? Was the family perfect because it was bored or bored because it was perfect? Or were all of them, without exception, parts of a single symbol, accepted and acceptable, of the quota of happiness we deserve, always partial but always complete because death is the absolute border, not nomadic and not muddy, and nobody is prepared to die leaving behind families that are ugly, ruined, and sad?

Jesús Aníbal responded internally to this question, telling himself that in the final analysis, he was married to the beauty of the family, and the great idea of inviting the scattered Sorolla and Quiroz kin calmed the growing hours of distance between husband and wife and encouraged hours of social coexistence that obliged them both to be on their best behavior.

"It's fine," said Ana Fernanda. "Let Cousin Valentina come from Michoacán. I didn't even think of her. She's so unattractive." And she added, applying her makeup in front of the mirror: "I agreed to the relatives so I can show off. Understand that, Jesús Aníbal. Don't think I'm doing it for you."

Cousin Valentina arrived without anyone noticing her and stayed in her bedroom until it was time for supper.

"Nobody noticed her?" Ana Fernanda said sarcastically. "I'm not surprised."

And it was true that in this fortyish cousin there was a kind of disposition not only to not be noticed but to disappear, transforming, like lizards, into a part of the tree or rock they were on. Nothing, however, precluded courtesy, and if Ana Fernanda remained seated and waited for Cousin Valentina to come over to kiss her cheek, Jesús Aníbal got to his feet, ignoring a certain acerbic expression on his wife's face—as if the cousin didn't deserve even the slightest show of good breeding—and welcomed Valentina, kissing her first on one cheek and then on the other, but between the two kisses, because of a movement of their heads, he kissed her lips, too.

He laughed. Not the cousin. She moved away, not blushing but with severity. In Jesús Aníbal's sense of smell, there remained a bitter, peppery trace, redeemed by a scent of musk and the cleanliness of a soap shop.

Standing, her hands crossed at her lower abdomen, dressed all in black in a long skirt and low boots, long sleeves and an unadorned neckline, Cousin Valentina Sorolla looked at the world from an imperturbable distance. Nothing seemed to move her regular features—too regular, as if minted for a coin commemorating the Bourbons, that is, only in profile. Because in order to look to the side, Valentina had no reason to move her head, since her eyes were separated on two equal sides by her sharp commemorative profile.

Nothing in her betrayed wit, mischief, or bad temper. She was a severe mask of severe absence from the external world. Like her body, her face was thin. Skin attached to bone with no obstruction except skin struggling to fuse with bone or bone yearning to reveal itself in skin.

All her hair pulled back into a chignon, a broad forehead and deep temples, a long nose that was inquisitive despite herself—a quiver betrayed her—and a dry, lipless mouth, shut like a money box with no opening. What coin could penetrate it, what brush clean her teeth, what kiss excite her tongue?

Cousin Valentina made the round of greetings with the silence of a distant bird in the sky, and Jesús Aníbal wondered about the reason for the uneasiness he felt when he looked at her. The fact was that Valentina did not resemble any of the relatives, either Quiroz or Sorolla, who had visited them. It was clear that, as the saying goes, she "ate separately."

Supper confirmed this. While the aunt from Veracruz, that sparkling conversationalist, narrated the chronicles of the Veracruzan carnival and the Monterreyan nephew, a fanatic about himself, recounted operations in high finance, Cousin Valentina remained silent as an uneasy Jesús Aníbal dared to embark on a conversation doomed to failure, though he certainly attempted to at least catch the eye of this peculiar relative. When he succeeded, it was he who looked away. In Valentina's eyes, he found a prayer for respite, the look of a woman conscious of her ugliness and fearful of ridicule.

That was when a *protective* attraction was born in the young husband, one that no other member of a family shaped by confidence in itself, from the extremes of pious devotion (we shall go to heaven) to professional success (we shall go to the bank), seemed to need, much less request, and certainly not from *gachupines* who came to Mexico, according to the popular saying, in espadrilles and a Basque beret.

Jesús Aníbal laughed to himself and looked at his cousin with a complicit air. Were they the two strangers in the bosom of this family, the displaced persons, the exiles?

Who, in reality, was Valentina Sorolla? Jesús Aníbal fell asleep with the question and had disturbing dreams, sometimes physically obscene, sometimes far too spiritual, though he eventually overcame their evanescence with one certainty: His cousin appeared in all of them.

When he was awake, during the daily masculine ritual of lather and razor that for certain men is the best time for reflection and planning, the young husband thought that his wife's beauty was evident just as his cousin's ugliness was evident.

However, in that very contrast, Jesús Aníbal found an obvious reflection that, once it was freed, took swiftly to the air. Who tells us what thing or person is beautiful or ugly? Who determines the laws of ugliness and beauty? Is a form beautiful that cannot manifest as anything more than form but dares to present itself as spirit? On the other hand, can a form be ugly that is clearly inhabited by spirit? And what gives soul to the form except the true truth, the external manifestation of spirit, without which the most beautiful body reveals, sooner or later, that it was simple copper painted gold, while the soul of an ugly form literally transforms it into something more beautiful than any exterior profile of the individual in question.

These were ideas that were unfamiliar to Jesús Aníbal in his own mind and were perhaps the sediment of his listening to poetry every day on the Periférico route between El Desierto de los Leones and the Juárez district. It was another way of repeating Garcilaso from memory, *I was born for nothing but to love you,* and Góngora, *all things serve lovers,* and Pedro Salinas, *if eyes could sense your voice, oh, how I would look at you,* and Pablo Neruda, *my heart looks for her and she is not with me . . .*

When he went down to breakfast, he looked toward the courtyard and saw Valentina walking there, head bowed, again dressed in black but with one peculiarity. She was barefoot. She stepped on the grass without shoes or stockings. Jesús Aníbal had the feeling that his strange cousin, apparently a frustrated nun, just as the cousin from Monterrey had described her, was fulfilling some penitence. Until he noticed, for the first time, a smile of pleasure on her dry lips. Then he did something unusual for him. He took off his loafers and joined Valentina on the grass. He learned the reason for doing this. The coolness of the sod granted a pleasure violated by the modest crudity of shoes. Walking barefoot in the grass is not only a pleasurable act, it is also an erotic one. The earth rose like a joyful caress from his feet to his solar plexus.

Valentina did not look at him, and Jesús Aníbal left for work with his shoes on and conscious of a dinner at home that night for the scattered relatives who were visiting them—the cousin from Nuevo León, the Veracruzan aunt, two Guadalajarans from Nayarit, Cousin Valentina from Morelia, Ana Fernanda, and himself, Jesús Aníbal. Nothing to worry about here. Ana Fernanda was the perfect homemaker, she would arrange the menu, hire the waiters, prepare the table, and assign places.

Everything as usual. Everything normal.

It was for this that the husband had thought up the program of family visits. Ana Fernanda was blossoming. She no longer had the single excuse of caring for Mama to turn away and distance herself from Jesús Aníbal, who was happy at first to sleep in a separate room far from the wails of Luisa Fernanda and, when the baby passed into the hands of a nurse, not to resume the ritual of the shared bed.

Now Ana Fernanda made herself and the house attractive. She was satisfied and left him in peace. Jesús Aníbal no longer had to worry about pleasing her in bed or during a conversation at the table.

The husband came home early to change his clothes and be on time for dinner. He went to the dining room to confirm the perfection organized by Ana Fernanda and was startled by a shout of alarm and an unusual uproar in the kitchen. He hurried in and found Valentina struggling against the siege of a young, dark, passionate waiter who was trying to embrace and kiss the cousin while she resisted with a fury diminished by the food in her mouth.

Jesús Aníbal forcefully pushed away the waiter, slapped him in the mouth, and the boy looked at him with profound resentment but said only, "I'm leaving."

But before he left, he turned to speak to his employer. "Dames shouldn't be in the kitchen when you're working. They just make trouble."

"The truth is, I'm a glutton, and I felt hungry," said Valentina, revealing another, somewhat childish side of her personality.

"Excuse me, Señor," the waiter continued. "I thought she wanted me to—"

"It's all right," said Jesús Aníbal with a reflexive impulse. "Stay. Do your job."

And he looked at his cousin. "I understand."

It's possible that the waiter hid a smile that continued the interrupted phrase "I thought I was doing the lady a favor," though the craftiness of his sly Mexico City glance said to Jesús Aníbal, "If you want her, keep her, after all, you're the boss."

Jesús Aníbal was really curious about participating in the play of glances—or the lack of them—among the waiter, Valentina, and himself, and he was satisfied, rejecting all temptation to flush with confused embarrassment.

During the dinner, the waiter, when passing the platter of turkey and dressing, could not help directing a glance at Ana Fernanda's décolletage but, without too much effort, avoided looking at the hidden breasts of Valentina, who, to forestall the servant's eyes, directed hers at Jesús Aníbal with a clear intention to express thanks for the protection offered that afternoon.

Everyone was chatting amiably, animated by Ana Fernanda's social gaiety, when one of the inevitable blackouts in the southern part of the city provoked an equally inevitable "Aaaah!" from the diners and Jesús Aníbal, moved by a force that not even he desired or understood, extended his leg under the table until his foot touched the tip of Valentina's.

His cousin withdrew her foot for a second but immediately, as if she feared the return of the light, resumed contact with Jesús Aníbal. They amused themselves in this way until the power returned.

They were all talking about their next vacations, about places they had visited or were going to visit. Only Valentina remained silent, as if she weren't going anywhere.

When everyone drank cognac, she chose a digestive tequila.

As they sat and talked after dinner, the host tried to avoid his cousin's eyes, though it was difficult for him, and he told himself that these things didn't happen by accident, there must be a deeper reason for two distant beings to become close so quickly, especially if they were not—and manifestly they were not—frivolous people, because Jesús Aníbal decided that walking barefoot or going into the kitchen for an early bite were delicious acts—did she think that? he thought—and in their own way, seriously free.

He prayed intensely for the darkness to return and the flirtation to resume. That did not happen. When he said good night, Jesús Aníbal's kiss on his cousin's cheek was fleeting, but what was prolonged was the union of nose against nose and the sensation that joined respirations produced in both of them.

"Good night."

"Until tomorrow."

And in a very low voice, Jesús Aníbal said, "Fate is on our side."

The host knew very well which bedroom had been assigned to Cousin Valentina. Jesús Aníbal waited for the hour of the wolf to leave his room and find Valentina's door. Would it be locked? No. He pushed it and entered a space lit by a candle beside the bed, more undulating than chaste.

Valentina stood waiting for him, barefoot, in a long nightdress with an embroidered bodice.

2. No, it wasn't because she had been invited for only three nights, and whatever happened now would dissipate very quickly, divided between distance and forgetting. For once, Valentina Sorolla would surrender to forbidden pleasure, certain there would be no consequences. And it wasn't because she was hungry for love and, in the arms of her cousin, discovered it not for the first but certainly for the principal time, and therefore it was worth it, with no further consideration. No, it wasn't because, by allowing herself to be loved passionately by Jesús Aníbal, she would free herself from a feeling of revenge for the frustrations of an entire life, damaged as much by her physical appearance as by the withdrawn behavior determined by that fact.

No, it was nothing that came out of her and her life. This was what baffled her, subjected her, frightened her. She was barely a rivulet flooded by the great passionate torrent of the man. It was he, Jesús Aníbal, the cousin she had not known about until now, who was the origin, on that night and the three that followed, of the erotic and emotional fervor that overpowered Valentina when Jesús Aníbal removed, with so firm a gentleness he seemed to tear them off, the skirts of stiff silk and the buttoned black shirt, furiously undid the chignon and kissed her until he suffocated her, laid her on the bed, told her sometimes with words sometimes with silences first give me a minute Valentina that's all I ask then give me the gift of an hour then let me spend the night with you saying and saying to himself Valentina your bitter peppery smell drives me crazy your hair hanging loose like a forest of snakes the beauty of your naked body so full so round so difficult to guess at under your nun's clothes, so dissonant with the severity of your features, you have a face that disguises your body the body doesn't correspond to the mask the mask converts the body into a dazzling discovery Valentina you know it don't cover your face realize it's your secret a face that conceals the secret of your body, how was I going to read you without daring to undress you, because it wasn't you Valentina who brought me to you I'm the one from now on who came here the one who found you and doesn't want to go away from you again I Jesús Aníbal bewitched by you by your newness so ancient so latent so patient waiting at the bottom of my soul you know Valentina? the truth is I was killing myself and if you and I loving each other is a deception then the lie gives me life and it's my life my love my woman Valentina Sorolla desired and despaired over, do you realize the earthquake you provoke in me the yearning you cause in me the tender ferocity born in me when I possess you Cousin Valentina? you could hate me for what has happened between you and me and I would only love you more the more you despise me but it won't be like that will it? don't try to explain yourself at all all you have to do is accept this: because you are who you are you have captured me you are my unfamiliar pleasure each spin of your time fills the empty hourglass that was my soul Valentina how nice we become aroused side by side try to mistreat me my love and you'll see that no matter how much harm you do me you'll never succeed in touching the good you bring me I kiss all of you and I move with kisses from your feet to your head I don't want to be the first or last man in your life I want to be the only man Cousin Valentina my love for you has a Spanish name it's diehard love finding you turns me into pigheaded Jesús, if you leave me I'd have nothing but days without tranquility you're my peace my freedom my navel my nails my digestion my dreams Valentina you free me from the burdens of conscience obligation faithfulness custom so I can be the lover of the ugly woman in the family comparable to no one unique in her passion who is all mine no one else's since no one would envy me no one would want to take you far from my sight and my touch I am unique in the passion that is all mine no one else's my pleasure unfamiliar pleasure my wide and ardent Valentina did you even know you carried inside you so much uproar so much delicate silky loving sensibility did you know? I didn't don't be surprised never think he did me a favor because it isn't true you did me a favor and freed me from all lies all pretensions ugly no never say ugly the way you just did be quiet unique that's what you are not like anyone else never say grateful again the way you did now the one receiving the gift is me Valentina if I'm with you it's because you do me a favor you grant me something I want to deserve by loving you the way I did on Friday and now Saturday and tomorrow Sunday before you go Valentina I can't bear that idea it's as if the arrow were piercing me like a Saint Sebastian before the bow of your solemn eyes my love that's why I love you because your eyes have dark circles and your lips are fleshless and your cheeks close to death and your hair a nest of vipers and your hands indecent claws on all my skin and your weight light under mine even lighter as if you and I the bodies of Valentina and Jesús had waited since infancy for the meeting promised by the stars of a man and a woman desperate to love each other the way you and I love each other cousin of my flesh forbidden cousin cousin obscene and pure at the same time Valentina if you leave me you know I will cry for you the sorrow of losing you will never disappear I will live and die for you because I am the discoverer of your true beauty the beauty seen only by the man who loves as I love you because I have discovered you and I cannot abandon the earthly body of my exploration I cannot veil with opacity and oblivion my privilege of being your cartographer your navigator your conquistador because your body is my land Cousin Valentina your body is my country because I am the lover who with you discovered the pleasure unknown until then because I love you Valentina because of my singularity and yours because no one would believe that someone like me would adore you or that someone like you would give herself to me and that is why each pleasure is a fragile sin and an incomparable thrill because you and I do not resemble anyone and that is what I was looking for without knowing it and what about you?

I thought I had been born to bother others and now I am going to think I am loved because I am different

and because you are ugly Valentina and also because you are ugly don't you want me to feel beautiful because of you?

no Valentina feel ugly so I can adore you for what nobody else would dare to tell you

I am ugly Jesús

ugly ugly ugly you're my perversion and my longed-for adventure an unforeseen love first give me a minute Valentina then let me spend the night with you then my whole life

ugly

offer me to your soul Valentina and I will give you mine

whom shall I tell that I love you?

whom, that we love each other?

3. Everyone withdrew after dinner. Only Valentina remained in the living room. Only for her the night had not ended.

Then he comes in.

Everyone has gone. They have all hidden themselves away to gossip.

Except Valentina still waiting for the sight that is the attraction: Jesús Aníbal.

His eyes tell her, "I want to find you alone again."

Only they look at each other.

The others try to avoid others' eyes.

She knows how a protective attraction is being transformed into a physical attraction.

She returns to her first moment with Jesús Aníbal.

She ignores everyone else.

She does not listen to the gossip.

The pretty woman desires the ugly woman's luck.

It seems a travesty.

Only a blind man would marry her.

It happens in the best of families.

And Ana Fernanda to Jesús Aníbal: "You traded me for that scare-crow? I don't have to pretend to despise you. But you are my husband in the eyes of God and man. I will never leave you. I will never give you a divorce. Get used to the idea. Dare to tell me I have done something wrong. Tell me something. Did you choose her because of your immense vanity, so you would know you are better-looking than she is? Because you could not stand being less good-looking than me, your wife? It was an unlucky day that we fixed up the house."

The relatives left.

Doña Piedita took to her bed, preparing, in her words, to go to "the hacienda in the sky."

Ana Fernanda did not invite anyone again and dedicated herself to bringing up her daughter, Luisa Fernanda, in accordance with the strictest Catholic morality.

Chorus of the Threatened Daughter

either you pay or we kill you
they say she was a very good student a good daughter she had
a boyfriend and everything they skated together they went on the
ferris
wheel the merry-go-round the octopus
the fair smelled of muégano candy and popcorn peanuts cotton candy
sticky sodas
the wheel turned and her boyfriend took advantage of the girl's fear
to put his arms around her and tell her if you don't kiss me I'll throw
you
out and to please him she opened his fly and
there were sticky candies there too
who pays for the fair?
don't they pay you for Sunday?
I don't have enough
oh well then find another cheaper boyfriend
don'tsqueezeit
mayyourotthere
what would happen to me without the fair on saturdays or without
the sodas
the popcorn the tamales
how will you pay for the fair without money
wait for me love I'll invite you to the fair don't rush
put a hundred clips of drugs in your knapsack
you'll sell them when school lets out
we'll give you a hundred pesos for every hundred clips you sell and
you'll
give us three thousand

she goes out
we can go together to skate here in perisur mall away from the
neighborhood
and the dusty streets and the whistle of drug
buyers and thieves when school lets out
some pickpockets stole my knapsack
it had the three thousand pesos I owed you
either you pay or we kill you
she covered everything but her head in blankets
if I don't pay them they'll kill me
they hit me all over look at the bruises papamama
they robbed me
they didn't kill me
I killed myself
because if I didn't kill myself they said they'd kill you papamama
for the three thousand pesos I owe them
ferris wheel merry-go-round drug dealers cocaine
popcorn marijuana sodas straw hats of glue
terrific

Conjugal Ties (1)

YOU'RE STILL WITH ME because there's nobody left but me who remembers your beauty. Only I have your young eyes in my old ones.

TIME belongs to me. He doesn't understand it. I close my eyes and time belongs to me.

WE'RE ALONE. You and I. Husband and wife. Newly-weds. We don't need anything. You don't let anyone in. Other people spoil everything. Only you and I, lost in an endless embrace. Chained dog barking in the courtyard. Only sound in the area. Your yellow dress tossed over a chair. The only light.

I DON'T HAVE the words.

How strange. We talk a great deal.

Inside I'm silent.

. . .

THERE WERE MISUNDERSTANDINGS. I made a date with you for twelve o'clock. What? You said two. No, twelve. Write down your dates. Dates? How many do you have in a day? With whom? With how many people? Why do you provoke my jealousy with equivocal answers? You always knew I was jealous. You even liked it. I like to feel jealous. That's what you told me. And why didn't you ever make me feel jealous with another woman? What? You were always faithful? Or didn't you have the imagination? I was busy with my career. I never had time for chasing after women. I was absorbed in my work. You know that. I wanted to get ahead. For you. For me. For our marriage. For the two of us. I had ambitions. My greatest ambition was to be director general. You held me back. What did I do? Nothing. That was the problem. No, tell me, really, what did I do? Your behavior. Your wanton behavior. But if I'm tied to you, do you think I have time to deceive you? Ah, then, if you had the time . . . But you watch me like a jailer. That's what brought you down. Hovering over me the whole day. First those phone calls from the office. Then you'd show up unannounced. Then the absurdity of opening closet doors, looking under the bed, saying aha! in front of an open window. Finally, you wouldn't leave the house. You watched over me day and night. And instead of calming down, you grew more and more jealous. Of what? Of whom? And you don't remember that jealousy inflamed my desire, the more I had you, the more I laid siege to you, like an enemy city, I laid siege to you with my tenderness and my eyes and my skin until you surrendered and then felt disgust for me and disgust for yourself for having done everything you shouldn't have what was forbidden what was dirty what degrades us to ourselves but not you, you took it for granted, it was natural, you had no idea of sin, my disgust wasn't yours, you felt something like ecstasy, whore, you displayed it to me, you didn't share my anguish, you laughed at me, where did you get all that business about "existential anguish," Álvaro, what did you think, that I was a book or a student thirsty for knowledge? why didn't you accept all sexual experiences, the most daring, the most calculated, but especially the most spontaneous, the ones that came to us out of the night, the postponed dawn, the unexpected afternoon? why did you interrupt my orgasm to tell me to look at the horrifying sight of two roosters slashing each other to death in a pit? where did you get the idea that a cockfight would excite me more than your sex? why give me explanations? cockfights always excited me, I had my first erection watching a fighting cock slash another fighting cock in an imaginary pit, no, it was in San Marcos, at the fair, but I wasn't there, the pit was the sand of my imagination, Cordelia, the battle took place in my head and you were incapable of penetrating it that's why I said to myself as long as she doesn't penetrate my imagination, I won't penetrate her body again, that's the simple truth, enough explanations, let's not give any cause for gossip, fire the maids, don't invite anyone to the house, I don't want busybodies in my life, I want the freedom to imagine the worst and make you pay for your sins, they're imaginary Álvaro, nothing of what you imagine has happened but it can happen, you can't deny that Cordelia.

MY GREATEST AMBITION was to be director general. Your behavior held me back. Can't you repent, can't you do that for me?

HE TAKES PLEASURE IN muzzling me and asking: What are you thinking about?

I WANT TO CONQUER your superiority of a well-brought-up girl, from a good family, discreet. And unbearable because of it.

HE EVOKES Cordelia's young perfumed hair. Now he pulls off her wig and guffaws. He chokes her with both hands and asks her to sing "Amapola."

BEG, BEG.

Why are you doing this to me?

I want you to pay for the simple fact of being an old woman and having lost your looks.

Have you no mercy?

Isn't cruelty better than compassion?

I'm tired, Álvaro, you exhaust me.

How could you marry me, a man without humor, ugly, vulgar, ignorant?

I don't know, Álvaro.

I know, my sassy little princess. You think that with you, princess, I'll overcome my own inferiority complex.

I'll think about it.

Whaaat . . . ?

HE CHAINS HER to the foot of the bed and observes her for hours waiting for her to say something or ask for water or to be hungry and she only looks at him with a kind of passive resistance that makes him suspect that her gamble is to endure the unbearable for years in order to dominate the tyrant in the end, wear him down until she conquers him. Like that troublemaker Mahatma Gandhi.

DO YOU KNOW, CORDELIA? There's no difference between the morgue and bed. Lie down like a corpse! And now fornicate.

HE LEAVES HER tied to the bed until he sees her surrounded by excretions and he closes his eyes to smell in all their purity her internal wastes, what she carries inside, not erotic delight, not sublime love, but all this that he looks at now and smells . . .

I'M COUNTING on blind obedience aging and hardening a woman, that's what I'm counting on . . .

HE THREATENS to pull out one of her nails with pliers. Once he dares to do it. A single nail. The one on the little finger of her left hand. Her wedding band shines even more brightly on the adjacent ring finger stained with blood. That seems beautiful to him. Let the little finger bleed and the ring finger look good. Aren't they husband and wife? He wouldn't do this to a prostitute. He wouldn't give her that much importance. Does he exult, thinking that with all these actions he is exalting the conjugal relationship to the maximum?

Do you realize I'm doing all this only to prove one thing to you?

What thing?

That I live only for you.

And the world?

What world?

Don't you realize that the world is much larger than this bedroom?

I don't want to know that.

You can't save yourself from the world, Álvaro. Don't you realize that?

You're the one who doesn't understand that you protect me from the immensity of the world and reduce it down to this corner.

I think you owe that to me.

What?

Understanding at least a corner of the world.

I don't want anyone to think you're married to me out of loyalty and habit. I want to know and I want you to know that you're here against your will. That you can't escape this house. Dammit, not even this bedroom. Prisoner.

Then why did you tell Leo on the phone that I'm here because I want to be?

How do you dare to call that bum here?

Well, Álvaro, life follows its course. I mean, beyond these four walls.

Look at them carefully. What they're like.

Yellow. A dirty, stained yellow. Full of white shadows where photographs used to be.

You'd call them lies. Photos of your childhood, your first communion, our engagement, fucking rowing on Chapultepec, fucking holding Madero's hand, fucking honeymoon in Nautla, fucking skiing on Tequesquitengo Lake . . .

A flooded valley, Álvaro. You can see a sunken church at the bottom of the lake. You ski past, and your feet brush against the dome.

Tequesquitengo.

The cross, the cross.

The cross where Our Lord Jesus Christ died, of course.

Yes, the instrument of execution. The cross or the electric chair or the gibbet or the wall. Ways to dispatch us to the next world without a God who comes down to save us. The cross. I laugh at the cross and at fiction. The cross is fiction. We might as well worship an electric chair. We might as well place a gibbet on the altar. We might as well carry a guillotine in a procession. We might as well distribute wafers with cyanide during Mass. *Ite vita est.*

CORDELIA THINKS and sometimes says (above all to Leo, less to Álvaro) that at first along with resignation there was affection, even a little respect, but as the arguments increased, she felt the temptation to hatred. She didn't want to embitter her life. She felt acidity rising from the pit of her stomach and became irritated with herself. Affection, respect, resignation were better for the spirit. But Leo you understand that a woman can feel herself at the crossroads (Álvaro makes puns about the cross the fiction) because she didn't obtain the total love that only came (well) for a time. Now the blood flows in my veins like cold water and I ask myself, I ask my husband, why don't you leave if you hate me so much? why don't you go and live alone?

DO YOU KNOW what irritates me most about you?

Tell me, Álvaro.

Your well-bred voice. Your voice that's so well bred. And do you know what I can't stand about you? Intimacy. Intimacy with you annoys me. Long story short.

The truth is, Leo, what attracted me was his appearance. Not him. Then I found out what he really was like. Too late, my friend. Then his appearance changed.

Why does he hold on to you?

Because only my eyes remember the way he was when he was young.

Don't sacrifice yourself anymore, Cordelia.

Do you see me as sacrificed? Don't think that. Do you see resignation in my eyes? You don't, do you? I'm calm. Do you know why?

No. Tell me.

I believe—that is, I imagine—that he knows more about what will come than about what's already happened.

Are you sure? He or you?

Both of us. I'm still with him because there's nobody left but me who remembers his youth and his promise. Only I have his eyes of yesterday in my eyes of today.

I NEED TO SLEEP with the window open. Close it. I need fresh air. It smells like a circus in here. I'll get pneumonia. Close it. Look at what a disaster the bathroom is. Why don't you keep your makeup someplace else? Why don't you clean the sink after you shave look at the dirty soap look at your hairs look at my brush full of your bleached hairs hang the towel up to dry spread it out don't leave it like that just thrown down put a mat beside the bathtub don't get the floor all wet yesterday I slipped and almost broke my neck why do you use so much toilet paper? don't you prefer to wipe your silky, high-handed ass with Kleenex? don't use my razors anymore to shave under your arms you leave them full of hair but I only use the one you've already thrown away why don't you remove the hair permanently and stop bothering me why did you rearrange my shirts? to make your life easier blue ones here white ones there short-sleeve shirts on one side sport shirts in the back because you wear them less often ah! do you want me to classify your panties your bras your panty hose because you can arrange my closet but I can't arrange yours right? why? because that's private Álvaro and I have nothing private, Cordelia? it's different it's different.

WE'RE NOT THE SAME you're right I have everything hanging on the outside you keep everything in those aromatic crannies, you're full of folds and more folds Cordelia and you know you smell like a fish market that's what you smell like a rotten red snapper that's how I feel when I make love to you that I'm fucking a dead fish left on the beach for a week a man shows himself he shows everything a woman hides everything she arranges everything in little quilted boxes but a woman disarranges your soul roll up your socks slowly bottom to top don't yank them don't put your shoes on before your trousers be careful not to stain your tie at the cleaners they ruin ties ties have their virginity too why were you messing with my tube of toothpaste? because it's very ugly to squeeze it from the top ah yes well I'm going to squeeze the tube from the top just to fuck up your little esthetic manias and give me the remote it's not mine I want to watch the news with Adriana Pérez Cañedo well Chespirito is on at the same time and I'd rather see Chilindrina where did you leave the *Reforma*? I threw it out why? I already read it and what about me? don't I have the right to read it, Álvaro? you don't understand anything, Cordelia, women are bovine creatures they graze and have calves and give milk, that's all and they don't know what's going on in the world and don't care . . .

AND YOU, ÁLVARO, don't urinate outside the bowl just look at the drops you've left on the floor . . .

ÁLVARO was obsessed with presenting himself as the éminence grise of powerful figures, he would come home full of himself and tell me:

"I proposed to the secretary . . ."

"I suggested to the subsecretary . . ."

"I made the senior official see . . ."

"The secretary's secretary, thanks to me . . ."

YOU STAY WITH ME because there's nobody left but me who remembers your youthful beauty. Only I have your young eyes in my old ones.

HOW DID IT HAPPEN? Was there a cause of all causes? What was first, what came later? Desire or jealousy? Ecstasy or disillusion? Misunderstandings or explanations? Suspicions or gossip? Desires or jealousy? Longing or disgust? Plenitude or rejection?

WHERE WERE YOU all afternoon? I've been waiting for you. You know I desire you in an untimely way.

Yes, you say I'm an untimely woman.

That's why I want you to be here when I desire you.

I'm sorry to disillusion you.

Bah, a man can't lose his illusions if he doesn't have any.

I don't understand you.

There are too many explanations.

That's true. Never complain. Never explain.

Not knowing where you are causes me tremendous anguish.

But I'm always at your side, you know that, my presence is in your imagination, in your desire, you always say that, I'm a prisoner in your head, I never leave there . . .

Your presence, darling, is only a bloody Kotex tossed in the toilet. Next time please pull the chain. Or send your menstrual filth to the cleaners, pig.

WHEN HE FOUND OUT, he didn't know what to do. Ignore it. Retaliate. Go out and kill him. He expected everything except her response.

You've violated my privacy. Those letters belonged only to me.

Álvaro couldn't believe it.

Only to you? Did the Holy Spirit write them? Did you write them to yourself? How long have you been quoting poems by Neruda?

Ha ha.

They're my letters. Mine. Understand that. Respect my privacy.

And if you found love letters sent to me by another woman, would you respect "my privacy"?

It's different, Álvaro. You have a profession, a public life, you go to work. You're in the world. But I live alone in this house.

Alone? Writing and receiving letters from a stranger?

Understand that I'm alone, alone deep inside. You don't give me all your time. I'm not reproaching you. But please understand that I need my time and my company, too. Yes, I need my privacy violated by your unhealthy curiosity. And everything going so well, my God . . .

Tell me, tell me what you're reproaching me for, Cordelia . . .

I'll tell you. You talk only about yourself, your career, your magnificent plans, your intelligence, your brilliance, the applause you receive. You're an applause meter. You're a valiant knight errant. Don Quixote. I'm your Sanchita Panzona. Well, no. Just as you live your life, I have the right to live mine.

I don't have a mistress, Cordelia.

Well, you ought to find one. Then we'd be even and no recriminations.

Is that all you can say to me?

No, of course not. Just imagine. I have my lover every day and you whenever I feel like it.

You've become a cynic.

Not a cynic. Desperate. How many times, beside you, did I have to pinch myself and tell myself, "I'm alive. I think. I want . . ."

Cordelia doesn't look away. He can't conquer her eyes.

That drives him mad.

I can bear only one tyrant. Myself, Álvaro.

All right. What's the point of telling you how it irritates me that you're so pleased with yourself.

What do you expect. I'm too alive.

She doesn't look away. He can't conquer her eyes.

This drives him mad.

NO, he didn't even give her the satisfaction of finding himself a mistress. He didn't want her to have any excuses. He wanted her to know that his cruelty was gratuitous and undeserved. He ties her to the bed. He gags her and asks what are you thinking? He chokes her and asks her to sing "Amapola." He says he wants to reduce her until the torments of curiosity (his) are lost completely.

You won't have any life but this one, locked up. At my side. Sequestered in your own house.

He let it be understood—he never said so explicitly—that this was the price she had to pay for his forgetting. Álvaro will forget Cordelia's guilt if Cordelia accepts gratuitous punishment, as if there were no sin between them. It was a painful way, she said to herself only because he said it first, "of beginning over."

I DON'T WANT anybody to think you're married to me out of loyalty, love, or habit. I want to know and for you to know, too, that you're here against your will.

What do you say out in the world, Álvaro?

That you prefer never to leave the house.

HE'LL CHAIN HER to the foot of the bed and tell her that this will be the punishment she deserved for the mere fact of becoming old and losing her looks. He'll gag her and ask what are you thinking about? He'll choke her while he asks her to sing "Amapola." He'll tell her there's no difference between the morgue and the bed. Lie down like a corpse! You'll close your eyes. You'll spare me your detestable vindictive gaze. You won't tell me that death is the maximum aggression against us because I'll keep you alive so you have no excuses. Until the final moment. I'll make you feel that death is only your possibility, not your reality. My malice will postpone your death. I'll prepare your death, dear wife. I'll separate you from death by prolonging your pain. I'll prepare your death. You won't be my phantom. You'll be my wife. Do you realize that I survive only to make you suffer?

WHEN I DARED to tell him—*Reforma*, Adriana Pérez Cañedo—that the secretary had done the opposite of what Álvaro told me he told him he should have done, he ripped the paper, kicked the TV, and began to isolate himself, to not go out, to look at me reproachfully: I knew his secret, I paid no attention to him, his airs were pure smoke, I condemned myself, if he no longer had power outside, he would show me he had it in the house.

AT THE LAST DINNER the two of them—Álvaro and Cordelia—attended together, they heard the honorable secretary say in a very low but exceedingly ill-intentioned voice:

Álvaro Meneses is a *lethal* bureaucrat. He's becoming redundant.

YOU HAVE LESS fizz than a Coca-Cola that's been open for a month . . .

I have an enormous empty space. That's what I have.

He said this and stumbled, falling on his face over the rug that still smelled of urine, and at that moment the dog was exiled to live tied up, howling with melancholy, in the courtyard.

HE BEGAN DISPUTING TERRITORIES WITH ME. He began extending his control over the closet, the bed, the bathroom, the TV, and I kept telling him your seclusion doesn't free you from the big cold world Álvaro (but really tell him that Cordelia) you're a child (don't be afraid of him Cordelia) you let yourself be judged too easily (you pick up the sections of the paper tossed to the floor and put them in order so you can feel victorious) you go around imagining what they're saying about you (tell him) what they think of you (think about it).

I'M AT A LOSS FOR WORDS.

You talk a great deal.

Inside, I'm silent.

HE MADE A POINT of masturbating in front of her. He laughed. He said, pleasures known to Onan unknown to Don Juan.

Did you think convention would control me? he said when he was finished.

No. What an idea. Not even love subjugates you, Álvaro.

I told him many things.

Will you let me tell you the truth?

No.

Excuse me. You're too weak for me.

Ah, you bitch. I'll show you . . .

I can endure only one tyrant. Myself. My own tyrant, Álvaro.

Shall I tell you something? Why you're so twisted? Why you never travel a straight path?

I'll ruminate on that, Álvaro.

This drove him crazy. He began to shout, tear his hair, ruminate, ruminate, he shouted, that's what cows say, why do you use those highfalutin words? why do you always talk like a well-bred girl? why do you constantly want to prove your superiority to me? because I was just a promising young man and you took charge of locking me away here . . . ?

You locked yourself away . . .

I locked myself away with you . . .

Nonsense.

You frustrated my ambition.

Just realize it, that's all.

I didn't become what I wanted to be.

You locked yourself away, I'm telling you . . .

I could have been somebody . . .

You are somebody. You're my husband. Isn't that enough?

It's your fault I'm a nobody.

What would you have done without me?

Become what I could have been.

Ah yes! The things I didn't do to please you . . .

Without you, Cordelia . . .

DIRTY CLOTHES dropped and forgotten. Floors slippery with forgotten filth. Toilets overflowing with shit. Sheets stained with blood. Rats conspiring in the corners. Spiders keeping watch from the ceilings. Cockroaches smoking marijuana in the kitchen. The sweet stink of abandonment. Without you. Without me.

. . .

I DREAMED I met you as a young man at a dance. A far-off dance long ago. Strauss waltzes. Tails. Crinolines. Cordelia Ortiz and her dance card. The line of suitors. A continental summer dance. Warm, distant, perfumed. Cordelia Ortiz and her blond curls arranged like tassels of wheat. Ah, how I desire her. Ah, how she charms me. I'm not even on her card. But I'm in her sight. She dances with someone else but looks at me. I'm the only one not wearing tails. I came unexpectedly. I'm dressed as a peasant. I can't stop looking at her. I get her to look at me. Now we don't stop looking at each other. Her eyes enslave mine. My eyes magnetize hers. We don't know if we're living for an instant or imagining an entire life. When she dances, she's so graceful, so fresh, so beautiful that measures of time disappear. She is now. She is always. She turns my internal clocks upside down. She concentrates all the time I've lived or can live. She makes me feel I don't need to go anywhere because now I'm here. She is my years, my months, my hours, in a minute. She is my place, all the spaces I've traveled through or can travel through. I am no longer divided. I am entire in myself and with her. I don't need to have her in my arms. The young Cordelia dances with others but looks at me. When I came in, I was an indeterminate man. From now on, she determines me. I understand this in a flash and already begin to hate her. With what right is this woman I don't even know going to determine me? I argue with myself, struggle against my doubts, I know I desire her, know my desire could be satisfied but still remain desire. I am like an island adrift that would like to unite with a continent. My insular desire can leave me there, surrounded by oceans. It can also unite me with the land I look at from my island and I see beaches strewn with black pearls and impenetrable forests and mountains broken into the steps of terraces and ravines that plunge into the deepest bowels of the earth. All of this I will have to conquer, the country called Cordelia, and once I conquer it, will I stop desiring it? No, I tell myself from the isolated island, from the shore of the dance that she dominates as if the floor were the entire universe, no, I'll obtain what I desire and will immediately want to dominate what I have desired because there is no gratuitous desire, there is no desire that does not desire to possess and dominate what is desired, make it mine, with no opening whatsoever for any possession that isn't mine. I desire Cordelia in order to have her first and dominate her immediately because otherwise how do I satisfy my desire? how, if I already possess her, am I going to stop desiring because I already possess? She is my wife. Don't they call a wife a "ball and chain," the handcuffs that bind the hands of the fugitive who attempted to steal the object of desire . . . ? The music stops. The lights dim. The orchestra withdraws to the sound of chairs carelessly overturned, feet accelerated by haste, abandoned music stands. The beaux are leaving downhearted, their black lines whipped by the approaching storm sending albino messages to the open-air ballroom. Only she remains in a circle of light that belongs only to her, to Cordelia Ortiz, my future wife, my beautiful prisoner, so no one will take her from me, she is my dream made reality . . .

WHY DO YOU PERSIST? Leo asks Cordelia and Cordelia responds: Because it is his way of showing me he lives only for me. He doesn't love himself. He becomes furious with me. Look, I tried to love him, to save him from everything unpleasant . . . I loved him once.

He hasn't reciprocated.

That isn't the point. The important thing is when I realized that Álvaro could love only me, I decided to put it to the test. To the point where I believed I was mad by my own will. The important thing is that by torturing me, he lives only for me. That's what counts, Leo. Would you do as much for me?

LEO DIDN'T SAY A WORD. Leo and Cordelia live together and don't need to state that they love each other.

You know my desire is that you don't ever see him again.

I know, and that's why I'm explaining my reasons for going back. Once a month. It's not too much.

I won't say anything, love. You know your game. But to see you come back each month in that state, well . . . I . . .

She places her index finger on his lips.

Hush—she smiles. Respect conjugal ties.

He doesn't love himself. He becomes angry with you. Don't go back anymore.

Leo, it took me years to decide. To leave or stay. Run away. I would say to him, Álvaro, give me just one hour of peace. Just one. I'm giving you my whole life. Do you know what he answered? He said: Do you want the truth? Well, you won't have it. I'll give you something better. The lie. Because in the lie there can be love, but in the truth, never.

SHE TURNED TO SAY GOODBYE. Álvaro opened the door for her and said:

I'm opening the door for you. Why don't you leave? You're free.

Have pity, Álvaro. Don't look for me anymore. Why do you oblige me to come back? Why do you torture me this way?

You're wrong—Álvaro didn't look at her, he moved his eyes around the yellow bedroom—I don't want to see you. Get out.

She was about to touch his hand.

I'm not afraid anymore that you'll lock me in, really. I don't care if I'm your slave.

Álvaro opens the door for her.

Why don't you leave? You're free. I've said it so many times. Fly away, little dove, fly away! My house is not a cage.

I'll never leave you, Álvaro.

Go. Consider me dead.

I want to take care of you. You're my husband.

I'm not going to think about problems anymore. When they come, I'll know how to face them by myself. Of course I will.

He said this with a look that was not resigned but tranquil.

He seemed, Leo, to know more about what's going to come than what already happened . . .

Why? What did he say to you?

He said he was at a crossroads because he hadn't gotten from me the total love that lasts only one night . . .

What did you say?

Nothing. He got down on his knees. He placed his head against my belly and I caressed it.

You didn't say anything to him?

Yes. I said, "I'll never leave you."

Why, Cordelia? Please tell me why you're going back to him. You're under no obligation. Do you want to be punished for the mere fact of having loved me?

No, Leo. It's that only his eyes remember how I was when I was young. He tells me that. "You stay with me because nobody but me remembers your youthful beauty. Only I have your young eyes in my old ones."

SHE TOOK OFF HER YELLOW DRESS. She didn't hear the barking of the yellow dog in the courtyard. She allowed him to caress her loose yellow hair for a long time. She planned never to come back.

Chorus of the Father of Rock

Father Silvestre Sánchez cries out in vain, the mass of young people shouts weeps advances like a Roman legion in togas in sandals boots and totally Palacio miniskirts with the name and likeness of the fallen idol Daddy Juan printed on their backs singing and shouting the words to his songs
think twice before you go
when the lights go out
pretty girls don't cry
it's too late
I told you so
while Father Silvestre attempts in vain to counter the cacophony with the ancient music of the requiem
quiet children behave this is a religious service
dona eis domine
requiem aeternam
lux perpetua
now Daddy Juan's coffin is in the open grave let me bless it before the gravediggers cover it in earth and then seal it carefully and the world is left in peace because you youngsters don't want your idol to be eaten by dogs or worms, isn't that right?
locked up in makesicko seedy
drowning in the shit of the cow the muck
fuckin with the nuts the gland
dancing to the mock the zooma
you're divine Daddy Juan you carry God on your back Idol, even though you are God
anathema let it be anathema
Ana the ma-le tit be Ana

Ana Ledibee
if you love Daddy Juan so much respect the ceremony girls respect the remains and the girls advance uncontrollably in an avalanche crying shouting Daddy Juan don't leave Daddy Juan let me toss you my panties, take my bra, here's my Tampax, sainted god, sweet little daddy,
only Juan said Jesús is God
before Mateo or Lucas or Marco found the courage
Daddy Juan is God
Daddy Juan is like the sun three things in one thing light heat and star
Ana Theme
Daddy Juan came like a ray of light into our lives
Christ Jesus is effluence protection and erection
Daddy Juan was created established and projected
God is the word
The word is Daddy Juan
God is the shepherd the door the truth the resurrection
Daddy Juan guide us open us tell us resuscitate
the mob at the grave passes beers from hand to hand to mitigate grief and augment goodbye singing the songs of Daddy Juan and pushing Father Silvestre let me officiate in the name of God quiet crow here there's no other God but Daddy Juan
here is Mexico Makesicko City here where they burned the feet of Cow the Muck where they stoned Mock the Zooma to death here the city was founded on water and rock and thorn and dust storms with glands and woven baskets the city of rock and roll perpetually at twelve on the Richter scale
here there's no other savior father but our sweet Daddy Juan surrounded by loose earth and irate dust and mute cypresses and leaden sun daddy-oh daddy-oh
until they push Father Silvestre into the open grave of Daddy Juan and the mob of fifteen-year-olds in miniskirts screaming and singing at the grave grabs the shovels away from the grave-diggers and begins to shovel dirt into the pit onto the body of

Father Silvestre mute now though openmouthed lying faceup on the cedar coffin with a silver guitar instead of a crucifix
it serves you right to suffer the priest murmurs under shovelfuls of earth, you sought out suffering my lord Jesus Christ, our lord Daddy Juan
when the lights go out they turn out the lights
I'm ready sings Muddy Waters in honor of Daddy John and Father Silvestre murmurs in response
it's too late stray cats we're underneath it all
ghosts appear in the grave of the mob
everything in a box, trapped in the case
I won't stand in your way make way for death Daddy Juan stray cats tollin bells for whom the bells toll for whom the belles toil for whom the balls roll for whom the blues roll and rock baby in a deep grave death is grave from womb to tomb from the cradle to the grave the cradle will rock and roll
when the lights go out Daddy Juan it serves you right to suffer
amen Father Silvestre pulvis eris et in pulvis reverteris

Mater Dolorosa

José Nicasio: Who was my daughter? I don't know where to begin. We all descend from someone else. We all come from somewhere else. Even the Indians aren't from here. Not even the Indians. They came from Asia millions of years ago. Nobody was here. That's why it's so wonderful to sit and watch nightfall from the steps of the ruins of Monte Albán. To tell yourself the mountains were always there, welcoming the sun every twilight as it lies down behind them, sending out the light of a pardonable rest. It shone on us all day. Now it disappears. Not behind but inside the mountains. The sun makes its bed in those hills. It lays down a pallet that we call "twilight." Capricious sunset. It changes colors every nightfall. It's intense red one time, misty blue the next, orange one afternoon, gray and old later. And this has been happening, José Nicasio, since before human beings appeared. Nature *was* without any need to be seen. It saw itself, in any case, and celebrated in solitude. The mountains of the Sierra Madre had no name then. Today do they know they are seen? Do they know that a man and a woman sat down one afternoon six months ago to watch the spectacle of nightfall in Monte Albán? How could I not understand, José Nicasio, that a young man and woman, two human beings, would remain there, insensible to schedules, enraptured by the spectacle. The mountains in silhouette. The sun fading. The valley already submerged in darkness. And the high vantage point of the ruins, the steps of the pyramid. How could I not understand. Two young people, a man and a woman, forget about schedules. They ignore the distant routine voices of the guards. It's time to close up. It's time to leave. The ruins will be closed off . . . Do the kingdoms of the past close, José Nicasio? The eternal monuments of a race, do they have schedules? The builders of the pyramids, were their comings and goings checked? Look, José Nicasio, look how I'm trying to understand. I'm trying to know. I think I know that the old gods are the guardians of their temples. The gods don't charge an entrance fee to their sacred places. Why would my daughter and you pay attention to the guard's whistle, it's time to go, the Monte Albán site is closing, it's time to go back to the city of Oaxaca, to civilization, to the roof and the bed and the struggle and the shower that waits for us. Leave the site to the gods. At least at night the temple will belong only to them, not to the intruders, José Nicasio and Alessandra. Tell me, why were you there?

Señora Vanina: Thank you for your letter. I certainly didn't expect so nice a gesture. Really so generous, Señora. In my solitude I don't expect anyone to communicate with me. Approach me. Visit me. Imagine what it meant for me to receive your very kind letter. Thank you for giving me this opportunity to explain myself. I swear to you there was no need. What is, is. What was, is over now. Have you noticed how we Mexicans use that famous NOW? NOW it was all right. NOW it was time. NOW I grew tired of waiting. NOW I'll leave here. NOW he died. Only that afternoon I told myself: NOW I've come back. NOW I can return to this place with different eyes after so long an absence. Return as if another man had gone to the place I went to, the land where I was born. Señora, how could I not be moved, agitated, Señora . . . ? When I was a boy in the village, I didn't even know there was such a place. In the village, we spent our lives growing what we sold on market days in Tlacolula. Have you ever been there? We all worked very hard so nothing would be missing on Sundays and Thursdays, the market days. If you stop by there, you'll see that nothing is missing. Cilantro, espazote leaf, tomatoes, sesame seeds, cheese, tree chilis, anchos, chipotles, guajillos, parsley and plantains, sapodilla fruit, melons, turkeys, even the famous edible grasshoppers of our country, everything the Lord Our God has given to Oaxaca so that we can gather the blessed fruits and take them to sell twice a week.

"God has given us everything because we're very poor," my father would say.

Go to the market, Señora Vanina, and try to hear Castilian in that murmur of Indian voices, which are high but sweet. They are bird voices, Señora, Zapoteca voices filled with *tlanes* and *tepecs.* We speak Castilian only to offer goods to the customers who visit us, dear customer, two pesos a dozen, this cheese shreds all by itself it's so delicious . . . Señora, you say we all come from somewhere else, and that's true. When I was a little boy, I began to play with colors and papers from the amate tree and then to paint on white amate wood and invent little pictures, then bigger ones, until my honored father said take them to the market, José Nicasio, and I did and began to sell my little paintings. Until the distinguished professor from the city of Oaxaca saw what I was doing and said this boy has talent and took me to live in the city (with the permission of my honored father) and there I grew up learning to read and write and paint with so much joy, Señora, as if I myself had been amate paper or an adobe wall that gradually is covered with lime and maguey sap until the wall of earth is transformed into something as soft and smooth as a woman's back . . . It wasn't easy, Señora, don't think that. Something in me was always pulling back to the village, the way they say a nanny goat pulls back to the mountains. My new happiness wasn't enough to make me forget my old happiness as a boy with no literature, no Castilian, barefoot with no clothes except drill trousers and a threadbare white shirt and mud-caked huaraches. And another white shirt stiff with starch and carefully pressed black trousers and shoes once a week so I could go to Mass like a respectable person . . . Now, in the city, I was a respectable person, I was being educated, I read, I went to school, I knew people who had come from Mexico City and friends who would visit the distinguished professor's studio. But I swear to you that an enormous piece of my soul was still tied to the life I left behind, the village, the market, the noise of donkeys and pigs and turkeys, the straw sleeping mats, cooking in the fireplace, poor stews, rich aromas . . . Except when I returned to the village on Sundays and feast days, it was like offending those who stayed behind, throwing it in their faces that I could leave and they couldn't. I swear it isn't just a silly suspicion. One day I went back out of sheer feeling, Señora, what you people call "nostalgia," and at first nobody recognized me, but when word got around,

"It's José Nicasio, he's come back,"

some looked at me with so much rancor, others with greed, most of them with distance, Señora, that I decided never to go back to the place I came from. But can we cut ourselves off forever from our roots? Isn't there something left that hurts us, the way they say an amputated arm continues to hurt . . . ? I couldn't return to my village. I could only return to the ruins of my village and from there calmly observe a world that was mine but no longer acknowledged me. The world before the world.

José Nicasio: Thank you for your letter. Thank you for having taken the time to answer me. What am I saying, when I received your message, I thought that man has all the time in the world. Will he learn to be patient? I asked myself from the beginning. Will he be able to hear me? Will he have a residue of tenderness, a thread of intelligence, to understand why I am writing to him? I believe so. I read your letter, José Nicasio, and believe I understand that you do. I also believe you are a rascal, *furbo,* as we say in Italy, sharp, as you say here in Mexico. You trumped me. You told me where you came from, the mix of luck and effort that got you out of your village and took you to the city and to success. José Nicasio: How unsatisfied you leave me. I understand you less than ever. I agonize trying to comprehend your behavior. I hope you're not offended if I tell you that as far as I'm concerned, your letter was never received. What interests me is your knowing who my daughter, Alessandra, was. I confess with some guilt that I had little patience where you were concerned. But I realize that if I write so you'll know who my daughter was, I'll have to put up with your telling me who you are . . . I told you we all come from somewhere else. You from an indigenous community in Oaxaca. My family, from the European exile that followed the Civil War in Spain. My father was a Republican. He didn't have time to escape. He ended up in prison and was shot by the fascists. My northern Italian mother, from Turin, could not leave her husband's grave behind without even knowing where they had thrown his body.

"All of Spain is a graveyard," she said and disappeared into the lands of Castile. I never heard from her again. A Mexican diplomat put me in a group of orphaned children, and we set sail for Veracruz. I reached the age of twelve, and a family of Spanish merchants adopted me. I married their son, who by now was completely Mexican. Diego Ferrer. A businessman. Alessandra was born of that union. You saw her. Her long honey-colored hair. Her Italian profile, with its long, slender nose, her eyes of Lombard mist, her waist that can be encircled by the fingers of two hands . . . She was distinctive. It was as if the ancestors, the dead of the house in Italy, were resurrected in her . . . Physically, she resembled my mother. But her spirit was her grandfather's. My husband watched her with astonishment as she grew. José Nicasio, Alessandra was a woman of extraordinary intelligence. She made such rapid progress in her studies that she surpassed the top student. Her calling was philosophy, literature, art, the universe of culture. Her father, my husband, looked at her with suspicion, with disbelief. Alessandra didn't marry. Or rather, she was married to the world of esthetic forms. Like you? Yes, but just imagine how different. She was born into a comfortable family. Do you believe that coming like you from a very low point brings greater merit to the effort to ascend? You're wrong. When you're born at a high point, the temptation to let yourself drift, *se laisser aller*, is very strong. Fighting comfort is more difficult than struggling against poverty. You had to achieve what you didn't have. She had to move away from what she already had . . . Her father, my husband, was apprehensive. He wanted a "normal" daughter who would go out dancing and meet boys of her own class, marry, give him grandchildren. He didn't have the courage to tell her this. My daughter's gaze was so strong it forbade familiarity, at home and away from home. Her eyes said to all of us,

"Don't come close. I love you very much, but I'm fine alone. Accept me as I am."

Diego, my husband, was not resigned. To "normalize" her, he called her Sandy, imagine, as if my daughter worked at McDonald's. Sandy! She was baptized Alejandra, but to emphasize her difference and irritate my husband, I always called her Alessandra.

It's true. Alessandra didn't participate, she didn't make friends, she lived enclosed in a balloon of culture. She used familiar address with the thinkers and artists of the past. It made me laugh to hear her speak not only of Michelangelo and Raphael but of Marcel or Virginia as if they were her intimate friends.

I defended my daughter's solitude. Her self-sufficiency. And above all, her promise. I told my husband, "If Alessandra does what you want and marries and has children, she'll be a superior mother and spouse, not an ordinary, run-of-the-mill housewife." At times my husband found consolation. The moment would come when Alejandra—"Sandy"—would settle down and lead a "normal life." But for me, her normality was to be how she was, a voracious reader, endlessly eager to know, as if her grandfather, my father, had survived the war and Franco's tyranny and continued, as a ghost, in the existence of his granddaughter—disciplined, focused, but ignorant of the world.

Innocent. Innocent but promising.

That was my daughter, José Nicasio. A promise inside a translucent sphere where the corrupt air of the human city could not penetrate. A promise, José Nicasio. Repeat that to yourself in your solitude. Repeat it night and day. I want these words to forever occupy the center of your life. You have to know who my daughter was. And please don't protect yourself, as my husband does, behind the lie of Alessandra's supposed human coldness. Ah yes, they say, she was a promising girl but barely human. She lacked warmth. She lacked emotion.

People who think that infuriate me, beginning with my husband, I'll tell you that with all honesty. It means not understanding that the "familiar address" Alessandra used with genius—or brilliance, I don't know—was an intense, erotic form of desire. My daughter loved, Señor. Not what everyone vulgarly attributes to that verb, physical attraction, not even the tenderness and warmth shared with other human beings. Alessandra loved Nietzsche or the Brontës because she felt them *alone*, alone in the graves of their books and their thoughts. Alessandra approached the geniuses of the past to give them life with her attention, which was the form her affection took: paying *attention*.

She didn't want to take anything from anyone. She wanted to give to the neediest. The dead? Yes, perhaps. It's true, "The dead are so alone." But she sought out the company of the less frequented dead. The immortals. That's what she told me. She wanted to look after, offer her hand to so many human beings, the artists and thinkers who are the subject of studies, biographies, yes, and lectures, but not of a *love* equivalent to what we give to a close, living being. Offer her hand to the immortals. That was my daughter's vocation. Perhaps that was why she was there, that afternoon, in Monte Albán.

José Nicasio: Don't condemn me without hearing me. I talked a great deal with my daughter. I warned her that love can isolate us from everything around us. But in its absence, we can be filled with the fear that something comparable exists. I believe my daughter wanted to love the incomparable and that all respect for the comparable filled her with disquiet. Is what I say true? Can you, if not judge, at least comprehend the words of a grieving mother? To think is to desire, I would tell my husband. He didn't understand me. Did you think about my daughter? Did you desire her, José Nicasio?

Señora Vanina: You've never seen me. You don't know me physically. I have no reason to hide what I am or where I come from. I'm ugly, Señora. I'm an ugly Oaxacan Indian. I'm short but muscular. I have a short neck, pushed down into my shoulders. This only makes the strength of my torso more prominent. If you could see how powerfully my heart beats. At times I believe that the front of my shirt betrays me. Right there, if you place your hand on my chest, right there you can feel the power of my heartbeats, Señora. I have an impatient heart, Señora. I moved up, I left my village and my people behind, and this makes me feel guilty, to tell you the truth. Unhappy. I have to constantly compare what could have been—what I left behind—and what I am. That's why I feel guilty. Shouldn't I have continued down there, in the village, in the Tlacolula market? Did I have the right to be more than all those people who saw me born, grow, play, work? In my heart this question always beats, Señora Vanina, an unsettling question that rises up to my neck where very thick veins throb to keep up my defiant head, I admit it, Señora, I have the face of an ugly Indian, flat nose, narrow forehead, and on my mouth an indecipherable sneer that I can't change no matter what I do. I look in the mirror and say to myself, José Nicasio, take off that sneer, smile, try to be nice. My face must have come to me from very far away. My mask, naturally, Señora. Let us understand each other. We are born with the face that time gave us. Hard time, almost always. Time to suffer. Time to endure. What face do you want us to put on . . . ?

You can see, my Indian nature comes out no matter how I try to hide it. It just comes out, like a wildcat crouching in my belly. I tell you that I see myself in the mirror and say, Change your expression, José Nicasio, put a nice friendly smile on your mouth, don't twist it like that, nobody's threatening you. And I try to do that, Señora, but it doesn't work, my head filled with colors and my chest filled with trembling tells me so. Don't look so fierce, José Nicasio, don't show so openly that you're taking revenge, not for your humble origin but for your present-day success, do you understand? Stop telling people excuse me for having moved up, I'm an Indian who carries on his back centuries of humiliation, an ordinary dark-skinned man, an indigenous Zapoteca who's not allowed to be on the sidewalk, they whip us down into the dust in the street . . .

Let me laugh, Señora. I go to the museums of Mexico and walk through the rooms of indigenous cultures—Mayas, Olmecas, Aztecas—filled with admiration for the art of my forebears. Well, that's where they want to keep us, Señora, hidden away in the museums. Like bronze statues on the avenues. What happens if King Cuauhtémoc climbs down from his pedestal on the Paseo de la Reforma and walks among the people? They burn his feet again . . .

Let me laugh, Señora. As soon as we're out on the street, we're filthy Indians again, submissive Indians, redskins. They seize our ancestral lands, force us into the wild and hunger, sell us rifles and aguardiente so we'll fight among ourselves. They invent a right to our women. They attribute every crime to us. They discover that their white women desire us in secret, and they come after us opening our backs so that dark blood spills even blacker blood. They shout Indian! at us or they shout redskin! when they come after us. Didn't you know, isn't Your Grace aware of all this? Your Grace. We're not "reasonable people." We're not "decent people." You kill us as soon as we turn our backs on you. The fugitive law is applied to us. Does Your Grace, a reasonable person, know what it means to be a stupid Indian, without reason, a stupid animal scorned in this country? A tongue-tied, splay-footed Indian.

And do you know what it means to escape the world of our fathers? First to Oaxaca because of my meritorious amate paintings. Then, thanks to the gringos who admire my work, to a school of Mexican handicrafts in San Diego, California, right on the border between Mexico and the United States. Far from my family's village in the privilege of Oaxaca, in the house of the distinguished professor who treated me like half a son, a proof of his generosity with the less fortunate. I heard him say so,

"I'm not racially prejudiced. Look at José Nicasio. I treat him like a son."

And now, far from my village, wandering the border. The wetbacks in California are dry when they arrive because there's no river between San Diego and Tijuana. There are barbed-wire fences. There's the migra. There are tunnels full of rats. There are garbage trucks where you can hide to cross over. There are vans abandoned in the desert, locked with padlocks and full of suffocated workers who paid a hundred or two hundred dollars to cross the border like animals. There's injustice, Señora. Something you can't save yourself from, even if you migrate to California . . .

But I already was "on the other side." In every sense, Señora. I was respected by the gringos because I had talent and knew how to work. They even invited me to their parties to show how democratic they were. I was what they call their "token Mexican," their nice demonstration Mexican, and they say a button's enough for a demonstration. I was the Mexican button.

The newly arrived Mexicans gave me ugly looks. I wasn't going to turn them in. Don't think I was going to displace them. I was out of place everywhere, in my Indian village, in the capital of Oaxaca, in San Diego, California. I've known nothing but discrimination, Señora, even when I'm accepted, I'm good only for soothing a bad conscience.

Look how far we've come, José Nicasio. Once we put signs outside restaurants NO DOGS OR MEXICANS ALLOWED. Once we called them *greasers*, greasy, filthy, untouchable.

And now you can't live without our work, I told them, and everybody took it badly, the gringos, the wetbacks, even myself.

Why do you shoot off your mouth, José Nicasio.

Learn to calm down.

Life has treated you well.

But the grimace was still there, Señora, as if nothing had happened.

. . .

José Nicasio: You're mistaken if you believe my daughter, Alessandra, discriminated against you. She was incapable of anything so vile. I'm not saying that Sandra was a Sister of Charity. She didn't display condescension. That kind of thing horrified her. She simply treated inferiors with respect and dignity. I mean, people different from her. She was conscious of the hypocrisies of our society and rejected them. How many times did I ask her to make friends with this girl, approach that woman, and she'd say, No, Mama, you haven't seen that the girl has already learned the art of dissembling, you haven't seen that the woman is a master of deceit.

How do you know, Alessandra? They're not bad people. I know them.

No, it's not that they're bad. It's that they're obliged to pretend they're good. They've been brought up to deceive and be cunning, to protect themselves from our society. I don't want to be like that. I prefer the company of the spirits . . .

Please, accept other people's limitations. Sooner or later, you'll have to be just a little familiar with society.

Never.

A mother is speaking to you, José Nicasio. I am speaking to you freely and with the futile hope that you yourself feel free. What I'm saying to you about Alessandra, I'm saying so you'll know who my daughter was. At the same time, I keep asking myself: Who was Alessandra? I thought I knew her character. That is what I'm describing to you. But I also knew that each character has its own exception. Is this what happened to you? That nightfall in Monte Albán, did you see the exception in my daughter? Did you discover the fault, the crack in a personality so carefully constructed?

Her father, my husband, a practical man, would become desperate.

"Tell me, Vanina, doesn't our daughter have a single defect?"

I would tell him no, Sandra was perfect, because I never was going to allow her own father to dissect her like an insect. For me, Alessandra was sacred. But I am not, and behind my husband's back, I had to look for the chinks of imperfection in my daughter.

Love.

Did Alessandra really love? Did her love for dead artists and thinkers hide a profound contempt for ordinary people? Forgive me, José Nicasio, was my daughter a social snob, a typical *bas bleu*? I implore you to forgive my frankness. My husband and I love each other. My husband is an excellent lover. He knows how to give me pleasure. Forgive me. I mean that Alessandra wasn't born of the routine obligations of marriage. No, my husband knew how to excite me, transport me, raise me to the pleasure enjoyed by a woman who knows herself not only desired, but physically *ecstatic.* Alessandra was born of pleasure. But she doesn't seem ever to have touched the pleasure I'm describing to you while she was alive.

I was afraid, observing my daughter's lack of sexual interest, that her coldness led back to me, to her mother, to that sadness that is the price of love not shared with those you love. Sandra had to know she was beautiful. At least I knew it. When she was already a woman, she would ask me to dry her after her bath. Running the towel along her wet body, I would tell myself how beautiful, how desirable my daughter is, does she know it, or is she still the little girl I would dry with the most delicate love during her childhood?

You know, José Nicasio, there is no human body that isn't visible and concealed at the same time. What is revealed in our bodies is as important as what is hidden. With my daughter, I had the secret feeling that the visible and the invisible were the same thing. She concealed nothing of her body because its mystery was only in her mind. That was for me, for the world, the invisible part of Alejandra. That was how she offered herself to me, her mother. I had to ask myself, how did she offer herself to a man? What will happen on the day Alessandra opens her visible body to a man who desires her only for her body and only later for her soul? Because in Alessandra, just as she was, there was no dissatisfaction.

Tell me, José Nicasio, do you believe you woke my daughter's latent bodily dissatisfaction? You, who describe yourself as an ugly man, forgive me for repeating it to you, almost a monkey, a dressed macaque, a simian with a narrow forehead and short neck and long arms? Forgive me. Forgive me. I want to see you the way my daughter saw you that afternoon. You, you couldn't wake the desire in my daughter. You, you, though you'll never admit it, desired my daughter that afternoon. You made her feel that a man's sex was threatening her. You wanted to be loved by a woman who did not desire you. Looked at by a woman who did not direct a glance at you. Greeted by . . .

You sexually assaulted Sandra. You took advantage of the solitude of twilight at Monte Albán to unleash your bestial instincts on my helpless daughter. Tell me it happened that way, José Nicasio. I need to know the truth. I've been sincere with you. I've written to you in prison so you'll know who my daughter was. You have to know whom you killed that afternoon in Monte Albán.

Answer me.

Tell me you understand.

I'm familiar with your situation. You became a U.S. citizen in San Diego. It was a necessary step, I imagine, to overcome discrimination, no matter how slightly. Now your ambition has worked against you. If you were a Mexican, they would have sentenced you to life, and in the end, influence would have set you free. Not in California. You'll be tried as a citizen of the United States. You'll be sentenced to death.

Tell me the truth before you die. Why did you kill my daughter?

Señora Vanina: Believe me, I am deeply grateful for your letters. Word of honor, I respect your courage and spirit enormously. I know what lies ahead. You don't need to remind me. I swear I want to tell you the truth. We were alone that afternoon, your daughter and I, watching the twilight in Monte Albán. It was clear that was the reason we stayed there when all the visitors had gone. To admire the sunset sitting on the steps of the Zapoteca temple.

What does a gaze mean, Señora? Is a gaze directed at the mountain the same as a gaze directed at a person? Do you look at a twilight and a woman the same way? I didn't want to look at your daughter, Señora, but I did want to look at her looking just as I was and know I shared with her the emotion of natural beauty. Perhaps I should have controlled myself. Perhaps I should have repeated the lesson of my entire life and continued to be the crouching man. The Indian who does not have permission to raise his eyes from the ground.

I rebelled, Señora. I wanted to look at your daughter. I looked at her. Not like a crouching man but like a haughty one. The arrogant one? The one made equal? Or the one redeemed? Judge however you like. The artist. The one who sees.

Now I blame myself. But you, Señora, do you forgive me for having sought out—the two of us alone, your daughter and I, at that moment of nightfall, in the midst of silence—the eyes of the girl seated three meters from me? Do you forgive me for having believed myself worthy of your daughter's eyes? Do you pardon my daring to seek out Alejandra's eyes in order to share the beauty of my country? Do you excuse my having stood without paying attention to the cry of alarm that escaped like a bird from your daughter's lips? Do you absolve me for my inability to transfer the amiability of my eyes to the bitterness of my lips?

Your daughter looked at me, Señora, and I would have liked to tell her:

I suffer because I cannot help anyone. What am I going to give to my old village of Indians? What am I going to give to the mestizo Mexicans who despise me because I remind them they are part Indian and run the risk of returning to the tribe? What can I give to the gringos who use me as an excuse for feeling like humanitarians? Am I partial everywhere, never an entire being: partial, a quantity between two parts, never an entire being?

Your daughter looked at me with fear. She looked at me saying, Don't touch me, don't come any closer, she looked at me saying, Stay where you are, don't leave your place. What is my place? Under, my place is under, always under, no matter how high I go, I'll always be *under*. And for that reason my hands rose, my arms could not restrain themselves, my nails felt like daggers, and I could only tell your daughter forcefully while I killed her with caresses, I'm your Indian,

I'm the Indian you don't want to see in yourself, I'm not killing you, I'm killing myself, I see clearly that if I kill you, I kill myself, if I condemn you, I condemn myself, but now I can't stop, my entire life is going downhill and I'm not going to fall alone, you're going to fall with me, you're going to pay for your fearful look at the Indian who dared to look at you, I know I can never possess you, what's your name, woman, call me man, call me Indian, I know you'll have me whipped if I let you go, I want you, but that doesn't give you the right to be afraid of me, you can feel what you like toward me, physical repugnance, social scorn, racial discrimination, but don't feel *fear*, not fear, please, for the sake of your life, don't be afraid of me, if you keep looking at me with fear, I won't be able to let you go, pressing my hands harder and harder around your neck, don't fear me for no reason, I'm not bad, I'm not bad, is that what you want to hear now that you can't talk anymore and only show your tongue and can't close your eyes filled with terror of the twilight because you know there won't be another day, because each night is the last night in the world, Alejandra, Alejandra, I kill you without even knowing your name, Alejandra, forgive me, forgive me for the pain you made me feel when, without opening your mouth, you said:

Don't come any closer. I'm afraid of you.

All my life I wanted to drive fear out of my head. Señora: Your daughter was afraid of me, but I was more afraid of her for fearing me, and I was afraid of myself for not knowing how to overcome my fear.

Please don't write to me again, Señora Vanina. You say I have all the time in the world. I'm going to believe you. God bless you. Thank you for writing to me. Thank you for paying attention to me.

José Nicasio, you have nothing to thank me for. I only wanted you to know whose life you had taken. Thank you for listening to me. Thank you for paying attention to me.

Alessandra, my dear daughter. I have communicated with the man who killed you. I wanted him to know whom he had killed. I didn't want him to go to his death without understanding *who you were.* I don't know if I achieved my purpose. I felt that something closed exists in this man, a door that no one—not even he—could open. That's why I'm writing to you. A letter with a mortal post office box. I feel dissatisfied, daughter, diminished because of everything I would have wanted to tell that man and couldn't. I don't know if it was a hidden contempt for his intelligence, which would damage the basis of my intuition: Señor, know who my daughter was, Alessandra, Alejandra, Sandra, Sandy. Know whom you killed. Be my accomplice. Be, before you die, the memory of my daughter's death.

Did he understand me? I couldn't tell him that you freed the executioner. Not with your sex. Only with your gaze. But I wanted to free the executioner, do you understand, my darling? Better yet, do you approve? Alessandra, my dear daughter, perhaps I said to that man,

Make a kingdom of your prison. Don't move again. Don't ever move again. Don't touch anything.

Do you remember, Alessandra? You had so much confidence in me, the confidence you always denied your father, that you reserved only for me, which is the reason *I had* to communicate with your killer, so he would understand whom he murdered. You remember: You were reading Pascal and quoted it to me. All the evils in the world come from our inability to remain still, seated in our chair.

Now I've written to a man locked in a cell in California about a woman walled up in a church in Coyoacán. We all come from somewhere else. We all leave Pascal's chair and allow ourselves to be carried along by the great magnetism of the world. I imagine that man whom I'll never see in person, and I see a dark pilgrim whose ancestors reached the land where the gods have their mountains, he migrated to Oaxaca and ended up in California.

The nation is called the U.S.A. What is the name of the Mexican locked in that prison? Can I comfort him from my own wandering, my dear, can I speak of my Spanish father killed by the Falange, can I speak of my mother fleeing the Italian Fascists? Can I speak in the name of my own orphanhood, sent as a girl to Veracruz in a ship loaded with orphans? Can I speak in the name of all this endless moving around of a humanity erring and errant, fleeing and fleet, incapable of remaining still because it believes that immobility is the opposite of freedom?

We are free because we move. We leave a wound called solitude and travel to another wound called death. There is a crossroads between the point of departure and the port of arrival. On that *carrefour*, my adored child, we always meet the other, the one who is not like us, and we find ourselves obliged to understand that if we move and meet one another, we ought to love one another on account of the contrast. Did you feel that contrast with your killer? Did he feel it with you, my love? Or do we perhaps go out into the world to fatally choose evil?

Fatally, because at the crossroads, we meet the other person and act *on* that person, giving free rein to our freedom, which is always the freedom to affect the lives of others. Perhaps José Nicasio, when he saw you that afternoon in Monte Albán, had a secret fear of not being *free* with you, betraying his freedom if he let you pass. He had to act before you, with you, but *he didn't know how*. You gave him the opportunity. *You were afraid of him.*

You decided for him, my adored child. He wanted to choose another person as a sign of his freedom. Except on that afternoon there was no one else but you. If José Nicasio hadn't approached you, he would have betrayed himself. He lived for that moment, do you understand? Imagine him alone before an alien, forbidden person, daring to look at her in search of a smile. Instead, he saw only the fear in your eyes. He saw the evil, Alessandra. Your fear of him was evil for him. He lived his life to win respect. Above all, the respect of not being seen as a man who was frightening, evil, hidden, ugly, Indian.

If he hadn't killed you, José Nicasio would have betrayed himself. He had to kill you to know that he existed. That he culminated his life saying,

"Don't be afraid of me. Please. Don't give me fear. Give me love."

And you gave him fear.

He killed you out of fear of himself, of his effort to come out of obscurity. You betrayed him with your rejection, my dear.

Now, kneeling before the urn that holds your remains, I tell you that perhaps you didn't know how to remove the fear from your consciousness. Your intelligence, so brilliant, had that enormous flaw. You were afraid. It's my fault. You gave me so much. If I can write these lines, it is because by educating you, I educated myself. But I, because of protective love, because of my protective devotion, could not tell you in time:

Don't be afraid. A day will come when intelligence isn't enough. You have to know how to love.

My dear daughter, have mercy on me.

This is my prayer.

I will live transforming your death into my reconciliation with the world you left me when you died.

Chorus of the Perfect Wife

before anything else exfoliation
hydration
elimination of impurities
so the bridegroom doesn't find a single imperfection
the scrub and you're ready to try on your wedding dress
choose: fairy-tale dream of gold or the goddess of spring
goodbye to singleness
all your girlfriends
are drinking coffee martinis
they're offering you a kit spa a kit moon a kit honey a honeymoon kit
they're giving you a bronzing express so you don't arrive white as a
    ghost
they're reading your cards pure good luck a hundred years of life
    eight children twenty grandchildren
you'll outlive your husband
waah waah
she cries alone in the church
don't listen to the priest's sermon against abortion against the pill
    against condoms pro-life
forget about the epistle of melchor woman is weak she owes
    obedience man is
strong man commands
you just hear the DJ at the banquet singing I will always love you
you just went into raptures in the magic garden of your wedding
    banquet
everything a dream everything so in mirrors instead of tablecloths
    hung with Swarovski

magnums of champagne seviche of mango rolls of pork iguana ice
cream
cactus cake
the superatmosphere the blowout plenty to drink a blast
waah waah
the golden couple
we don't stop dancing
getting frisky
lots of kissing and cuddling
everything so in
I will always love you
put on a cherub face
lucky you your fiancé I mean husband I mean monkey hairy beast
horrible King Kong
mama mamamama mamama
allons enfants de la patrie
a photo sitting on the toilet
perverted prick
we're going to Cancún

The Mariachi's Mother

1. You know her. Nobody knows her better than you. But now you wouldn't recognize her. How could she be? Doña Medea Batalla stripped? A mature woman—sixty, seventy years old—naked in a police cell? The gray-haired grandmother without clothes except for a diaper pinned on her, you say? Her chest defeated as if by a too frequent haughtiness? Thin strong arms accustomed to work and not to penitence?

What work, you ask? In the neighborhood, many occupations are attributed to Doña Mede, who begins her back-and-forth at the market very early in the day. She wants to be the first to choose the potatoes and dry chilis and grasshoppers and locusts in season. Then she withdraws to her one-story house between a tire-repair shop and a hardware store, at the rear of a parking garage, and takes the real treasure from her rebozo. A snake rattle.

Doña Mede knows she survives thanks to the rattle, which is a potion for long life. Each snake has five rattles. With two doses a week, you enjoy good health.

This is a secret you may not have known, and I'm telling you now so you can begin to understand. Because in the case of Doña Mede, everything is supposition and guesswork, since she makes a point of keeping—concealing—her secrets inside her rebozo, allowing neighborhood gossip to fly. They say she's a seamstress. Haven't you seen her go into the house with a bundle of clothes and then come out with packages that could be shirts or blouses or skirts? Or she's a potter. Have you heard her turn the wheel and then go out to wash the clay from her hands at the faucet outside her house? Or a midwife. Where does she go in such a hurry when a little kid from the neighborhood comes running and says come, Doña Medea, come now, hurry, my sister's yelling and says you should come and help her? Or a witch, a Protestant preacher, a procurer for nonexistent local millionaires, and more miracles are hung on her than the ones she gives thanks for with constant special ex-votos to the Virgin here in the Church of the Immaculate Conception.

A straw-colored braid adorns the nape of her neck and her back. You remember that when she was a young woman, her hair was black and pulled back tight, hanging down to her buttocks and driving the men wild. Now they say she has one foot in the grave. Though they've been saying that for many years.

"Doña Mede has one foot in the grave."

"She'll go flying to the cemetery."

"Doña Mede's ready to breathe her last."

"One of these days Doña Mede will kick the bucket."

"Death already rented her body."

"The next world is in her eyes."

It isn't true. You know Doña Medea doesn't have death in her eyes, she has sadness. You know the lady's comings and goings don't reveal her real concern. She has another, secret desire. Does it have to do with the men she knew in her life? Who knows if you know. Doña Medea has pure desolation in her eyes.

You've heard there were men in Doña Medea's life. But you never saw their faces, and neither did anybody else. One thing is sure: This woman lost all her men in cheap pulque taverns.

It was her destiny. And destiny is like a hare. It jumps out when you least expect it. And nothing less than the rabbit of fatality jumped out at Doña Medea in the taverns. This is a crowded district, you know that very well. It's as if lives become confused here. Names are lost. Men change their lives and their names without having to or being afraid to. Like movie stars, wrestlers in masks, criminals. El Santo. El Floridito. El Pifas. El Tasajeado. Evil names, all of them. El Cacomixtle. But then, like compensation, there are all the blessed names. Holy Child of Atocha, Christ of the Afflicted, Virgin of Remedies.

That's how flashes are given out, because for Doña Mede, flashes were what people called themselves or what they were called by others. Flashes in the city. Sudden flare-ups. Grass fires.

"And how did you get such a strange name, Doña Medea?"

"Because of Empress Carlotta."

"What does she have to do with it?"

"My mother saw a movie with an actress who always played Carlotta."

"What was her name?"

"Medea. Empress Medea de Navarra."

"Isn't it Novara?"

"Navarra, Novara, at this late date, what difference does it make? We all have the names that somebody else dreams up for us. That's God's truth!"

Men change their names and their lives. That's why it's strange that all of Doña Mede's loves have been pulqueros. Not exactly the owners but the victims of pulque taverns. In La Solitaria she lost a husband among the silver mirrors and wooden barrels. In La Bella Bárbara another man drowned in pulque mixed with oats. And they say a third husband was swallowed up by a mixture of lukewarm eggs, cascabel chili, and watered milk at the pulque tavern El Hijo de los Aztecas.

That's why nobody knows the father of Doña Mede's only son. The mariachi.

2. Do you know why Doña Medea Batalla finds herself in the police station, dressed only in a diaper? Because, you'll say, that's just what she needed. Just that? It isn't that her life was so full of affliction. Doña Medea, except for her amorous adventures in the pulque taverns, was always a tidy woman. Her day usually begins with a visit to the markets. She spends the entire morning looking without buying, choosing without paying, sensing that the noisy peace of the old city marketplaces compensates her for life, or at least calms her curiosity about living. She walks up to the stalls, and modern toys, the Barbie dolls, the Dragon Balls, the SpongeBobs, make her laugh. She recalls with affection the dolls in the old days. The bullfighter puppets in their pink stockings, the Mamerto cowboys with their big mustaches and huge hats, the fat Torcuata ladies in their wide skirts and rolled-up braids.

She asks them to play vinyl records of the old boleros and rancheras. And against all her feelings to the contrary, she wants to get angry, she wants to cry, she finally gives in, the mariachi music traps her, silences her, makes her cry, and enrages her, too.

To calm down, she goes up to a food stand, and as she eats, she airs recollections that are very much appreciated by the restaurant owners who offer her food free of charge while Doña Medea talks about the past. It's as if a great river of memories flows without ever stopping, because in the faces of the new cooks and servers, Doña Medea sees her own youth and senses the same feelings of love, sadness, hope, rancor, and tradition that are recounted in song lyrics. *Moles,* pozoles, enchiladas. Feeling nourishes, food is felt. That happens, as you know very well. Good Lord!

Doña Medea moves through the market and doesn't buy anything because she feels everything that comes in through her eyes is hers. That's why, as far as she's concerned, there are no objects without a price. Everything that is used contains a lost value that returns in a magical, unexpected way to a shopwindow with dusty wedding dresses, a record of ranchera music, an ex-voto giving thanks to the Virgin for having saved us from certain death . . . She is devoted to the Immaculate Conception of Mary, and every day she visits the small church presided over by the Mother of God. You know her, and you know she's not just any devout old woman. Her devotion has a mission. Why does she enter on her knees? Why does she light candles? Why, in short, does she pray to the Virgin? And why does she read the ex-votos with so much attention, as if she were hoping to find in one of them—only one—the message she is waiting for, the telegram from heaven, the announcement that the Virgin sends to her and no one else?

She stops to read that ex-voto. A certain death. Have you noticed how the undertaker at the funeral parlor on the corner salivates as he watches her walk by? She laughs at this. The undertaker wants to frighten her, Doña Medea explains. He's measuring her for the coffin. But she still has a good while to go before she lies down in a casket.

"Don't be such a meddler," she says to the undertaker.

"And don't you be so deferential." And with a smile, "Listen to me. Come and see me. I ought to take your measurements once and for all."

"Don't be a fool. Death doesn't matter. The terrible thing is dying."

"I'm here waiting for you, Doña Medea. You should take more precautions."

"Well, just be very patient, because when you come with your little box, I'll already be resurrected."

The truth is that Doña Medea doesn't want to surrender to eternal darkness just like that. The guacamole doesn't drip out of her taco. She sees other women to compare herself to and guess their destinies. She classifies them accurately. Some seem like beasts of burden. Others are thought of as clever. Doña Medea can smell from a distance the predatory women who conspire all day and the ones who seem so resigned they don't even complain.

The entire neighborhood is a swarm of ambitions, desires to leave, to get out of the swamp of the city. That's what you say, Señor.

"A city without hope, destroyed inside and out, but fed by illusions that, with luck, allow the luxury of being more abused than a fatality that gnaws away at everything until it leaves the residents in the neighborhood with no recourse except crime. Violence as the final refuge of hope, no matter how strange this sounds."

"Suddenly, violence is afraid of Doña Medea. Because she has constructed her entire life as a defense against two things."

"What are they?"

"One, the throb of violence she feels all around her, which she defeats with her ordinary routine."

"And the other?"

"Ah, that's her secret. For now all you need to know is that she sleeps with the Picot Songbook as her pillow. She believes the words come in through the hole that Don Lupino, the druggist, says we have at the base of our skull, and in this way the danger vanishes like the snake rattle in her mouth. What she's really afraid of, without understanding it completely, is the urban wave that can wipe out everything, licentiate, drag her to a destiny that isn't hers, implicate her in mistakes she hasn't made . . ."

Until she ends up in diapers in the hands of the police, a woman who has always gotten along wonderfully with the gendarmes who need, who knows, to know a person like her who can give them back their confidence in life. Oh!

She says all this to herself, and you recriminate her, and rightly so.

Violence appeared some time ago in Doña Medea's house. Sorrow treacherously knocked on her door. With warbling knuckles and a goldfinch's voice. Pure farce. She already carries violence inside herself, with no need for everything that has happened.

Violence at home.

And violence on the street.

Sorrow everywhere.

3. That's why the old woman moves around the markets and the food stands, that's why she chats with marketwomen and policemen. That's why she listens to the music of Agustín Lara and José Alfredo Jiménez. In order to believe that life in the neighborhood has a solution. That it's the same today as it was yesterday. And if it isn't, then to exorcize the threat she feels on her skin and in her bones, everything that exists here and that she doesn't want to admit, as if a good yellow *mole* would be enough to establish joy and serenity in life. As if, by naming them, the murmuring of a bolero could chase away all the evils of existence . . .

Well, it turns out that Doña Medea Batalla is a woman with antennae, and she knows very well that not only unpleasant but downright wicked things are going on. Behind the spotless facade she has erected, there is a good deal of filth and suffering and crime and resentment. She knows that if some have gotten away from here, others have remained, making a virtue of necessity, whether it's the crook who finds a way to get a rake-off from misfortune or the scoundrel on the bottom who decides to be smarter than the scoundrels on top.

"Will you do a job for me?"

"A rival in love?"

"No, an enemy in business."

"Tell your son to take the tied-up dog for a walk."

"That's the signal?"

"Walk the mascots."

"Fear doesn't ride a donkey."

"Zero tolerance?"

"What do you mean? Zero remorse."

"What did you say? I can't hear you."

"Clear up your voice with some mallow tea."

"Ah, now I understand you."

"Really?"

"One hundred percent."

"Just don't torture yourself."

"Sure. Progress is slow."

"Isn't it?"

"And never walk under trees at night."

"It's driving me crazy."

Of course she understands all this. That's exactly why she is the way she is, does what she does. To live a life different from everybody else's. To believe that even though her example of charitable availability benefits no one, at least it creates something like an aura of kindly normality in a neighborhood with no standard but evil.

"You know that already."

Which is why on that night, moved by a strange mixture of reasoning and presentiment, Medea Batalla leaves her poor house, which no one else has entered since her son left.

What's going on?

Why is everyone leaving their houses, why are businesses closing, why do all the traffic signals stay green? Why are the streets flooded with people, with shouts, with howling sirens?

She knows the people in the neighborhood. She just hasn't known them so enraged. The neighbors move forward, men and women, they move forward like a single tiger, they move forward with no order but with the strength of a groundswell. They move forward and surround the police. The police threaten with raised fists and voices without timbre, muffled by the growing uproar. People tighten the circle, you aren't the police, you're kidnappers, we've come to protect you, from what? We can protect ourselves. They told us there are drugs here, you people are drug traffickers. Look, you crooks in uniform, we rule ourselves here, the fewer cops the better, we know how to protect ourselves. The circle is closing, and Medea Batalla, without wanting to, becomes part of the wave. They pull her, they push her, they shove her aside violently, they flatten her like gum against the moving wall of the entire neighborhood surrounding the five policemen who protest with less and less energy. There are drugs, we're going to search the houses, we're going to protect you. We can protect ourselves, you're not police, you're kidnappers, you're cradle snatchers. Zero violence,

Señora, zero remorse, cops, we know who you are, for weeks you've been taking pictures when school lets out. Child robbers, you don't get out of here alive. Beat them to death. Don't let them escape. Look at that one trying to get on the roof of the car. Grab him. Pull him off. Kick him. Knock him down. To the ground. Hit him. Motherfuckers. The assholes are bleeding. Now douse them with gasoline. Set them on fire. Nothing should be left of them but the ashes of a shadow, the decal of their profile, the ghost of their bones. Burn them alive. Let them fry. Let them sizzle.

There were shouts of jubilation when they poured gasoline on the police and set them on fire. Doña Medea joins the chorus of joy. The neighborhood has defeated the violence that came from outside with the violence that comes from inside. Two of the police burn alive with screams that silence the sirens. The television cameras transmit everything. Live. The helicopters of His Honor the Mayor and His Excellency the President fly like crack-crazed bumblebees over the mob, letting it happen, confirming in the eyes of the neighborhood that we're right to kill the officers of the law. That the neighborhood rules itself and knows the score. From the air, could they see clearly the police burned by the people in the neighborhood? Will they come to collect what's left of the law: the blue trousers and shoes with metal tips? Sizzling in a burning pyre. Bonfires of branches and straw.

"Burn them!"

"We don't need the government!"

"We're neighborhoods free to buy and beat up, mock and murder, bellow and bite the dust!"

"After them!"

"Watch out, you rich sons of bitches, you bastard politicians!"

"After them!"

"Get a good look at us on your TVs."

"Look at us without any papers."

"Better off that way."

"Oh dear God." Doña Medea falls and is dragged along by the noise of the crowd. "Don't let them use my bones for a club."

The lynching is seen by the entire country, but Doña Medea has eyes for only one man. A man birthed by the crowd because the crowd doesn't know that in the smoke and the blood and the shriek of the sirens, there is another voice muffled by blows.

She hears it. How could she not hear it. She's listened to it her whole life. If it shouts now with rage and despair and defeat, it once sang very nicely. It was a very pretty voice. Now the voice is being muffled by blows in the nocturnal crowd from the neighborhood watched over by the forces of law and order that are provoking the power of disorder in the smoke and fog from tires set on fire and cars overturned and policemen burned alive sizzling with the smell of hair and rubber and indigestible guts. Releasing with their death the collective smell of deep-frying ears of corn warm tortillas armpits feet farts overalls rebozos sawdust hay leather wet wood burning tiles. Bursting from knifed stomachs are the countless insignias of death.

4. From the time he was a boy, Maximiliano Batalla sang very well. He would go out to the courtyard, and while he showered with buckets of water, he sang popular songs. When he was a boy, they came to propose that he sing in the choir of the Church of the Immaculate Conception. He said no because his songs were only for his mama.

Doña Medea (how naive of me) believed that this filial song would last her whole life because the strength of a son depends on the strength of his mother. No matter how aggressive the son's and how anguished the mother's. It's inherited. After all, Maximiliano had been weaned with pulque, and so he was free to go out and search for milk. Medea looked at Max, and the boy must have felt that so much love compensated for a poverty subject to the national proverb:

"We've been eating tortillas and beans for centuries, son. How little we need to survive."

If Maximiliano was happy, it was because he didn't ask for anything. A calm child, perhaps resigned. How little we need to survive.

Now, years later, Doña Medea believes she committed a serious, a very serious, mistake. Giving Maxi a doll she happened to find in the market. A Baby Jesus dressed as a cowboy.

A happy child.

Except at the age of fifteen, he came home visibly upset and sprang the question on Doña Medea:

"Who's my father?"

She shrugged. Maximiliano was so gentle and intelligent that the question seemed superfluous in a relationship as tender as the one between mother and son. Except that this time the kid insisted:

"I want to know whose son I am."

"You're my son," Doña Medea responded with smiling naturalness.

"And the Holy Spirit's?" the boy said with an attitude of false devotion.

"Go on," Medea said with a smile, totally missing the point. "Sing 'Cucurrucucú Paloma.' "

" 'Paloma Negra' would be better."

"No, that's very sad."

"Well, they say I'm the child of sadness."

"Who says that?"

"Can't you guess? At school."

"Tell them to go—"

"Fuck themselves? But I already live with my fucking mother."

"Oh, son! What devil's gotten into you?"

"The devil of shame, Señora."

Maximiliano lasted another year in the shanty at the rear of the parking lot. She tried to calm him down. She took him to church to encourage him to sing in the choir. Maxi lied through his teeth to the priest. Medea resigned herself. She gave him a cowboy outfit just like the one on Baby Jesus. She papered the bedroom with photographs of Jorge Negrete and Pedro Infante that she found at the flea market. She made vows to the Immaculate Conception so her son would love his mother again. She always knew—you know her—that these external acts weren't enough, weren't important. If the boy's love had been lost, she wasn't going to get it back with little gifts. Something beat in the heart of Doña Medea, which was the certainty that no matter how independent or distant her son became, he would need his mother to bring out the strength that even the most powerful were missing. Call it whatever you like. Tenderness. Patience. Acceptance of the unexpected. Calibration of the definitive stumbling block.

In Doña Medea's imagined scenario, Maximiliano was going to be the son who protected his mother. When they asked him about his father, Maxi got into fistfights with his classmates, and he fought hard, no one was braver. The head of the school told Medea about it in a recriminatory way. She felt pride more than anything else, because she knew that her son's rage had its roots in the nervous strength of his mother. In the reserves of pure resistance in Doña Medea. Maximiliano learned to fight because his mother was protecting him, even if he didn't know it.

I believe you understand that this certainty never abandoned the mother. And she had great need of her faith when her son left without saying goodbye.

She didn't see him again. She heard about him through the kind of chorus that, without wanting to, accompanies every city dweller and is transmitted from voice to voice, passing through indifferent ears unaware of their function as transmitters of news until, with no intention at all, it reaches the distant ear of the person for whom it is intended. In this way, the city and its neighborhoods form an involuntary aureole of desires, memories, conundrums, redundancies, playful instances that create an arc suspended over each neighborhood, each street, each family, and each life. We know it, you and I feel it. There is absolutely no need to separate the personal from the collective, the lived from the dreamed, what needs to be done from what has already been done. The city is generous and embraces everything, from the smallest to the biggest, from the most secret to the most public, from the most personal to the most social. There's no point in trying to divide and separate anything from what a great city like ours creates. Only ideology separates without respecting the whole, my friend. You know that.

Ideology makes comrades of imbeciles and wise men. But you already know that.

And so, thanks to the silent chorus of the city, Doña Medea learned that Maxi had joined a mariachi band on Plaza Garibaldi, and because he was the baby of the group, they gave him a luxurious black cowboy outfit with silver buttons and the eagle and serpent embroidered on the back. A tricolor tie and a black hat edged in silver.

He looked so young and handsome that they pushed him to the front of the group because he attracted the rich girls driving by in big convertible Lincolns in that time before widespread violence, and they would hire him to sing to the call of "My God how cute he looks when they dress him up like a cowboy" and to catch the whisper of "I woke again in your arms."

This was how Maximiliano Batalla became a man, except for the benders on the Callejón de San Camilito. Being a man doesn't mean not being a child anymore but beginning to be a criminal. There are about five hundred musicians registered at Plaza Garibaldi to offer their services to those who request them, whether beside the car parked right on the square, or to serenade a girl in Las Lomas de Chapultepec, or sometimes, with luck, to play at a posh get-together, and other times, but without luck, to liven up a dull party.

It doesn't matter. Guitars, trumpets, violins, and double bass guitars are enough to live an absolutely terrific life and embody, night after night, the mariachi's lyrics.

The mariachi sings a happy tune.
Sound of the guitar, bass guitar croons.
The violin sighs, and I do, too.

Except that at the age of twenty, with five years as a mariachi behind him, Maxi had come to feel that the suit of lights—comparable only to a bullfighter's—and the free sex with motorized women and girls and the occasional drinks in cantinas were no longer enough. Because in Maxi there was a hidden need, and this was the need for danger. He came to feel that if he wasn't exposed to danger, what he did made no sense. And had no future or past, since danger was as much an inheritance from his mother as the defiance she deserved.

How and when he left the group that chose him when he was a boy after he had left home, to join the mariachi band called the Taste of the Land, you and I are in no position to tell. The fact is that the young man of twenty-one, very clean-shaven, very smooth-skinned, without the pockmarks of adolescence or the scars of experience on his angel's face, and no false modesty in his devil's body, and with a pair of eyes stolen from the altar to the Holy Child Reappeared, became the perfect bait for the band of cryptomariachis who used him, with his innocent appearance, to hire out the services of their orchestra for five thousand pesos in advance. Maxi took the money and left the clients in the lurch. Just like that. With the superior idea of earning a living without working. Though Maximiliano Batalla liked to sing and would have done it with no need to steal. But his colleagues didn't like that idea. The sweet thing was to make the dough without wearing out your voice. The money was divided up among the other four false mariachis, a thousand pesos apiece.

It was only a matter of time before the five swindlers were caught, and though El Florido and El Pifas managed to avoid prison, El Tasajeado (for being ugly) and El Cacomixtle (for being stupid) were sent to jail, while they offered handsome Maxi the chance to redeem himself by joining the undercover police force, where his angelic appearance and sentimental voice would be perfectly suited to policemen who dedicated themselves to extortion, intimidation, and bearing false witness. Who wouldn't believe beautiful Maxi?

They posted him in the neighborhood where he was born. He objected. He'd be recognized. They would, literally, fuck him over. They threatened him. That was why he would be there: because he knew everybody, and nobody, after ten years, would recognize him. He left a little weenie and came back a full-fledged prick. That was the joke. He'd go from house to house threatening and proposing. Everybody's fine if you give us half the drugs, the alcohol, the girls, or if you prefer, the blow, the booze, and the babes. Taking contributions, paying the tax on peace, the police officers and Maxi were becoming rich when they committed the huge mistake of watching the little district school on the pretext that the same things being sold there were what they had come to offer.

And then the neighbors, criminals as well as honorable people, asked themselves, What do these bastards want? To take our children by surprise, plant drugs on them, force them into prostitution? In their doubt, the community decided to act, set an example, and do away with the five officers.

Two were burned alive.

Three were beaten.

Among them, Maximiliano Batalla.

A blow to the neck with a club knocked him down and left him permanently mute.

5. Doña Medea took him, bleeding and dazed like the Holy Christ of the Afflicted, in her arms. Staggering, mother and son reached the ramshackle living quarters hidden at the rear of a parking lot. Maxi leaned against the cars, staining the windshields with his red hands, howling like a beautiful animal that knows it is not only wounded but lost and not only lost but extinguished forever. He was the ghost of the mariachi. At the very most.

He couldn't see clearly through the cloud of blood that covered his eyes. Perhaps he didn't even know where he was, unless he recognized the familiar smells, though these were pretty common. Epazote leaves. Thyme. Marjoram. All the herbs in Doña Medea's kitchen, which was everybody's kitchen. Because she—you know her character—had not identified herself. She helped her son in the way Veronica would have helped Christ. Invisible. Silent. Unexpected but tolerated . . . Because beaten virility is not defeated virility but manhood prepared to start the next fight. Though looking at Maxi, Doña Medea didn't believe this cock would crow again.

Something happened that was both remarkable and foreseeable. As the days passed, her son began recovering his senses. Doña Medea administered herbs, bandages, pozoles, and essences of rattlesnake. Badly beaten and close to death, Maxi at first could hear the comings and goings of his unknown mother without attributing them to her. Then he smelled the stews, and perhaps he recognized something familiar in the flavor of the soups that Medea fed him with a spoon. Finally, the swelling of his eyes went down, and he could look around. Then one of two things happened. He acknowledged and refused to admit or didn't acknowledge and admitted. What was it he accepted if that was true? That he wasn't master of his own person. His mortally slow movements betrayed him. He didn't know where he was. Or he pretended not to know.

Medea did not acknowledge him and did not allow herself to be acknowledged. A very ancient wisdom in her person told her it was better not to. If Maxi wanted to acknowledge her, he would have to do it on his own. She would not lend herself to any emotional bribery. Such was the strength of her character that after the dreadful experiences of recent days, she extracted from herself, as if from those old abandoned mines whose only treasure is mystery, the silver that for so long had been thought exhausted.

Maxi heard. Maxi smelled. Maxi felt. At last Maxi saw. Medea waited eagerly for her son to sing. She did some useless things. She played a Cuco Sánchez record. She stirred up the canaries. She whistled the tango "Madreselva." All in vain. Maxi stayed there, lying on the cot with two serapes covering him and the Picot Songbook as a pillow. A distant look and a closed mouth.

This was when Medea told herself that great evils demand great remedies.

She went to see the woman who managed a nearby restaurant to ask to borrow the wheelchair reserved for disabled patrons. Back in her house, she struggled to sit Maxi in the chair and pushed it out to the street.

She knew very well where she was headed.

She wagered her destiny and her son's on the auspicious date of November 22, the day of Saint Cecilia, patron saint of musicians.

She entered the Church of the Immaculate Conception. An entire wall was dedicated to the ex-votos expressing gratitude for miracles ranging from saving someone from an automobile accident to resurrection two days after death. Would Medea Batalla have the occasion to add her own ex-voto to the gallery? Would the Virgin return a mariachi's voice to her son?

Mother and son reached the altar. Maximiliano seemed entranced and distant, as if being alive were miracle enough. Doña Medea hoped for the miracle. She didn't take it for granted.

She knelt in front of the image of the Virgin dressed in blue with embroidered stars and the half-moon at her feet. It was a miracle-working image. People said it had brought back to life the daughter of an acrobat at the fair who fell from her chair and was run through the chest by stakes but was saved when the image of the Virgin appeared at the top of the Ferris wheel.

Now Medea asked for a new but lesser miracle: that the Virgin return his voice to her son. That Maxi sing again. That the mariachi not remain mute, with catastrophic consequences for everyone: the world, the nation, music, Maxi, and Mede.

Medea spoke to the Virgin by speaking to her son. "It doesn't matter if you don't love me, Maxi. Your real mother is the Virgin."

And to the Virgin: "Mother of God, give my son's voice back to him so he can praise you."

And to Maximiliano: "Go on, Maxi, go on, don't you see that Our Lady is asking you to do it? Don't be stubborn!"

Then they say—you haven't heard about it?—that the miracle happened. The Virgin extended her hand to Medea Batalla and gave her a bunch of tiny keys. "This is so you can enter my house, Medea."

She took the keys, kissed them, placed them on Maxi's lips, and said: "Go on, son. Sing. The Virgin has given you back your voice."

But Maxi didn't open his mouth. He only opened his eyes, still partly bewildered and partly absent. And yet the Virgin looked at him. Maxi did not look back. But Medea did. The mother looked at the Virgin as she would have liked her son to look at her. In that look, Medea brought together her entire life, her excessive loves, the joy of giving birth twenty-five years before, the relief of the snake's rattle, the tiny tasks of washing other people's clothes, the midsize ones of making pottery, the large ones of assisting women in the neighborhood to give birth. Everything assembled in that moment of the meeting of the Virgin and the son, son of Medea and son of María, the mariachi who lost his voice because of a blow from a club on the day of the riot, the singer who now, if the Virgin really was a miracle worker, would recover his voice right here.

There was an enormous silence.

Everything was illuminated.

Each ex-voto caught fire like a lamp of hope.

The candles shone.

Maximiliano remained silent.

Medea opened her mouth and began to sing:

Peacock you are a courier
going to Real del Oro,
Peacock if they ask you,
Peacock tell them I'm weeping
tears of my own blood
for a son whom I adore.

Medea sang in front of the candles with an unconscious desire for her breath to extinguish them. But the candles did not go out. They grew with Medea's song. They became animated with the life of her voice. A voice that was clear, strong, and sonorous enough to animate a yard full of roosters. A man's voice, a mariachi's voice. A voice that came out of the mariachi's mother, illuminating the ex-votos, the candles, the keys that the Virgin gave her, the bit of the key with the image of the supper in Jerusalem.

A voice that filled the entire city with light.

6. Doña Medea Batalla is naked in a cell at the police station. All she is wearing is a diaper held up with pins. She was pulled along in the general roundup on the day of the disturbances. The cops, the blues—the

gendarmes, as she called them, betraying her own verbal antiquity. But the residents closest to the trouble were brought in, stripped, locked up. At least they allowed her to keep the shameful diaper that she was resigned to using to protect herself from incontinence.

Now Medea is waiting for you to come and rescue her. To pay the fine. She had to give your name. Who else could she mention? The undertaker at the funeral home? The managers of restaurants? The lovers who died in pulque taverns? The mariachi band the Taste of the Land? The son she thought she caught a glimpse of in the mob the night before?

Of course not, Señor. Only you. You who were twenty when she was forty, and every man in the neighborhood followed her because of her fresh, dark beauty, guided by the black braid that reached down to Medea's buttocks, don't you remember, licentiate, Señor Stuckup? Did you lose your memory, Don Fop? Don't you remember anymore how pretty Medea was and the decision she made to have a son only with you, the father of the mariachi? Have some shame. Only you can come to save her. Don't be a prick. Acknowledge him. Take responsibility. For once in your damn life, Señor. Forget about who you are and become the man you were. For your mother's sake.

And don't give me the same old story:

"We're in Mexico. Pray."

You'd be better off taking a snake rattle.

Chorus of the Naked Honeymoon

Regino and Regina came to complain at the lost-luggage office at the airport, traveling on their honeymoon from Tuxtla Gutiérrez to Acapulco by way of Mexico City, how can they go without their suitcases, what's going on, where are they, whew, sir, madam—Regino, Regina—don't be impatient, in half an hour we'll have them, in the meantime why don't you have a nice cup of coffee, listen, the thirty minutes are up, what happened? where are they? and Regina thinking about the gorgeous underthings her girlfriends gave her with erotic intentions at the shower in Tuxtla and the airport, well, the suitcases haven't come yet, you know, a car crash, where? in Chiapas on the runway at the airport so they never got on the plane no but the news is that the suitcases were destroyed but it was all new clothes, a bride's clothes, do you know what I'm saying? ay, Señorita, what I recommend, please, I'm Señora, Señora, is that you don't pack anything you'll miss, but it's my bridal trousseau, ay, if you only knew the kinds of things that get lost here, who knows what happened to your truss but sometimes what disappears are artificial limbs, medieval armor, even contraband dolls with drugs hidden in the removable head, what haven't we seen here! and you're complaining about losing a nightgown, show my wife more respect, yes Señor it's just that, you know, there are more than two million people who lose suitcases every year at the airport so our advice is that people travel wearing what they'll need I mean underwear shirts and socks and a small bag for packing what the family doesn't want to lose and if you like take pictures of what you're carrying in the suitcase and this way there's no loss, you know, all the suitcases are the same all of them are black because that's what's fashionable and thank your lucky stars because once more than five hundred suitcases arrived for a Mr. Mazatlán because the gringos in

Los Angeles thought it was a passenger and not an airport so if you want you can file a complaint with the warehouse in Scottsboro Alabama which is the cemetery for all lost suitcases in North America and listen what's this couple complaining about as if they needed clothes for a honeymoon in Acapulco, what do they need that for

Sweethearts

Manuel Toledano boarded the ship in Venice to travel Trieste-Split-Dubrovnik for the next five days. The *vaporetto* took him from the hotel on the Grand Canal to the inner harbor, but in the traveler's eyes, the ducal city remained an enduring, duplicated mirage. Leaving Venice behind, Manuel moved away from a fantasy that was transformed in his memory into a ghost of itself. He thought for a moment that perhaps the specter of Venice had more reality than the illusory municipal reality of streets, canals, squares, and churches.

The established *dogana* was a memory that all the trappings of Venice—the magnificence of the Pearl of the Adriatic—were the fruit of an ancestral simulation, a long-lasting taste for Italian theatricality. Venice wagered its dramatic stage setting—a sumptuous backdrop—on something that in the end was a commercial center as naked as the dock where Toledano set foot this morning with the sensation of stepping on forgotten solid ground, confirming in this way that Venice *was floating*, and the traveler there had to become accustomed to the rocking of stone.

The city, however, reserved for him, after farewells at customs, a last illusion, a radiance that rose like a veil over Venice: light, respiration, heartbeat, foam of the air, salivation of the sea.

After settling into his cabin, Manuel went for a walk on the deck. He did not want to miss the arrival in Trieste and the appearance, equally spectral, of Miramare, the longed-for seat of the sad imperial couple, Maximilian and Carlotta.

When the port came into view, Manuel discovered the palace and felt a lightning flash of pity for the innocence and illusion that separated those young princes, at once ingenuous and ambitious, from a life of hereditary tranquility in Europe and hurled them into a death of shrapnel and madness in Mexico.

They were, after all, only two unfortunate sweethearts.

"Look at the palace, baby . . . Oh, don't be annoying. You're so clumsy!"

There was a calamitous sound of abandoned chairs followed by a resigned sigh that turned into labored breathing. Manuel came around the corner on the deck and saw the woman attempting to pick up a capsized chair. He hurried to help her. The irritated lady could recline once more on her deck chair.

"*Grazie*," she said to Manuel.

"You're welcome, Señora," Manuel said, smiling, but she didn't return his amiability; she looked at him with curiosity and turned back to her feigned reading of a fashion magazine.

For an instant, however, their eyes had met with a question that Manuel, returning to his false lookout post at the railing (travelers travel as if the proper operation of the train, the plane, or the ship depends on them), dared to formulate in secret that the lady was Mexican, her verbal localisms betrayed her. Did he know her? Had he seen her before? And she, did she recognize him?

Manuel smiled at Trieste. Too often he had been mistaken, searching in the most hidden little light in aging eyes, in the weariest tone of a voice that had once been fresh, for a friendship from his youth . . .

Sometimes he guessed correctly: Are you Borras Barroso, basketball champion at the Francés Morelos Secondary School? And sometimes not: Didn't you sit in the first row in the class on civil law at San Ildefonso? With men, it was a simple matter: yes or no. With women, it was more complicated: Don't be fresh, Señor, your tactics are stale, excuse me, you're mistaken and what a shame, I would like to have known you when you were a young man, or frankly, you're an overconfident old man, very well preserved but a little inappropriate.

Sixty-five well-preserved years. Like marmalade . . .

The lady concentrated on her reading. Manuel looked at her out of the corner of his eye. They were probably the same age as well as the same nationality. Perhaps, with luck, at supper they'd be at the same table, there would be an opportunity to approach her naturally, courteously, without ridiculous or dangerous pretexts.

She didn't appear at supper. The steamer was docked in Trieste all night. Perhaps she went down to a restaurant in the port. She. He kept thinking—had he seen her before? Where? When?

Memory ought to have supplementary lenses capable of superimposing, through layer after layer of skin, the faces prior to the present face, until the final face of death was unveiled. By the same token, this process ought to operate in reverse until it also showed the first profile, the one of a longed-for youth, along with the unrenounceable feeling that we once were young and because of that we once were happy, strong, attractive, unique . . .

But the past is a mist that moves invisibly over our heads without our realizing it. Until the day it rains.

Manuel's heart still throbbed with the sensation of youthful fulfillment. He was not alarmed by that. He was astonished. Calendars, mirrors, above all the glances of those who no longer recognized him, could not vanquish the image that Manuel Toledano had of himself. His *interior* sight kept alive an *anterior* sight, that of his youth. It was a vision that he judged faithful, summonable, persistent in a thousand and one characteristics of his face remodeled by time.

If others did not see the Manuel Toledano that had been, he did. He was the best, most knowledgeable guardian of his own true image: that of his youth.

And she? Was his interior and anterior sight that of a memory that preserved, in faithful archives, the faces of his closest relatives, lost friends, forgotten sweethearts?

And she . . .

The following day, walking on the deck and avoiding the heroic Adriatic sun with a hand placed like a visor over his forehead, Manuel took advantage of the situation to direct surreptitious glances at the lady masked by her fashion magazine and unmasked by an impatient distraction, as if reading were the disguise for something else, a constantly deflected vigilance, a duty both troublesome and imperative . . . The woman turned the pages of the magazine without looking at them. She almost scratched at them as if memory were a sharp nail.

Finally—inevitably?—their eyes met, hers blinded by the glare from the sea, his by the shadow of his own hand. Manuel smiled at the lady. "Excuse me. It's just that I heard you yesterday and told myself you're Mexican."

She nodded without saying a word.

He insisted, conscious that he was engaging in a dangerous piece of audacity. "That's not all. I have the impression we've met before."

He laughed at himself, half closing his eyes. Now came the resounding verbal slap, no we've never met, don't be insolent and inappropriate, that ploy is very old.

She looked up. "Yes. I had the same impression."

"I'm Manuel Toledano—"

"Manuel! Manolo!"

He nodded in surprise.

"Manuel, but I'm Lucy, Lucila Casares, don't you remember?"

How could he not remember? Through Manuel's head passed images at once sweet and violent, of his early youth, nineteen or twenty years old, ardent nights cooled only by the stars. Beaches. The perfume of young flesh, sweat washed by the sea and restored by kisses. Dancing pressed close, motionless, on the floor of the club La Perla in Acapulco. Illusive perfumes. Dead aromas.

Lucila Casares. He looked at her with infinite tenderness, now without a trace of surprise or wariness. He did not see a woman over sixty, his contemporary. He saw the girl with curly hair of an indefinable color, blond but dark, copper over gold, wheat over barley, small, sensual, conscious of every movement she made, Lucila of the soft arms and golden legs and the face lit forever by the tropics. Manuel felt the foam of melancholy on his lips. "Lucila . . ."

"It's a miracle, Manuel!"

"Chance?"

"Whatever you call it. How wonderful!"

She made a coquettish gesture with her hand, gently patting the reclining chair next to hers and urging Manuel to sit down.

Manuel was afraid of one thing. That information about the present—the current life of a man and a woman in their sixties—would displace the delicious return to his early youth, the young love they both enjoyed so much. He, Manuel. She, Lucila.

"Is it really you, Manolo?"

"Yes, Lucila. Look, touch my hand. Don't you recognize it?"

She denied it, smiling.

"That doesn't change. The palm of the hand," he insisted.

"Ah yes, the lifeline. They say it gets shorter with age."

"No, it gets deeper."

"Manuel, Manuel, what a surprise."

"Like before, like Acapulco in 1949."

She laughed. She brought a finger to her lips and widened her eyes in feigned alarm.

He laughed. "All right, Acapulco always."

He felt he had a right to remember, and he asked her to join him. The Adriatic, a calm, high-colored sea, also offered an unrepeatable sky this morning. "Just think, I heard you before I knew you."

"And when was that?"

"During the holidays in '49. I was in the room next to yours at the Hotel Anáhuac. I heard you laugh. Well, what they call 'giggle' in English, that fresh, youthful, ingenuous laugh . . ."

"Deceptive," Lucila said with a smile, raising an eyebrow mischievously.

But the meeting that same night at the cocktail party was no deception. He saw her approach, ethereal, radiant, with those tones of gold and copper that illuminated her from head to toe, a pretty girl, he saw her come in and said, "That can only be her, the girl in the next room," and he went up to her and introduced himself.

"Manuel Toledano. Your neighbor, Señorita."

"That's too bad."

He asked why, disconcerted.

"Yes," the girl went on. "Walls separate us."

They didn't separate again during that unforgettable December in the year 1949 that was prolonged, following the festival of San Silvestre, in the January vacation and the tender, astonishing repetition of the first meeting, at the cocktail party, only you and I talked to each other looked at each other the others at the party didn't exist they were talking nonsense from the first moment only you and I were there Lucila and Manuel Lucy and Manolo.

The days were long. The nights too short.

"We danced on the floor of La Perla, do you remember?"

"Do you remember the music they were playing?"

"I'm taking the tropical way . . ."

"The night restless, unquiet . . ."

"In the breeze that comes from the sea . . ."

"No, you're wrong. First it says 'With its perfume of dampness . . .' "

They both laughed.

"How vulgar," said Lucila.

A small Acapulco, adolescent like them, half grown, always divided between hills and beach, poor and rich, native and tourist, still possessed, Acapulco, of a clean sea and clear nights, families that loved one another, and first courtships: warm, gentle water at Caleta and Caletilla, wild water at Revolcadero, pounding waves at the Playa de Hornos, silent waves at Puerto Marqués, stone cliffs at La Quebrada, recently opened hotels—Las Américas, Club de Pesca—and very old hotels—La Marina, La Quebrada—but sand castles, all of them.

"Boleros let us dance very close together."

"I remember."

"In the breeze that comes from the sea . . ."

"We hear the sound of a song . . ."

A vacation spot both daring and tranquil, wavering between its humble past and probable heavenly future. There already vibrated in the air at the airport another Acapulco of big planes, big millionaires, big celebrities. In 1949, not yet. Though the domestic calm of that time could not hide a social chasm deeper than the ravine of La Quebrada itself.

"I remember," Manuel said with a smile.

"It's true," Lucy said.

The perfume of two bodies in bloom. The smell of the Acapulco sun. Manuel a contagious perspiration. Lucila a sweet perspiration. Both transformed by the brand-new experience of young love . . . A day when Lucy is sometimes with us and sometimes Manolo.

The perfect symmetry of the day and of life during a month's vacation in Acapulco.

They spoke with preserved emotion, separated from the world by the voyage and joined to the earth by shared memory. Acapulco during the vacation of 1949. Acapulco is the awakening of the new decade of the fifties. A time of peace, illusion, confidence. And the two of them, Lucila and Manuel, embracing at the center of the world. What did they say to each other?

"I don't remember. Do you?"

"What two puppies say to each other." Manuel laughed. "What they do . . ."

"You know I was never happier in my life, Manolo."

"Neither was I."

"It's wonderful that in five weeks you can live more than in fifty years . . . Forgive my frankness. Age authorizes what it was once forbidden to say."

Detailed memories tumbled out, the beaches back then, Caleta during the day, Hornos at dusk, the children playing in the sand, the fathers walking along the sea wearing long trousers and short-sleeved shirts, the mothers in flowered dresses and straw hats, never in bathing suits, the fathers vigilant, watching the adolescents moving away from the beach, swimming to Roqueta Island where paternal glances did not reach where young love could ally itself with the one visible love young love in heat surrender of the soul more than of the body but senseless uncontrollable pounding of the pulse the flesh the look of closed eyes—do you remember Lucy do you remember Manolo?—the touch uncertain more than experienced and sensual exploratory and auroral, Lucy, Manolo, while from Caleta the fathers look anxiously toward the island and ask only will they be back in time for lunch? and the mothers will open their parasols even wider and the fathers will wave their panama hats asking them to come back come back it's time . . .

"Was it like that, Manolo?"

"I don't know. The first meeting is always a day without memory."

"There were many days, a love that seemed very long to me, very long . . ."

"No, remember it as a single day, the day we met."

Lucila was about to take Manuel's hand. She stopped herself. She said only: "What long fingers. I think that's what I remember best. What I liked most about you. Your long fingers."

She stared at him with a cruel gleam that took him by surprise. "So much asking myself, Whatever happened to him? Is he happy, unlucky, poor, rich?" She smiled. "And I had only one certainty left. Manuel has very slender, very long, very lovable fingers . . . Tell me, were we so inexperienced back then?"

He returned her smile. "You know that in czarist Russia, couples older than fifty needed their children's permission to marry."

She bowed her head. "Forty years later and you still reproach me?"

No, Manuel denied it, no.

"You know I died for you?"

"Why didn't you tell me so then?"

She didn't respond directly. She fanned herself wearily, not looking at him. "Perfection is what they expected of me." She let the fan fall on her lap, next to the fashion magazine. "Who's perfect? Not even those who demand it of you."

"You hurt me very much, Lucila."

"Imagine how hard it was for me to tell you, 'Go, I don't love you anymore.' "

"Is that what your parents asked you to do?"

She was perturbed. "I had to tell you that so you'd go away, so you wouldn't love me anymore."

"No, tell me really, did you believe it?"

"What do you think?" She raised her voice without intending to.

"Did they ask you to?"

"Yes, but that wasn't the reason I turned you down."

Manuel kept to himself what he knew. Lucila was supposed to marry a rich boy from high society. Manuel was "decent people"—that was what it was called—but with no sizable bank account. That was the real reason, a categorical order, break off with that pauper, this Manuel can't give you the life you deserve, romantic love ends, you get older, and what you want is security, comfort, a chauffeur, a house in Las Lomas, vacations in Europe, shopping in Houston, Texas.

"Then what was it?"

She sat erect, proud. " 'Go. I don't love you.' " She looked straight at him. "I thought I'd keep you that way."

"I want to understand you . . ." Manuel murmured.

Lucila lowered her eyes. "Besides, that excited me. Letting you go . . ."

"Like a servant."

"Yes. And getting excited. To see if you rebelled and refused to believe what I said and pushed me against the wall . . ."

"It was your parents' decision."

". . . and carried me off, I don't know, kidnapped me, would not be defeated . . . It was my decision. It was my hope."

Waiters served consommé and biscuits. Manuel sat thinking, self-absorbed and struggling against that undesirable thought: seeing in the separation of two young sweethearts only an episode in the autobiography of an egotist. There had to be something more. He sipped the consommé.

"We made a date, remember?" said Manuel.

"And kept postponing it," said Lucila.

"How could we lose hope?"

"So much wondering: Whatever happened to him? So many self-recriminations: Why did I let him go? I wasn't happy with the husband they forced on me. I was happy with you, Manuel."

They looked at each other. Two old people. Two old people remembering distant times. Did they both think that when all was said and done, none of it had happened? Or that, given the fact of chance, it could have occurred in very different ways? Looking at each other now as they never had when nostalgia was exiled by presence, both of them thought that if none of it had happened yesterday, it was happening now, and only in this way would they be able to remember tomorrow. It would be an unrepeatable moment in their lives. With its actuality, it would supplant all nostalgia for the past. Perhaps all yearning for the future.

"The sweet sorrow of separation. Who said that?" he murmured.

"The sorrow, the sorrow of losing you," she said very quietly. "And the obligation to hide my feelings . . . Do you know I was dying for you?"

"But why didn't you tell me so back then?"

Lucila abruptly changed the subject. No, her marriage hadn't been happy. Though she was, because she had three children. All girls. She smiled. And he? No, he was a die-hard bachelor.

"It's never too late," Lucila said with a smile.

He returned the smile. "At the age of sixty, it's better to marry for the fourth time, not the first."

She was about to laugh. She restrained herself. There was a superficial but respectable sadness in his words. A sentimentality necessary to both their current lives. Still, Lucila noticed a certain coldness in him as soon as they moved from the evocation of their youth to the destiny of their maturity.

"How was it for you, Lucila?"

"I lived surrounded by people whose company was preferable to their intelligence."

"Dispassionate people."

"Yes, decent people. Sometimes I'm grateful not to be young anymore."

"Why?"

"I don't have to seduce anymore. And you?"

"Just the opposite. Being an old man means being obliged to seduce."

"What's an old bachelor looking for?" Lucila took up the subject again in a playful voice.

"A quiet place to work."

"Did you find it?"

"I don't know. I think so. I have no family obligations. I can travel."

He decided not to say where. He was afraid of compromising this miraculous encounter. Opening the door once more to postponed assignations, as if they were twenty years old again and about to break off their relationship because of external pressures. The imposition of wills that did not understand the love of two young people without the experience to live their lives.

Who understood? Those ignorant of the miracle of lovers who weren't strangers when they met. Guessed at. Perhaps desired with no name or profile yet. For them, the first time was already the next occasion.

"I imagine you don't live in Mexico City."

"No. I go back to Mexico City every once in a while."

"Why?"

"Before, because of a nostalgia for tranquility. Unhurried schedules. Even slower meals. Everything was so human then. Now I go back because I fear death."

"What?"

"Yes. I don't want to die without seeing Mexico City one last time."

"But these days the city is very unsafe. It's hostile."

He smiled. "Not for a romantic, damaged man like—" He stopped and abruptly changed the subject and his tone. "Let me tell you that I foresaw your love. I had always carried it inside me." He stopped and looked into her eyes. "How could I renounce what already existed before I even saw you? Admitting it could endure only when I lost you?" He stopped on the brink of what he despised most. Self-pity. Perhaps she would think what he wasn't saying. Damaged by love for the wrong woman and not able to avoid . . .

"Loving her . . ."

"What?"

"Look at the sea." He pointed. "Don't you see some nuns swimming fully dressed?"

Finally, she laughed. "You always amused me, Manuel."

"I lost the compass. Without you, I had to reorient my entire life."

"Don't say that. Don't even think it."

"No. And you?"

"I live in New York. Mexico City is too unsafe. They kidnapped the husband of one of my daughters. They killed him. We paid the ransom. Even so, they killed him. My other two daughters are still in the capital because their husbands work there, with bulletproof windows in their cars and armies of bodyguards. I need them. Especially my grandchildren. I visit them. They visit me." She laughed softly. "Oh, Manuel."

She sobbed. He embraced her. Between sobs, she said, "I've spent years looking sideways at what was approaching and not daring to look at it straight on, not daring to look at what was approaching, now

I think it was always you, like a phantom of my youth, why does everything we shouldn't do exclude exceptions while what we like to do is always exceptional?"

"Not me," he replied with a kind of growing certainty. "I go on hoping. I go on hearing that noise at my back. I'm not sure about anything. Even before I guessed at you in the next room in Acapulco, I had always carried the anticipated delight of you deep inside me. The only thing needed to dislodge the phantom was you."

He embraced her tightly. He placed his lips on her temple. "How do you want me to renounce something that has always existed? By admitting it could endure only after you left me?"

He released her, and for a moment both sat looking at the sea, she thinking that there is nothing more melancholy than disillusioned youthful passion, he thinking that when we sacrifice immediate emotion, we gain the serenity of being remote, both of them wondering, without daring to say so, if they had lived nothing but an adolescent fantasy or an act indispensable for growth.

"How good that we met," Lucila insisted at last with a sincerity she didn't want. "Each of us could have died without seeing the other again, do you realize that? You know"—her voice modulated—"sometimes I've thought with joy and sorrow, both things, about everything we could have done together, you know, read, talk, think . . . Go to the movies together, to a restaurant . . ."

"I don't," Manuel replied. "You know we saved ourselves from habit and indifference."

He said it in a way he didn't want to say it. Cutting, disagreeable, hiding the reasons she didn't know about and that he would never say to the girl from 1949 but with violent shame he said to the woman of today, it wasn't only your decision, Lucila, not only your parents were opposed to me, my mother was, too, my mother would stand behind me in the mirror while I was shaving, take me by the shoulders, embrace me with a butterfly's touch that I felt like the mortal grip of an octopus and say you look so much like me my baby look at yourself in the mirror that girl doesn't deserve you her people aren't right for you they'll humiliate you leave her now I don't want you to suffer the way I've suffered since your father left and died dear boy think it over carefully, will you?

"Why did we separate, Manuel?"

"Because you demanded total surrender from me."

"I did?" She smiled the smile of a woman accustomed to complying.

"Forget my friends. Forget my work. Forget my mother. Enter your exclusive and excluding world."

Lucila reacted with a strange desire not to disappoint Manuel. "And you didn't know how. Or couldn't, is that right?"

"All of us, every one of us, wanted to do other things and were lost, Lucy. Let's be happy with what we managed to accomplish. Families oblige us to recognize our differences. You left a rich poor man for a poor rich one." He stopped for a second to turn and look straight at her. "Is the wait for love to come more tortured than sadness for love that was lost? If it's any comfort to you, let me say that it's nice to love someone we couldn't have only because with that person we were a promise and will keep being one forever . . ."

"You didn't tell me." Lucila spoke with a touch of contempt. "What do you do?"

He shrugged.

"Final words," Lucila concluded.

"Yes." Manuel took his leave, bowed courteously, and walked away on the deck, murmuring to himself, "We became parasites of ourselves," uncertain about this meeting, disturbed by doubt.

Lucila smiled to herself. How many things had been said, how many, so many more, had not been said. How was I going to tell this man, You know, I live hoping that someone will tell me the day's events, you know, those little things that fill our hours, so I can say the really important thing to myself?

"You know? You're going to die. This is your last vacation. Milk it for all it's worth. You're going to die. Invent a life."

She was grateful for what had happened. The memory of adolescence and young love completely filled the void of separation and frustrated affection. It wasn't bearable to die without knowing. About death but also about love. Communicate it to anyone, to the first person who passed with the veil of ignorance covering his face and the gloves of the past disguising his hands . . . Tell these things to the first person who came along, an acquaintance or a stranger. And if it was a stranger, tell it with the astute complicity of the solitary traveler longing, like her, to share the memory of what never was.

On the other hand, walking toward the prow of the ship, Manuel Toledano thought that the more untouchable a memory, the more complete it turned out to be.

He hurried his pace to return to Lucila. He stopped when he saw her in the distance, accompanied by an adolescent girl. He turned so he could approach without being seen from a passage that led to the deck.

"Who were you talking to, Granny?"

"Nobody, Mercedes."

"I saw you. I didn't want to interrupt."

"I'm telling you, it was nothing. Just glances. Think, honey, how often we exchange glances with someone and then go our separate ways."

"And nothing happened?" Mercedes said mischievously.

"No. Nothing happened."

"Then what did you talk about?"

"What a nosy kid!" Lucila exclaimed. "About places that no longer exist."

"Like what?"

"Acapulco. Foolish things."

"And what happened?"

"Nothing, I said. Learn to give emotions to places. Even if they're nothing but lies." The grandmother caressed the girl's cheek. "And now go on, Meche. Let's find your naughty little sister. It's time for lunch. Go on."

Manuel listened to them until the girl helped her grandmother up and both of them walked away. Perhaps he'd meet them again during the trip. Perhaps he'd have the courage to confront Lucila and say:

"We didn't really know each other. It's all fiction. We decided to create a nostalgic past for ourselves. Nothing but lies. Attribute it to chance. Don't worry. There was no past. There's only the present and its moments."

He looked at the Dalmatian Coast. They were approaching the port of Spalato, in reality a huge palace transformed into a city. Emperor Diocletian lived here in courtyards that today are squares, walls that today are restaurants, chambers that today are apartments, galleries that today are streets, baths that today are sewage pipes.

From the deck of the ship, Manuel did not see these details. He saw the mirage of the ancient imperial city, the fiction of its lost grandeur restored only by the imagination, by the hunger to know what once was better than what is and what could have been more than anything else.

From mirage to mirage, from Venice to Spalato, the world of memories was turning into the world of desires, and between the two beat a heart divided by love that was put to the test between past and present.

Then the Adriatic wind blew, the damp, warm sirocco carrying the threat of rain and fog. Dry in its North African origins, the sea impregnates it with smoke and water.

Not yet. The wind was gentle, and the Dalmatian city sparkled like one more illusion of the god Apollo.

Manuel only murmured:

"I still think about you."

Chorus of the Murdered Family

My father and my mother
died in the massacre of El Mozote
on December 11 1981
since the army of the dictatorship couldn't conquer the guerrillas of
the Farabundo Martí Front
they decided to kill the innocents to frighten the population
they sent word they would invade us but wouldn't kill
those who stayed in their houses
only those wandering around the streets and outskirts
those they would kill like rabbits
then the Atlácatl Battalion financed and trained by the USA
made a surprise attack and slaughtered all the inhabitants of
El Mozote
men women children
on the tenth of December the soldiers of the battalion
entered
El Mozote
dragged everybody from their houses
gathered them in the main square
ordered them to lie down on their stomachs
kicked people
accusing them of being guerrillas
demanding that they tell where they hid the weapons
but there was only seed plow nail hammer tile
after an hour they ordered them to go back to their houses and not
show even their noses
we crowded into the houses we were hungry

all we heard were the men from the battalion in the streets laughing
drinking
celebrating their victory
then at dawn
on the eleventh of December
they dragged us from the houses
gathered us together on the level ground in front of the Church of the
Three Kings
kept us standing there for hours and hours
then they put the men and boys in the church
the women and little kids in an abandoned house
we were about six hundred people
they put us men facedown and tied our hands
and again they asked us about hidden weapons
and since we didn't know anything the next morning they began to
kill us
they cut off the heads of the men in the church with
machetes
one after the other
so we could see what was in store
then they dragged the bodies and heads to the sacristy
a mountain of heads looking without seeing
and when they got tired of cutting off heads
they shot the rest of us outside
leaning against the red bricks and beneath the red
roof tiles of the school
that's how hundreds of men died
the women they marched to Cruz Hill and Chingo Hill
and fucked them
over and over and over again
and then they hung them stabbed them
set fire to them
the kids died crying hard

the soldiers said the kids that are left are very cute
maybe we'll take them home
but the commander said no
either we kill the children or they'll kill us
the children screamed as they killed them
kill all the bastards kill them good so they can't holler anymore
and soon there were no more screams
my grandmother hid me in her skirts
we saw the slaughter from the trees
I swear that when the Atlácatl Battalion passed
the trees moved to protect
my grandmother and me
then it was known all over the region
that the soldiers of the regular army
came back to clean up El Mozote
from the farmhouses you could smell rotting flesh
they took the bodies out of the Church of the Three Kings
and buried them all together
but it still smelled of sweet corpse
pigs walked around eating the ankles of the dead
that's why the soldiers said don't eat that hog it ate human flesh
nobody picks up the dolls, the decks of cards, the side combs, the
    brassieres, the shoes scattered
all over the village
nobody prays to the bullet-ridden virgins in the church or to the
    heads of decapitated
saints
in the confessional there's a skull
and on the wall an inscription
the Atlácatl Battalion was here
here we shit on the sons of bitches
and if you can't find your balls
tell them to mail them to you at the Atlácatl Battalion
we're the little angels of hell

we want to finish off everybody
let's see who imitates us
me and me and me and me and me and me
the mara, the gang?
the children of the soldiers of '81
the children of those slaughtered in '81
nothing is lost in Central America
the slim waist of a continent
everything is inherited
all the rancor goes from hand to hand

The Armed Family

When General Marcelino Miles marched into the Guerrero Mountains, he knew very well what ground he was walking on. He was in command of the Fifth Infantry Battalion, and his mission was clear: to finish off the so-called Vicente Guerrero Popular Army, named in honor of the last guerrilla of the Revolution for Independence, shot in 1831. "His lesson was ours," General Miles muttered at the head of the column struggling up the slopes of the Sierra Madre del Sur.

He had to persuade himself under all circumstances that the army obeyed, that it did not revolt. For over seventy years this standard had established the difference between Mexico and the rest of Latin America: The armed forces obeyed civilian authority, the president of the republic. That was clear as day.

But this morning the general felt that his mission was clouded: At the head of the rebel group was his own son, Andrés Miles, in armed rebellion following Mexico's great democratic disillusionment. From the time he was very young, Andrés had fought for leftist causes, within the law and in the hope that political action would achieve the people's goals.

"A country of one hundred million inhabitants. Half of them living in dire poverty."

It was Andrés's mantra at supper, and his brother, Roberto, gently took the opposing view. Social peace had to be maintained at any cost. Beginning with peace in the family.

"At the price of one delay after another?" Andrés protested, sitting on his father's left, naturally.

"Democracy makes slow progress. Authoritarianism is faster. It's better to settle for a slow democracy," Roberto said with an air of smugness.

"Fastest of all is revolution, brother," Andrés said irritably. "If democracy doesn't resolve matters by peaceful means, the left will be forced to take to the mountains again."

General Miles, the mediator between his sons, had a longer memory than they did. He remembered the history of uprisings and bloodshed in Mexico, and his gratitude for seventy years of one party and peaceful successions that in 2000 had allowed it to achieve a democratic alternation.

"Alternation, yes. Transition, no," Andrés said energetically, refraining from banging the teaspoon against his cup of coffee as he turned toward his brother. "Don't close the doors on us. Don't badger us with legal trickery. Don't underestimate us in your arrogance. Don't send us back to the mountains."

Andrés was in the mountains now, at the head of an army of shadows that attacked only at dawn and at sunset, vanishing at night into the sierra and disappearing during the day among the men in the mountain villages. Impossible to pick out a rebel leader from a hundred identical campesinos. Andrés Miles knew very well that to city eyes, all peasants were the same, as indistinguishable as one Chinese from another.

That was why they had treacherously chosen him, General Miles. He would be able to recognize the leader. Because the leader was his own son. And there is no mimetic power in the gray, thorny, steep, trackless, overgrown tracts of land—the great umbrella of the insurrection—that could disguise a son in an encounter with his father.

Under his breath, General Marcelino Miles cursed the stupidity of the right-wing government that had closed, one after the other, the doors of legitimate action to the left, persecuting its leaders, stripping them of immunity on the basis of legalistic deceptions, encouraging press campaigns against them, until they had the leftists cornered with no option except armed insurrection.

So many years of openness and conciliation ruined at one stroke by an incompetent right, drowning in a well of pride and vanity. The growing corruption of the regime broke the chain at its weakest link, and Andrés declared to his father:

"We have no recourse but violence."

"Be patient, son."

"I'm only one step ahead of you," Andrés said with prophetic simplicity. "At the end of the day, when we've run out of political options, you generals will have no choice but to take power and put an end to the passive frivolity of the government."

"And along the way I'll have to shoot you," the father said with severity.

"So be it," Andrés said and bowed his head.

Marcelino Miles was thinking of this as they climbed the foothills of the Sierra Madre del Sur. He would do his duty, but it was against his will. As the troops advanced, using machetes to cut their way through lianas in the impenetrable shadow of amates and ficuses intertwined with papelillo trees and embraced by climbing vines, in his mind, love for his son and military duty similarly fought and were entwined. Perhaps Andrés was right, and once again, the sacrifice of the rebel would be the price of peace.

Except what peace? General Miles thought (since one had to think about everything or nothing to triumph over the arduous ascent of an unconquerable mountain, watchword and symbol of a country as wrinkled as parchment) that Mexico didn't fit into the closed fist of a mountain. When it opened its hand, out of the wounded skin poured thorns and quagmires, the green teeth of nopal, the yellow teeth of puma, streaked rock and dried shit, acrid odors of animals lost in or habituated to the sierras of Coatepec, La Cuchilla, and La Tentación. At each step, always within reach, they sought the intangible—the revolutionary army—and what they found was something concrete: the excessive, aggressive evidence of a nature that rejects us because it is unaware of us.

How could Roberto Miles not oppose his brother, Andrés? The general had brought up his sons in modest comfort. They never lacked for anything. They didn't have an abundance of anything, either. The general wanted to prove that at least in the army, the national pastime of corruption had no place. He was a Spartan from the south of Mexico, where the difficulties of life and the immensity of nature are the salvation or perdition of human beings. The person who maintains a minimum of values that the forest, the mountains, the tropics cannot subdue, is saved.

Marcelino Miles was one of those men. But from the moment his superiors transferred him from Chilpancingo to Mexico City, his sons' tendencies were revealed outside the rules (his pact with nature) the father had imposed.

The forest and the mountain were the ironic allies of Division Commander Miles. He fulfilled his duty by climbing the sierra with the help of machetes. He fled his obligation by thinking that guerrillas never engage in formal combat. They attack the army in its barracks or ambush it in the wild. Then they vanish like hallucinations, clouded mirrors in the terrifying, impenetrable magic of the forest.

They attacked and disappeared. It wasn't possible to foresee the attack. The lessons of the past had been learned. Today Zapata wouldn't fall into the government's trap, believing in good faith that the enemy had come over to his side and would meet with him in Chinameca to seal the double betrayal. The feigned betrayal by the government army of its leader, Carranza. A clear prediction of the certain betrayal of each Zapata.

Betrayal was the name of the final battle.

Now there was a deficit of ingenuousness, just as yesterday there had been an excess of trust. Marcelino Miles thought this bitterly, because if he, Marcelino Miles, offered amnesty to his son Andrés in exchange for his surrender, the son would see a trick in the father's generosity. The son would not trust the father. The son knew the father was obliged to capture and shoot him.

Two calculations presented themselves to General Marcelino Miles's mind as he led his troops through the mountains. One, that the populations of the mountains and the plain offered their loyalty to the insurgents. Not because they had identified with the cause. They didn't support them out of necessity or conviction. They were loyal to them because the guerrillas were their brothers, their husbands, their fathers, their friends. They were *themselves* in other activities as normal as sowing and harvesting, cooking and dancing, selling and buying: bullets, adobe bricks, corn, roof tiles, huapango dances, guitars, jugs, more bullets . . . It was the familial link that strengthened the guerrillas, sheltered them, hid them, fed them.

The general's other calculation, on this night of droning macaques and clouds so low they seemed about to sing, covering the column and driving it mad as if the real siren song came from the air itself and not from the distant, atavistic sea, was that sooner or later, the countryside would grow weary of the war and abandon the rebels. He prayed that moment would come soon: He wouldn't have to capture and try his own son.

He was fooling himself, he thought immediately. Even if the villages abandoned him, Andrés Miles wasn't one of those who surrendered easily. He was one of those who went on fighting, even if only six guerrillas were left, or two, or only one: himself. Andrés Miles with his tanned face and melancholy eyes, his shock of hair prematurely grayed at the age of thirty, his slim, nervous, impatient, crouched body, always ready to leap like a mountain animal. Obviously, he didn't belong to the pavements, he wasn't a creature of the sidewalk. The wild called to him, nostalgic for him. Since his childhood in Guerrero, he would occasionally get lost when he climbed the mountain and not be heard from for an entire day. Then he would come back home but never admit he had been lost. An admirably stubborn pride had distinguished him from the time he was very little.

Was his brother better? Roberto was clever, Andrés intelligent. Roberto calculating, Andrés spontaneous. Roberto the actor in a smiling deception, Andrés the protagonist in a drama of sincerity. Both victims, the father suspected with sorrow. As an adolescent, Andrés had committed to the leftist struggle. He didn't marry. Politics, he said, was his legitimate wife. His lover was his adolescent sweetheart in Chilpancingo. At times he visited her. Other times she came to the capital. Andrés lived in the house of his father, the general, but he didn't bring the girl home. Not because of bourgeois convention but because he wanted her all to himself and didn't care to have anyone judge her, not even himself.

On the other hand, Roberto, at the age of twenty-eight, had been married and divorced twice. He changed wives according to his own idea of social prestige. He began in a high-technology company, decided to start his own electromagnetic equipment business, but his ambition was to be a software magnate. Things were not going too well for him now, which was why he returned, a divorced man, to his father's house, following the "Italian" law—today universal—of living at home for as long as possible and in this way saving on rent, food, and domestic help. He always had women, since he was good-looking—"cute," his father said to himself—but he didn't bring them home or mention them.

One woman united father and sons, the mother, Peregrina Valdés, dead of colic before the boys reached adolescence.

"Take care of them for me, Marcelino. I know your discipline, but also give them the love you gave to me."

Roberto was very different from his brother. Lighter-skinned, with a green-eyed gaze walled in by suspicion. He shaved twice a day as if to file down all the rough spots on a face that demanded trust without ever receiving it completely.

The warm memories of his family did not prevent the general from acknowledging the discouragement of his troops. Every day, inch by inch, they explored the Guerrero Mountains. The general was methodical. Nobody could accuse of him of negligence in his mission, which was to seek out the rebels in every corner of the sierra. Miles knew his effort was useless. First, because the rebel band was small and the mountains immense. The revolutionaries knew it and hid easily, constantly changing their position. They were the needles in a gigantic haystack. The general explored the sierra from the air and could not make out a single road, much less a village. In the vast extension of the mountains, not even a solitary wisp of smoke betrayed life. The dense growth admitted no space other than its own compact green nature.

And second, because the troops under his command knew that he knew. Each day they resumed the trek, aware they would never find the enemy. No one dared to say aloud what he was thinking: that this useless campaign of General Miles saved them from confronting the rebels. Until now they had fired only at rabbits and turkey buzzards. The first were fast and offered an exciting game of marksmanship. The second devoured the dead rabbits, stealing them from the soldiers.

The pact of deception between the commander and the troops allowed Marcelino Miles to enjoy the gratitude of his men and avoid recriminations from headquarters. Let them ask any soldier if the general had or had not carried out the order to search for the rebels in the sierra. Let them just ask. The commander's well-being was also that of the troops.

They had spent six weeks on this ghostly campaign when something happened that the general hadn't expected and the troops never would have imagined.

Quartered in Chilpancingo after three weeks of exploring the wild, Marcelino Miles and his soldiers had an air of duty fulfilled that authorized a couple of peaceful days for them. Though the general understood that the troops knew as well as he did that the guerrillas were not in the mountains, the physical effort of climbing and exploring redeemed them from all blame: What if now, right now, the rebels slipped up to the top and now, right now, the general and his people captured them there?

If this double play passed through the minds of Miles and the soldiers, all of them concealed it without difficulty. The general commanded, the troops obeyed. The general was carrying out to the letter his duty to explore the sierra. And the troops were doing theirs, covering every inch of the steep, solitary, overgrown terrain. Who could accuse them of shirking their duty?

Roberto Miles. He could. The general's younger son, Roberto Miles, dressed in a guayabera and holding an insolent, phallic cigar between his teeth. Roberto Miles sitting at a table on the hotel terrace with a sweet roll and a small espresso growing cold as he waited for his father to appear and not show—because it wasn't his nature—any surprise at all.

Marcelino sat down calmly next to Roberto, ordered another coffee, and asked him nothing. They didn't even look at each other. The father's severity was a mute reproach. What was his son doing here? How did he dare interrupt a professional campaign with his presence, not merely useless but inopportune as well? His presence was impertinent, disrespectful. Didn't he know his father was pursuing his older brother through the sierra?

"Don't look for him anymore in the sierra, Father," Roberto said as he sipped the coffee with voluntary slowness. "You're not going to find him there."

The general turned to look coldly at his son. He asked nothing. He wasn't going to compromise—or frustrate, he admitted to himself—his intimate project of *not finding* the rebel, of deceiving headquarters without incurring any blame at all.

Let Roberto talk. The general would not say anything. A profound intuition ordered this conduct. Not to look. Not to speak.

When he looked at himself in the mirror the next morning, the general thought his slender little mustache, as thin as a pencil line, was ridiculous, and with a couple of strokes of the Gillette, he shaved it off, seeing himself suddenly free of the past, of habits, of useless presumptions. He looked like a defeated commander. His undershirt was loose, and his trousers hung on him unwillingly.

He reacted. He tightened his belt, rinsed his sweaty armpits, and put on his tunic buttoned with conflictive anger and disinclination.

Andrés Miles was now in prison. He smiled at his father when they arrested him in the house of his sweetheart, Esperanza Abarca.

"There's no better disguise than invisibility," the older son said with a smile when he was detained. "I mean, you have to know how to look at the obvious."

He placed a small Dominican banana in his mouth and surrendered without resistance. He had only to see the equally sad faces of his father and the troops to realize that what they did, they did against their wills. It was almost as if the father as well as the soldiers had lost in one stroke the reason for this campaign aimed at what had happened now—the capture of the rebel leader, Andrés Miles—and reached an unwanted conclusion that brought all of them face-to-face with a fatal decision. Eliminating the rebel.

"Just don't apply the fugitive law to me," Andrés said with a smile when they tied his hands.

"Son . . ." the father dared to murmur.

"General, sir," his son answered with steel in his voice.

And so Marcelino Miles spent the whole night debating with himself. Should he try his son according to the summary procedure dictated by the military code? How comfortable it was for the political authorities to shoot the rebel and leave no trace . . . make him disappear, provoke a passing protest, and assure the eventual triumph of forgetting. How complicated to bring the rebel before judges who would determine the proper punishment for insurgency and uprising.

How destructive to paternal morale to attend the son's trial and oblige himself to present the infamous evidence: His brother had betrayed him. Wouldn't it be better for Roberto to stay out of the case, for the father to assume complete responsibility?

"I captured him in the sierra. My men will testify to that. Mission accomplished. Let justice be done."

He remembered Roberto's face when he betrayed his brother.

"It's as clear as two and two make four." Roberto dared to be ironic. "Don't tell me, Father, that it never occurred to you the rebel might be hiding like a coward behind the skirts of his old lady here in Chilpancingo?" He laughed. "And you lost in the sierra, just think . . ."

"Why, Roberto?"

The ironic mask shattered. "Did you calculate, Father, the cost of having a brother who appears day after day in the papers as an insurgent fugitive? Have you thought of the very serious damage all of this does to my business? Do you believe that people, people, General, sir, the government, businessmen, gringo partners, all of them, do you believe they'll have confidence in me with a guerrilla brother? For God's sake, Papa, think about me, I'm twenty-eight years old, things haven't gone well for me in business, give me a chance, plea—"

"Capturing him was only a question of time. You had no patience with me," Marcelino Miles said, making a great effort to be conciliatory.

"Naaaaa," his younger son mocked him openly. "Nonsense! You were acting like a fool, to put it kindly, you—"

The general stood, hit his son Roberto in the face with his whip, and headed for the prison.

"Let him go," he told the captain of the guard. "Tell him that this time he should really disappear, because the second time will be the end."

"But General, sir . . . If headquarters finds out, you'll—"

Miles interrupted him brutally. "Who's going to tell what happened?" he asked in a voice as hard as basalt.

"I don't know . . ." stammered the captain. "The soldiers . . ."

"They're loyal to me," the brigadier general answered without any doubts. "None of them wanted to capture my son. You can testify to that."

"Then, General, sir, your other son." The captain's firm tone returned. "The one who turned him in, the one—"

"Do you mean Judas, Captain?"

"Well, I—"

"My son Cain, Captain?"

"It's your—"

"What do you think of the fugitive law, Captain?"

The captain swallowed hard. "Well, sometimes there's nothing else—"

"And what do you think is worse, Captain, rebellion or betrayal? I repeat: Which one stains the honor of the military more? A rebel or an informer?"

"The honor of the army?"

"Or of the family, if you prefer."

"There's no question, General, sir." Now Captain Alvarado blinked. "The traitor is despicable, the rebel is respectable."

Nobody knows who shot Roberto Miles in the back as he was going into the hotel La Gloria in Chilpancingo. He fell dead on the street, surrounded by an equally instantaneous flow of thick blood that ran with sinister brilliance from the snow-white guayabera.

General Marcelino Miles communicated to headquarters that the rebel Andrés Miles had succeeded in escaping military detention.

"I know, Mr. Secretary, that this family drama is very painful. You must understand that it was very difficult for me to capture my own son after six weeks of combing the mountains looking for him. I couldn't imagine that my other son, Roberto Miles, would put a pistol to the head of the upstanding Captain Alvarado and force him to allow his brother, Andrés, to escape."

"And who killed Roberto, General?"

"Captain Alvarado himself, Mr. Secretary. A valiant soldier, I assure you. He wasn't going to allow my son Roberto to stain the honor of an officer."

"It's murder."

"That's how Captain Alvarado understands it."

"He thinks so? Or he knows so? He only thinks so?" the secretary of national defense said with controlled passion.

"General, Captain Alvarado has joined the rebels of the Vicente Guerrero Popular Army in the Sierra Madre del Sur."

"Well, it's better for him to join the guerrillas than the narcos."

"That's true, General. You see that four out of ten leave us to go with the narcos."

"Well, you know your duty, General Miles. Continue looking for them," said the secretary with a smile of long irony in which General Marcelino Miles could detect the announcement of a not very desirable future.

Marcelino Miles returns with pleasure to the sierra in Guerrero. He loves the plants and birds of the mountains. Nothing gives him greater pleasure than identifying a tropical almond from a distance, the tall lookout of the forests, catching fire each autumn to strip itself bare and be renewed immediately: flowers that are stars, perfume that summons bumblebees, yellow fleshy fruits. And also, close up, he likes to surprise the black iguana—the garrobo—looking for the burning rock of the mountain. He counts the five petals of the basket tulip; he's amazed that the flower exists outside a courtyard and has made its way into the dense growth. He looks up and surprises the noisy flight of the white-faced magpie with its black crests, the long throat of the social flycatcher and its spotted crown, the needle beak of the cinnamon-colored hummingbird. The clock-bird marks the hours with its dark beak, conversing with the cuckoo-squirrel with its undulating flight . . . This is the greatest pleasure of Marcelino Miles. Identifying trees. Admiring birds. That is why he loves the mountains in Guerrero. He doesn't search for Andrés. He has forgotten Roberto. He is in the army because of his passion for nature.

Chorus of the Suffering Children

why did we run away?
because my papa wouldn't let me be with other children nobody
could come to play
with me I couldn't go anywhere
because my father hit us both my mama and me
because my mother was afraid and so was I
because locked in my room I hear the insults the blows
because I have nightmares
because I don't sleep
because my father doesn't respect my mother and if he doesn't
respect her he can't respect
me
because my papa makes me take a freezing-cold shower so I'll behave
because my papa makes me watch porn movies with him on TV
because if my papa insults my mama why can't I?
why did we run away?
because they abused us they whipped us they threatened to cut us
because they threw us out of the house
papa and mama, abusive father, single mother, father and mother
divorced, addict fathers, drunken fathers, unemployed fathers
because papa and mama have no other mirror than
us their lost youth
because papa and mama resent their lives and
they ruin ours so we won't dare
to be better
because we don't have grandparents and our grandparents
have no
grandmother

because my husband wanted a male heir and
he made me get an abortion when the doctor told him
that my baby was a girl like me
ultrasound ultrasound there are no fetal secrets anymore
mountains of fetuses
more fetuses than garbage
a little girl is undesirable she'll wind up going off with her
husband she'll lose the father's name
educating a girl is throwing water into the sea the husband
will have the benefit of the education we gave her with so much
sacrifice
ungrateful the two of them
(the sex of a fetus is no longer a secret)
(the garbageman baptizes the sex)
save yourself from happy families
look at your parents: only violence settles things
look at your parents: don't respect women
look at your parents: your father killed you because he
wanted to kill your mother and you were near at hand
and now where?
escape your dumbass family the school that makes you stupid
the suffocating office the loneliness of
the streets
kid, become a cycleboy! they give you a motorcycle you
laugh
at the traffic lights the curses
the police the endless delays
zigzag cycleboy kill pedestrians freefreefree
fastfastfast
adrenaline express
bulletcycle cycleboy urban cowboy
though you're the one who regularly dies every day
the only one among a thousand cycleboys who are
saved one day to die smashed up one by one

in the following days
        and now where?
        join the flashmobs the lightningrace find out
where's the hookup today
        escape: arrive and join in leave no more than two
minutes at a time this is the fiesta of
        passing friendship of impossible communication
of instantaneous flight
        suck up the coke and run
        there's no way out
        run before they play taps for you
they throw you in jail
        they apply the fugitive law to you
        quick quick the kiss the greeting the pass
        and now where?
        damn motherfucker wandering around
        don't you have a home? I don't have a home because
            nobody's looking for me and nobody's looking for me
            because I don't have a home
        how many are there? how many flies are there in an outhouse
with open windows?
        why don't you go back?
        because I'm not a damn kid anymore I'm a man
like my father
        why don't you go back? Because I'm getting mixed up
help me

The Gay Divorcee

Guy Furlong and José Luis Palma met in the old Balmori movie house on Avenida Álvaro Obregón, a sumptuous art deco palace with the best sound equipment of the day and a seductive gleam of lustrous bronzes, mirrors, and marbles. They happened to sit next to each other. The first brush of knees was avoided with nervous urgency. That of elbows, forgiven. That of hands, spontaneous, when they clasped during the laughter demanded by the screen, awkward only for a moment—the instant just before the meeting of their eyes that, with its intensity, eclipsed the erotic ballet of Fred and Ginger on the screen.

The Gay Divorcee was the title of the film with the Rogers-Astaire team. Then came *The Gay Desperado,* with an Italian singer disguised as a Mexican *charro,* and later, *Our Hearts Were Young and Gay,* the autobiography of a

Broadway actress. Except back then the word "gay" meant only "happy, carefree, lighthearted," while contemptuous, insulting terms were reserved for homosexuals. Queer. Pansy. Faggot. A whole gamut of them. Forty-one, because of an old club of bourgeois transvestites with that number of members. *Adelitas,* for being "popular with the troops," considering the relative ease of hiring indifferent soldiers for last-minute performances. *Jotos* in Méjico with the "j" of García Lorca and with the murdered poet *pájaros* in Havana, *apios* in Seville, *floras* in Alicante, and *adelaidas* in Portugal.

And back in Mexico, *jotería* to classify an entire sexual group. A pipe makes his mouth water. He likes his rice with the stem. He enjoys boiled Coca-Cola. The storm of nominal and adjectival scorn that poured down on Mexican homosexuals perhaps only hid, crudely, the very disguised inclinations of the most macho of machos: those who deceived their wives with men and brought venereal disease into their decent homes. Enchiladas with cold cream. Male hookers.

José Luis and Guy, from the very beginning, by an agreement unspoken but acted upon, established themselves as a couple removed from both dissimulation and excuses. It was auspicious that the movies brought them together when they were only eighteen years old. They still weren't emancipated, but their early relationship pushed them to find as soon as possible the way to leave their families (indifferent to the situation because the lovers decided it that way) and live together. Guy achieved it first, since his success as an artistic promoter produced good commissions that allowed him to establish an agency called Artvertising, which quickly had a list of distinguished clients. In the meantime, José Luis completed his law studies at the age of twenty-three.

It was auspicious that the movies brought them together. In the silver images of the Balmori, they had discovered a capacity for wonder that set fire to their love and kept it alive. They divided their attraction to films among the several unreachable models offered to them by the irreplaceable darkness of the cinematographic cave. They let pass the pretty ones like Robert Taylor, the rough ones like James Cagney, the extroverts like Cary Grant, the introverts like Gary Cooper, and settled into their admiration, secret in its androgyny, of Greta Garbo, the woman men wanted to be but the woman no man would ever become. Mademoiselle Hamlet, as Gertrude Stein called her (or was it Alice Toklas?). The sphinx. Her face filled with wintry absence projected from the screen like an offering and a challenge. Leave me alone, like bullfighters, but make me yours, like courtesans.

As soon as they moved into a nice apartment with neoclassical architecture in the Roma district, Guy and José Luis placed some photos of Garbo in strategic spots, though their principal paintings were given to them by Alfonso Michel and Manuel Rodríguez Lozano. A still life that throbbed with vital breath in the exuberant, disheveled, husky Michel (a midwife to painting) and a funeral procession in blacks, whites, and grays from Rodríguez Lozano (its gravedigger).

Together they found their professions. Guy Furlong opened an art gallery on Calle de Praga to give a space to painters who used an easel and to prove that murals were not the only art in Mexico. José Luis established a law office on Avenida Juárez that soon specialized in discreet divorce negotiations, division of property, awarding of custody, and other troublesome matters in the life of a family that ought to be kept away from public opinion.

"To be who we are, we need money," José Luis said judiciously, and of course Guy agreed.

In order not to worry about money, they had to make money. Without ostentation. The important thing was to keep alive desire, the capacity for wonder, to share time, to create a common background of memories and an evanescent oasis of desires. If love was divided among several unreachable models, affection was concentrated on a single intimate model. Themselves.

The two boys established certain rules for their life in common. Guy said it one night:

"The first time you made love to me, you accepted me once and for all, without any need to test me or constantly reaffirm the ties that bind us. Between us, there are more than enough complications."

It really wasn't necessary to reaffirm a love given as spontaneously as the flow of a fountain, though with constant references to everything in the life of the world that pleased them and identified them. Their intimacy was the thing that was sacred, untouchable, the impalpable diamond that, handled too much, could change into coal. In the secret chamber of their intimacy, Guy and José Luis established a relationship as close to itself as water is to its continent. "Death Without End," the great poem by José Gorostiza, was one of the couple's vital bibles. Form was content and content form with no more motive than the patterns of delight in touch begun that increasingly distant afternoon in the movies. The joy of mutual contemplation. The knowledge of the respect owed to each one and to the couple.

As for the world . . . they weren't naive. They knew they were in society, and society tests us, it demands periodic examinations, especially of homosexual lovers who dare to be happy. José Luis and Guy prepared good-naturedly to endure the world's tests, aware that they wanted to have contact with the group but avoid (as if it were mange) promiscuity.

"You're not a flirt," José Luis said to Guy. "You just display yourself. You like to show yourself off. You're right. You're handsome, and you ought to let yourself be admired. I'm happy you're like this. I'm happy people admire you."

"Don't fool yourself," Guy responded. "People need to know me to love me. If a person doesn't know me, he probably won't like me."

They laughed at these topics and admitted:

"There can always be somebody who seduces us."

Until now, no one had come between them. The serious, amiable behavior of the boys, their stability as a couple, made them likable. They dressed well, they spoke well, they were doing well in their respective careers. They saved criticism of other people for private moments. They weren't gossipmongers.

"Did you see the faces Villarino was making? He was putting moves on you."

"You like people to admire me, didn't you say that?"

"Show yourself off now that you're young. Take a good look at Villarino so you never become a flirt when you're old. How awful!"

"No. How ridiculous!"

Both had been educated in English schools, but they never referred to what is called "the English vice." They did accept, however, a rule of conduct learned by means of educational blows with a cane to the gluteals:

Never complain. Never explain.

Ni quejarse ni explicarse. The demands of love imposed themselves naturally, without any need for complaints or explanations, in the very act of love. Demands before love tended to kill pleasure, withdrawing its implicit satisfactions, losing them in the harsh antagonist of love, which was logic, though this only reinforced the professional competence of the two men.

And so there was a very attractive equilibrium in their lives, measured out between their work and their private life. Which doesn't mean that my friends Guy and José Luis didn't have a social life in the very lively Mexico City of the forties and fifties to the mid-sixties. They participated in various groups founded to the almost biological rhythm of the decades and their newsworthy duration, their inevitable decline, the attachments to and detachments from social groups and, in particular, the solid middle class to which they both belonged. They were present at the end of the fiesta dominated by Diego Rivera and Frida Kahlo, two large multicolored piñatas that skillfully avoided the sticks of governments, political parties, or social classes. Artists ate apart. They owed nothing to anyone except art. Frida and Diego swung picturesquely at an unreachable height to which you had access only if your name was Trotsky, Breton, or Rockefeller, or if you were a modest cantina owner, the projectionist at the movies, or the indispensable hospital nurse. In the forties, José Luis and Guy were present only at the end of that boisterous party, the tail of the comet that pulled along in its generous wake the lights of artistic creativity, sexual confusion, and political arbitrariness.

Then they moved among the romantic violins of Reyes Albarrán's

Rendez Vous and the Jockey Club, which became the most discreetly gay and refined place to meet on Sunday thanks to the management of Jaime Saldívar, a man endowed with inseparable amiability and elegance, capable of making himself followed, like the pied piper of Hamelin, by newly minted princes and the patriarchs of ancient lineages. Although the mix of European *epavés* from World War II and the stars of a Hollywood undecided between Roosevelt's New Deal and McCarthy's witch hunt met at the Ciro's of the dwarf A. C. Blumenthal, a partner of the gangster Bugsy Siegel, and in what remained of the intimate wartime cabarets: Casanova, Minuit, Sans Souci . . .

Then came the adventures of the Basfumista group, fervent, anarchic, invented by the painter Adolfo Best Maugard, a former assistant to Sergei Eisenstein in Mexico and endowed with a vestal in residence, Mercedes Azcárate, and a slim blond philosopher, Ernesto de la Peña, who knew some twenty languages, including that of Christ, and was master within the group of a distracted vocation for alarm in a society still capable of being surprised and forgetting from one day to the next about its own newness. Basfumismo never defined itself beyond the Chaplinesque call for attention before a dehumanized society.

It was the last clarion call of the 1940s, before the immense city devoured every attempt to come together under the roof of culture and acquire a personality by means of avant-garde circles. On the horizon, the Rosa district was already dawning, a mix of St. Germain des Prés and Greenwich Village around a Café Tyrol presided over every afternoon by a Colombian writer, Gabriel García Márquez, who had lived in Mexico City since 1960, and baptized by the painter José Luis Cuevas, a cat who seduced with scratches.

But by then Guy Furlong and José Luis Palma were the only Mexicans who still wore tuxedos to eat dinner. They were distinguished by a reluctance to abandon the styles of their youth. Both of them based elegance on style, not fashion. The bad thing was that by the sixties, wearing a dinner jacket at a cocktail party or a vernissage meant running the risk of being confused with the waiters. The old seducer of adolescents, Agustín Villarino, had turned in his documents to eternity sometime earlier. Not, however, without leaving a successor in Mexico City, his nephew Curly Villarino, and here our story actually begins.

Guy and José Luis did not want to be left behind. The groups and conclaves mentioned here tacitly proclaimed their modernity, their cosmopolitanism, and their youth. Three purposes that condemned them to disappear. The modern is destined to vanish quickly for the sake of its own decaying currency and in favor of the next brand-new novelty that, whether it's called postmodern or retro and rejects or evokes nostalgia, simply repeats the warning of death to fashion in the *Pensieri* of Giacomo Leopardi: Madama la Morte, Madama la Morte, don't ask me who I am: I am fashion, death . . . I am you.

Then the spree began to fall apart in a charmless slumming in run-down, high-living cabarets in the Guerrero district and in San Juan de Letrán. El Golpe, King Kong, El Burro, Club de los Artistas . . . and if one wanted to dance the mambo on Sunday with one's servants, the Salón Los Angeles dissolved, with delight in loud revelry and false democracy, the barriers between classes. The cabarets for danzón and dance hostesses died a natural death, the Río Rosa, next to the Bullfight Ring, and the Waikiki, whose only vegetation was the cactus on Paseo de la Reforma. Thanks to its consecration by Aaron Copland, the Salón México survived with its famous sign: DON'T THROW LIT CIGARETTES ON THE FLOOR, THE GIRLS CAN BURN THEIR FEET.

Cosmopolitanism customarily required a center of worldwide attraction, like Paris in the nineteenth century or New York in the twentieth. The fall of colonial empires after World War II meant the end of one or even two cultural metropolises in favor of a revindication of traditions, each anchored in a calendar distinct from the Western. For a Mexican, in any case, it was easier to refer to the Mayas or the Baroque than to the contributions of Kenya, Indonesia, or Timbuktu, the new capitals of the disguised anthropology of third-world revolution.

As for youth, it was being transformed into a solitary avenue that José Luis and Guy stopped walking with the impression that they were ghosts. It was difficult for them to abandon the obligation to be the representatives of *a* youth. What was left was the dejection of losing—abandonment, death, lack of will—the people who, half in self-congratulation, called themselves "our crowd," "our set." These compliments were not, however, the requiem for Guy's and José Luis's constant certainty: We didn't let ourselves go with a group of dispensable people, we weren't interchangeable, we were *irreplaceable* as a couple.

In the midst of these changes, both kept the friends who hadn't succumbed to violence or been liberated into death. A man needs sad friends to whom he can tell what he doesn't say to his lover. A man needs patient friends who give him the time that a lover denies him. A man needs the friend who talks to him about his lover and evokes a kind of shared warmth that requires the presence of a third person, a special confidant. And above all, a man must respect the relationship with the friend who isn't his lover and gives the assurance that passion could overwhelm him.

For Guy and José Luis, their relationship with friends secretly established an obligation, which was to avoid promiscuity. It was implicit that a friendship, no matter how close, would never cross the frontier of physical love. In their youth and early maturity, Guy and José Luis proposed taking part in everything but in moderation, without vulgarity, without failures in respect. They told each other that a couple needs others but ought to reserve to itself the dialogue between you and me, never surrendering intimacy to the group, to others. And above all, it must respect the relationship with the friend who isn't a lover and gives the assurance that passion could overwhelm him.

Both Guy and José Luis, now lagging behind the avant-garde, believed that this friend was Curly Villarino, a bridge between our couple's sixty years and the thirtysomething of everybody else. Guy and José Luis suffered the feeling of having lost the group, the circle that accompanied them between the ages of twenty and fifty, decimated now by age, death, indolence, the loss of a center, and the move to the outskirts of a Dantesque city: the wild forest.

In short, each group brings with it the question: "What impression are we making?" The Jockey's aristocrats, L'Aiglon's gilded youth, the Rosa district's artists and intellectuals. All of them wanted to make an impression, and in this aspiration lay the defeat or triumph of its members. Both transitory, except that those who failed had to choose between returning to their families or, following André Gide's proclamation—families, I detest you—give themselves over to a bohemia that was sad, poor, solitary, scruffy, and as dependent on what they could beg as the most "subjugated" son at home. Only a few stayed afloat in the heavy seas of yesterday's groups, asserting their talent thanks to the hard exigencies of indiscipline, the purges of monogamy (sometimes serial), and carefully measured-out absences from the ravenous homeland. Mexico City threatened to devour alive each one of its inhabitants, whether victim or victimizer.

Instead of a single center—between the Zócalo and Angel—the capital spread in concentric circles increasingly distant from what Guy and José Luis considered the "heart" of the city. The Rosa district would end up prostituted and brothelized, exiling its mobile geography of restaurants, cafés, and boutiques to Avenida Masaryk, from where it would soon move to the center, expelled now by gangs of car thieves, pilferers of watches, entire families of crooks who specialized in breaking into houses, robbing banks, handling burglary tools, murdering for pay, beating with clubs, stabbing, pimping, and prostituting. Old pensioners without a pension, fugitives from justice, con artists . . . What remained of the ancient City of Palaces? A huge supermarket filled with cans of blood and bottles of smoke? Blood and hunger, basic necessities of the city-monster.

"The consumer society," wrote Georges Bataille in *La Part maudite*, "was invented by the Aztecs. They consumed hearts."

Guy and José Luis believed they had saved their hearts from Mexican ritual cannibalism. At the age of fifty-six, they could look with nostalgic apprehension at their youthful meeting in the Balmori movie theater and tell each other, "I think we saved ourselves, we think we haven't been touched by undesirable emotions, we think that by this time nothing can disturb us . . ." They condemned the city to death.

They did not count on the opposition of Curly Villarino, committed to reviving the days of an aristocratic freedom reserved, at this point in history, only for a handful of multimillionaires and members of European and Arabic royal houses. That is what Curly's calling card was: a summons to the nostalgia of Guy and José Luis for their youth, a sweet evocation of a lost time that he, Curly Villarino, seemed to or pretended to reincarnate for the exclusive benefit of the two friends.

"All my uncle Agustín's friends have died. Only you two are left from that time, Guy, José Luis, my dears. You are my seductive perfumes."

He said it in so childlike and lovable a manner. With his voice and manners, he made you forgive his somewhat outlandish appearance of a fat boy who never finished growing. The baby fat on his cheeks swayed from side to side with the emphatic movement of his pink cherub's lips, though the fat seraph was contradicted by narrow myopic eyes behind a pair of small eyeglasses in the style of Schubert that, Curly *dixit*, would eventually replace the oversize aviator's glasses favored by the deplorable decade of miniskirts, mammoth belts, and bell-bottom trousers.

Curly's entire spherical existence was crowned by a mass of curls, once blond but now streaked with gray, that resembled the inspired wig of the great Harpo Marx. But if the latter was famously mute, Curly talked incessantly, wittily, and freely. It charmed my friends that when he was introduced, Curly said to them:

"I am not impartial, don't believe that even for a minute. You two are my classics. And I need a 'classic' in order to live and die. I think you" (he looked at them innocently) "are the culmination of the race. You are from *mon genre,* if such a thing can be repeated. No, seriously. Everything would be perfect if we were immortal. Since we aren't, let us at least be unending. I mean, let us ask: Why do they tolerate us homos? Answer: in order not to discriminate against us. If we accept this truth, let us admit its consequences. I devote myself only to looking for opportunities that 'normality' would deny me."

And after a long sigh:

"Sometimes I find them, other times no. We are all like submarines that cut through posh marinas checking on whether the yachts have anchors, how many barnacles are clinging to them, if the ship is old or new. Then—I warn you—*I attack*. I attack in earnest. With torpedoes. I warn you so that no one can call it a deception. If I suspect a couple isn't getting along, I am going to try to seduce them . . ."

Guy and José Luis remarked that Curly was an amiable buffoon, reminiscent of the most notable excesses of another time. Nowadays singular personalities were lost in the sulfurous urban magma, groups disintegrated, and the only recourse was to search the haystack for the brilliant needle of the brilliant eccentricity that once was.

"Do you realize that we're beginning to talk like a couple of doddering old men?" asked Guy.

José Luis didn't reveal either melancholy or fatalism. "That's why we like Curly. He's young, but he's in sync with us."

"We didn't need clowns before," Guy said with a frown.

"No, but only because everybody was comical except you and me."

"Do you feel that self-congratulatory about our behavior?"

" 'Self-congratulatory' isn't the word. Don't be pedantic. Perhaps serious, serious in the midst of the circus. 'Serious' is the word. We never deceive, and we don't allow ourselves to be deceived. If you take a good look at our life, Guy, you'll admit that we were observers but never full participants."

"You mean we never allowed our private relationship to be confused with our social life?"

"Something better. We were witnesses in order to survive."

"Do you think we've survived? As measured by what?"

"As measured by what we proposed being. A faithful couple, Guy. I believe we both know very well that we've never failed in our loyalty. Promiscuity was all around us. We never fell into it."

"Don't be so sure," joked Guy. "There's still time."

On the verge of turning sixty, Guy and José Luis had solidified their personal relationship as well as their professional lives and their dealings—increasingly rare—with a society in which they no longer recognized themselves. Rises and falls were too abrupt. Famous names turned infamous. Anonymous people achieved their fifteen minutes of Warholian fame before somersaulting and disappearing. The hateful norms of a hypocritical Catholic morality had disappeared only to be replaced by a no less hypocritical cult of immorality: pleasure, money, consumption hailed as a proof of freedom, and sophisticated indifference behind a mask of sincerity even in those who did not practice it but felt compelled to celebrate it. There were no well-rooted islands left. Everything was like a vast, drifting political and social Xochimilco crossed by boats with names written in flowers that withered from one day to the next. The men in power changed. The vices of power remained.

Curly, then, was an island of cheer as well as nostalgia for a lost world: the world of Guy's and José Luis's youth. He brought them the private pleasure of an audacious joke, a caricatured excess, which the *expectant* nature of the Furlong–Palma couple demanded, almost as if it were an acquired right. Curly was their show.

Of course the plump young man surpassed himself in word and deed. That is, he alone took the place of several generations from their social past. It was part of his charm. It was inevitable. He was, for Guy and José Luis, a reminiscence. Like a minor Oscar Wilde, Curly fired off paradoxes and bons mots left and right.

"Life would be perfect if I were immortal."

"Promiscuity is taking pleasure in yourself."

"Sex doesn't bring happiness, but it does calm the nerves."

"Amity is so drunk she's even drinking from the vases."

"Nothing's as exciting as exposing yourself to a man in church."

"The problem with Rudy is that he's orthopedic."

"Gustavito has a bore inside his head."

These malicious witticisms were received with laughter, Guy's happier than that of José Luis, who—as he confessed to his lover—was beginning to weary of Curly's verbal excesses.

"He can be very impertinent. That isn't our style."

"Don't pay attention to him, José Luis. Impertinence only hides his vacuousness. Did you expect profundity from a boy like that?"

"Not profundity. Not impertinence, either."

"Let it pass. Who would replace this blessed Rigoletto fallen from heaven?"

"Or come up from a sulfurous pit, how can anyone tell . . ."

They felt sorry for him one night when they were having supper together in a restaurant on Calle de Havre, and Curly's eyes became dangerously distracted. Guy's back was to the dining room. José Luis, beside Curly, could appreciate the obscure object of desire.

A dark-skinned boy went back and forth with ancestral agility, as if a remote ancestor of his had been responsible for bringing fresh fish from the coast to Emperor Moctezuma in his palace on the plateau.

He was nimble, swift, graceful, without an extra gram on his face or body. Curly looked at him with a desire that was increasingly difficult to hide, to the point where he stopped chatting with his friends and absently committed the unforgivable error of sitting with his mouth open, his gaze lost in the waiter's movements, something that provoked José Luis to laugh and remark that a "closed mouth catches no boys," which provoked Curly's irritation followed by this action that revealed, to whomever wishes to measure it, the nature, *naturata* and *naturante*, of the witty fat man.

The fact is that Curly, as the young indigenous waiter walked past, dropped his napkin to the floor and looked at the boy with a mixture of indignation and scorn.

"What are you waiting for?" said Curly.

"Excuse me?" responded the waiter.

"Stupid Indian. Pick up the napkin."

The waiter bent over and picked up the napkin lightly spotted with lipstick, as Guy and José Luis could observe with smiles, but not the servile object of Curly's wounded contempt. The servant.

"Learn to serve," Curly continued. "Learn to differentiate." And stressing the two words, he concluded: "I am *a gentleman*."

He said it with an insufferable arrogance that mortified Guy and

José Luis, whose glances, one directed at Curly and the other at the waiter, were both filled with someone else's excuses and sorrow. The boy bowed gravely to Curly and withdrew to continue his work.

"They're our only aristocrats," José Luis commented when the waters had calmed.

"Who?" asked a red-faced Curly.

José Luis did not respond, and in Curly's eyes, this registered as a serious offense.

"Did you realize?" said José Luis, holding a *New Yorker* when they were back home. "Since he couldn't punish you for seeing him turned into an imbecile with his mouth hanging open, he turned on the weak one, the waiter."

Guy buttoned his pajamas and said nothing.

"He's a shameful coward" was José Luis's judgment. "I don't know if it's worthwhile to keep cultivating him."

"Yes," Guy said with a yawn. "Probably he's already served his purpose."

"Which was?" suggested José Luis, setting aside the magazine.

Guy shrugged. "Frankly, it's all the same to me if we see him or not."

"Ah," exclaimed José Luis, accustomed to less ambiguous or contradictory answers from his companion. "Then you think it's a matter of one of those *surmountable* incidents."

It wasn't a question. It was a statement.

The conversation was following brand-new paths. Generally, Guy and José Luis were in agreement because they knew they were united against a world that would have liked to be hostile if they themselves did not make it habitable. The couple's agreement in the face of society translated into an affirmation of the couple in their intimacy. One thing, as they knew very well, defended and empowered the other.

Now something was happening that obliged Guy to say sarcastically, "Do you know what they call us in secret?"

"No," José Luis said with a smile.

"Tweedledum and Tweedledee, the twins Alice meets who say the same thing at the same time."

"But they never make stupid remarks." José Luis escalated the dialogue.

"Don't torture me." Guy smiled again.

Then they went to sleep without speaking or even touching each other. The next morning, while they were shaving side by side in the art nouveau bathroom, Guy broke the ice.

"If you prefer, we won't see him anymore."

"Who?" José Luis said from behind the lather.

"Please, José Luis."

"I couldn't care less."

"That's not true."

"I give you my word. In any case, I'm not going to let that flan with legs ruin our life. We don't owe him anything."

"Nothing," Guy said without conviction. "Nothing at all."

Curly did not fail to appear that same morning with a bouquet of roses and a handwritten note: "My dear friends. Why are you indifferent to me? Like the Brazilians, I watch over your absences. With love, C.V."

They decided to invite him to dinner the next day. Good manners demanded it. Not appearing to be offended demanded it even more. And denying power to Curly demanded it most of all.

As required, they wore tuxedos.

"Out of nostalgia," said Guy.

"Out of habit," added José Luis.

"Out of laziness," laughed Curly, dressed in red velvet with a ruffled shirt. "Do you two know? I know you know that boy turned me down, and I've come to ask you not to tell anyone about it."

Guy said nothing. José Luis became indignant at so vulgar a provocation. He dropped his silverware with a clatter.

"I expected better taste or at least better irony from you," he said to Curly.

"I'm in no mood for irony tonight," Curly said with a sigh. "I'm suffering from lovesickness."

The chubby man turned toward Guy.

"But you know about that, don't you, darling?"

José Luis couldn't believe it. Guy blushed. José Luis weighed in to the defense.

"We know only what it's important for us to know. You're putting in the banderillas and we won't tolerate it."

"No?" The young man smiled. "Well, look, José Luis, you can stick me with banderillas, lances, and swords, and I won't be irritated. Talk it over with your little friend and see if he tolerates it from you."

"I don't understand. What are you talking about?" José Luis asked Curly, though he was looking at Guy.

"For God's sake," Guy replied. "Don't make a tempest in a teapot."

Curly laughed out loud.

"I don't believe it! Please stop presenting me with such glorious opportunities. Gang up on me, I beg you. Defend yourselves against your little spy Curly Villarino, the busybody who knows everything and divulges everything. Isn't that right? Oh, discretion isn't my forte!"

Suddenly, he changed his tone.

"What do you want me to tell you. That only novelty excites me? That I'm desperate because the night before last I didn't seduce the busboy? That I don't need witnesses to my amatory failures? That I've come on my knees to beg you to remain silent? That I'll find the way to fuck you over if you betray me to other people?"

Then José Luis told me that "other people" was too vast to refer to a circle growing smaller and smaller. The fact is that on the day Curly came for dinner, he initiated a lament to my friends. Both of them, united in their old custom of remaining on the margins of other people's passions, of being a discreet couple, one that was solitary if necessary but never condemned to participate in what would be called a radio soap opera yesterday, a TV soap opera today, and a melodrama always. And melodrama, as you know, is comedy without humor.

"That I've always been an outsider?" Curly continued. "Always marginalized? That I'll leave the closet and no one will follow me?" Suddenly, he snapped his fingers, imitating the click of castanets. "Or be the life of the party?" He laughed artlessly. "And sometimes the death of the party."

He put on a funereal air and stood up. "I know. You want me to leave. You don't want me to foul your sweet little love nest. Fine, my dear fags. I won't beg. You think you've conquered me. Fine. We'll see." He made a ridiculous pirouette, sometimes lifting off the ground despite his large bodily mass, revealed in that act as a balloon filled only with self-satisfaction. "Fine. I'll go. But my box of surprises isn't empty yet. Wait a little. A bee stings harder the longer he retains the venom."

Guy's unusual spiritual distance during the days that followed was understood by José Luis as uneasiness rather than irritation due to the scenes provoked by Curly. Still, in his more intelligent moments, José Luis decided to treat what seemed serious as if it were frivolous, what seemed profound as if it were superficial. He didn't change his behavior, the rhythm of his daily actions, the usual chatter of lives that were too intimate and too old not to understand that the times of the most level normalcy did not exclude but underscored the moments filled with physical love as well as intelligent discourse between two human beings.

José Luis, somewhat pensive, asked silent questions of Guy. What is our relationship made of? Desire and jealousy? Or innocence and disdain? Will you always love me in the natural way you have until now? Or are you going to make me feel that you're indulging me? Isn't indulgence the most deceptive form of tolerance?

("We've never tolerated each other, you and I. We wouldn't have lived together for so long if we only tolerated each other.")

His glance happened to fall on a photograph taken when they were young. Guy and José Luis side by side, smiling but serious, not embracing, displaying the seriousness of their relationship because it wasn't demonstrative, it was discreet. It was enough for him to see himself in his twenties, when the relationship was already an irreversible fact, to know that he and Guy always knew how to survive the bad times, and this conviction deflected the irritations found in every shared, intense, prolonged life. They put off explosions of bad temper. They exiled misunderstandings. They banished tedium and indifference. Precisely because all of that was found in the relationship, not because it was missing.

Perhaps the inevitable was treated by the couple not as something not talked about—hypocrisy—but as something just the opposite—imagination. Bad humor saved by an opportune joke. Misunderstandings elevated to the level of vain possibility. Tedium deflected by a reference to the movies, to literature, to art, to everything that, being theirs, should have been everybody's.

This was the difference. Now it would seem that the roles they had once shared were turning into monologues. José Luis resisted being the actor of jealousy opposite the protagonist of desire in Guy's distant glance. He was afraid that jealousy would turn into scorn as Guy's desire disguised itself, ridiculously, as innocence.

The fact is that José Luis, knowing Guy so intimately, could distinguish the temperatures of desire in his lover. What disturbed him was that, after a few days, he could not identify the object of that desire. Because he, José Luis, was not the object or the subject of Guy's familiar palpitations.

José Luis was in his office at nightfall when Curly phoned to invite him to supper in his penthouse near here, opposite Diana the Huntress. José Luis tried to confirm what the now not very trustworthy Curly had said, but Guy was no longer in the gallery. And he hadn't returned home. José Luis changed and went to Curly's supper alone.

"Welcome to the Pink Pantheon," Curly said with a smile to José Luis. "And remember my slogan: *sex copuli, sex dei . . .*"

With his forelock tilted like the Tower of Pisa, Curly was wearing his host's attire. A plush velvet jacket, white ascot, Scottish plaid trousers, and black slippers, one with the image of the sun, the other the moon. He wore no socks.

"Ah," he said with a sigh. "What can I offer you? You have to drink to put up with me, José Luis. I swear, tonight I feel stranger than a green dog, and I don't see more in my future than martyrdom with dark glasses."

"You're in Technicolor." José Luis smiled as he took the margarita that Curly served him.

"And in wide screen, love," said Curly. "Just have a look." He approached the large picture window in the penthouse and tugged at the cord of the drawn curtains. "There's no better view of the city," he remarked as the curtains separated to reveal the terrace and two men embracing, kissing each other, one mature, the other young. Their faces were hidden by the long kiss until light from the living room fell on the lovers' closed lids, obliged them to open their eyes, turn their heads, and show themselves to Curly and José Luis.

"Courage, José Luis. Don't worry." Curly smiled. "Sex is like a hangover: It lasts eight hours."

If he had seen him in the days that followed, José Luis would have told Guy what he wrote to him in a letter that was never sent.

"Believe me, I understand you. You've never lost the need to attract. As I once told you, you're not a flirt, you simply need to display yourself. Since I understand that, it doesn't bother me too much that you've taken the next step at least once. We always avoided it. We never excluded it. In the end, did we deceive ourselves? Did we let ourselves be poisoned by what we had always evaded—jealousy, disillusionment, accusation? I see our picture taken when we were thirty, and I put myself in the adverse situation. Do you remember Agustín Villarino? He had lost his youth and sought out young men who would return it to him. He infuriated us. We laughed at him. Not death in Venice, you said then, but death in Xochimilco. You'll say these are cruel words. It isn't my intention to hurt you. I only want you to understand that I understand you. We managed to grow old together. My request is very simple. Don't ruin *everything*."

He found out that Curly had taken Guy and the boy to a rented house in Acapulco. José Luis expected a letter. What he received was a phone call.

"Excuse me. I had to. I thought you'd indulge me."

"I was going to write."

"I didn't receive anything."

"Isn't my intention enough?"

"I don't know if you realized it."

"Realized what?"

"Saffron is just like you."

"With that name? Don't make me laugh."

"Well, it's the name Curly gave him."

"Then he can't be just like me."

"He's like you at the age of twenty, José Luis."

"Please, leave the past in peace."

"I wasn't prepared for this."

"Neither was I."

"Did we deceive ourselves?"

"Who knows. It's always too late to know when we move from one phase to the next in our lives. When we realize it, the first act is over, and the play is about to end."

"I'll tell you something else, it might be a comfort to you. This boy is unreachable."

"Excuse me while I laugh. You reached him. Or he reached you."

"Understand me, José Luis . . . I called you humbly . . . I need . . ."

"You've turned into an imbecile. Or a baby."

"It depends on your preference. We have to endure the bad times."

"Don't tell me you're coming back to me. How? Tenderly, longingly, regretfully?"

"We're an old couple, José Luis. We'll overcome the crisis. Didn't you tell me once that I'm handsome, that I like to display myself, that you enjoy my being like that?"

And after a silence: "Don't hate me, José Luis."

"I don't hate anybody."

He hung up the phone because he was about to add (he tells me): "I don't hate anybody. I love you." And he didn't want to say those words. Guy's resonated in his head: "He's just like you when you were young."

At nightfall, José Luis went out for a walk. A desire both determining and difficult led him to Avenida Álvaro Obregón and the place where the luxurious movie house Balmori had once been located.

Now it was an empty lot where metal ruins stood. Twilight birds flew over the site as if looking for a nest in memories of yesterday. Greta Garbo. That unrepeatable smell of celluloid, sticky muégano candy, melting chocolates, programs made of pink-colored paper, sounds like a bird's wings. That first touch of hands watching Fred and Ginger dance against a background of snow falling in Manhattan. Greta, Ginger, Fred. As he looked at the ruined theater, José Luis felt that the models we admire and pursue come out of ourselves. They are not imposed on us. We invent them, and they magically, gracefully appear on a white screen. Except they are our own shadows transformed into light. They are our most satisfactory portrait. They remain young even in death.

"I wander the streets like a ghost. I've left my image in a ruined movie house. Come and acknowledge it if you dare. I've lost everything but the memory of you. I no longer have a body. What I have is the desire to see you again, to talk to you again."

Guy: A straight, slightly prognathous profile. Wavy hair, without the thin spots of age. Eyes that show interest in everything they see. He is sure he touched the sky one day.

José Luis: Round face. Pronounced baldness. Very large eyes, pools of a sharp, quiet intelligence. The despair of schemers. He never feels the need to challenge his companion. His rule is to avoid promiscuity. He would like to be located at the heart of a constellation.

Chorus of a Son of the Sea

the tip of the peninsula opens like the biggest fan in the world
the freezing distant pacific ocean crashes into the hot storms of
sinaloa
displaying two hundred degrees of surf
Nicanor Tepa stands on the board waiting for the monster wave nine
feet high
he takes it with audacity elegance reticence simplicity strength
always from the left
you never take a huge wave from the right
from the right the wave falls on the surfer crushes him drowns him
from the left Nicanor Tepa conquers the wave turns into wave
a vast white veil holds up Nicanor's body
the white foam crowns his dark head
the tension of his muscles isn't felt it is resolved with jubilation in his
triumph over the
wave of blue crystal
it is august the great month for headlands in baja
in september Nicanor Tepa will travel to san onofre beach in
california and its
forty kilometers of waves inviting him to tame them as if the sea
were an
immense whale and the wave only the spout of the monster spewing
sea spray
twenty-four meters into the air
in october Nicanor is in the burial ground of the freezing sea of
Ireland in the bay of
Donegal and its waves of turbid green broken and enlarged by the
barrier

reefs
and in december he'll arrive in Hawaii to win the Triple Crown
championship exposed
to the incessant hammering of the bay of Waimea and its waves
thirty-six meters
high
Nicanor begins the new year on the peninsula of Guanacaste in Costa
Rica and
in february goes down to Australia to the longest sandbar in the
world where three gigantic
waves gather and explode and allow him to glide like a gull over
the heights of the sea
that hurls him at the end of the monsoon in Tahiti with its electrical
storms
flashing into the sea where Nicanor conquers the most fearsome of all
waves
the Teahupú
and now the wave shatters against the head of Nicanor who made a
mistake taking it from
the right
and he comes to under a high-tension spiderweb in a hovel in the
Capulín
district
and he tries to grasp the volcanic rock so he won't drown in the
marsh
and he wakes in his one-room windowless shack
and he'll go out right away to see if he can catch what's fallen from
the trucks going to the
market
and he forms his pyramid of peanuts on the highway that goes to the
airport
and looks without interest at the venders of gum plastic toys lottery
tickets
hairpins

and tells himself in silence that if he were bolder he would clean windshields and even eat
fire at the crossroads
you have to eat fire to revive the six little brothers dead before their first
birthday typhus polio rabies
you have to bring in an ocean wave to demolish the district without potable water to carry to the
sea the mountains of garbage
but Nicanor Tepa trusts in luck
he resumes looking at the surfers' calendar now they should go to Jeffreys Bay in South
Africa
Nicanor lifts one after another the pages of his calendar of waves
july in Fiji august back to the headlands immediately again san onofre and then
ireland until the new year in costa rica but in december the year ends
and Nicanor Tepa has no calendar for next year he found this one in a
trash can at a hotel in the airport
that he flies out of to Indonesia Tahiti Australia Hawaii
and Nicanor falls asleep exhausted dreaming that he'll change what he can and bow his
head before what he can't change and have the wisdom to
know the difference
he is surrounded by dry bitter broken earth
Nicanor grasps the volcanic rock
Nicanor sinks into the huisache swamp
then the gigantic wave of sleep falls on his head

The Official Family

1. President Justo Mayorga was awakened by the abrupt, huge, unlocatable noise. He opened his eyes with more suspicion than surprise. His first impulse always was never to give in to alarm and look for a redeemable error or a condemnable act. The procession of functionaries who had been fired, punished, ignored because they had *erred* still passed through his drowsy mind. Other people's mistakes guided, even in dreams, his presidential decisions and—he yawned without wanting to—opened lists where disloyalty was only one chapter, the lowest and most insidious, of the catalog of faults the president always had close at hand. There never was a shortage of Judases.

He looked with early-morning distance at his strong hand, broad but with long, slender fingers. He knew how to use it effectively in his speeches. Only one hand, the right, is required: clenched in a fist—strength; open—generosity; palm down—calm, calm; palm up—warning? request? with the fingers slightly bent toward his own person—come, approach, I love you, don't be afraid of me. Justo Mayorga had given up using both hands in his speeches. On the largest screens and in the smallest squares, the use of both hands at the same time seemed not only hackneyed but counterproductive. It indicated that the orator was *orating*, and when he orated, he deceived, making promises he knew he would never be able to keep. He asked for faith from the incredulous and doubt from believers.

On the long journey from local Culiacán delegate to national office at Los Pinos—twenty long years—he had learned a form of vigorous but serene speech-making using only his right hand as rhetorical art and keeping the left in his jacket pocket, on his silver belt buckle, and on only one celebrated occasion, on national television, grasping his testicles to skewer his opponent in an election debate:

"I have more than enough of what you're missing."

Now, when he was awake, he felt his balls bristling at the infernal noise that had come—he looked quickly at the clock, recovering his keen faculties—to wake him at three in the morning. Earlier presidents of Mexico might think of things like armed attack, military uprising, popular demonstration. Justo Mayorga was not paranoid. The noise was infernal, but not even the devil could get into Los Pinos, that's what the well-guarded barred windows and well-trained military staff were for.

And yet . . . no doubt about it. The din that woke him came from his own space, the presidential residence Los Pinos, and not from the interior of the house but—President Mayorga opened the windows to the balcony—from outside, from the avenue through the garden watched over by icy, immobile statues (because some are warm and dynamic) of his predecessors at the head of the state.

He soon had the evidence. He went out to the balcony. Two cars were racing at top speed along the alameda of Los Pinos. An unchecked suicidal speed competing with life more than with the courage of the two untamed drivers who, to a lethal degree, accelerated the low-slung cars, one black, the other red, both capable of revivifying all the statues in the garden, from tiny Madero to gigantic Fox.

A very Mexican idiom—Mayorga thought of it—said, to indicate native stoicism and impassive strength, that something or someone "bothered me the way the wind bothered Juárez."

The president of the republic did not lose his serenity and did not explicitly invoke the Hero of the Americas. He pressed the proper buttons, put on his robe, and calmly waited for his military aides to give him an explanation. One of them smiled stupidly. The other did not.

"It's your son, Mr. President," said the serious one.

"Enriquito," the idiot said with a smile.

"He's racing with a friend."

"Richi, you know? Richi Riva."

"We thought you had authorized it."

" 'Don't worry. My father knows.' That's what he said. Quique and Richi." The aide-de-camp with a limited future in the presidential residence gave a stupid smile.

2. Enrique Mayorga felt offended, uncomfortable, flat-out annoyed that his father, the president, had made a date with him for breakfast at nine in the morning without taking into account the scant hours of filial sleep, not to mention his hangover, his eyes like a bedbug's, his tongue like a rag.

To make matters worse, President Mayorga had seated Quique's mama at the table, the first lady, Doña Luz Pardo de Mayorga, Lucecita. Father and mother sat at the two ends of the table. Enrique sat in the middle, like the accused between two fires, naked under the Calvin Klein robe with the yellow and green stripes. Barefoot. The only things missing, the boy thought, were the hooded executioner and the guillotine.

He scratched at the bristles emerging on his neck and thought with pride that his Adam's apple was not trembling. "What the hell is it now?"

The president got to his feet and gave his son a resounding slap in the face. Enrique swallowed hard and waited.

"Do you know who you are, you moron?" said Justo Mayorga, still standing, looking down at his diminished offspring.

"Sure. Enrique Mayorga, your son."

"That's what you know, you idiot? Only that?"

"The son of the president," Quique managed to say in quotation marks.

"And do you know who I am?"

"Don Corleone." The boy laughed before he was slapped a second time.

"I'm a man of the people." With a powerful hand, the president lifted his son's chin, and the boy could feel the controlled trembling of his father's long, sensual fingers. "I come from the bottom. It cost your mother and me a lot to reach the top. When I was a boy in Sinaloa, I lived in a hut with a roof so low you had to go in on your knees. Yes, Señor, when I was a boy, I slept with the straw roof up my nose."

"And now, Papa, you want me to live like you did?"

The third slap of breakfast.

"No, Señor. I want you to be responsible about my position, not make me look ridiculous, not give my enemies ammunition, not let people think I'm a weak or frivolous man who spoils his son, a rich kid who doesn't work or do anyone any good."

Enrique was attached to the idea that the words and slaps weren't going to upset him. But now he kept silent.

"From the bottom, kid. Through diligence, dedication, studies, night classes, humble jobs but a great ambition: to move up, to serve my country—"

"Without friends?" Quique interrupted. "Alone, all by yourself?"

"With your mother," the president said in a firm voice.

"Your slave," Quique said and smiled, but Doña Luz nodded and signaled her husband with her finger.

"My companion. Loyal and discreet. Attentive to my needs and not putting obstacles in my way."

"Justo . . ." murmured Doña Luz with an unknown intention.

"I can't have friends," Justo Mayorga said savagely. "And neither can you."

"Without friends," his son repeated, sitting up straight in his chair. "The Loner of Los Pinos, that's what they call you. Listen, don't you like anybody? Why don't you have friends?"

Justo Mayorga returned to his seat. "A president of Mexico has no friends."

Doña Luz shook her head, imploring or understanding. Her tastes were always ambiguous.

"I achieved everything because I had no friends." He paused and played with the crumbs from his roll. "I had accomplices."

"Justo . . ." Doña Luz stood and walked to her husband.

"A president of Mexico can govern only if he has no friends. He can't owe anything to anybody." He looked at his son with cold severity. "And nobody's going to tell me I can't govern the country if I can't govern my own son."

He stood. "I don't want to see your pals around here again."

3. Don't be discouraged, Richi Riva said to Enrique Mayorga, hugging him to the rhythm of the yacht anchored in Acapulco Bay, it's all right, we won't run races at Los Pinos anymore, but as long as your papa doesn't send you away with the bodyguards, we can keep having a great time, look, here we are, the two of us alone on my yacht, and as the saying goes, gloomy night falls and you and I have our lives in front of us, don't let yourself get trapped by the old geezers, play it smart, look at Acapulco in the distance, how fantastic, how those lights shine and each one is like an invitation to let yourself go, Quique, give in to your emotions, that's something nobody can take away from us,

that's what makes all the papas green with envy, because they don't know how to have fun anymore, but you and I, Quique baby, look at Acapulco waiting for us, imagine the wild night that's waiting for us, we can go wherever we feel like, you have the protection of the federal army, Quique my friend, who else in this country can say "The army is my babysitter"? we're untouchable, bro, don't let yourself be trapped, everything's under control as long as you're with Richi Riva, your best bud, we'll go to whatever disco you want, your goons will open the way for us, we're the greatest and we have everything under control, pick the babe you like best, send the lieutenant to bring her to the table, what else is power for, you jerk? look at the supply right here in the disco, what do you prefer, society girls, good-looking broads, top models, or plain European whores? ah what the hell, go on, order those bleached blondes to stop in front of us on the floor and moon us, to pull down their panties and show us their buns, go on Quique baby, don't be shy come onto the dance floor with me, let's give in to our e-mo-tions, the gringa doesn't want to come over to our table? tell the lieutenant to threaten her with the uzi, fuck, don't let yourself be trapped by power, use it Quique my friend, let the eagle lift you up and the serpent get you excited, don't let yourself be trapped, don't be afraid, I ordered the soldiers to occupy the roof of this dive and if you get tired of the hood we'll just move on to a cooler one, let's see, Lieutenant, bring us that broad and if she refuses threaten her with the uzi and if there's a boyfriend (the broad's, not yours, Lieutenant, it's no innuendo) take him away by force and if he gives you any trouble shoot him on the beach ah fuck don't wake the wildcat I have inside, Quique my friend, because you should know I want to move at full speed with the whole world, I want to be nice and have everybody love me, and the only thing I want is to get along with the galaxies, I swear, I love to have good relations with bad friends, it's my specialty, fuck, don't beat yourself up so much Quique my friend, make a stand, you're the son of the prez, you can do whatever the fuck you want, just surround yourself with soldiers, that's what the national army's for, so you and I can have a hell of a time in a cool world, now let's go, this hole stinks, Mancuernas is expecting us, you know, the one with the retro haircut? the one who pets me and caresses my cheek and tells me Richi you have a sweet and dangerous face, but your eyes are glass . . .

4. Señora Luz—Lucecita—let them arrange her hair carefully but she avoided looking at herself in the mirror because I don't want to know the face I have after three years in Los Pinos and I'm just waiting for the moment I go back with Justo to a life that's more peaceful for me, for him, for our son, I came with Justo from Sinaloa to Los Pinos, I've been a loyal companion, I've never asked anything for myself, I've only worked to clear the way for Justo so he doesn't stumble on my account, I've never shown any personal ambition, I've only worked for my husband's success, tried never to overshadow him, never to say anything that would hurt him, nothing that creates storms of publicity or causes any gossip, I'm not complaining about anything, life has been good to me, I could have been a little provincial woman for the rest of my life, I never had any ambition except to support my husband and understand his passion to serve Mexico, and he's so all alone, as he never tires of telling me, alone and with no true friends, only accomplices, as he says, the president doesn't have friends, the president doesn't love anybody but he uses them all but what about my son? don't I have the right, after so much sacrifice, to love my own son, to indulge him a little, to protect him from his father's severity? doesn't my son deserve, precisely because he likes the wild life so much, a little of the tenderness his father and his friends and his women don't give him? I want to be a reserve of tenderness for my son, they've assigned me the works of charity appropriate for an honorable first lady who knows her place, but I need to give charity to my husband so he at least learns to love at home and to my son so he doesn't get trapped in the dead end of being angry with his parents, why do I protect my son, I ask myself when I'm alone, does he even deserve my protection? maybe I do it for egotistical reasons, I don't open my eyes to avoid my current face in the mirror while they style my hair because that way I can be another woman, I save myself from the politics that make us

dirty and the power that steals our souls and I protect the most authentic thing I have left today and that's my memory of youth, my nostalgia for the provinces, for beauty, for youth, the coast of Sinaloa, the evocative names of Navolato and La Noria, El Dorado and El Quelite, Mocorito and the Mesa de San Miguel, late afternoons on the Sea of Cortés the five rivers that flow to the sea, the valleys of sugar and rice, the music of La Tambora in the little square of Santiago Ixcuintla, everything I knew as a girl and never forget because without childhood there's no nostalgia, without youth there are no memories, and my love for the man who tore me away from tranquility and carried me in his strong arms up the mountain, whispering to me, Justo Mayorga whispering to me, Luz Pardo, his sweetheart from Mazatlán, be happy my love, hope for everything and don't understand anything and I'm not complaining because I lived the warmth of life with him, hoping for everything though I didn't understand anything but always telling myself, Luz, you have the right to happiness whatever happens try to be happy today don't let power make you think that everything beautiful and interesting in life, everything nice in life, is in the past, don't lose your private self Lucecita because if you let it escape it will never come back no matter how much power you have, don't give in to that secret desire of yours, the desire to be absent, don't become completely invisible, make people think you share your husband's dream of giving hope again to Mexico after all the calamities that have happened to us, return their faith to Mexicans, I want to help the president my husband in that though I know very well the two of us he and I are only actors in a farce, he smiling and optimistic though reality denies it, I smiling and discreet so the people forget about so much failure and hold on to the dream that Mexico can be happy, that's what we're working for, that's why we smile at the cameras, to make people believe the ongoing lie, the dream renewed every six years and now we did it this time everything will turn out fine, oh I'm complaining, yes, how quickly everything passes and what else can I hold on to except love of my husband performing the eternal comedy of the happy orderly stable country and my poor son not understanding anything, trying to break the order established by his father, not realizing that this lasts only six years and wanting him not to know that if he doesn't make the most of things now he'll go back afterward to that small ranch which means being a nobody after being everything on a big ranch, I have to maintain those two illusions of my husband's power and my son's pleasure and I don't know how to tell them by indulging and supporting them that neither one will last, that power and pleasure are mere sighs and I was really happy only when I was hoping for everything and didn't understand anything, when everything was warm like a beach at home and I didn't know yet the cold truth that happiness doesn't come back no matter how much power you have . . .

5. Sitting at his desk with the tricolor flag planted behind him like a parched nopal, President Justo Mayorga read the urgent communiqué. The agrarian leader Joaquín Villagrán had occupied the federal Congress with an army of workers carrying machetes and demanding—nothing less—radical policies on all fronts to bring the country out of its endemic poverty. There were no insults on their banners. Only demands. Education. Security. Honest judges. From the bottom. Everything from the bottom. Jobs. Work. From the bottom. No waiting for investments from the top. No asking for loans and canceling debts. School and work, from the bottom. Sharecroppers, day laborers, trade unionists, artisans, members of village communes, Indians, workers, small contractors, poor ranchers, village merchants, rural schoolteachers.

And the movement's flag. An Indian sitting on a mountain of gold. "Mexico is the country of injustice," said Humboldt in 1801, the president recalled. The Indian, the campesino, the worker had joined together and taken over the seat of Congress. Who would get them out? How? With guns? Congress is surrounded by the army, Mr. President. Because in Mexico no one governs without the army, but the army is institutional and obeys only the president.

"While the president represents the state," the secretary of defense, Jenaro Alvírez, informed Justo Mayorga. "Because we soldiers know how to distinguish between transitory governments and the state that endures."

He stared at Mayorga. "If, on the other hand, the president stops representing the state and defends only his own government . . ." He smiled affably. "We Mexicans are like a large extended family . . ."

General Alvírez hurled his suspension points like bullets. And Justo Mayorga closed the folder with the day's information and gave free rein to his interior murmur, I don't do business with my conscience, I'll do whatever I have to do, right now I don't know what I should do, the situation is serious and I won't resolve it the way I have other times by firing secretaries of state, removing functionaries, blaming others, letting it be known that I've been deceived by disloyal colleagues, the usual Judases, the fact of the matter is I don't have any colleagues left I can blame, the ball stopped on my number on the roulette wheel, it's not a day for distractions, it's a day for internal courage, I must be strong in my soul to be strong in my body, outside, on the street, I have to repeat to myself that being president is not owing anybody anything and being grateful for even less in order to appear in public as if I were the dream of the man in the street which is to be president of Mexico, what every Mexican thinks he deserves to be, the chief, this is a country of chiefs, without chiefs we wander around more disoriented than a parakeet at the North Pole, that's the truth, I have to be cold inside to be heated in my external performance and it irritates me that my son's frivolity now seems like a fly in a storm, the idea that keeps coming back pains me, my son is my worst enemy, not the leader Joaquín Villagrán who's taken over the Congress, not the army under the command of General Jenaro Alvírez surrounding the Palace of San Lázaro and waiting for my orders,

"Remove the agitators,"

my good-for-nothing son and his friend Richi Riva have draped themselves in the middle of my mind and I want to get them out so I can think clearly. I can't be the mental prisoner of a couple of frivolous kids, I don't want anybody to say how will he govern the country if he can't govern his son, ah you pissant little bastard, you're giving me a feeling of failure that paralyzes me, I haven't known how to teach you my morality, don't be anybody's friend, you can't govern with frivolity and sentimentality, being president is not owing anybody anything . . .

"Mr. President. The army has surrounded the Congress. We're waiting for your order to remove them."

6. For the whole blessed day, Luz Pardo de Mayorga wandered like a ghost through the empty rooms of Los Pinos. Her intimate, enduring alliance with Justo Mayorga made her as sensitive as a butterfly trapped under a bell jar. Something was going on. Something besides yesterday's unpleasant breakfast. Who knows why, this afternoon she would have liked to be absent. She had dressed for lunch, but her husband sent word he wouldn't arrive in time. There was no one in the residence except the invisible servants and their feline secretiveness. Doña Luz could fill the afternoon hours however she chose, watching soap operas, playing the CD of the boleros she liked best,

We who loved so much,

who made a wondrous sun of love . . .

she hummed very quietly because in this house—the president had told her—even the walls have ears, be careful Lucecita, don't show your feelings, keep the rancor you feel in your heart, because you can't be authentic, because you're the prisoner of Los Pinos, because you'd like it if your husband weren't so powerful, if he got sick you could show him the real affection you have for him, if you were braver you'd demand that he understand Enrique, that he not feel so resentful if the boy has a good time and you don't anymore, Justo, you don't know how to have a good time anymore and you can't stand pleasure in anybody else, try to imagine my soul split in two, between the love I feel for you and the love I feel for our son, don't you say you love only your family, nobody else, that a president doesn't have the right to love anybody, only his family? you'll allow me to doubt, Justo, you'll permit me to think that your political coldness has come into our house, that you treat your son and me like subjects, no, not even that, because with the masses you're seductive, affectionate, you put on a mask with the people, and with us who are you, Justo? the time has come to say who you are with your wife and son . . .

"Don't dress up too much. Be more circumspect."

"I only want to look nice."

"Don't fondle me so much."

Justo Mayorga leaned over to kiss her temple. Then he saw something he hadn't seen before. A tear suspended in the corner of his wife's eye. He felt transported, irrelevant, on his way elsewhere. He looked at that single trembling tear, suspended there without ever falling, without rolling down her cheek, he saw it kept there since her youth, since they were married, when Luz Pardo promised herself never to cry in front of her husband.

"I can't conceive of losing you and continuing to live. It would make no sense."

7. Attack, Mr. President. In half an hour we can empty the Congress. Don't do anything, Mr. President. Just surround them until they give up because of hunger. Don't make them into martyrs, Mr. President. If they go on a hunger strike, more people will come to encourage them than there are soldiers surrounding them. Abandon the place, Mr. President. Be noble. Leave them there until they get tired and leave on their own.

Attack. Surround. Don't do anything.

The dusty wind of a February afternoon shook the trees in the park and the curtains of the official residence. Father, mother, and son sat down for supper. First there was a long silence. Then the first lady remarked that a storm was brewing that night. She bit her tongue. She didn't want to refer to anything more serious than the weather. Restless, impulsive, irritated, Quique broached the subject of what the point was of getting to the top and not enjoying life.

"Don't worry, son. Three more years and we go back to the ranch."

"You, not me," said the rebel, then immediately modulated that.

"I'm not going to any ranch. Even if you drag me. I'm staying here in the capital. Here's where my pals are, my life, I don't need you two."

"Inside here we have no idea what's going on out there," the president said calmly but enigmatically. "Don't kid yourself."

"You're not going to stop me from being Richi's friend." Quique raised his voice provocatively. "With Richi I stop being the president's damn son, I'm myself." He got to his feet violently. "Without mommies and daddies all over me."

"Watch your mouth in front of your mother," said the president without becoming irritated. "Beg her pardon."

"Pardon me, Mom." Quique approached Doña Luz and kissed her on the forehead. "But you two have to understand me." He lifted his supplicating, haughty head. "I'm different, with Richi I'm different."

Señora Luz armed herself with courage and, looking first at one and then the other, she raised her voice for the first time in her life, knowing she would never do it again, though now her husband's impressive calm authorized her to speak forcefully, to break the glass that enclosed their lives.

"Do we really deserve one another? Do the three of us love one another? Answer me."

She wiped the corner of her mouth with a napkin. An undesirable foam had gathered there, like the waves of Mazatlán, because of the strength of things, because of the law of the tides.

"Give me something," shouted Luz Pardo. "Why don't you ever give me anything? Don't I deserve anything?"

She didn't cry. She never cried. Only that afternoon did she allow the tear she owed Justo Mayorga to escape. Now her desperate weeping choked in her trembling chin. She got up from the table and walked away, saying in an inaudible voice, "Answer me . . ."

She managed to hear her husband's words. "I don't want disorder in my house," and then, when Justo Mayorga came into the bedroom and found her lying down, he asked, "Didn't you watch television?" And she: "I don't have the heart, Justo, understand me."

The president turned on the set. He sat down next to Doña Luz and took her hand. On the screen Justo Mayorga was seen approaching the palace of Congress, ordering General Alvírez, "Let me alone, I'm going in alone," and entering the Congress occupied by rebel workers, Justo Mayorga alone, with no aide, no armed men, alone with his courage and his head high, that was how the entire nation saw him go in on TV and that was how they saw him come out later leading the agrarian leader Joaquín Villagrán by the hand, smiling, waving his free hand—the right one, always—raising his left together with the right hand of the leader, announcing, "We've reached an agreement."

But the agreement didn't matter to the crowd gathered in front of the Congress, what mattered was the president's bravery, the guts to go in alone into the mouth of the lion and get an agreement with the union leader, the important thing was that the people loved him, the people were right, the president was a real man, everything bad that happened was because the president didn't know about it, if the president knew, if the bureaucrats didn't lie to him, see, he goes in all alone and comes out holding the leader by the hand and so tomorrow we're all going to the Zócalo to cheer our president who's very macho, Justo Mayorga on the balcony of the palace, with only one arm—the right one—raised, conceding without shyness and in silence, yes, I'm the chosen one of the masses, I'm the proof that the man on the street can reach the top, look at me, admire me, the president is the lucky charm of the Mexican people . . .

"Never say it out loud, say it to yourself the way you're saying it now, in secret, like an intimate confession . . . I'm the lover of my people . . ."

And in an even more secret voice, "Power postpones death, it just postpones death . . ."

8. Richi Riva was put on a Qantas plane to Australia. Quique Mayorga Pardo tried in vain to break through the barrier of bodyguards who prevented access to the ramp: "I'm the president's son!"

The soldiers had turned into a hostile, impenetrable world.

Quique drove his Porsche back to Los Pinos. He parked it in the garage. He got out. He slammed the door. He clenched his teeth, held back the tears, and began to kick the red sports car, powerful kicks, denting the body.

9. "What did I give the leader Villagrán? Nothing, Lucecita. I wrapped him around my finger. The usual promises. The important thing is that people saw me go in alone. They know their president's hand doesn't tremble. Without firing a shot. When I went in, they were shouting 'Death to Mayorga!' When I came out, nothing but 'Long live Mayorga!' Pure guts, Lucecita, pure guts. They'll be quiet for the rest of my term. Then we'll go back to the ranch."

Chorus of the Family from the Neighborhood

He left the house because they beat me they stripped me they forced me
My father my mother
Because they both died and there was nobody but me in
the house
Because I don't have relatives
Because the guys told me don't be an asshole come to the street you're alone in your house they beat you they give you a hard time they call you rat
In your house you're fucked you're lower than a cockroach
I feel so alone bro like a damn beaten insect
So low bro
So attacked bro
Give me shelter with no roof on the street
Be safe take root on the street
Don't even look at people who aren't from the street
Here you're safer than in your house bro
Here nobody asks you for anything
Here there aren't any fucking responsibilities
Here there's only the turf
Here we're the family of the turf between El Tanque and El Cerro
Don't let anybody by who isn't family from the neighborhood bro
Anybody who steps over the line smash him in the face
We're an army a hundred thousand children and adolescents running free
Alone without a family in the streets
Stuck on the street

Do they want to get away from the street?
There's no place else
Some came to the street
Others were born in the street
The family is the street
We were born to the street
Your mama aborted in the middle of the street
They kicked her in the middle of the street until the fetus dropped out
In the middle of the street
Because the street is our womb
The gutters our milk
The garbage cans our ovaries
Don't let yourself be tempted bro
Fucking packing for a super
Fucking cleaning windshields
Fucking peddling
Fucking guy who wipes the windshield asshole
Fucking kid for falling-down drunks
Fucking damn pimp beggar
Refuse bro
Live on air on alcohol on cement
Better to go dying like a damn cockroach
In streets tunnels garbage cans
Than think you've been defeated

The Father's Servant

1. This town is suffocating. One would say that at an altitude of over three thousand meters, the air would be purer. This isn't true, and one can understand it. The volcano is a priest with a white head and black tunic. It vomits the same thing it eats: ashen solitude. The proximity of heaven oppresses one here on earth.

The legend insists on repeating that Popocatépetl is an alert warrior who protects the nearby body of the sleeping woman Iztaccíhuatl. They didn't tell Mayalde the story that one has known since childhood. The priest brought her up here to live, in the foothills of Popocatépetl, on the same day the girl had her first menstruation, and he said to her: "Look. It's the sacrilegious stain. We have to go far away from here."

"Why, Father?"

"So you won't sin."

"Why would I sin?"

"Because you've become a woman. Let's go."

They left the sacristy of Acatzingo with its beautiful Franciscan convent and came to live here, where you look at snow and breathe in ash. It was the isolated spot closest to Puebla, and since no one wanted to come where one was, they gladly sent him.

"Are you taking your niece, Father?

"Did you think I'd abandon her? She depends on me. Without me, she'd be a poor orphan. She owes everything to me."

"Ah!"

"Though let me clarify, Bishop. She isn't my niece. Don't burden me with that old story."

"Ah! Your daughter?" the bishop asked with raised eyebrows.

The priest turned and left the bishopric.

"That man is turning into a recluse," remarked the prelate. "He doesn't know how to get on with people. He's better off going to the mountains."

It wasn't that Father Benito Mazón had sought out a parish in the foothills of a volcano to isolate himself from people. The fact is people withdrew from him, and this suited him perfectly. In the end, he came out ahead. No matter how disagreeable Don Benito was, God was not only agreeable but indispensable. Only Father Mazón, with his eyes of an uneasy wolf, iguana's profile, and paper-thin habit, had the ability to administer the sacraments, baptize, sing a requiem, and certify a death. People in the village depended on him in order to live with a clear conscience. And he depended less on one. Even if nobody attended the miserable little adobe church on the edge of the volcano, Benito would receive his stipend, and of course, the same village that distrusted him for being disagreeable would not let him die of hunger. One.

Well, the fact is that we parishioners—one—feel animosity toward Father Benito Mazón. He seems to live indifferent to one. One reproaches his hypocrisy in introducing the girl Mayalde, who is sixteen years old, as his goddaughter. One knows that goddaughters tend to be priests' daughters. Should he be given credit for the charity he has shown in putting a roof over the girl's head? Or must one display indignation at the hypocrisy?

One does not have easy answers. In the end, habits follow their own course, with or without complete explanations. One suspects. One intuits. One fears. In the end, one shrugs one's shoulders. One.

"It's worse to have bad habits than to have no habits at all," Father Mazón whispered in outrage to our most devout woman, Doña Altagracia Gracida, during the act of confession.

"And where does the girl sleep, Father?"

"Be careful, woman."

The parish in the mountains was barely a house, made of adobe bricks, with a wood-burning stove, a small living/dining room, a bedroom, and an outdoor bathroom. The church was just as modest. But the adjoining chapel was a small, richly decorated Baroque delight, almost as splendid (almost) as the lamented Acatzingo. This was how it should be. Father Benito worships God because he believes that God is horrified by the world.

Mayalde's beauty created a small storm of indecision in the village. She was a fresh, lovely girl, comparable in her look of purity to the snow that crowns the mountain before it is obliterated in ash. A light-skinned brunette with very large black eyes, as if she wanted to see beyond the frame of her oval face and then immediately, as if conscious of the vanity signified in using beauty to gain happiness, she lowers them to attend to her tasks in the humble house that scrapes the sky. She is used to it. She doesn't expect anything else from life. One might think that the priest always treated her badly in order to treat her well. That is what he always told her:

"If Our Lord Jesus Christ suffered, why shouldn't you?"

Then he sat her on his knees. "Do you think I don't suffer, Mayalde, seeing you suffer?"

All manual tasks were her responsibility. When Father Mazón walked by and saw her washing clothes, making the bed, or dusting polychromes in the church, he would say things like:

"You'd like to be a lady, wouldn't you?"

"I spoiled you too much when you were little. Now I'm going to get rid of all that spoiling."

"Clean the church. It'll do you more good. I'm going to check each holy vessel as if you were drinking my milky cum from it."

Then he sat her again on his knees. She feared these moments of affection because Father Benito agonized so much to be good and then treated her badly to compensate for the failing of tenderness.

"You're a mule. A sterile freak. But you work very hard and endure the cold of the mountains."

She didn't smile openly for fear of offending him. But the damn priest made her laugh inside, and she mocked him as she tended to the birds in their cold cages, gathered scarce mountain flowers and put them in water, went to the market and came back, humming, with baskets full of vegetables, pigs' feet, warm tortillas, and serrano chiles.

"The girl is simpleminded," we would say in the village.

She knew that this way, by being so obliging, she provoked Father Benito. She wasn't a good-for-nothing. And she wasn't a beast of burden. When she went down to the market, one admired her cadenced walk, the lightness of her flowered dress, the guessed-at feminine forms, firm and rounded. Mayalde was, for one, the elusive magic of the village. She smiled at everybody.

"She's simpleminded."

One thought, however, that her coquettishness was fidelity to Father Benito Mazón. That was what one told oneself.

One day Father Benito broke the flowerpots and freed the canaries. She remained very still, staring at the priest and imagining that she, if she decided to, could change into a flower or fly like a bird.

Father Benito did not want to admit that nothing defeated Mayalde. He felt like telling her, "Go on, my girl. Go back to your mother. Tell her to treat you well and that I remember her. You know I'm no good at being your father. We'll see if she even bothers to see you. Though I doubt it. You should have seen how glad she was to get rid of you."

For her part she thought, I make him angry because I love things, I love the flowers, the birds, the markets, and he doesn't. I serve him, but he doesn't enjoy it. He's a sour old man with vinegar in his blood.

It was clear to Mayalde that Father Benito wanted to enjoy things. She bathed outside under an improvised shower in a small courtyard, and she knew the priest spied on her. It amused her to play with the schedule. Sometimes she bathed at dawn; other times she bathed at night. The priest always spied on her, and she soaped her sex and her breasts before pretending alarm at being caught, covering herself quickly with her hands and laughing without stopping as she imagined the confusion of the priest with the narrow eyes of an uneasy wolf and the iguana's profile.

"Put aside evil thoughts," the priest would tell her when she confessed. And he would add with growing exaltation: "Repeat after me, child. I am a sack of foul-smelling filth. My sins are an abomination. I am pernicious, scandalous, incorrigible. I deserve to be locked away in a cell on bread and water until I die." And rolling up his eyes to heaven: "My fault, my fault, my most grievous fault."

Mayalde observed him with a smile, convinced he had lost his mind. The girl shrugged in amazement and kept her own counsel.

Father Mazón would sing these damn hallelujahs that have been repeated in Mexican churches for the past five hundred years and eventually move away from Mayalde, the object of his recriminations, and conclude by praising himself, remembering what they had told him at home when he disclosed his ecclesiastical vocation:

"Benito, there's nothing theological about you."

"Benito, you look more like a scoundrel."

"Benito, don't tell us you're not pretty horny."

He agreed with the last two propositions but decided to put them to the test by subjecting himself to the disciplines of the first: entering the priesthood.

His relationship with the beautiful Mayalde joined together his three temptations: the divine, the worldly, and the erotic. How far had it gone? In the village, one didn't know for sure. The situation itself—priest with supposed goddaughter or niece who, in the end, turned out to be secret daughter—had occurred so often it couldn't withstand another version. The strength of the tradition obliged one to think certain things. It also allowed us, a few of us, to propose the exception.

"That only happens in old movies, Doña Altagracia. Let's say she really is his niece or an orphan or whatever all of you like and prefer, and the priest simply and openly exploits her as a maid without enjoying her as a concubine."

Some said yes, others no. One, who tries to be fair, would not admit baseless gossip or unproven suspicions. But when Mayalde came down the mountain to the market, a melancholy silence surrounded her. The village smelled of wet dog, of lit hearth, of roasted food, of burro dung, of ocote pine smoke, of untouchable snow, of unpardonable sun. She moved as if she weren't touching the ground. She was pursued by the evil thoughts of some, the suspicious silence of others, the ambiguous solitude of everybody. Was Benito Mazón a man of God or a damned sinner? In any case, only he dispensed the sacraments in this forgotten village. And if he gave us the host and extreme unction, what wouldn't he give to the pretty girl who lived with him?

A few of us had been educated and did not believe the falsehoods of the Church. But nobody—not even one, who is an atheist, to tell the absolute truth—dared challenge the weight of religious tradition in the villages. The sky would fall down on us. Centuries and centuries of proclaiming ourselves Catholics has its importance. Being an atheist is almost a failure of courtesy. But one thinks that what the believer and the indifferent ought to share is charity and compassion. It isn't justice that unites us. One knows Christians who go out of their way to be unjust. To inferiors. To children. To women. To animals. And who, beating their chests, proclaim themselves Christians and go to Mass on Sunday.

One is not like them. One tries to be sincere with the world and with oneself. One wants to be just even though one is not a believer. One thinks that even if one is not Catholic, justice is the most Christian thing there is. Because of justice, one helps others, and mercy is only a little medal they pin on us afterward.

Because of simple charity, then, one pretends not to see and lets him pass at night as one observes from the darkened window the limping young man who looks around in distress without knowing which way to go until one comes out in the midst of the silent ringing of the Angelus and directs him:

"Go up the mountain a little way. Follow the bells."

"What bells?"

"Listen to them carefully. Up there you'll be received with charity."

I sent him away from the village because one knows very well who one's neighbors are. The boy, his leg injured, with dirty bandages around his knee, torn clothing, and muddy boots, was going to be suspect, no matter who he was and where he came from. One is not accustomed to the sudden appearance of people one doesn't know. One is predisposed against the stranger. Even more so in a village of less than a hundred souls lost in the volcanic heights of Mexico, a village of ash and snow, icy air, and numb hands. A village enveloped in a gigantic gray serape as if in a premature though permanent winding-sheet.

But if the stranger seeks refuge in the house of the priest, it means he has nothing to hide. The Church blesses those it receives. The boy could climb down from the church to the village without arousing anyone's suspicions. What he couldn't do was appear like this, hurt, confused, and exhibiting a youthful beauty as somber and dazzling as that of a black sun.

"Climb the hill. Take refuge in Christian charity. Ask for the priest. Find an explanation."

"I was mountain climbing and I fell," Félix Camberos said simply, for that was the name the boy gave when Father Benito Mazón opened the door as dawn was breaking.

"It's very early," the priest said disagreeably.

"Mountains are overcome early in the morning." Félix Camberos smiled, for better or worse. "Just like piety."

"All right, Mayalde, see to the stranger," said the priest, feeling strangely trapped in a contradiction he did not understand.

Benito Mazón had seen the figure of the boy, and in his heart, he had reasons for charity as well as suspicion. They merged in the figure of Mayalde. Who would tend to the injured boy? Why not the priest? Because he would have to kneel before the injured man in a posture his arrogance rejected. He would have to display humility to a man younger than himself. And above all, handsomer. The priest caught Mayalde's glance when Félix appeared. It was the face of a voiceless moon expressing everything by means of waxing and waning movements, as if a tide from heaven had carried the stranger to this desolate place.

Mayalde had not controlled her own face when she saw Félix. Father Benito noticed this and decided to place the young man in the girl's care. Why? The reason seemed as apparent to the priest as it does now to oneself. Benito Mazón's iguana's profile and wolf's eyes were the opposite of the statue's profile and puppy's eyes of Félix.

Father Mazón felt an uncontrollable impulse to place Mayalde in Félix's hands and expose her to temptation. He savored the decision. It exalted him. He felt like a missionary of the Lord who first offers us the joy of sin in order to immediately impose the difficulty of virtue and to arrogate to himself, by means of confession, the right to forgive. Between one thing and the other, between sin and virtue (Mazón gloated) crawled a serpent made of temptation. The priest would not have to conquer it. But the girl would. This possibility was enough to assure her soul many hours of martyrdom, of harassment, of severity when he and Mayalde were alone again and he could corner her and feel the pleasure of humiliating and accusing her, and finally, with luck, the defeated girl would no longer resist.

Father Mazón went out to attend to his divine duties, and Mayalde remained alone with Félix. The girl was very discreet.

"Take off your trousers. Otherwise I can't tend to your knee."

Félix obeyed gravely, though he smiled and blushed just a little when he sat in front of Mayalde, displaying his brief, tight undershorts. She looked at him without curiosity and proceeded to clean the injury on his leg.

"What are you doing here?"

"Mountaineering."

"What's that?"

"Climbing the mountain."

"How far?"

"Well, up to the snow, if I can."

"And you fell?"

Félix's hesitant voice did not escape the concentrated attention of the secretive girl.

"Well, I slipped," the boy finally said with a laugh.

"Ah." She looked at him mischievously. "You slipped up." She gave him an affectionate tap on the leg. "Well, you're set, Don Slippery."

That afternoon the volcano threw out a few tongues of flame, but the ashes were soon extinguished by the summer's evening rain.

"How strange that you came here in August," Mayalde said to Félix. "That's when the snow goes away. In January it comes right up to our door."

"That's exactly why." Félix smiled with something like a distant star in his eyes. "I like to attempt what's most difficult."

"Oh my," Mayalde said in a quiet voice as she touched Félix's hand. "It must come from God."

She had a desire, too, just like Father Benito.

"Why 'oh my'?" Félix smiled. "What comes from God?"

"Bad thoughts." Mayalde looked up.

When Father Benito went down to the village to give extreme unction to the baker, Mayalde had already given her virtue to Félix. The baker took a long time to die, and the young couple could love at their leisure, hidden behind the altar of the Peacemaker. The ecclesiastical vestments served as a soft bed, and the persistent odor of incense excited them both—him because it was exotic, her because it was customary, both because it was sacrilegious.

"Don't you feel very secluded here?"

"What do you mean? Why?"

"This is like the roof of the world."

"You managed to get up here, didn't you?"

"I don't know. There's another world away from here."

"What's there?"

"The ocean, for example. Haven't you ever been to the ocean?"

She shook her head.

"Do you know what color the ocean is? I'd like to take you away with me."

"The priest says water doesn't have a color."

"He doesn't know anything. Or he's deceiving you. The ocean is blue. Do you know why?"

She shook her head again.

"Because it reflects the sky."

"You have a pretty way of talking. I don't know if it's true. I've never seen the ocean."

He kissed Mayalde, holding her head with both hands. Then she said: "Once I wanted to get away from life. Then you came."

2. The one who arrived at nightfall was Father Benito Mazón. He struggled up the hill, panting in the rain, his wolf's eyes more uneasy than ever. He had delayed his return. He wanted to give every opportunity to the young couple. He had endured the tolerance one offered him by giving back his own intolerance. He returned armed with an indifference that had fallen into the trap of his crude bitterness. The parishioners require a sacrament; they find it repugnant that he is the one who gives it to them, and he knows they have no choice.

He returned late because in the village he had spoken amiably with the civil and military authorities. One was amazed at so much courtesy in someone as dry and arrogant as Father Mazón.

Father Mazón, walking back, looks again at the desolation of the ash-colored volcano, compares it again to being abandoned by God, and would like to see things clearly, not with these clouded eyes . . .

The man of God arrived and took off his straw hat, revealing tow-colored hair. Water ran down his cloak of corn leaves.

He looked coldly but without suspicion at the couple. "How's that leg doing?"

"Better, Father."

"When are you leaving us?"

"Whenever you say. I won't stay a minute longer than you want. I'm grateful for your hospitality."

"Ah, but first you put it to the test."

Félix couldn't avoid a smile. "Your hospitality exceeds my expectations."

The priest let the water run down his cloak and said to Mayalde without looking at her: "What are you waiting for?"

She came to remove his improvised raincoat.

"She's an obedient girl," the priest said severely.

She didn't say anything.

"Go on, prepare supper."

They ate without speaking, and when the table was cleared, Father Benito Mazón asked Félix Camberos if he was a student or a mountaineer.

"Well," Félix said with a laugh, "a person can be both things."

But the priest insisted: "A student?"

"Not a very good one." Félix modulated his smile.

"Everyone chooses their life. Look at Mayalde. She's mad to become a nun. I assure you it's true, by the nails of Christ."

This caused great hilarity in the priest, indifference in the young man, and stupefaction in the girl.

"Father, don't say falsehoods. It's a sin."

"Ah," Mazón said in surprise. "Are you rebelling, little girl? Don't you want to go to a convent to get away from me?"

She didn't say anything, but Father Mazón was already on the track that one knows.

"Well, I swear to you, your rebellion won't last very long. And do you know why? Because you're submissive. Submissive in your soul. Submissive to men. Because submission is stronger in you than rebellion."

Felix intervened. "But affection is stronger than submission or rebellion, don't you agree?"

"Of course, young man. Here you can prove it. In this house there is only love . . ." The priest paused and toyed with the blue and white Talavera cup he always had with him, supposedly to keep from forgetting his humble origins, before he raised his wolfish eyes. "Haven't you proved that yet, boy?"

"I think I have." Félix decided on irony to counteract the priest's snares.

"Wasn't it enough for you?"

"Affection is a good thing," said Félix. "But you need knowledge, too."

The priest smiled sourly. "You're a student, aren't you?"

"A student and a mountaineer, as I told you."

"Do you think you know a great deal?"

"I try to learn. I know that I know very little."

"I know God."

Abruptly, the priest rose to his feet. "I am on intimate terms with God."

"And what does God tell you, Father?" Félix continued in an agreeable tone.

"That the devil comes into houses by the back door."

"You invited me in through the front door," Félix responded with exacting harshness.

"Because I did not know you were going to steal the host from my temple."

"Father." Félix also stood, though he had no answer that wasn't a lie. "You have to control yourself if you want to be respected."

"I don't control myself or respect myself—"

"Father." Mayalde approached him. "It's time you went to bed. You're tired."

"You put me to bed, girl. Undress me and sing me to sleep. Prove that you love me."

He said it as if he wanted to transform his wolf's eyes into the eyes of a lamb. Félix circled the dining room chair as if that piece of furniture gave him balance or checked, like a barrier, his desire to break the chair over the priest's head.

"Father, restrain yourself, please."

"Restrain myself?" Father Mazón replied with a nasal growl. "Up here? In this wilderness? Here where nothing grows? You come here to ask me to restrain myself? Has anyone shown restraint with me? Do you understand me? What do you think the knowledge is that you're so proud of, student?"

"It's what you people have denied all your life," exclaimed Félix.

"I'm going to explain to you the only thing worth knowing," the priest replied, letting his arms drop. "I come from a family in which each member hurt the others in one way or another. Then, repentant, each one hurt himself." He looked at the student with savage intensity. "Each one constructed his own prison. Each one, my father, my mother, especially my sisters, we beat ourselves in our bedrooms until we bled. Then, together again, we sang praises to Mary, the only woman conceived without sin. Do you hear me, Señor Don University Wise Man? I'm talking to you about a mystery. I'm talking to you about faith. I'm telling you that faith is true even if it's absurd."

The priest held his own head as if to stabilize a body that had a tendency to race away. "The Virgin Mary, the only sweet, protective, and pure woman in the corrupt harem of Mother Eve. The only one!"

Mayalde had withdrawn to a corner like someone protecting herself from a squall that doesn't end because it is only the prelude to the one that follows.

Mazón turned to look at her. "Not only a woman, an Indian. A race damaged for centuries. That's why I keep her as a maid." He looked with contempt at Félix. "And you, thief of honor, learn this. Life is not a sheepskin jacket."

"It's not a cassock, either."

"Do you think I'm castrated?" Benito Mazón murmured, both defiant and sorrowful. "Ask the girl."

"Don't be vulgar. What I think is that there is no physical limit to desire," said Félix Camberos. "There is only a moral limit."

"Ah, you've come to give me lessons in morality!" shouted the priest. "And my desires? What about them?"

"Control yourself, Father." Félix was about to put his arms around Mazón.

"Do you think I don't spend my life struggling against my own wickedness, my sordid vileness?" shouted the priest, beside himself.

"I don't accuse you of anything." Félix stepped back two paces. "Respect yourself."

"I am a martyr," the priest exclaimed, his eyes those of a madman.

3. That same afternoon, when the two of them were alone, the priest sat a docile and mocking Mayalde on his knees and told her that God curses those who knowingly lead us down the wrong path. He caressed her knees.

"Think, child. I saved you from temptation and also from ingratitude. Don't you have anything to say to me?"

"No, Father. I have nothing to say."

"Get rid of the wild ideas that boy put in your head."

"They weren't wild ideas, Father. Félix put something else in me, just so you know."

The priest pushed the girl off his lap. He didn't stand up. "Forget him, girl. He's gone away. He didn't love you. He didn't free you from me."

"You're wrong, Father. I feel free now."

"Be quiet."

"You're a very sad man, Father. I'll bet sadness hounds you even when you're asleep."

"What a chatterbox you've turned into. Did the deserter give you lessons?"

Mayalde was silent. She looked at the priest with hatred and felt herself being pawed at. The priest didn't have anybody else to humiliate. What was he going to ask of her now? Would he humiliate her more than he did before Félix Camberos's visit?

Perhaps there was a certain refinement in Father Benito Mazón's soul. He didn't mistreat Mayalde. Just the opposite. One knows he said things about thinking carefully if life with him had favored her or not.

"Do you want to go down to the village with me? When the sun shines, it makes you feel like leaving this prison. Let yourself be seen, fix yourself up. I'll dress you."

"So I won't talk, Father?"

"You're an absolute idiot." The priest whistled between his teeth. "You don't know what's good for you. I'm a man of God. You're less than a maid." He began to hit her, shouting, "Wild ideas, wild ideas!"

The black cover over his body seemed like a flag of the devil as the priest shouted, "Man of God, man of God!" and Mayalde, on the floor, did not say a word, protected herself from the blows, and knew that in a little while the priest's rage would begin to give out like air in an old, broken bellows, "Wild ideas, wild ideas, what did that boy put in your head?"

And in the end, out of breath, his head bowed, he would say to her (one knows it): "You're an absolute idiot. Nobody wants to see you. Only me. Thank me. Get undressed. Have you called anyone else Daddy?"

When, barely two years later, Mayalde came down the mountain to tell one that Father Benito had died accidentally when he fell over a cliff, one was not surprised that the features and attitude of the eighteen-year-old girl had changed so much. It is clear to one that the priest kept her prisoner after the incident with the student Félix Camberos. The young woman who now approached looked stronger, robust, proven, capable of anything. Nothing like a prisoner.

"What happened to the priest?"

"Nothing. A slip. A misstep."

"Where do you want to bury him?"

"Up there. In the ashes. Next to where Félix Camberos is buried."

There the two of them are, side by side, on an abrupt slope of the mountain that looks pushed up toward the sky. From that point you can see all the way to the city that is generally hidden by the volcanic mass. The city is large, but from here you can barely make it out. One can imagine it as a conflagration. Though in the midst of the fire, there is an oasis of peace. The urban struggle concentrates on itself, and one forgets it if one takes refuge in an isolated corner, an island in the multitude.

We descended one day, she and I, from the slopes of the volcano to the great city that awaited us without rumors, curses, suspicions. But recollections, yes.

She could not forget, and she infected my memory.

When I married her after the priest died, I decided to take her far away from the little village in the mountains. I stopped talking behind the mask of the one who kept me far from the desire to make her mine. I became an "I" determined to show her that the uses of life are not sins you have to run away from by taking refuge in the mountains, that the false saint takes pleasure in humiliating himself only to inflict his arrogance on us, that humility sometimes hides great pride, and that faith, hope, and charity are not things of the next world. They should be realities in this world of ours.

I told her that Félix Camberos fought for these things.

I don't really know if the beautiful Mayalde resigned herself to abandoning the adjoining graves of Father Benito and the student Félix. There was a sense of transitory guilt in her glance that I attempted to placate with my love.

In the end, all that remained were these words of my wife, spoken years later:

"All of that happened in the ill-fated year of 1968."

Chorus of Rancorous Families

and not only El Mozote
on May 22 1979 we protested on the steps of the cathedral and the
army came and fired and three hundred of us died
blood pouring down the steps like water in a red waterfall
on January 22 1980 cotton workers
electricians office clerks teachers
machine-gunned cut off between two avenues
He
in the Sampul River trapped in the water fleeing
on one side Salvadoran soldiers firing at us
on the other side Honduran troops blocking our way
the Salvas grab children toss them into the air and cut off their heads
with machetes
they call it operation cleanup
the next day the Sampul River can't be seen
it is covered by a mass of turkey buzzards devouring the corpses
better dead than alive fool
we saw it in the villages
they talk about it in the shacks
go on look go see your father's
two bodies
half a body on one corner
the other half on another corner
come see fool your mother's head
stuck on a fence
look at the sky fool
look at the dragonfly jet fighters 37
they bring you little presents

they bring you six thousand pounds of incendiary bombs and
explosives
they bring you white phosphorus rockets
they shoot at you with 60mm machine guns
they're the spotter planes
they see people
they're the huey helicopters
when they don't see people they fire at livestock
huey oxen
it's better to run away
whole families on the roads
it's better to have a fiery sky fall on you
it's better to die in despair on the road in the daytime
than to fall into their hands
they tortured my father with a plastic bag filled
with flour on his head
talk
they mutilated my father cutting off his testicles
they hung weights on my father's balls until they maimed him
forever
but we're still there in our miserable villages
the women wash boil grind
we kids are couriers
we carry the news
they killed Gerinaldo
Jazmín won't return to the village
we kids played ambush
Rutilio and Camilo and Selvín
then we grew up however we could
we formed gangs of rancorous orphans:
there is rancor
and nobody hides it
there are the fourteen families' mansions in San Benito beach
houses cocktails at the country club Hollywood musicals

at the Vi movie theater
there are the mobs of one-eyed lottery-ticket sellers bootblacks
shooshine the lucky little number the blind man
on the streets
and the fourteen only read condensed novels from reader's digest
and the fourteen listen to music by mantovani even when they take a
shit
and they are protected by soldiers nothing but dark-skinned little
farts with no
forehead no chin with boots that hurt and belts
that pinch
who follow the orders of strutting whites
who don't dirty their hands
and the gang was formed there
children and grandchildren of guerrillas of soldiers of widows
of other courier children
the ones who got together night after night to wait for news
about the disappeared
then tell us
who cares about my death?
what's more fucked up?
being dead?
or being poor?
that's what we want
everybody poor
and that's why they're afraid of us now
since we stood up to the death battalions
the huey helicopters
since we were kids we thought think now you're dead and your
worries are over
maybe only when you're dead do you see your papa again and your
mama
your little brother
so be initiated into the gang

take the vomiting test
you stick your finger in the back of your mouth
touch your uvula
if you don't puke we jam a snapdragon to the
back of your palate and a corncob up your sweet ass
be initiated
with a savage beating
to see if you can take it
kicks to the balls
they cut off your father's son of a bitch kicks to the belly
they kicked your pregnant mother bastard fucker until you
came out
kicks to the knees
they cut off your grandfather's legs to make him talk
kicks to the shins
your grandfather cut off my grandfather's
now pull down your pants and take a shit in front of everybody
put on a happy face
imagine you're not shitting you're killing
get used to the idea bro that killing is the same as the euphoria
of shitting
you'll be the sergeant you shit
you'll be the captain you turd
but don't stop thinking about all of them
the fourteen families
the mob
the killers and torturers in the battalions of death
just like you
the guerrillas who killed in self-defense just like you
the gringos arming giving classes on death weapons of death
now remember a single soldier from the battalion: forget about him
now remember a single guerrilla at the front: forget about him
life begins with you
in the gang

get used to that idea
nobody cares about your death
try to remember a single ácatl
try to remember a single farabundo
forget about them
erase the words patriotism revolution from your head
there was no history
history begins with the salvatrucha gang
your only identity is your tattooed
skin
swastikas totems tears a little death
knives stones rifles pistols daggers
everything's good
burn the earth
leave nothing standing
we don't need allies
we need the jungle to hide rest invent
we learn to walk like shadows
each mara gang member is a walking tree
a shadow that moves toward you
toward you carefree asshole
do you think you saved yourself from us?
do you think you saved yourself from us?
just smell the acid of our tattooed skin
just taste the rust of our navels
just put your finger in the mudhole of our assholes
just suck the curdled cum of our pricks
just sink into the red butter of our mouths
just twist around in the black jungle of our armpits
we are the gang
we save salvatruchas everything all of you nice and clean and neat in
your sunday best hid shaved cleaned deodorized
and on top of that tattooed skin
and the warnings on our skin

tears and teardrops painted on our
faces by death
while all of you read advertisements in the press on television
peripherals
we announce ourselves with our bitter stinking rancorous tattooed
skin
read the news on our skin

The Secret Marriage

Every time I want to tell you the truth, something interrupts us.

Don't worry, Lavinia. We're alone, my love. I've given orders not to be interrupted. What do you want to tell me?

I'm very unhappy. No, don't interrupt me. I want your love, not your sympathy.

You have both. You know that. Tell me.

Can I begin at the beginning?

I'm all yours. So to speak.

Leo, you know about my life, and you know I never lie to you. I want to talk to you about him. As you say in your discussions, I want to recapitulate. I only hope I can be brief. After all, we've been together nine years. I want you to be aware of my relationship to Cristóbal. I won't hide anything from you. You know almost everything, but only in pieces. I want you to put yourself in my place and understand why my relationship with him has lasted so long. You have to imagine what it meant to me at the age of twenty-nine, when you begin to feel the terror of turning thirty, to renew my life thanks to a passion that was fresh, new, and above all, dangerous.

I swear to you, Lavinia—

Don't interrupt, please. I was at an age, nine years ago, when you still believe you can begin your life over again, throw the old baggage over the side, and remake yourself from head to toe. I confess I already carried that inside me. Restlessness, the little worm, whatever you want to call it. My career had given me successes, compensations. Being a top publicist is something. It's enough for a lot of women. They marry their careers.

They say a professionally successful woman always has a lover in her bed: her career.

Agreed. A career is very erotic. And yet I was dissatisfied. My career was just my dish of *mole*. But the sauce needed spice. Well, I was fertile ground, as they say . . . The fact is that on the afternoon he came into the office, our eyes met, and we both said in silence what we repeated to each other afterward in a quiet voice, you understand, both of us in half-light. Love at first sight. An infatuation. I'm telling you this with no shame at all. Cristóbal came into the office, and I undressed him with my eyes. I guessed what he looked like naked, and he did the same to me. We found out that night. Do you care if I tell you about it just the way it happened?

No. I like it. If you kept anything secret from me, you'd be an egotist.

You're a savage. In the bedroom, he took off my panties, picked me up still dressed, with tremendous strength he picked me up and took me with my legs wrapped around his waist . . . I've never felt pleasure like that. Except with you.

Thanks.

But not the first time. With you, I had to get used to you. With him, I was afraid so much pleasure right away could only produce a kind of backlash of reduced sensations as time passed and we became accustomed to being together.

The law of diminishing returns.

But no. The truth was that the initial excitement lasted a long time. Danger helps, of course. Trysts, places that are nice but of necessity secret, fear of being discovered.

One's companion always viewed as a temptation, not as a habit.

Exactly. Heaven on earth, isn't it? Everything's so unpredictable, so risky, so destructive to everyone if you're discovered, that . . . Well, I admit it all feeds the vanity of a woman who feels herself needed, admired, without the humiliating sensation of just being there like a piece of furniture.

It's the good thing about being the mistress and not the wife.

Why?

The wife makes the bed after love. The mistress has a maid who makes it for her.

Don't kid around, Leo. I'm talking to you seriously.

Like a piece of furniture, you were saying . . .

Waiting for the man to sit on you, eat on you, urinate on you without even looking at you. Cristóbal made me feel unique. Queen of a kingdom with only two subjects, he and I, both subject to the desires—all the desires—of the other, which, because it was what the other wanted, belonged to both and to each, to me, to him . . .

Fornication is a universal and inalienable right.

At first he filled me with enthusiasm. He made me ecstatic. He told me things like "You have a fragile beauty and an intense sadness." How could I not love him? It's an ornate sentence, vulgar perhaps, but you're not told that every day, Leo, you're told what time we'll see each other, I'll be back at seven, order me some tacos, where did you leave the keys, you're not told that your beauty is fragile and your sadness profound, no, not that . . . Nobody but a passionate man tells you he doesn't know if you're beautiful because you're proud or proud because you're beautiful, things like that. I would watch him combing his hair and get terribly excited. He combed his hair with his fingernails, you know? I spied on him when he tidied up in front of the mirror alone pushing his hair back alone before returning alone to the bedroom alone with the strength of an animal and with my own secret animality maintaining the very human love of the looks I gave him without his knowing I was looking at him. We made love, and he called me whore bitch in heat shameless tight cunt with a clit as cute as a golf course he told me all that with no shame and finally:

"If you deceive me, I want you to be faithful to me. If you're faithful to me, I want you to deceive me."

In everything, almost, you're very frank. And you have a good memory.

What? Do you think something like this can be forgotten?

Not everyone knows how to mix memory and desire. When the second ends, the first goes away.

Leo, the most attractive vanity can become repellent. Habitual surprise can stop surprising one day. No, he's always given me the best. The best hotels, the best restaurants, the most beautiful trips, everything first class, always. I have nothing to complain about. But do you know something, Leo? Even the unexpected became routine. I can't reproach him for his desire to pay attention to me, to always take me to the most elegant places. The moment came when I wanted everything except the exceptional. Because I began to anticipate the extraordinary, you know? Then the ordinary threatened to come back. With indomitable strength, the strength of the exceptional. Normalcy began to appear in every first-class section of Air France, every suite at every Ritz, every table at El Bodegón, truffles began to make me itch, pheasants left me cross-eyed, lobsters grabbed at my hands to pull me back to the ocean floor . . . Love can suffocate us, Leo. It's like eating candy all the time. You have to give tedium its due. You have to be grateful for the boring moments in a relationship. You have to . . . You have to stop anticipating the extraordinary. You have to learn to foresee the foreseeable.

It's the best thing about love.

You said it! What happens is that nobody foresees the moment when you no longer want to be as happy as you were and you desire a little of that unhappiness called ordinary life. Well, what you give me, Leo.

X kills Y and Z kills X.

You pay attention to me—

I'm referring to proofs.

You never talk about yourself. You listen to me.

I pay attention only to you, Lavinia.

Aren't you ever offended?

You and I never had to pretend. Not before, not now.

I admit there are confidences I don't like to hear.

I'm just the opposite, Lavinia, I love hearing yours. Please go on.

Do you know what I began to detest in him?

No.

His laugh. The way he laughed. At first I thought it was part of his charm. You're pretty solemn, if truth be told.

Just serious. A little serious.

He had an elegant laugh. Spontaneous. Joyful. Everything well rehearsed.

Have you ever heard sad laughs?

Something worse. There are laughs with significance.

I don't understand.

Of course you do, you know. Those people who never laugh at somebody else's jokes and die laughing at their own, though nobody else finds them funny. I mean, Cristóbal began to laugh to redeem his defects. I realized he wasn't only laughing at a joke or to lighten a tiresome situation. Not to liven up the conversation and even life itself. He laughed to excuse himself. When he did something wrong. When he said something inopportune. When he forgot an anniversary. When he was late for an appointment. When he fired a servant without consulting me first. When he didn't like my makeup, my dress, the book or magazine I was reading, he laughed. He laughed at me. He excused himself for throwing out my lipstick or giving half my wardrobe to the

Red Cross or grabbing away the book by Dan Brown or my copy of *Hola!*, laughing as he said bad taste, trash, I have to educate you.

What did you say?

Hey, don't play Pygmalion with me. That popped out. It was our first disagreement. After that, he enjoyed criticizing me with an eye-dropper, always smiling.

Did you say anything to him?

I'm untorturable. That's what I told him. It was a mistake. He began to annoy me more and more. I didn't let him. Your successes bore me, I told him. Don't tell me about them anymore. Stop presenting yourself to me as a man who makes important decisions every half hour. Your decisions bore me. Every night you come into my bedroom shouting "Land ho!" You had a good time colonizing me, Cristobalito. Don't you ever put off a decision? Don't you ever reflect, don't you ever take your time? And not only that, Leo. Slowly I began to realize that behind the boasting about successes, Cristóbal wanted to impress me with a very powerful love, bigger than any affection for me. Love of manipulation. Loyalty to lies. That's what was behind his boasting.

How did you find out?

It was incredible, Leo. Priscila Barradas, my best friend, you know, the fat woman, made a date with me at the bar in the lobby of the Camino Real. We were drinking margaritas and gossiping very happily when suddenly, fat Pris very calmly stood up and walked out to the lobby. Cristóbal came into the hotel, and she stopped him, holding his arm, whispered something into his ear with her nasty bean breath, and he looked toward the bar nervously, not meeting my eyes—not like the first time, you see?—and hurried away. Shameless Priscila went after him, leaving me flat, sitting in front of a margarita getting warmer and warmer. Oh yes, and leaving me to push up daisies, the old bitch.

Next time order cognac.

That night I reproached Cristóbal for his infidelity. He laughed at me. My conclusions were false, he said. Priscila was the wife of our friend José Miguel Barradas. She simply came over to give him a message from José Miguel. And why didn't the vulgar cow come back to say goodbye to me? Cristóbal laughed, as usual. To provoke you, he said, to make you jealous. Yes, I said, you have to have friends who are very married who don't want to trade their husband for yours. This amused Cristóbal very much. He made passionate love to me again, and again he disarmed me.

And your friend Priscila? Surely you saw each other again.

She's a fat, cynical pig. When I mentioned it to her at a cocktail party, she said, "I think being the only woman who can love your husband is a supreme act of egotism."

What did you say?

One husband's as good as another, as far as you're concerned. Be happy with what you already have, fatso.

And then?

We pulled each other's hair. It happens in the best circles.

And Cristóbal?

I'm telling you, he made passionate love to me and disarmed me. I'm a poor dumb cow.

As the song says, the one you like so much, "Let's fall in love, why shouldn't we fall in love?"

It was at first sight, Leo. Do you have to wait for second sight to take the first step?

"Let our hearts discover—"

Little by little. Condemned to discover the truth a little at a time. What we should have known from the beginning, before we set sail. At least find out if there are lifeboats. Is love fated to be the *Titanic* of one's life?

Did you see the movie? The only surprise is that the ship sinks. I mean, if you had known then what you know now, would you have given up on love?

Forget it. Okay, novelty is not only exciting, it also blinds. Hah, as if I didn't know, a publicity executive.

"We were not made for each other." A variation on the lyric. Cristóbal was exceptional. He's become familiar.

I tell you, his successes bore me. I'd like to see what face he'll put on if he fails. Of course, he'll never admit defeat. Other people fail. He never does. Oh well. I observe him and tell myself I prefer doing something and making a mistake than not doing anything and having passive successes, like an oyster on the ocean floor until it's pulled up for someone to eat. Perhaps this is what happened to him, and naturally, he would never admit it. He counted on me, on my complicity or passivity or erotic need, who knows. The fact is he acts, knowing he can count on me. Imagine the shame of it. He talks and lets me know I'm the force that sustains him.

Mother Earth, let's say.

A damn domestic Coatlicué, the mama goddess with her skirt of snakes waiting for the macho Mexican adventurer. Bah, this whole game of statues wears me out, Leo, we're always turning into stone idols, household idols, with no adventure, no illusion, not even danger, not even . . . I don't know. I feel imprisoned by the mistaken loyalty of continuing a failed relationship. I'm bored with this.

No, Lavinia. Please go on. Just think that with any man, love is like inspiration. Nothing but hard work.

You talk the way they do in one of your soap operas.

That's what I live on, Lavinia.

And the inheritance from your aunt Lucila Casares.

That's true. My aunt in heaven peeks out to watch me enjoy myself.

What was the lady like, your aunt Lucila?

Watch my soap *The Sweethearts.* She's the protagonist.

That vulgar old woman sighing for her adolescent loves?

The same. All I did was transcribe what she said in her diary.

And the little boyfriend from Acapulco, who was he?

I don't know. She calls him Manuel, that's all.

A reject. A guy without will.

Do you even watch my soaps?

I don't. My maids tell me about them. This Manolo is vulgar, he's *cursi*.

Well, our Spanish word *cursi* comes from "courtesy" and from "curtsy." Being well bred.

Then I prefer being a savage, Leo.

Just go outside. But never forget that love is hard work.

With any man?

Yes. With him. With Cristóbal.

Or with you?

With me, too.

Even though the days go by, one after the other, always the same, an endless procession until one day your life is only a little sand at the bottom of a bottle tossed into the sea?

Yes.

Isn't there anything to do?

Yes. Change the game all the time. It's the only way to hold on to a man.

Is that why I have you?

Yes. Do the same with Cristóbal. Constantly change the game. You've let yourself fall into the very routine you reproach him for. You're too faithful, too passive, pining for the first moment of love. You have to realize it won't come back. Invent some new first moments.

Ah, are you saying that for yourself?

You have me forever. With me, you don't need any tricks of love or fate. You'll never be able to leave me.

Are you, beside everything else, my best friend?

I think so, Lavinia. As long as you remember this: There's nothing more seductive than a friend. You know all his secrets, what he likes, what he dislikes. That's why you shouldn't tell your friends everything.

What does friendship have to do with happiness? In any case, what does love have to do with happiness?

Don't look for a definitive answer to anything. Don't keep asking yourself where we're going. Let yourself go, Lavinia. We've spent five years loving each other.

It never should have happened.

Our love?

Never.

Your marriage?

Yes. It was inevitable.

Believe that, Lavinia. Continue with Cristóbal. I swear that our being the lovers we are depends on it. Be faithful to your husband.

Faithful?

In the deepest sense. Continue with him faithfully so you and I can always love each other in secret, with the excitement of the first hour.

Poor Cristóbal . . . I don't know. I don't know if . . .

Don't finish the sentence, Lavinia. You and I don't need to finish sentences.

It was a mistake for us to meet.

Suspension points . . .

Forget it . . .

Chorus of the Daughter Who Killed Herself

The girl went to the cemetery with the pistol that belonged to her
  papa who
abused her the pistol was blacker and harder than her father's cock
I hope he understood that after the
girl put a bullet through her head and then
(just like in the movies)
stood up revived
(just like daffy duck road runner the crazy bird and tom the cat who
  falls from a skyscraper smashes into a mountain is folded into an
  accordion is flattened into a tortilla is shit on and always revives
  resumes his usual form pursues pursues pursues the mouse jerry)
just like in the movies
to tell him what's up you old prick you thought I wasn't capable of
killing myself killing myself
look at me dead and learn your lesson daddy and don't punish your
little girl because she broke the vase and hung from the towel rack
and don't fight anymore papa and mama because then papa comes in
with smoke coming from his nostrils and drool from his mouth to
  take his revenge
on me for his argument with mama
don't fight anymore because I swear I'll throw myself off the roof
don't make me desperate anymore daddymommy
    do you think I'm made of wood?
I touch my skin I pinch myself I feel don't you know that I feel?
there are four hundred of us kids who kill ourselves every year in the
  Rep Mex
Wanna bet you didn't know that?

The Star's Son

1. You stand at the mirror in your bathroom. You look at yourself in the mirror. You look for D'Artagnan leaping from the balcony to the back of the horse waiting for him in the lane. You hope to see the Black Corsair swinging from the mast of the *Folgore* at the attack on Maracaibo. You imagine, in your mirror, the Count of Monte Cristo—you yourself, young, with those motionless gray hairs daubed at your temples like a sea of stone—and you see in your mirror Alejandro Sevilla, yourself, filming *The Seven Boys from Ecija,* and you are all seven of them, you alone are all you need to incarnate the seven generous Spanish bandits of the eighteenth century. You are the hunchback Enrique de Lagardere, the gentleman in disguise to deceive the court of Louis XIII and save the honor of Blanche de Nevers . . . except that now, Alejandro, you can't shake off the imaginary

hump, it's stuck to your body, the deformity isn't made of rubber anymore, it's made of bone, and then you shake your head so the mirror will give back to you the dashing figure of the masked Zorro, ready to defend violated justice in Old California.

You no longer are.

No matter how much you shake your head.

Neither Zorro nor the count of Lagardere comes back. You can no longer be the third or fourth musketeer, and the last time you tried to do D'Artagnan, you leaped from the balcony of your beautiful Constance, and instead of landing gallantly in the saddle (as in the old days), your bones dropped like a sack onto the mattress that divine mercy (the film studio Mexigrama) placed there to prevent accidents.

"Alejandro, give up making costume adventure movies."

You refrained from telling them that you are the star, that the films were the colossal image of your life, and the studio never offered you a production worthy of your person. You are not the producer's servant or the director's valet. You are Alejandro Sevilla, the top star of Mexican film. You have been for thirty years. You dubbed the voice of Charles Boyer. You made inroads into Hollywood films. You were famous for having been Marlene Dietrich's lover, and whether it was true or not doesn't matter: Marlene has been forgotten, Boyer is dead, and you refuse to believe you have loved a ghost or dubbed the voice of a corpse.

The image makes you believe, Alejandro, that you will always be young and will live forever . . . except that in the past, no beginning starlet refused when you asked for her sweet siren's ass and now even the extras turn you down, or laugh at you, or give you a tremendous slap when you say, "Give me your furry diadem." And didn't Peggy Silvester, the Hollywood actress, say she wouldn't work with you, that you were a has-been, a relic of the past, and besides, you had bad breath?

"We can offer you a mature actor's roles. You know, the understanding paterfamilias to the younger generation. Or a misunderstood neurotic of the older generation."

You laughed. The studio depended on you, you didn't depend on the studio.

You were the first to demand—and obtain—a portable dressing room so you could relax with the sirens and their diadems, rest, memorize lines, drink just a little . . . Now they have to put your dialogue on a large placard, and sometimes your movements, the placards, and the cameras don't coincide, and disconcerted, you look at yourself in the mirror and tell yourself, I am D'Artagnan, Zorro, and the Seven Boys of Ecija all in one, and you know you are the great impersonator, a shadow without his own profile, you are Alejandro Sevilla only because you are the Black Corsair, and when in the end you fall from the mast and suspect they are laughing at you behind the scenes, you go to the movies in a scarf and dark glasses to see yourself on the big screen and there it's true that the audience is laughing out loud, they shout, "Get off, you old bum, go to the home for mummies, vegetate vegetarian," and the producer of all your pictures since your debut in *He Suffers for Love,* your longtime friend, does not bite his tongue and tells you, "Alejandro, the actor first has to be in order to seem, but in the end he has to disappear in order to go on being."

You answer that at least your voice, your voice that is so characteristic, so melodious, so well enunciated (you dubbed for Charles Boyer) could be used, you don't know, for newsreels, for travelogues like Fitzpatrick's, no, Alejandro, the voice has wrinkles, too.

Every door was being closed. You weren't even offered roles as a maître d'hôtel. At least I know how to put on a tuxedo, you contended. Then let a luxury restaurant hire you, was the reply. Today restaurants aren't what they used to be, you sighed to yourself, because nobody else would understand. The Ambassadeurs closed, its old patrons died . . . The 1-2-3 closed, its bartender drowned in Acapulco . . . The Rivoli closed, destroyed in the earthquake of 1985 . . .

"Either you change your generation, or this generation will trade you in for another star who's younger."

You leaped from the balcony of Constance Bonacieux, the horse ran off, you contended, the horse should not have moved but it moved, you had a terrible fall, they took you off the picture and your only recourse was to think either you stay inside your mobile dressing room, disguised as a musketeer, mummified forever . . . or you go back, after so many years, to your house.

After so many years.

Then your face disappears from the mirror and other faces return to it, as if emerged from the quicksilver, as if born of the mist . . .

2. You had all the women, Alejandro. All of them. But you loved only one. Cielo de la Mora. She was very young when she came to the studio. She was from Nicaragua. They were filming *The Return of Zorro,* and she fit perfectly into the colonial California setting, adorned with a high, elegant comb and ringlets, dressed in a crinoline. And with a birthmark next to her mouth. You took advantage of the romantic scenes to move in with the iron rod (to use your peculiar expression) and gauge the response. Even the most indignant succumbed. Who knows why, but you respected Cielo de la Mora from the very beginning. You dared only to sing into her ear, "that birthmark you have, my sweet heaven, next to your mouth, don't give it to anyone else . . ."

"It belongs to me," she completed the stanza.

In other words, from that moment on you felt in charge.

There was mystery in her, veiled by a somber though striking beauty, eyes half closed but alert. A look you didn't dare decipher. The others, yes, they were legible. Actresses accepted your advances in order to advance themselves. They were using you, and you knew it. You gave singular value to each "lay." Sincere or insincere, unique or unrepeatable, it made no difference. Other women loved you for yourself, for being a leading man, for being handsome (you look in the mirror and give yourself a satisfied pat on the jaw, recalling Alejandro Sevilla at the age of thirty, when a man is in his prime, the irresistible Alejandro Sevilla, magnetic, athletic, magical, poetic, sarcastic, master of the world, the star of Mexico).

You knew how to intuit women, read them, guess their weaknesses, not take them seriously, discard them without mercy. They were your babes, your cuties, broads, dames, in the long run anonymous, forgettable because they were decipherable. Only Cielo de la Mora appeared to you as a mystery, she herself an enigma. You had no illusions. Behind the mysterious eyes of the splendid woman with very black hair and very white skin, was there another mystery that wasn't simply the mystery of her eyes?

As a screen star, you had in your favor what an actor in the theater doesn't have. The great close-up, the approach to your face and especially your eyes. You believed you were—you told yourself—a specialist in "a woman's glances." You would intone, with a slight change in lyrics, the famous bolero while you shaved first in the morning and again at eight at night, to avoid five o'clock shadow, as the Gillette commercial called it.

A woman's glances
that I saw
close to me . . .

Some were shamelessly flirtatious, the glance of "come close, what are you waiting for?" and there were some, equally shameless, as chaste as a nun's. Glances that announced an experience their owners hadn't had and glances that feigned an innocence that wasn't theirs, either. Rarely, very rarely, indifferent glances. The opposite sex was never indifferent to Alejandro Sevilla. And at times the masculine gender paid you homage, Alejandro, imitating your postures, your words, the clothes you wore on the street when you stopped being a musketeer.

"Your ambiguous attitudes kindle the flame of my jealousy."

"Frankly, darling, you leave no mark on my personality."

"I suffer from a twilight love."

"It's of no importance."

"Keep the change, waiter."

Cielo de la Mora was different. It isn't that she had no mystery (for you, all women have it, and if not, you invent it for them) but that she maintained an imperturbable calm in the face of your advances and amatory acrobatics. It isn't that she didn't take you seriously. And you couldn't say she was mocking you. She was your normalcy. Serene, worthy of her luminous name, she was completely blue inside and out. No siren's ass or furry diadem. She was attractive because of her contemplative serenity, a seriousness and sobriety in her manner.

She didn't resemble any other woman.

That's why you fell in love with her.

Cielo didn't ask for matrimony, and neither did you. Marriages between film actors were only for publicity, and you didn't need promotion or have a reason to give any to Cielo. In the end, you wanted her, with her face of a waning moon, to depend only on you, her sun. You would take care of giving her parts in your movies. With high combs for Zorro, crinolines for D'Artagnan, high Napoleonic breasts for Monte Cristo, red shawls for the Black Corsair: Cielo de la Mora was your chromatic partner. She obeyed you in everything, letting it be known that a prior agreement existed between you and her.

She disobeyed you only twice.

She decided to have a child with you. Surprised, you weighed the pros and cons of paternity. The most favorable part was increasing your following, both feminine and masculine. Irresistible images for both sexes. The doting father carrying a baby, showing him off proudly, lifting him high in the midst of the flashbulbs of the boys in the press.

Besides, Cielo would be out of action for five months. Eliminated from the cast and offering you a magnificent excuse to take up again the conquests your celebrated union with Cielo implicitly denied to you. You'd be careful to keep your adventures discreet. You'd threaten talkative starlets with a sudden end to their careers.

"You know, gorgeous, my word will always be worth more than yours. Sex and silence or sex and being fired. It's up to you, babe . . ."

It wasn't that Cielo de la Mora would have been upset to learn about another of Alejandro Sevilla's infidelities. After all, they weren't married. And in the end, who else had decided to have the baby? Who else had stopped using birth control? Who else had taken the sedative for her nerves?

"I really was very nervous, even though I didn't show it."

Which was why, when the baby was born, the mother blamed only herself. She tried to assimilate her horror by watching Roman Polanski's film *Rosemary's Baby* over and over again and trying to imitate Mia Farrow's maternal feelings. Each gesture of maternal love, however, repelled Cielo de la Mora in the deepest part of her being, obliged her to falsify her desire for serene distance before the world, to openly choose the mother's love expected of her or the sexual repugnance that had returned to the place of conception. To love or hate. Cielo felt cornered, obliged to make drastic resolutions, abandoning her preferred role as serene (and even submissive) observer of the world.

"Forgive me, Alejandro. Don't touch me."

"Control yourself, Señora. That little problem won't be repeated."

"Don't touch me, I'm telling you."

"Let's give time a little time."

The national film industry brought her to you. The national film industry separated her from you. Once she had recuperated from the birth, though not from her melancholy, you included Cielo in the cast of your first contemporary movie. You gave in to the pleas of the producer, the public wants to see you dressed in ordinary clothes, by now they think that even at home you walk around like a musketeer, don't fuck around, Alejandro, you owe it to your public . . .

One scene in the movie took place in an opera house. Cielo de la Mora was sitting in a box. You looked at her with your binoculars, and she looked away. She was wearing a very low-cut strapless lamé gown. When the performance was over, you approached her on the street. You were wearing a heavy overcoat in addition to the indispensable gray felt hat. But she appeared without a coat, with her bare shoulders and Olympic diver's neckline. The director hit the ceiling and shouted. Where was the mink, the fur coat the actress was supposed to be wearing?

"It's very hot," Cielo said.

"It doesn't matter. The script says, 'She comes out carefully buttoned up against the cold north wind on a wintry night.' "

"It's ridiculous. It's hot. Only in Nicaragua do women wear fox to the opera in spite of the heat."

"Darling," you intervened, carefully buttoned up, "it's precisely to give the impression that Mexico isn't a tropical country, a banana republic, but that it's cold here, like in Europe."

She laughed at you, turned, and got into a taxi while you murmured: "It's to show that we're civilized—"

"It's to hide what we really are," she said from the taxi.

3. In her goodbye letter, Cielo de la Mora said things like these. She had fallen in love with a photograph. "Even before I met you, even before I had seen you on the screen. An actor has to be admired from a distance. The truth is, fame muddies ordinary affection. At least let's save the child from our quarrels. From hostility. From humiliations."

You remembered other things you had forgotten.

"Whenever I want to tell you something that matters to me, Alejandro, you say you're in a hurry, you leave, you don't listen to me."

And now she was writing to say she was leaving you for good.

"How can I explain my desire to get away, to stop being the woman I was with you, to begin a new life?"

She didn't take the child with her. Everything else was an excuse. The truth is, she abandoned the child. Before Sandokán was born (given this name in homage to the adventure novels of Emilio Salgari), you told yourself in secret that you wouldn't marry Cielo.

"Suppose I marry her and she gets a divorce and then leaves Mexico with the child."

Now she had gone, but without the child. Free. Like a bird that knows only the calendar of the seasons, the call of warm air, the rejection of the cold habitat. Leaving three-month-old Sandokán in your care.

You deceived yourself. You thought, like a good father, that you would tend to your son with affection. It was another of your interminable stupidities, Alejandro. You don't realize the number of moronic things you do. They're like the idiotic rosary of your existence. I know you'll never accept this. You beat yourself up. How are you going to admit that your life is a farce, that it exists only in the way it exists for Cielo de la Mora, as an inert portrait of celebrity? Now you had a great chance to redeem yourself as a man, as a father, as a human being: Let it all go, Alejandro, leave your career and dedicate yourself to your son, Sandokán.

If at some moment this idea passed through your mind (and I believe it passed, it's clear to you it did), it lasted less time than the proverbial winter swallow. Your good intentions did not survive forty-eight hours. An invalid child, monstrous and deformed, did not fit in the big screen of your life. Now you could put the blame on Cielo de la Mora for having taken thalidomide, her innocent pills for her nerves. There was no valid justification. There is none for the deficiencies of a son. The mother had abandoned father and son. She fled in exchange for nothing, because nothing was waiting for her: no fame or money, no (perhaps) new boyfriend (at least you wanted to believe that). The mother could not bear (malgré Mia Farrow) the company in a concealed cradle of the baby with little arms sprouting out of his armpits, the child condemned to depend on others, his tiny hands close only to his face but not to his sex, or his ass, or a cup, or a knife, or a movie script. The pages of the most recent script—*Sandokán the Tiger of Malaysia,* your son's homonym—were opening in your hands. You felt immense anguish (unusual for you). The pirate leaps from one ship to another, fights with his sword, cuts the mooring lines of his own vessel, rescues Honorata van Gould, makes her his, fornicates with her, Alejandro, you say, Honorata give me your sweet siren's ass Honorata let me kiss your furry diadem, you can, Alejandro, he, your son, never, not ever. Life was *denied* to him. At that moment you understood why Cielo de la Mora had left. She feared the death of Sandokán. She feared it because she herself wanted to offer it to him: Die, little baby, so you won't suffer in life, I'm drowning you, baby, so you can go back to heaven, I'm abandoning you, honey, so you won't blame your mother or know her or even know her name.

4. "Never talk to him about his mama."

You said that to Sagrario Algarra, the old character actress of Mexican movies, who was prepared to take care of Sandokán Sevilla de la Mora while you took care of filmofornication, and the mother, well, consider her dead.

As a young woman, Sagrario Algarra had played the long-suffering mother and the loving grandmother. She became celebrated—indispensable—as the "featherbrained woman" in old melodramas. Paradoxically, when she aged, she could no longer play—because she feared being identical to them—old women's roles. She became coquettish. She decided to rejuvenate. Perhaps she wanted to avenge her anticipated old age in the movies and recover in her own biographical seniority the illusion of the youth "that art denied me."

She would say this with a sigh.

"Your career is over, Sagrario," you would reply with compassion.

"Yours, too, Alejandro, it's just that you don't know it yet."

You're tenacious, it's true. You're stubborn. It's difficult for you to abandon what you have been, what fame has given you, money and the capacity for squandering both things: fame and money. What isn't at all difficult for you is to abandon your son, leaving him in the care of Sagrario Algarra, be frank, Alejandro, you keep Sandokán at a distance because you don't tolerate disease in any of its forms, especially if it deforms. How could it be otherwise? You represent virile health, duels with a blade, pursuits on horseback, leaps from one mast to another, the sword that marks the walls of California with your eponymous Z.

Besides, you agonize over the difficulty of approaching your son and explaining to him the absence of his mother; what could you tell the child when he believed that Sagrario was his mama and Sagrario protested that she was not a mother because she had no grandmother?

"Your mama abandoned us, she went off with another man, that's why I abandoned her, too, Sandokán, I wasn't going to be less than her, I'm Alejandro Sevilla the superstar, I'm the one who abandons women, no woman abandons me."

And resigned:

"I abandoned her. I wasn't going to be less than her. I'm not some dumb prick."

Sagrario Algarra laughed at him: "Don't be stupid, Alejandro. Don't say that to your son."

"Then what? Where do I begin?"

"Tell him the truth. You aren't a great star anymore. Understand? You're in the same situation as your son. Both of you have been abandoned."

"We still have you, my faithful Sagrario."

"The hell with that faithful bullshit. I've had enough. I'm leaving. You stay with your little monster."

"In any event, thanks for taking care of him for me."

"Thanks? Ask the kid if he thanks me for watching him while he sleeps, visiting him every night with a light in my hand, curious, Alejandro, sick to know what he did at night with those little hands that couldn't reach his sex, how he masturbated, if he rubbed up against the mattress or maybe under the shower, you know, waiting for the running water to excite his penis and punishing myself, Alejandro, for my lack of courage, for not taking his sex in my hands, jerking him off myself, or sucking it, Alejandro, and since I didn't have the courage, I punished him and I punished myself, I was violent with him, at midnight I would take him to the bathroom so a cold shower would drive out his bad thoughts, humiliating him, Alejandro, laughing out loud and asking him, 'Who ties your shoes for you?' Go on, try it yourself."

She wiped her nose with a dishcloth. "I wanted to be a stepmother, not a mother. A she-wolf, not a grandmother. Use your son to get out of the prison of my old movies."

Sagrario Algarra assumed facial features illuminated by a strong nocturnal radiance. It was her best part (her bespart). Innocent granny transformed into stony Medusa.

"And what did you tell him about me?"

"That you would come to see him one day. What did you expect me to say?"

"And it was true. I did come, Sagrario."

"But you always pretended to be somebody else. The musketeer, the corsair."

"It was to amuse him. A child's fantasy is—"

"You confused him. One year you made him think that Christmas was December 28, another year that it was November 20, taking advantage of the sports parade, all depending on your convenience, a bad man, a bad father."

"Take it easy, Sagrario, this isn't a movie."

Was the old actress so shrewd that she knew to announce her departure from the apartment in the Cuauhtémoc district on the same day Mexigrama told Alejandro Sevilla his career no longer had a future?

Exit Sagrario. Enter Alejandro.

Sandokán looked at his father without surprise. Sagrario had taken him to see all of Alejandro Sevilla's films from the time the boy was five until now, when he was turning sixteen. Still, when you entered the huge room with no separating walls, remodeled so the boy would not have to open doors or go up and down stairs—an apartment that opened onto a small garden of flowerpots and unmovable tiles, a kind of penthouse on the roof of the building, hermetically separated from the lower floors by a private elevator—you saw that your son did not know or recognize you. His glance had more rationality than the voice of the producers: "Retire, Alejandro, don't be a fool."

You can never describe to anyone, Alejandro, the embarrassing difficulty of that reencounter, if not first encounter, with a boy whom you hadn't seen for five years, when Sandokán had not yet entered puberty and you didn't know what to say to prepare him as you supposed a good father should. The fact is, you knew only the lines of the parts you hated most—the mature father of the family giving advice to his rebellious, carousing, rock-and-roll children—and a strange delicacy never before seen in you kept you from talking to your son. You had imagined him as a deformed replacement for James Dean.

You shouldn't have been afraid. The boy began to speak as if he had waited a long time for this moment to arrive—because the time of the encounter was exactly that, an apparition, a phantom, a ghost that brought together in an instant all the dead hours, resuscitated all the defeated calendars only for the reality of this moment, and moved all the clocks ahead just to move them back to the time that had been lost.

You looked at each other without saying anything. Your son's eyes were directed at the wall.

"Thank you for the Christmas present, Papa."

It was a mobile in the style of Calder, and Sandokán's eyes said clearly that nothing had occupied more of his time than the observation of the always distinct movements of the large, multicolored toy that gave a second air to the very atmosphere of the uniform room. A space without obstacles between the bed and the chairs, the table and the terrace, the electronic equipment whose use Sandokán immediately demonstrated with the agility that his condition gave to his bare feet. He was dressed in a long white undershirt that covered his sex and buttocks, allowing him to urinate and defecate without using his hands.

The boy laughed and turned on a kind of mechanized roll of towels, letting it be understood that this was enough to clean himself.

Embarrassed, you went to help your son. Sandokán rejected you. His initial friendly smile had turned into a grimace.

"You told me to hang the mobile from the ceiling just to frighten me, didn't you?" You couldn't even mutter a reply. You choked on the words, and there was no immediate correspondence with the dialogues appropriate to an encounter between father and son in the movies.

You said nothing, looked for the bed that Sagrario Algarra had abandoned, opened your suitcase, and began to arrange your things. Sandokán watched you in silence. You moved forward as if you were entering a new life, which is why you find yourself at this moment looking at yourself in the mirror of the small bathroom adjoining the large room, looking there for D'Artagnan, for the Count of Monte Cristo, and finding only a sixty-one-year-old man who is losing everything, his hair, his teeth, the firmness of his flesh, the impetuosity of his glance . . .

Your fame, was it the truth or a lie for your own son? You didn't know. You had to discover your son beginning with a deluded question: Does my son know me only through my fame? Said another way: Does my son love or hate me?

Things began to reach their level and proportion during the weeks that followed. Sandokán mocked you, warned you, "Be careful, Papa, I put a needle in the soup" or "Watch out, I put glass in the orange juice." It wasn't true. Sandokán could not do anything in the kitchen. From now on that was your job. In a single stroke, you came down from the illusory world of fictitious adventures to the unfortunate world of small domestic misadventures. You did not have the money to pay a full-time maid, you had barely enough for a weekly cleaner, a dark-skinned young girl in flip-flops who didn't recognize you, or even look at you, no matter how ridiculously you assumed a musketeer's poses with a broom in your fist in front of her.

In the meantime, you realized that Sandokán put on an innocent face, but a malevolent intention lodged between his eyes and his mouth. If there is hatred in Sandokán's expression, you surprise yourself discovering that if hatred is a manifestation of evil, it is possible to find unexpected beauty in the face of someone who absolutely does not wish you well. You surprise yourself, Alejandro, formulating a clear idea that becomes an outgrowth of your long speeches in the movies.

Your idea of the boy distracted by his physical deformity, you hadn't noticed the classic beauty of his face. Now you know why. Sandokán is identical to his mother, your Nica wife Cielo de la Mora. The jet-black hair. The transparent white skin. Even the birthmark beside his mouth.

Naturally, you didn't want to find your wife in your son. The young man had never seen a photograph of his mother. The only woman he had seen up close was the sour Sagrario. He can't compare—and if he knew, if he knew that his mother had reappeared in the living portrait of her son, would Sandokán be more lovable, more understanding with the papa who had come home without a cent, my boy, because I threw it all away on tramps and traveling, on the great spree of my life, dammit, even on Sagrario's salary, I didn't know how to save, I didn't know how to invest, for me there was no tomorrow.

"Because there was the moment of your pictures, Father, there time doesn't pass, there you never grow old."

You attribute this to your son. You think that if what you think he thinks is true, your son has seen your movies, it isn't Sagrario's pious lie.

"Yes, Sagrario took me to see you whenever you were showing." Sandokán laughed. "I never thought I'd know you in person."

"But I've come a few times, son."

"Always in disguise. Not now. Now I see you for the first time. I don't know"—he stopped smiling—"if I prefer the truth to the lie."

At that moment you decide you are not going to surrender, Alejandro. Something new in you—abandoning the play, leaving representation behind—sprang up in you unexpectedly, guiding you in an imperfect way toward your son's personality, which was the path of affection. And for you this was a huge, joyful revelation.

"Know something, Papa? I had a dream that I'd escape, run away from the house. But I couldn't do it alone. Then . . . look . . . open . . ."

He indicated a suitcase under his bed. You opened it. It was filled with postcards.

"I asked Sagrario to find me cards from everywhere. She knows a lot of strange people. Look. Istanbul, Paris, Rio de Janeiro . . ."

He smiled in satisfaction. "I've been everywhere, Papa, and besides . . ."

He sat down in front of a lectern. A volume lay open on it. Sandokán pressed a pedal, and the pages moved.

" 'On February 24, 1813, the lookout in the port of Marseille announced the arrival of the *Faraón,* proceeding from Smyrna, Trieste, and Naples . . .' "

He looked at you. "You see? I've been to the same places you have. Except the book is earlier than the movie. I beat you!"

Sometimes Sandokán isn't lovable. He tries to hurt you.

"What have you given me, Papa? What do you want me to give to you? How are you going to pay me for being abandoned? Just tell me that."

"Don't repeat my dialogues," you say irritably.

"Seriously, Father, do you understand? You had everything, I've had nothing."

The boy says this with a wooden face.

At other times you're busy doing what you have never done. You cook. You keep the house clean. You pretend this is another role, just as if you were—it might have happened—the headwaiter at a restaurant.

Sandokán interrupts. You tell him to let you work. He turns his back.

"Whenever I want to tell you something that matters to me, you say you're in a hurry."

Where have you heard that same complaint before?

Your son wants to join you, aggressively. He falls flat on his face. You run to help him. He resists. He struggles with you. In the end he embraces you. You embrace each other.

"You ought to be dead," the son tells the father, and you refrain from repeating the phrase because it compromises Cielo, your wife, Sandokán's mother, who also tried to kill her son in the cradle before she fled.

"Have pity on me," you say instead to your son, knowing that these are, in turn, the words the boy wants to say and cannot.

Sandokán looks at you with unexpected, invasive tenderness. "You know? Now both our feelings are hurt."

He culminated his remark by extending his leg in order to trip you. This becomes Sandokán's greatest diversion. Making you fall. At first you are resigned. It is difficult for you to scold him. You don't dare to slap him. Little by little, you prefer to accept the prank. Finally, you celebrate it. You laugh each time Sandokán, with the agility of a pirate from the Island of Tortuga, extends his leg and makes you fall. The strength the boy has developed in his legs is surprising. Beneath the comfortable shirt he always wears, you see two robust limbs, very developed, almost hairless, statuesque, almost marble-like, streaked with blue veins. So that half of his body lives intensely, from the neck up and from his navel down. So that perhaps you were right to stop Cielo de la Mora from drowning your son in the bath or throwing him into a trash can or . . .

This means you will let Sandokán make you fall, and you will laugh because in this way, you celebrate the life of the boy, his presence in the world. Nothing less than that: his presence in the world. And little by little, Alejandro, you begin to realize that your son's individuality was the most faithful mirror of the life that still was yours, that leaving the movie sets was not a death certificate, as you believed before, but a window that opened to let air, sun, birds, rain, pollen, bees into the closed tomb of a movie set reeking of sawdust, cardboard, glue, the hair of wigs made with the tresses of corpses, period costumes never sent to the cleaner, stained under the arms and between the legs, the clothing of extras, the others, the surplus, the replaceable, the dispensable.

Now you're the extra in your final film, Alejandro. Except that your secret resignation—or can it be your will?—to disappear into the vast anonymous nation of failure has been frustrated by the encounter with your son, by the spirit of *comedy* that Sandokán displays in a situation that, instead of causing pity, he transforms into a prelude to a limited though hoped-for adventure: that of reuniting with you and initiating your real life together.

Hoped for and despaired over: Each fall that Sandokán makes you take is an invitation to the pending adventure. Is the child in fact father to the man? Where did you read that? Who said it to you? You confuse your dialogues on the screen with your words in life. You look in the mirror and accept that you'll never escape this dilemma: speaking as if you were acting, acting as if you were speaking. Now, when you fulfill the rite of shaving each morning, you begin to believe that your old face is being lost, though not in a banal way because of the simple passage of time, but in another, more mysterious way, closer to both real life and theatrical representation. You feel that you have surpassed all the faces of your life, those of the actor and those of the man, those of the star and those of the lover, those of the role and those of flesh and blood.

All your faces are becoming superimposed in this poor, worn mirror with the rusting frame and insincere reflections. You are, in this moment you live through with fear like a throbbing announcement of approaching death, everything you have been. You are resigned to this fatality. You are grateful for it as well. You never imagined that the perfect film—simultaneous and successive, instantaneous and discursive—of all your moments would be presented to you in life. You enjoy this, even if you are resigned to the fatality of summarizing your entire past. Even if you suspect it signifies that you won't have a future.

It is the moment when your son appears behind you in the mirror and looks at you looking at yourself. And you look at him looking at you. He looks at himself in you. He places his small, stunted hand on your shoulder. You feel the pressure of his cold fingers as part of your own flesh.

5. The Plaza de los Arcos de Belén near the Salto del Agua attracts the same working-class audience that frequents the so-called frivolous theaters in the center of the city as well as the anonymous bars, the dens where they still sing boleros, the dance halls where the danzón and the cha-cha-cha survive, the old lunchrooms with awnings that serve pozole, the few Chinese cafés that remain.

It is a peculiarity of this city that the arches and the canal that once ran through here celebrate the memory of an old lacustrine capital whose springs began to dry up until the entire valley was transformed into a saucer of dust surrounded by thirst and dead trees. Not long ago they finished setting up here one of those fairs that in every neighborhood of the immense capital of Mexico are, at times, the only solace of people of no means, which are the immense majority. My father and I see the numerous reality of our people in the Zócalo on the night of September 15, in the Villa de Guadalupe on December 12, on Sundays in Chapultepec, at any hour in the great human serpent of Tacuba in the center, of Andrés Molina in Santa Anita, of the Highway de la Piedad, the Highway de Tlalpan, the Highway Ignacio Zaragoza going to Puebla, and the Indios Verdes going north.

There are people.

There is an audience.

The fair at the Arcos de Belén has been assembling all kinds of attractions, from the wheel of fortune to the octopus, from the carousel to fortune-telling birds, from hawkers of remedies—sciatica, impotence, nightmares, calluses, bad blood, good life—to the wizards and diviners stationed at the corners with their crystal balls and star-covered pointed hats and several mariachi groups (the young star of the ranchera Maximiliano Batalla) and bolero singers (the retired songstress Elvira Morales). Weight lifters, failed tenors, big-bellied odalisques, certified veterans of the Revolution and improbable horsemen of the Empire, declaimers of immensely popular verses (Toast of the Bohemian; Nocturne for Rosario; Margarita, the Sea Is Beautiful). Reciters of the Constitution, memorizers of the telephone book, voices with the singsong of the lottery, with the buzz of neighborhood gossip, the acidity of balcony slanderers, the tears of unemployed circus clowns.

People come here five times a week, five nights in a row (the authorities don't give seven-day permits in order to exercise authority in something). They come to have a good time with the spectacle of the armless teenager who, with long, strong legs, trips the old musketeer who threatens him with a little aluminum sword, and each time the old man attacks the boy, he extends his leg and makes the musketeer ostentatiously take a tremendous fall, to the delight of the audience. Applause whistles and shouts.

"How much?"

"Whatever you wish."

6. In this way, my father and I managed to save enough to buy a VCR, and now the two of us can enjoy old movies brought back to life, clean, remastered, and in Dolby Digital, together we can see Edmundo Dan-

tés escape the Castle of If in the shroud of Abbot Faria, D'Artagnan presenting the jewels of the Duke of Buckingham to the queen, Emilio de Rocabruna approaching the coast of Maracaibo under the black flags of the corsairs.

"Who's the girl who falls in love with Zorro, Father?"

"Why do you ask?"

"I think she's very pretty."

"She's just a foreigner, Sandokán, a bit player, a soubrette, as they used to say in the old days. She's of no importance."

Chorus of the Children of Good Families

Fito bored sunday afternoon
he's unfailing
he doesn't pass unnoticed
he's good-looking
he's superfine
a terrific time incredibly stoned
high as an eagle
cool cool cool
but he's bored
he comes from a decent family nice fine
he has manners
he has servants
his mom and dad call them rude coarse untrustworthy trash bums
indians
but would never say it
his mommy and daddy feel more than disgusting
disgust: mexica louts
that's why he organizes the group of pissers
to water the roses for them and give enough to their vegetables
the ones who are unfailing the nice ones the crème hey hey
now guys we fly over the wall
don't fly over it, better aim at it
wanna see who has better aim hey?
no Fito my friend, hold on a little, drink another magnum all by
yourself and when you can't
hold it anymore we'll aim at the wall but just remember that first we
drink

until we die and before we die we aim at the wall to see who pisses more and better
because Fito got bored with sunday afternoons with the society girls at the cool
parties where he's very good-looking and superfine
where everybody has a terrific time
except him
he wants strong sensations
to tell all the nice people like him to go to hell
all the society girls
and that's why he comes to pee on his father-in-law's wall
with his golden buddies
aiming at the wall
whoever pees the farthest wins a trip to las vegas with babes who make you stand up and salute hey hey
and that noise?
and that noise ay?
and that ay—dammit!
naco guys with their knives and machetes assaulting the children of good families
hey where'd they come from?
from penitenciaría and héroe de nacozari and albañiles and canal del norte
how did they get here?
by subway my fella citzens
since there's been a subway we come out like ants scorpions moles from the black holes
of the siddy
with knives and machetes to assault
come to cut
in one slice the ones that have stopped
to slash the ones that are sleepy
to cut cock you bastards
now get them together

the pigs
let the boars in and the dogs
let the animals eat sausages
let them bleed
look at them vomit
look at them covering the wounds
look at the blood running down their thighs
look at them look at them look at them
sunday afternoon what a handsome birthday boy in the show on the
 tube everything very lively
a terrific time
an unbelievable time
at the father-in-law's wall
and whoever shouts put his own chile in his mouth
you never thought about that bastard
about sucking yourself bleeding bastard
and now what will your girlfriends say a bunch of rich fuckers
and now how will you father more fucking children rich castrated
 fuckers
sons of mufuckin
it's a dream right?
it's a nightmare isn't it?
seal off all the subway exits
let's go with the cute girls for the weekend
let's run away
to get married have children go to the club fly to nuyor
send the children to school
fondle their nursemaids
and now the only children will be ours
fucking children
there are millions of us
nobody can stop us

The Discomfiting Brother

1. Don Luis Albarrán had his house in order. When his wife, Doña Matilde Cousiño, died, he was afraid that as a widower, his life would become disorganized. At the age of sixty-five, he felt more than enough drive to continue at the head of the construction company La Pirámide. What he feared was that the rear guard of that other security, Doña Matilde's domestic front, would collapse, affecting his life at home as well as his professional activities.

Now he realized there was nothing to fear. He transferred the same discipline he used in conducting his business to domestic arrangements. Doña Matilde had left a well-trained staff, and it was enough for Don Luis to repeat the orders of his deceased wife to have the household machinery continue to function like clockwork. Not only that: At first the replacement of the Señora by the

Señor caused a healthy panic among the servants. Soon fear gave way to respect. But Don Luis not only made himself respected, he made himself loved. For example, he found out the birthday of all his employees and gave each one a gift and the day off.

The truth is that now Don Luis Albarrán did not know if he felt prouder of his efficiency in business or his efficiency at home. He gave thanks to Doña Matilde and her memory that a mansion in the Polanco district, built in the 1940s when neocolonial residences became fashionable in Mexico City, had preserved not only its semi-Baroque style but also the harmony of a punctual, chronometric domesticity in which everything was in its place and everything was done at the correct time. From the garden to the kitchen, from the garage to the bathroom, from the dining room to the bedroom, when he returned from the office, Don Luis found everything just as he had left it when he went to work.

The cook, María Bonifacia, the chambermaid, Pepita, the butler, Truchuela, the chauffeur, Jehová, the gardener, Cándido . . . The staff was not only perfect but silent. Señor Albarrán did not need to exchange words with a single servant to have everything in its place at the correct time. He did not even need to look at them.

At nine in the evening, in pajamas, robe, and slippers, when he sat in the wingback chair in his bedroom to eat a modest light meal of foaming hot chocolate and a sweet roll, Don Luis Albarrán could anticipate a night of recuperative sleep with the spiritual serenity of having honored, for another day, the sweet memory of his loyal companion, Matilde Cousiño, a Chilean who had until the day of her death a southern beauty with those green eyes that rivaled the cold of the South Pacific and were all that had been left to her of a body slowly defeated by the relentless advance of cancer.

Matilde: Illness only renewed her firm spirit, her character immune to any defeat. She said that Chilean women (she pronounced it "wimmen") were like that, strong and decisive. They made up for—this was her theory—a certain weak sweetness in the men of her country, so cordial until the day their treble voices turned into commanding, cruel voices. Then the woman's word would appear with all its gift for finding a balance between tenderness and strength.

They had a happy love life in bed, a "carousing" counterpoint, Don Luis would say, in two daily lives that were so serious and orderly until the illness and death of his wife left the widower momentarily disconcerted, possessed of all obligations—office and home—and bereft of all pleasures.

The staff responded. They all knew the routine. Doña Matilde Cousiño came from an old Chilean family and was trained in ruling over the estates of the south and the elegant mansions of Providencia, and she inculcated in her Mexican staff virtues with which they, the domestic crew of the Polanco district, were not unfamiliar and normally accepted. The only novelty for Don Luis was having, when he returned home, elevenses, the amiable Chilean version of British afternoon tea: cups of verbena with teacakes, dulce de leche, and almond pastries. Don Luis told himself that this and a good wine cellar of Chilean reds were the only exotic details Doña Matilde Cousiño introduced into the mansion in Polanco. The staff continued the Chilean custom. Given Mexican schedules, however (office from ten to two, dinner from two to four, final business items from four to six), Don Luis had elevenses a little later, at seven in the evening, though this sweet custom cut his appetite for even the monastic meal he ate at nine.

Doña Matilde Cousiño, as it turned out, died on Christmas Eve, so for Don Luis, December 24 was a day of mourning, solitude, and remembrance. Between the night of the twenty-fourth and the morning of the twenty-fifth, Señor Albarrán dismissed the servants and remained alone, recalling the details of life with Matilde, perusing the objects and rooms of the house, kneeling at the bed his wife occupied at the end of her life, playing records of old Chilean tunes and Mexican boleros that choked him with romantic and sexual nostalgia, going through photograph albums, and preparing rudimentary meals with odds and ends, gringo cereals and spoonfuls of Coronado jelly. He had a sweet tooth, it was true, he saw nothing wrong in sweetening his bitterness and something sinful in stopping at a mirror hoping to see the face of his lost love, and the sorrow that ensued when he discovered only a closely shaved face, an aquiline nose, eyes with increasingly drooping lids, a broad forehead, and graying hair vigorously brushed straight back.

The doorbell rang at eight on the evening of December 24. Don Luis was surprised. The entire staff had left. The days of asking for lodgings were over, destroyed by the city's dangers, and still the voice on the other side of the door of corrugated glass and wrought iron sang the Christmas song,

iiiiin the name of heaaaaa-ven
I ask yooоou for loooodg-ing . . .

Don Luis, incapable of admitting his incipient deafness, approached the door, trying to make out the silhouette outlined behind the opaque panes. The voice, obviously, was a caricature of childish tones; the height of the silhouette was that of an adult.

"Who is it?"

"Guess, good guesser."

Dissolute, unruly, strewing the same destructive actions no matter where he was or whom he was with, at home or outside. The news had arrived: He was the same as always. Thirty-four forgotten years returned at one stroke, making Don Luis Albarrán's extended hand tremble as he wavered between opening the door to his house or saying to the suspect phantom,

"Go away. I never want to see you again. What do you want of me? Get away. Get away."

2. Reyes Albarrán had been given that name because he was born on January 5, a holiday that, in the Latino world, celebrates the arrival of the Santos Reyes, Melchor, Gaspar, and Baltasar, bearing gifts of gold, frankincense, and myrrh to the stable in Bethlehem. Centuries before the appearance of Santa Claus, children in Mexico and Chile, Spain and Argentina, celebrated the Day of the Kings as the holiday with

presents and homemade sweets, culminating in the ceremony of the rosca de reyes, the ring-shaped kings' cake inside which is hidden a little white porcelain figure of Baby Jesus.

Tradition dictates that whoever cuts the piece of cake that hides the baby is bound to give a party on the second day of the following month, February, and every month after that. Few get past the month of March. Nobody can endure an entire year of Christmas parties. The last time he saw his brother, Don Luis received from him a rosca de reyes with twelve little dolls of Baby Jesus, one next to the other. It was a treacherous invitation from Reyes to Luis: "Invite me every month, brother."

Matilde said it: "On top of everything else, he's a scrounger. I don't want to see him again. Not even as a delivery boy."

When Luis Albarrán, moved by an uncontrollable mixture of blameworthy argumentativeness, buried fraternity, seignorial arrogance, unconscious valor, but especially shameful curiosity, opened the door of his house on that December 24, the first thing he saw was the outstretched hand with the little porcelain doll held between thumb and index finger. Don Luis felt the offense of the contrast between the pulchritude of the doll and the grime of the cracked fingers, the broken nails edged in black, the shredded shirt cuff.

"What do you want, Reyes?" said Luis abruptly. With his brother, courtesy was not merely excessive. It was a dangerous invitation.

"Lodging, brother, hospitality," a voice as cracked as the fingers replied from the darkness. It was a voice broken by cheap alcohol: A stink of rum lashed the nostrils of Don Luis Albarrán like an ethylic whip.

"It isn't—" he began to say, but the other man, Reyes Albarrán, had already pushed him away to come into the vestibule. Don Luis stood to one side, almost like a doorman, and rapidly closed the door as if he feared that a tribe of beggars, drunkards, and sots would come in on the heels of his undesirable brother.

He repeated: "What do you want?"

The other man guffawed, and his Potrero rum breath floated toward the living room. "Look at me and you tell me."

Don Luis stood outside the bathroom listening to his brother singing "Amapola" in a loud off-key voice, splashing with joy and punctuating his song with paleo-patriotic observations: "Only—Veracruz—is—beautiful, howprettyismichoacán, Ay! Chihuahua! What! Apache!" as if the guest wanted to indicate that for the past three and a half decades, he had traveled the entire republic. Only because of a trace of decency, perhaps, he did not sing "Ay Jalisco, don't brag."

And if not the entire republic, Reyes had traveled—Don Luis said with alarmed discretion—its lowest, most unfortunate neighborhoods, its black holes, its spider nests, its overgrown fields of bedbugs, lice, and chancres, its maw of ashes, mud, and garbage. It was enough to look at the pile of dirty, frayed clothing riddled with holes, and its grayish tone, with no real color or form: Reyes Albarrán had left all this—the rags of wretchedness—at the bathroom door. With repugnance, the master of the house smelled his acrid armpits, the crust of his asshole, the bitter intimacy of his pubis.

He closed his eyes and tried to imagine the handsome, intelligent boy who, at the age of twenty-four, ruled over the most exclusive bar in Mexico City, the Rendez-Vous, facing the traffic circle of the Angel of Independence, when the capital had two and not twenty million inhabitants, when all the known people really did know one another and would meet at the Rendez-Vous, where, with luck, night after night, you would see one of the many celebrities who, in those days, frequented the exotic Mexican metropolis—John Steinbeck, Paulette Goddard, Aaron Copland, Virginia Hill. The so-called most transparent region, still wearing the halo of the recent glories of European exile and the distant fires of the Mexican Revolution.

Reyes Albarrán not only made cocktails. He was a cocktail. He mixed languages, references, gossip, jokes, he played the piano, he sang Agustín Lara and Cole Porter, combed his hair with pomade, imitated Gardel, introduced surprising mixtures of alcohol with irresistible names—the Manhattan, the sidecar, the Tom Collins—attempted to bring together necessary and dissimilar couples, urged homosexuals and lesbians to show themselves without complexes, impelled boys ruined by the Revolution to fall in love with girls enriched by the same event, deceived the Hungarian princess dispossessed by Communism into marrying the false rogue without a cent posing as a petro-millionaire from Tabasco. Between drinks, he imagined them all, learning on their wedding night that between the two of them—the princess and the rogue—they couldn't put two eggs in the refrigerator.

"My specialty is launching penury in pursuit of wealth," he would say, the sophisticated Reyes Albarrán with his elbow on the bar and a gin fizz in his hand.

But the clientele—*hélas!*—began to understand that the owner of the Rendez-Vous was a mocker, a gossip, a cruel and talkative man, even if he tended bar with burlesque religious solemnity, serving each drink with an "ego baptiso te whiskey sour" and closing the establishment at the hour prescribed by law with a no less mocking "Ite Bacchus est."

He loved, in other words, to humiliate his clients while pretending to protect them. But since the clients eventually saw the light, rancor and suspicion accumulated around Reyes Albarrán. He knew too many secrets, he laughed at his own mother, he could put an end to many reputations by means of gossip columns and whispered slander. They began to abandon him.

And the city was growing, the fashionable places changed like serpents shedding skin, social barriers fell, exclusive groups became reclusive or inclusive, the names of the old families no longer meant anything, those of the new families changed with each presidential term before they retired to enjoy their six-year fortunes, engagements to be married were determined by distances, the new Outer Ring dictated debuts, dates, angers, punctual loves, lost friendships . . . Luxury and the places that were frequented moved from the Juárez district to the Zona Rosa to Avenida Masaryk, right here in the Polanco district where the shipwrecked survivor of the postwar period, the pomaded and seductive Reyes Albarrán, had been tossed up one Christmas Eve to knock on the door of his solid old brother, the punctual and industrious Don Luis Albarrán, a recent widower, undoubtedly in need of the fraternal company of the equally needy bartender who had ended as a drunkard, forgetting the golden rule: To be a good saloon keeper, you also have to be a good abstainer.

A drunkard, a pianist in an elegant boîte who ended up pounding the keys in the brothels of the Narvarte district like Hipólito el de Santa, a pomaded seducer of European princesses who ended up living at the expense of rumberas in decline, a waiter in funky holes and, with luck, dives close to the Zócalo, the Plaza Mayor where, more than once, he was found sleeping, wrapped in newspapers, awakened by the clubs of the heartless Technicolor gendarmerie of the increasingly dangerous metropolis. Cops, blue, tamarind, all of them on the take, except what could they put the bite on him for except hunger? Stumbling through the entire republic in search of luck, not finding it, stealing bus tickets and lottery tickets, the first bringing more fortune than the second, carrying him far and sinking him into being broke until the doctor in Ciudad Juárez told him, "You're no longer the man you were, Señor Albarrán. You've lived a long time. It isn't that you're sick. You're just worn out. I mean exhausted. You can't do any more. The wind's gone out of you. I see that you're over seventy. I advise you to retire. For your own good."

If some buried tenderness remained in Don Luis Albarrán toward his older brother, Reyes Albarrán (the "Don" didn't come off even as a joke), the implacable Chilean Doña Matilde Cousiño had kept him from bringing it to the surface: "That filthy beggar doesn't set foot in my house. Don't let yourself be ruled by affection, Lucho. Your brother had everything, and he threw it all away. Let him live in his shanties. He doesn't come in here. Not while I'm alive. No, Señor."

But she wasn't alive now. Though her will was. That night Don

"Lucho" Albarrán felt as never before the absence of his willful wife. She would have thrown the discomfiting brother out on the street with a sonorous, very Chilean:

"Get the hell out of here, you damn ragged beggar!"

3. As tends to happen to most human beings, Don Luis Albarrán woke up in a bad mood. If sleeping is an anticipation of death, then it is a warm, comfortable, welcoming announcement. If dreaming is death, then it is the great open door of hospitality. Everything in that kingdom is possible. Everything we desire lies within reach. Sex. Money. Power. Food and drink. Imaginary landscapes. The most interesting people. Connections to celebrity, authority, mystery. Of course, an oneiric counterpart exists. One dreams of accidents. Dreams are dimensions of our circulation, and as Doña Matilde would say,

"Lucho, don't be an asshole. We're nothing but accidents of our circulation."

Except that accidents in a dream tend to be absurd. Walking naked down the street is the prototype. Or they can be mortal. Falling from the top floor of a skyscraper, like King Kong. Except at that moment the angel sent by Morpheus wakes us, the dream is interrupted, and then we give it an ugly name, *pesadilla*. Borges, said the very southern and well-read Doña Matilde, detested that terrible word and wondered why we didn't have a good word in Spanish for a bad dream, for example, *nightmare* or *cauchemar*.

Don Luis recalled these ideas of his Chilean dreamer regarding dreams, and he prayed as he was falling precisely into the arms of Morpheus:

"Get away, *pesadilla*. Welcome, *cauchemar*, hidden sea, invisible ocean of dreams, welcome, *nightmare,* nocturnal mare, mount of the darkness. Welcome to you both, drive the ugly Spanish *pesadilla* away from me."

Don Luis awoke that morning convinced that his bad mood was the usual one upon opening his eyes and that a good Mexican breakfast of spicy huevos rancheros and steaming coffee from Coatepec would be enough to return him to reality.

The newspaper carefully opened on the table by Truchuela, the butler, noisily displayed news much worse than the worst personal dream. Once again the world was on its head, and the *pesadillas, cauchemars,* or *nightmares* of the previous night seemed mere fairy tales compared to ordinary reality. Except that this morning the austere face of Truchuela, as long and sour as that of any actor cast in the role of a butler with a long, sour face,[1] was more sour and longer than usual. And in case Don Luis didn't notice, Truchuela filled the cup to the brim with coffee and even dared to spill it.

"The Señor will please excuse me."

"What?" said a distracted Don Luis, bewitched by his effort to decipher the tongue twisters of high Mexican officials.

"Excuse me. I spilled the coffee."

No expression of Don Luis's justified what Truchuela wanted to say:

"The Señor will forgive me, but the unexpected guest in the blue bedroom—"

"He is not unexpected," said Don Luis with a certain severity. "He is my brother."

"So he said," Truchuela agreed. "It was difficult for us to accept that."

"Us? How many are *you,* Truchuela?" Don Luis replied with a growing irritation, directed at himself more than at the perfect servant imported from Spain and accustomed to waiting on the superior clientele of El Bodegón in Madrid.

"We are *all of us,* Señor."

From this it appeared that Reyes, installed in the blue bedroom in less than a morning following the return of the staff, had demanded:

a) That he be served breakfast in bed. A request fulfilled by the

[1]The Mexican Luis G. Barreiro or the Englishman Alan Mowbray—Author's note.

chambermaid, Pepita, whom Reyes ordered to let him sleep postprandially (Truchuela's preferred expression) until noon before returning (Pepita) to run the water in the bath (tub) and sprinkle it with lavender salts.

b) That the cook, María Bonifacia, come up to the top floor (something she had never done) to receive orders regarding the menu to be followed not only today but for all breakfasts hereafter (marrow soup, brain quesadillas, chicken with bacon and almonds, pork in wine sauce, and also pigs' feet, everything can be used, yellow *mole,* stuffed cheese from Yucatán, smoked meat, jerked beef, and ant eggs in season.

" 'Señor Don Luis eats simpler food, he isn't going to like your menu, Señor—?'

" 'Reyes. Reyes Albarrán. I'm your employer's brother.'

"Yes, Señor Don Luis, he said everything 'in quotation marks,' " the butler affirmed.

"And what else?" Don Luis inquired, certain that no new petro-war of Mr. Bush's would be worse news than what came next from the mouth of Truchuela.

"He ordered that the gardener, Cándido, be told that there are no roses in his bedroom. That he is accustomed to having roses in his bedroom."

"Roses?" Don Luis said with a laugh, imagining the prickly pears that must have been the habitual landscape for his unfortunate vagabond brother.

"And he has asked Jehová the chauffeur to have the Mercedes ready at three this afternoon to take him shopping at the Palacio de Hierro."

"Modest."

" 'I'm totally Palacio,' said your . . . brother?" The impassive Truchuela broke; he could contain himself no longer. "Your brother, Señor Don Luis? How can that be? That—"

"Say it, Truchuela, don't bite your tongue. That vagrant, that bum, that tramp, that beggar, that *clochard,* they exist everywhere and have a name, don't limit yourself."

"As you say, Señor." The butler bowed his head.

"Well yes, Truchuela, he is my brother. An unwelcome Christmas gift, I admit. His name is Reyes, and he will be my guest until the Day of the Kings, January 5. From now until that date—ten days—I ask you to tell the staff to treat him as a gentleman, no matter how difficult it may be for them. Put up with his insolence. Accept his whims. I'll know how to show my gratitude."

"The Señor does honor to his well-known generosity."

"All right, Truchuela. Tell Jehová to have the car ready to go to the office. And to come back for my brother at three."

"As the Señor wishes."

When he was back in the kitchen, Truchuela said, "The Señor is a model gentleman."

"He's a saintly soul," contributed the cook, María Bonifacia.

"He's nuts," said the gardener, Cándido. "Roses in January are only for the Virgin of Guadalupe. Let him be happy with daisies."

"Let him go push them up," an indignant Pepita said with a laugh. "A bum dying of hunger."

"Push them up? What, the daisies?" Cándido asked with a smile.

"Yes, but not my butt, which is what he tried to do when he asked me to dry him when he got out of the tub."

"And what did you do?" they all asked at once, except for the circumspect Truchuela.

"I told him to dry himself, dirty old man, jerk with big hands."

"He'll complain about you to the boss."

"No, he won't! He just laughed and shook his wrinkled dried-up prick with his hand. It was like the ones on those old monkeys in the zoo. 'Keep your chipotle pepper to yourself,' I said to the indecent old creep. 'Little but delicious,' sang the old son of a bitch."

"Pepita, don't risk your job," said the prudent María Bonifacia.

"I can have plenty of jobs, Doña Boni, I'm not ready to be thrown away like you."

"Respect my gray hairs, you stupid girl."

"Better if I pull them out, you miserable old woman."

The three men separated the women. Truchuela laid down the law:

"Don't let this unwanted guest have his way and make us enemies. We're a staff that gets along. Isn't that true, Pepita?"

The chambermaid agreed and bowed her head. "I'm sorry, María Bonifacia."

The cook caressed Pepita's dark braided head. "My girl. You know I love you."

"So," dictated Truchuela, "we'll serve *Don* Reyes Albarrán. No complaints, kids. Just information. We obey the boss. But we let the boss know."

Unusually for the month of January, a downpour fell on the city, and everyone went to tend to duties except the gardener, who sat down to read the crime newspaper *Alarma!*

4. Don Luis Albarrán had decided that the best way to dispatch his discomfiting brother was to treat him like a beloved guest. Charm him first and then dispatch him. That is: January 6, bye-bye, and if I saw you, I don't remember. This was the grand plan of the master of the house. He counted on the patience and loyalty of the servants to bring his scheme to a successful conclusion.

"I have no other recourse," he said to the spirit, accusatory from the grave, of his adored Doña Matilde.

Certainly, Don Luis tried to avoid Reyes as much as possible. But an encounter was inevitable, and the discomfiting brother took it upon himself to have his supper served in Don Luis's bedroom in order to have him captive at least once a day, in view of Don Luis's daily flights to the office (while Reyes slept until noon) or business lunches (while Reyes had himself served Pantagruelian, typically Mexican lunches) or his return from the office (while Reyes went "shopping" at the Palacio de Hierro, since he had no money and had to content himself with looking).

Until Don Luis saw Jehová come in with a outsize tower of packages that he carried up to the bedroom of *Don* Reyes.

"What's that?" an irritated Don Luis inquired.

"Today's purchases," Jehová answered very seriously.

"Today's purchases? Whose?"

"Your brother's, Señor. Every day he goes shopping at the Palacio de Hierro." The chauffeur smiled sardonically. "I think he's going to buy out all their stock." He added with singular impudence: "The truth is, he doesn't buy things just for himself but for everybody."

"Everybody?" Don Luis's irritated perplexity increased.

"Sure. A miniskirt for Pepita, new gloves for the gardener, a flowered Sunday dress for Doña Boni, Wagner's operas for Truchuela, he listens to them in secret—"

"And for you?" Don Luis put on his most severe expression.

"Well, a real chauffeur's cap, navy blue with a plastic visor and gold trim. What you never bothered to give me, and that's the damn truth."

"Show some respect, Jehová!"

"As you wish, Señor," replied the chauffeur with a crooked, mischievous, irritating little smile that once would have been the prelude to dismissal. Except that Jehová was too good a chauffeur, when most had gone to drive trucks across the border in the era of NAFTA.

In any case, how did he dare?

"How nice." Don Luis smiled affably when Truchuela brought him his usual light meal of chocolate and pastries, and for Reyes, sitting now across from his brother, a tray filled with enchiladas suizas, roasted strips of chile peppers, fritters, omelets, and a couple of Corona beers.

"Sure, give it your best," replied Reyes.

"I see you're well served."

"It was time." Reyes began to chew. He was dressed in a red velvet robe, blue slippers, and a Liberty ascot.

"Time for what?"

"Time to say goodbye, Luisito."

"I repeat, time for what? Haven't I treated you like a brother? Haven't I kept my Christmas promise? You will be my guest until tomorrow, the Day of the Kings, and—"

"And then kick me out on the street?" The discomfiting brother almost choked on his laughter.

"No. To each his own life," Don Luis said in a hesitant voice.

"The fact is, I'm having a fantastic time. The fact is, my life now is here, at the side of my adored *fratellino*."

"Reyes," Don Luis said with his severest expression. "We made a deal. Until January sixth."

"Don't make me laugh, Güichito. Do you think that in a week you can wipe away the crimes of an entire life?"

"I don't know what you're talking about. We haven't seen each other in thirty years."

"That's the point. You don't keep very good accounts." Reyes swallowed a chalupa and licked the cream from his lips with his tongue. "Sixty years, I'm telling you . . . You were so solemn as a boy. The favorite son. You condemned me to second place. The clown of the house."

"You were older than me. You could have affirmed your position as firstborn. It isn't my fault if—"

"Why should I drag out the story? You were the studious one. The punctual one. The traitor. The schemer. Do you think I didn't hear you tell our father: 'Reyes does everything wrong, he's a boy with no luck, he's going to hurt us all, Papa, get him out of the house, send him to boarding school.' "

Reyes was swallowing chalupas whole. "Do you remember when we both went to Mass together every Sunday, Luisito? Ah, we were believers. It's what hurts me most. Having lost my faith. And you're to blame, little brother."

Don Luis had to laugh. "You astonish me, Reyes."

"No." Reyes laughed. "I'm the one who's astonished. You're only stupefied. You must have thought you'd never see me again."

"You're right. I don't want to see you again. On the sixth, you—"

"I what? Recover my innocence?"

Luis looked at him gravely. "When were you ever innocent?"

"Until the day you said to me: 'Asshole, we go to Mass every Sunday, but we don't believe in God, we only believe in ourselves, in our personal success, don't go around thinking Divine Providence will come to help you. Look at yourself, Reyes, so overgrown and so devout, look at your younger brother, I tell you, I go to Mass to please Papa and Mama, the family, while you, Reyes, you go because you believe in God and religion, what a joke, the younger brother is smarter than the older brother, the baby knows more than the big galoot. And what does the baby know? That you come into this world to be successful with no scruples, to beat out everybody else, to move ahead over other people's good faith or conviction or morality.' "

He took a foaming drink of beer, tilting back the bottle. "Nobody believes my story, brother. How can it be that the little brother *corrupts* the older one? Because you corrupted me, Luis. You left me with a *malignant* relationship to the world. I saw you move up, marry a rich girl, manipulate politicians, negotiate favors, and in passing rip out my innocence."

"A carouser. You had a vocation for dissipation."

"How could I believe in the good with a diabolical brother like you?"

"A tree that grows twisted—"

"God made you like that, or did you betray God Himself?"

"Soul of a delinquent—"

"Did you betray God, or did God betray you?"

Don Luis choked on a biscuit. His brother stood up to pound him on the back and didn't stop talking.

"I wanted an ordered, simple life. Your example stopped me. You moved up so quickly. Ha, like the foam on this brew. You were so greedy. You know how to use people and then throw them into the trash. Your diabolical wife gave you feudal tips. The arrogance of Chilean landowners. And you spiced up the stew with Mexican malice, fawning, climbing, betraying, using."

"Water . . ." Luis coughed.

"Ah yes, Señor." Reyes moved away the glass. "Everything in order to reach the age of sixty-five with a gorgeous house in Polanco, five-count-'em-five servants, eight board presidencies, a dead wife, and a boozing brother."

"You are what you wanted to be, a poor devil." Don Luis coughed. "I didn't force you."

"Yes." With a blow of his hand, Reyes knocked the tray of chocolate and biscuits to the floor. "Yes! You challenged me to emulate you, and I didn't know how." His eyes filled with tears. "You lent me the dough to set up a bar."

"And you got drunk making your customers drunk, you poor idiot," Don Luis replied, using his napkin to wipe the mess of chocolate and crumbs from his shirt and lap.

"I wanted to be consistent in my vices," Reyes said with misplaced pride. "Just like you."

"Pick up what you knocked down."

Reyes, smiling, obeyed. Don Luis stood, went to the desk, sat, wrote out a check, tore it from the checkbook, and offered it to Reyes.

"Take it. It's ten thousand dollars. Take the check and get out right now."

His brother took the check, tore it into pieces, and threw them in Don Luis's face. "There's no need. I can imitate your signature. Ask them in the shops. I bought everything on your signature, friend. Ask your servants. Everything I've bought has been with your checks signed by me." He brought his face and his mouthfuls of tortilla up to his brother's face. "You look confused. That's why I'll say it again. Signed by you." He moved away, satisfied. "It's an art I learned in order to survive."

In one hand, Reyes flapped Don Luis's checkbook like the wing of a wounded bird, and in the other, he waved a silver American Express card. "Look, brother. Life consists in our getting used to the fact that everything will go badly for us."

5. "No, what do you mean, Don Luis, your brother is a saint. Imagine, he ordered a marble stone for my dear mother's grave in Tulancingo. I always wanted that, boss, seeing how everybody walks on a grave without a stone, nobody respects a grave marked with little stones and a couple of carnations. And now, thanks to Señor Reyes, my dear

mother rests in peace and devotion. And I say to myself, María Bonifacia, God bless the boss's brother."

"Well, Señor, I've been driving your Mercedes for what? Twelve years? And at the end of the day, what do I have? Taking the bus and traveling an hour to my house. You never thought about that, did you? Well your brother did, he did. 'Go on, Jehová, here are the keys to your 1934 Renault. You have a right to your own car. What did you think? You'll never ride a bus again. Of course you won't.' "

"Imagine, boss, I go back to my village on Sunday, and they welcome me with wreaths of flowers saying THANK YOU CÁNDIDO. You know that on the road to Xochimilco, there's water but no land. Now I have land and water, and my children can take care of cultivating flowers, thanks to the piece of land your brother gave us, that saint."

"Oh, boss, I'm sorry for the bad impression of your brother I gave you. For years in my village of Zacatlán de las Manzanas, we've been asking for a school for the girls because as soon as they're twelve, they're deflowered, as they say, and loaded down with kids, and they have to go to work in a rich man's house, like me. And now the village has a school and a gift of scholarships so the girls can keep studying until they're sixteen, and then they leave with a diploma and are secretaries or nurses and not just maids like me, and they come to their weddings pure, your brother's so kind, Don Luisito!"

"The complete works of Wagner. Do you realize what that means, Señor Don Luis? The dream of my life. Before I'd save enough for an opera here, a bel canto selection there . . . No, damn it, begging the Señor's pardon, now the complete works of Don Ricardo, let's hope I live long enough to listen to all the CDs, a gift from your brother. Don Luis, it was a lucky day when he came to live in this house."

6. Morning after morning, Don Luis Albarrán woke with his head full of good intentions. Each evening, Reyes Albarrán came with a new, bad, and worse intention.

"I'm going to imagine that you're a dream," Don Luis told him with an evil look.

"Don't hide from the world anymore, Güichito."

"I'm afraid of unfortunate people like you. They bring bad luck."

"We're brothers. Let's bury the truth in the deepest grave."

"Get out of here."

"You invited me. Be sensible."

"Sensible! You came into my house like an animal. A beast lying in ambush. You're a parasite. And you've turned all my employees into parasites."

"The parasites of a parasite."

"Leave me alone. For just one day. Please," Don Luis shouted and rose to his feet, exasperated.

"What are you afraid of?" replied Reyes very calmly.

"Unfortunate people. The evil eye. Unfortunate people like you bring us bad luck. Bad luck is contagious. A jinx."

Reyes laughed. "So you have the soul of a Gypsy and a minstrel . . . Look, your cynicism toward religion, which I reminded you of the other day, came with a price, Luisito. Since we didn't perform the penance of the Church, we have to perform the penance of life."

"Penance? You filthy bum, I don't—"

"Do you even look at your servants? Have you smelled your cook up close, saturated with the aromas of your damn huevos rancheros for breakfast? Tell me the truth, brother, how many people *do you know*? How many people have you *really* gotten close to? Do you live only for the next administrative board?"

Reyes took Luis by the shoulders and shook him violently. The businessman's glasses fell off. With one hand, Reyes tousled Luis's hair.

"Answer me, junior."

Don Luis Albarrán stammered, stunned by bewilderment, injury, impotence, the mental flash that told him, "Everything I can do against my brother, my brother can do against me."

"And even worse, Luisito. Who looks at you? Really, who *looks* at you?" Reyes let Luis go with a twisted smile, half boastful, half melancholy. "You live in the ruin of yourself, brother."

"I'm a decent man." Don Luis composed himself. "I don't harm anybody. I'm compassionate."

"Compassion doesn't harm anybody?" The discomfiting brother pretended to be amazed. "Do you believe that?"

"No. Not anybody."

"Compassion insults the one who receives it. As if I didn't know that."

"Cynic. You've shown compassion to all my servants."

"No. I've given them what each one deserved. I think that's the definition of justice, isn't it?" Reyes walked to the door of the bedroom and turned to wink at his brother. "Isn't it?"

7. "Permit me to express my astonishment to you, Don Luis."

"Tell me, Truchuela."

"Your brother—"

"Yes."

"He's gone."

Don Luis sighed. "Did he say what time he'd be back?"

"No. He said, 'Goodbye, Truchuela. Today is the Day of the Kings. The vacation's over. Tell my brother. I'm leaving forever, goodbye.' "

"Did he take anything with him?" Don Luis asked in alarm.

"No, Señor. That's the strangest part. He was wearing his beggar's clothes. He wasn't carrying suitcases or anything." The butler coughed. "He smelled bad."

"Ah yes. He smelled bad. That will be all, Truchuela."

That was all, Don Luis Albarrán repeated to himself as he slowly climbed the stairs to his bedroom. Everything would return to its normal rhythm. Everything would go back to what it had been before.

He stopped abruptly. He turned and went down to the first floor. He walked into the kitchen with a firm step. He realized he was seeing it for the first time. The servants were eating. They got to their feet. Don Luis gestured for them to sit down. Nobody dared to. Everything would go on as it always had.

Don Luis exchanged glances with each servant, one by one, "Do you ever look at your servants?" and he saw that nothing was the same. His employees' glances were no longer the same, the boss said to himself. How did he know if, in reality, he had never looked at them before? Precisely for that reason. They were no longer invisible. The routine had been broken. No, it wasn't a lack of respect. Looking at each one, he was certain about that.

It was a change in spirit that he could not distinguish but that he felt with the same physical intensity as a blow to the stomach. In a mysterious way, the routine of the house, though it would be repeated punctually from then on, from then on would no longer be the same.

"Will you all believe me?" said Don Luis in a very quiet voice.

"Señor?" inquired the butler, Truchuela.

"No, nothing." Don Luis shook his head. "What are you preparing in the oven, Bonifacia?"

"La rosca de reyes, Señor. Did you forget that today is the Day of the Kings?"

He left the kitchen on the way to his bedroom, on the way to his routine, on the way to his daily penance.

"From now on, everything will put me to the test," he said as he closed the door, looking at the photograph of the beautiful Chilean Matilde Cousiño out of the corner of his eye.

Yes, he said to himself, yes, I have known love.

He slept peacefully again.

Chorus of the Inspected Family

they gave him his death certificate on coffee-colored paper with a
hammered frame a water mark and the national seal of the eagle
and the serpent visible against the light
who's going to die?
I am
in fifteen minutes we declare you dead, it costs you fifteen hundred
pesos
who certifies it?
we have here the directory of medical forms, the doctor signs even
though he doesn't see the body, it'll be another fifteen hundred
pesos
three thousand?
it's very little to die in peace, the doctor's name and the medical
document confirm your death
what will I die of?
choose, it can be because a fish bone got caught in your throat
I never eat fish
very simple, the preferred death is by infarction, it leaves no trace
but my family, where will they pray for me?
the best thing is ashes in an urn
and my family?
they can be a dog's ashes, nobody will know
with this my widow can collect my insurance and pensions?
what, didn't you tell us you wanted to die so you wouldn't see your
wife and children anymore because they interfered with you?
yes, but I don't want to leave them out on the street
don't worry, we arrange everything with "those inside"
good, now I want to come back to life

of course, in fifteen minutes we'll have your new birth certificate, complete with official documentation and, if you like, a voting document and a taxpayer record
you pay taxes even when you're dead?
tell us, what name do you want
let me choose
here's a list from A to Z
well an A and a Z
Amador Zuleta
done
"Amador Zuleta" left the civil registry in Arcos de Belén renewed, breathing deeply, with a roll of bills in his pocket and a ticket on the Red Arrow line that would take him far from his former life, far from the capital, to the north, to a new life, an unknown family, loved for the mere fact that it was different and distinct from all the habits and phrases repeated ad infinitum of the family he was abandoning Mexico City–Ciudad Victoria–Monterrey–Nuevo Laredo
Amador Zuleta stood at the beginning of the longest highway in the republic and began to run to run to run

Conjugal Ties (2)

1. Leo Casares delights in the contemplation of his own space. The apartment on the top floor of an office building on Calle de Schiller. Leo chose it because by day the place is occupied by transitory employees, and by night the most absolute solitude reigns. Leo in his penthouse. Where he lives. His habitat. The private space of a bachelor with no family. The place where times meet freely. The past and the future in the present. The present in the past. The future of the present. Leo proposed to have the apartment reflect a constant will: to convoke all the moments of his life in a current of actual sensations. He spent years choosing furniture, lamps, curtains, tables, mirrors, and above all, *paintings* to give the sensation of permanent flow.

He would have liked each thing to be its own present on the condition of recalling and foretelling. A space like a crystal ball. Among all the objects in the apartment, Leo has chosen a painting as representative of his will. It is a work by the Japanese painter Katsushika Hokusai. It occupies an entire wall of Leo's bedroom. It is a portrait of a changing landscape. A wave rises, hiding the fogbound line of the coast. Or perhaps it is the coast that clouds the reality of the wave. The shore is incorporated into the surf. The sea disguises itself as shore. The elements fuse and are confused. The gray of the sea might reflect the green of the coast. The dawn of the dunes might nullify the chiaroscuro of the sky.

Leo contemplates the painting for hours. He is convinced that he sees in it what he wishes to see, not what the painting attempts to represent. He wonders if Hokusai has the same power over other viewers. How do women see it? "My women," says Leo in a quiet voice. "My two women." How?

2. The good thing about a mobile phone is that it allows you to lie, let us say, with mobility. You're not tied to the umbilical cord of a precise place. If your husband suspects, he answers the mobile; my husband leaves the message or I, the liar, answer it. Not a soul can find out. I was with you but told him I'm in the car on the way to the hairdresser.

Adultery was never so easy, Lavinia.

Don't use that ugly word.

What, then?

The *affaire*. You know, you just say the *affaire*.

My *affaire*, our *affaire*? And what will happen on the day when not only the number you're calling from but your face appears on the screen of your husband's telephone?

Shut up! I'll have to wear makeup even in the shower! But that isn't the point, Leo. Do you think Cristóbal will care if he finds out?

Please don't play with me. The danger is that he will care, and then he'll decide to conquer you.

Reconquer me, you mean.

Lavinia, forget about the arithmetic of coitus. A modern woman ought to deceive her husband as many times as he deceives her. Do you care?

I don't know. I'd like to take the lead. You understand.

What's stopping you?

You, my love. I'm unfaithful to you only with Cristóbal, no one else. Why am I telling you that! I'm unfaithful to you, and that's the truth.

Am I enough for you?

Look, Leo, a woman is always prepared to be adored. What counts is the intensity of the adoration, not the number of adorers. What a mess! You and my husband are more than enough for me, I swear.

Still, he and I give you different things.

Don't tempt me, Leo. I'm here in your arms, and the only thing that makes me feel I'm right is everything I despise in my husband. It's clear as crystal.

It's not very exciting to know you're the better-than-nothing of a discontented wife.

Don't be an idiot. Listen to me. You know how to talk. You know how to seduce with your tongue, aha! Cristóbal is the master of flat conversation. "What did you say?" "Why didn't you tell me?" "What were you going to say?" It's exasperating. To be waiting for a dialogue that never happens.

Does your husband make up for his silences in some way?

It isn't silence. It's repetition.

In other words, it's silence with noise.

Sometimes I don't follow you, Leo. All I know is that Cristóbal is an excessive, arrogant, pedantic man who thinks he's the papa of all jokesters. Let me tell you. If I want to take him to a party and he doesn't want to go, I say, "Come on, Cristóbal, everybody's going," and he just gives me an icy look and says: "No, I'm not going." Do you believe his petulance? Another thing: I'm so tired of the phrases he repeats over and over again. "I'm not asking you to believe me, Lavinia." "It would be better for you, Lavinia." "It's all right with me, Lavinia."

"Seeing is believing, Lavinia." "Just in case, Lavinia." "The man hasn't been born, Lavinia." He's a balloon of self-esteem. Tarzan's papa. Let me tell you.

Why don't you deflate him?

I don't think he's deflatable.

Make him think it would be cruelty on your part to resist him.

Shall I tell you how he'd respond? He'd treat me with contempt in public. He's already done it. If he thinks I'm doing well with him, he becomes irritated inside and waits for the opportunity to humiliate me in front of others. Then he feels victorious.

Of course, you don't dare attack him in public.

You know I don't. My upbringing wouldn't let me.

And in private? Don't you ever break your rule of conjugal perfection to criticize him in private?

I can't. Cristóbal has a terrible weapon against me. He threatens to make me a witness of what I can't see. That silences me.

Do you suspect?

I imagine. I imagine something intolerable that I don't want to be exposed to. Leo, I don't know anymore what I should feel, being married. With you, I do know what I feel.

Well, instead of matrimonial red tape, I give you love and admiration.

But you can't make them public.

In your heart, what do you reproach your husband for, Lavinia?

For not being able to hold me. There it is. The truth, what do you think? He could only oblige me. Understand? I'm tied to obligation. Pure and simple.

Can't you break off your relationship to your husband?

Don't be cynical, Leo. I've proposed leaving him and living with you. You've told me a thousand times not to, that living together would ruin what we have—

A perfect *affaire*!

That's what you say. How can you ask me now to leave my husband if I know you wouldn't accept me as your wife?

Darling, who told you to leave your husband and marry me?

Who's talking about marrying? Living together, that's all, my love.

You don't understand, Lavinia. I'm talking about you leaving your husband, not for me but for another husband.

Then what about you and me?

The same as always, darling. You married to Monsieur Quelconque, Mr. Nobody, and you and I free lovers forever after, with no domestic deadweight.

Really, just like now.

Except with a different *partenaire*.

Does that excite you, you cynic?

We'd be lovers and not create problems for anybody.

We wouldn't gain anything.

We wouldn't lose anything, either.

Then tell me what we gain if we don't lose.

Being apart so we want each other more. Distance increases desire. It's almost a Church dogma. Abelard and Heloise. Tristan and Isolde. You know.

I say we already have that. Explain what we would gain if I change husbands but continue as your lover.

I'll tell you later.

You're pushing me, Leo.

Toward what?

I'm just letting you know. Don't push me too much, my love.

3. Leo looks intently at the painting by Hokusai. That Oriental sea—the rougher it becomes, the more cold it gives off. A white sail rises from the waves, which are so intense, and the sail so fragile, that one would doubt the existence of anything else: the undiscovered country, said the Bard, from whose bourn no traveler returns. Is that sail tossed on the agitation of the elements an act of mercy? Does it keep us from seeing the imaginary land hidden by the fog? Not to mention landing on it? Is the mist a friendly invitation to remain where we are, not to go *beyond*, to that *là-bas* of the imagination where temptation and danger,

satisfaction and disappointment, the life of death tremble like flames? Beyond. Taking the next step. Not settling for the crooning hush of the sea and its white sirens. Hush: crush. Crush the song of the sirens with drowned resonances and hostile foam. Hush the streams that come down from the sierra looking for the way to the sea. Crush the sirens so they don't daze us. Daze and detain. Leo would have liked to set foot on the coast. Would he dare? Had he lived his life so far as a delicious conjuring trick, not daring to take the next step, the step from game to life, from shadow to wall, from appearance to touch, from touch to true absence? From observation of the sea to the certainties of terra firma, where all imaginary dangers are transformed into the greatest danger: no longer sensing any danger at all?

4. It's all true, Leo. Álvaro insults me, abuses me, doesn't appreciate me, mistreats me, but at the same time he complains violently that the world insults him, people abuse him, injustice victimizes him, and destiny mistreats him. That's his posture. He's simply giving me what the world, destiny, and people have given him. The worst thing is that deep inside, he believes this identifies us and, in a way, makes us partners in misfortune, so to speak. He makes us depend on each other in unhappiness. He and I. He creates an effect filled with blame.

Except that he can make you miserable, and you don't know how to harm him, Cordelia.

Are you insisting I abandon him completely?

I said no such thing. I'm not asking you to leave him. I'm asking you to do him harm.

Isn't it enough that he knows about us?

No. And I'll tell you why. Forgive me, Cordelia. Yesterday I went to visit your husband.

You saw Álvaro? Why? What happened?

First of all let me clarify: He called me. He reached out to me.

I don't understand. What did he want?

To require my presence.

Why?

To clarify my relationship with you.

And what did you tell him?

That it is reflection in absence that makes a husband undesirable, not his proximity.

Did he understand you? Because I don't really understand you.

Let both of you understand me, then. The great romantic rule is that distance stimulates desire. Tristan and Isolde. Abelard and Heloise.

I know. You always refer to those couples.

It's the great romantic rule. Unacceptable to modern promiscuity. We want immediate satisfaction. And we get it. Except that what is gotten right away is consumed quickly and then thrown in the trash. I don't know how a society can be called conservative when it doesn't conserve anything. We are engaged in an imperfect duel with the world.

Don't leave for the hills of Úbeda.

I mean that if the consumer society is the way it is, Abelard and Heloise are impossible. The rule takes a leap to tell us that absence separates us and makes us undesirable. We want to consume each other. If we can't, we don't hate each other, we simply ignore each other. Whoever isn't immediately available becomes old and decayed forever. Love has an expiration date, too, just like a bottle of milk. Everything conspires to disenchant us.

You forget that one can love somebody without that somebody knowing it.

Ah. That's the case with your husband.

It may be, if you insist.

Naturally. I insist. Of course I do.

Nothing you've told me includes my case.

Tell me.

Being the object of love that is ignorant of the fact.

I don't follow.

Álvaro doesn't know that even if I leave him for you, I'll go on loving him. And even though he hates me because of you, I don't know if Álvaro will go on loving me.

You know and he doesn't?

He doesn't know that I know.

Why?

Because he doesn't have an imagination for the good. He thinks and feels only in darkness.

Why does he bring me into it, Cordelia?

Because Álvaro doesn't love or hate. He fears vulnerability. He wants to know he's protected.

I repeat: Why me? I believe I'm the least qualified to give your husband protection.

You're thinking sentimentally. Remember who gave him a job at the Department of the Interior.

The secretary.

Who recommended him?

I did, because you asked me to.

Who are you?

Adviser to the secretary.

Who dismissed my husband?

The secretary, because Álvaro was insubordinate.

Did you approve the dismissal?

There was nothing else I could do. It was a bureaucratic decision. Don't think it was on account of you. Besides, it isn't that he was insubordinate. He simply didn't measure up. I'm sorry.

It doesn't matter. For my husband, you're the *factotum*. You hire. You fire. You seduce the wives of your employees. And just as you seduce them, you can abandon them. And then, Leo, then he would be there, ready to receive me with feigned anger, with disguised tenderness, he, Álvaro Meneses, who is who he is only because of favors received, becomes the giver, do you understand? The Good Samaritan, the sentimental Midas, oh, I don't know! He receives. He gives to me. That's his well-being.

You're the object of love who ought to be unaware of it.

Do you know something? I'm tired of the comedy of pain, devotion, and fidelity. Passion exhausts me. The problem with my husband is that things weren't as satisfactory as I hoped or as indifferent as he expected.

What did you want, Cordelia? Being a couple is an illness. It's a sickness. It isn't true that the couple is the perfect egotism between two people. The couple is shared hell.

You and I?

The exception that proves the rule.

Aren't there three of us, if we include Álvaro?

Tell me something, Cordelia: At some point in your marriage, did you ever have the feeling that you and your husband were a single person?

Yes. How horrible. As soon as I felt that, I began to step back.

Was I the way to distance yourself from the similarity to your husband?

In part. Not completely. Not always. It doesn't matter. The more you resemble yourself, the less you resemble your spouse. That's what I thought then. With you, there are no physical antipathies. Very strange. With you, there are no doubts about the amorous relationship.

Inevitable doubts?

Maybe.

Are you sure? You didn't break with Álvaro. Not completely, I mean.

I love each one in his own way. You and he.

Would you take the next step?

It depends. I don't know. What are you talking about?

About egotism disguised as generosity. I'm talking about giving. About giving oneself. About giving oneself completely. About going beyond the couple . . .

5. Leo could concentrate on the painting by Hokusai. On the other hand, it was difficult for him to concentrate on the two women, Lavinia

and Cordelia. In the painting, he could see what he wanted to. It was a transparent painting, pure glass open to the whim of one's eyes and the strength of one's imagination. For example: In the picture, it is raining on the landscape. To Leo's eyes, the rain is smoke. In the painting, the world floats past. To Leo's eyes, the world tends to be fixed, immobile, in the most immediate reality. Leo's daily reality? Or the reality of the imaginary painting? Aren't they, both of them—everyday reality, the virtual reality of art—permanent flux, everything flows? Leo understands it this way even though he doesn't feel it. Leo is the victim of a parceling of hours into immobile minutes that, no matter how they follow in succession, are identical among themselves or, at least, to themselves. But Hokusai's sea, though immobile in the painting (or within the painting), is like the gigantic spirit of the world. That surf along the Japanese coast, enclosed within the four sides of the painting, overflows them, the sea ascends to the sky, invades the beaches, sinks to the bottom of itself, devours itself in each singular, repeated wave.

The sea, like the figures in Piero della Francesca, looks *elsewhere, ailleurs, là-bas.* Leo knows there are no geographical *là-bas* to flee to, as Gauguin and Stevenson did. Gauguin's grandchildren receive the Paris papers by plane every day. Stevenson's grandchildren watch a serialized *Treasure Island* on television. The *là-bas,* the *other place,* the great undiscovered country, exists only in each person's soul, but there are beings with no soul, that is, with no imagination. And even those who have more than enough, which is what Leo thinks about himself, who use it up rapidly, soon become sated with their own fantasy and then feel the need to go *beyond,* farther than where they have already gone.

An enormous lassitude invades the entire being of Leo Casares when he thinks this, and then he returns to his bedroom and continues to look at the painting. The world is floating by. Grab it!

6. First he spoke with each woman and later with both of them together in the penthouse on Calle de Schiller. He had spoken to each about the other without revealing the nature of their relationships to him. They

were friends, barely acquaintances. To each—it was the most difficult point—he explained the particular beauty of the other. He admired each for her beauty—one so different from the other—and when he told this to the other, he did not add what the one listening—Lavinia, Cordelia—wanted to know, each more beautiful than the other. And since they could not say that about themselves, they waited for him to say: "She is very beautiful, but you're more beautiful." Or "not as beautiful as you." Or at least "there's no comparison to you." He kept this back. At the most, he told each one: "A woman is interesting not because she's beautiful but because she's *another* beauty."

He knew, looking at each one in turn, that he was looking for a woman who would have a little of Lavinia and a little of Cordelia. Since that woman did not exist, Leo preferred having both. The problem that was becoming acute, distressing, exciting, and filled with expectation was knowing how to bring them together, put them face-to-face, and observe what would happen when the two women who were his lovers met without knowing that each was a sexual partner of Leo's. Would they intuit it? Say it? When two are one, each experiences what Mallarmé calls "the evil of being two." What does the poet mean? That the amorous couple would like to be a perfect, indissoluble unity, and when they achieve it, they experience evil, the absolute evil of knowing yourself a lover and knowing, fatally, that you are separated from what you desire most in spite of having it?

Leo debates this question with himself, the lover of two women who do not know each other and whom he now invites to have a drink at the same time—seven in the evening—in the apartment that each one—Cordelia, Lavinia—knows and considers hers because each one has moved from the living room to the bedroom and from the bedroom to the bathroom and each one has used the same soap, the same shower, the same towel, the same bidet, and sometimes the same toothbrush (Cordelia never forgets to bring hers, Lavinia does: "What would my husband, Cristóbal, think if he found a toothbrush in my Louis Vuitton bag?").

Until now Leo has kept them apart thanks to a fortunate though hazardous act of juggling. Two balls in the air. One ball in each hand. Leo becomes irritated. In his life as a great dilettante, a great *enthusiast,* each step ahead has been transformed over time into a step backward if the next step forward is not taken in time. It is what he is experiencing now. Lassitude. Abulia. Lack of surprise. Wonder exhausted. The sea dries up. There is only a cliff that sinks to the bottom of a great cemetery of sand. A ravine whose crown is the great bare desert. The sea basin has to be filled again. Where is the surf, where are the sweet laments of the sea, where is the new, unheard-of, voracious foam that his existence demands in order to move forward? In order not to commit suicide in the name of unknown novelty?

Leo replaces on the mantelpiece the photograph hidden during Cordelia's and Lavinia's visits. It was the portrait of a man in his forties, handsome, with a thin face, his chin resting on two hands with long, very slim fingers. The dedication read: "To my adored son Leo, your father, Manuel."

7. Leo told them the good thing about absence when a couple falls in love but lives apart is that it keeps desire alive.

Lavinia did not agree. She said that absence does not stimulate desire, it kills it. And she added picturesquely: "If you're smart, don't stay apart."

Cordelia intervened with the opinion that absence is like the sweet but unbearable reserve of the next encounter.

"I've wanted to be at a distance without desiring," Leo claimed, leaving unstated the conclusion that neither woman would or could reach.

"I'd rather say stupid things than feel sorrow," Lavinia said in an eccentric way.

"Do you mean that's why you say them?" Leo said with a nasty smile.

"I don't dare oppose older people like the two of you," Lavinia said, returning his smile.

Leo guffawed in irritation. "I like women who, in spite of being women, are different."

Cordelia shrugged and made a disapproving face. Did Leo think that being a woman was a uniform? Weren't men, in any case, more similar to one another than any two women? Lavinia laughed. "We wear feathers like savages, we raise and lower our skirts following the dictates of fashion, whatever that means, we don't become bald, we don't have to shave (our faces), and our underwear isn't predictable, we're divine!"

Leo and Lavinia wanted to break the ice emanating from Cordelia's labored breathing. Suddenly, this simple conversation (this complicated presence of the three of them in the home of a shared lover) had placed Cordelia at an age disadvantage, something she was not accustomed to accepting, especially because it was the repeated insult her husband, Álvaro, threw up to her.

It was obvious that Álvaro's wife was twice the age of Cristóbal's. Except with Leo, Cordelia had never felt the contrast that the youthful presence of Lavinia imposed on her now. The two women were aware of the difference. They also confirmed that age did not matter to Leo.

His shaved, bluish skull, firm jawline, the spiderweb surrounding eyes by turn icy and smiling (mocking?), the impertinence of arched eyebrows, the sensuality of lips that were mocking (smiling?), everything gave this man whatever age he wanted to be, now with Lavinia, now with Cordelia.

The remarkable thing was that with both present, he did not stop being the man he was with each separately. They knew it. He knew it. Leo moved his pawns on a board that he controlled but one on which the pieces moved with an economy of chance very similar—he reflected—to the most dangerous kind of independence. At that moment he knew it was time for him to act, boldly, even impetuously, by surprise but with no vulgarity.

That is, for the moment when they had a drink together, Leo deferred his personal movements.

The two women left at the same time, not coming to any agreement except the decorous necessity of not remaining alone with Leo.

Before they leave (they have already picked up their handbags, and one has smoothed her skirt, the other her trousers, both of them their hair), Leo asks them:

"What do you think of Hokusai's painting? What does it say to you?"

Lavinia and Cordelia look at each other, disconcerted.

8. He wanted to execute everything to perfection. The distribution of spaces allowed all kinds of combinations. Taking the large bedroom as the center of the game, one entered it through a hall door or through two bathrooms at either side of the master bedroom (nuptial chamber?), both supplied with everything necessary: closet, hangers, shoe racks, changes of clothing, caftans. The usual. The doors of the bathrooms opened to the left and the right of the bedroom. The bedroom itself was an upholstered, carpeted cave perfumed by the Persian aroma of tapestries more than by any artificial flowering, giving freedom to bodies to perspire, to smell, if necessary, to stink in order not to lose the animality of the relationship, not to sanitize it until it was extinguished in a mere required function of mental substitutions because of a lack of physical incentives.

Leo Casares put on a blue-and-white-striped robe and amused himself thinking about how the two women would come out of each bathroom into the bedroom, each with an appointment, the other not knowing, the twin bathrooms separated by a single bed. He had exercised all afternoon at the gym without taking a shower afterward. He wanted to proclaim in an olfactory way his animal masculinity. He refused to displace probable offenses with splashes of lavender. He wanted to enjoy and be enjoyed within the Augustinian precept, so inculcated in Catholic school, of sex as the act of beasts. He felt the need to verify, with two women at the same time, that animal nature could coexist with the human, if Cordelia would finally accept anal intercourse or if Lavinia would be satisfied with frontal. Anal like animals. Frontal like heroes. But pleasure among the three of them, like gods.

He guessed correctly. At ten sharp, as he had asked each one, Cordelia opened the door on the left, Lavinia the door on the right.

Lavinia, as was her custom, appeared naked. Cordelia, as was hers, came in enveloped in a white caftan. In the center of the bedroom, Leo waited for them in a robe. He looked at one, then the other. He looked at the far wall of the bedroom. Hanging there was the Japanese painting of sea and sky, wave and cliff. He did not look at the women. He looked at the painting. Let them act. Let them understand that this was the next step in the relationship. That Leo wasn't asking them to love another man, different from him and also from their husbands, Álvaro and Cristóbal. That this was no longer enough to excite him. That the new rule was this: you and I, the three of us together, two women and a man.

This was what we needed. This was the necessary step toward the unknown, toward what comes next. The meeting of land and sea and sky. Would Lavinia and Cordelia understand that from this moment on, both were hostages to the man's desire? Would they dare to consummate that desire, or would they frustrate it and consequently break everything, erase the image of the painting, return to a situation not only earlier than the couples Leo-Lavinia, Leo-Cordelia, but also solely conjugal, Lavinia-Cristóbal, Cordelia-Álvaro, since he, Leo, would disappear forever from the lives of both women if they did not advance toward him now?

He avoided looking at them. That was what Hokusai's painting was there for. To fix Leo's attention on a work of art untouchable by sex, barely caressable by fingers, though destructible by hands. To distance Leo, at that moment, from an unhealthy curiosity to see the two women, observe their attitudes, guess at their intentions, judge Lavinia's young body in contrast to Cordelia's mature one, see how the two women saw each other or know if they even looked at each other, if they avoided looking at each other, if they had eyes only for their austere, distant, perhaps incomprehensible, perhaps seductive or seducible lord and master and voluntary slave Leo Casares.

Would the two women read Leo's thoughts? Would they realize that this mise-en-scène eliminated jealousy, extinguished envy, exiled banal prejudices? Who would dare, here and now, in the bedroom elevated to a personal sanctuary for Leo, who would dare offend the other two? Whoever gives offense, loses. And if one leaves, the couple remains. And if yesterday's couple doesn't remain, a new couple will be found tomorrow. A new game, always beginning, culminating now or never.

"It's a win-win situation," Leo murmured, summarizing what he knew they also knew, because after all, in fragments, here and there, over time, each couple (Leo-Lavinia, Leo-Cordelia) had said it or intuited it or thought it. Except that even in the most perfect geometry of joy deferred or premeditated cruelty, the demon of pleasure puts in an appearance, and Leo was doing battle with him now in order to stare at the painting and avoid looking at or being looked at by them.

"Of course beauty exists," he said in a very quiet voice. "But only for a moment."

The imperfect actuality of the beautiful had to be sacrificed. He thought about it. Did they know? Leo felt on the verge of an almost supernatural happiness and of too physical a misfortune. He felt doubts. The women revealed nothing. It had been easy to concentrate on each one separately. Would it be difficult to pay attention to both at the same time? In what order would the pleasures of each occur, the inevitable couple, the potential trio? Was the orgasm the little death or a transitory suicide? At that moment suicide and death attempted to personalize themselves in the feverish yet lucid mind of Leo. What did he want? To be rid of the husbands, Cristóbal and Álvaro? Or of the wives, Lavinia and Cordelia? Leo had prepared this scene in order to take the next step, to put to the test not the conjugal fidelity he knew had been overcome but the intensity of emotions, which he imagined had been postponed. He did not have to look at Lavinia (naked?) or Cordelia (caftan?) to know that the situation did not eliminate the villain of the piece, the green monster of jealousy. He did not need to see them to know this because he felt it in his own heart.

This was what alarmed him. That he imagined the step following the ménage à trois. It was the step toward reconstituting the couples. Not the return to conjugal ties. Not even the permanence of the trio but an alliance of the two women against him, against Leo, the two of them alone against the solitary man who proposed tonight to make love to both women only to reach the culminating point and abort the ecstasy, interrupt the pleasure in order to exasperate both and oblige them to desire once more, again, and again, and again . . .

He did not want to look at them just then. He would have liked to tell them that blind distance maintains the mystery, that he wanted them both far from him in order to continue to read them. He realized he had already said that. That instead of advancing in his purpose, he was moving backward, like a crab. That his imagination obliged him to go forward in order to overthrow any habit past, present, or future, to move toward perhaps unreachable possibilities without understanding that his desire for them could be a desire to begin all over again in order to love better.

Knowing what he already knows?

Forgetting everything?

What was the next step?

Everything configured an imperfect duel. Leo refused to look at them. He prayed that this scene would not make them tired of him, of themselves, of the irretrievable earlier situation. All of this flashed through his head; accepting habit was the greatest defeat, unacceptable to him. True, in the end, it was all an imperfect duel between desire and its consummation: repeatable or unrepeatable. Leo, with almost Edenic innocence (that's right, with fragile compassion for himself, he thought), wanted only today's satisfaction to leave us unsatisfied so we could desire and achieve the next day's satisfaction.

Would the women understand it this way? Why didn't they say anything? Why didn't they move? Would one of them—Cordelia or Lavinia—dare to destroy the proposed trio, tacitly believing that in this way they would return to the earlier couple? Or had he, Leo, destroyed forever all possible relations with them? Did they (Lavinia, Cordelia) realize that Leo had done them the favor of showing each one that her life was false, that the artifice offered by Leo was *the truth*, in spite of the artifice, just as in the Japanese painting?

"Everything I've done is for the sake of happy families."

How was he going to say this if he himself was incapable of believing it? Of believing *anything*? Even that these women might be happier with their husbands than with him?

This idea provoked irrepressible laughter in him. He decided to face them, laughing, gauging them, the two women. He, triumphant. This would be the propitious moment to bring the situation to a head. A laugh to absolve them and absolve himself, dispelling everything as a huge joke, an *exquisite corpse* of Leo's surrealist spirit. Or perhaps dazzling, almost diabolical laughter, defying the women's imagination, a fatal invitation to a shared copulation that would renew and even exceed relations among the three. The great pact, euphoric, gallant, transgressive, of Leo, Lavinia, and Cordelia.

He let them look at the Japanese painting. He turned on his heel to face the two women he had just imagined behind him, immobile, each one coming out of a bathroom, walking toward the bed they would share. Or moving away from the bed, returning to the bathrooms, disappearing . . .

"You need to have a great lack of imagination to break off an amorous relationship," Leo said to himself in a very low voice.

9. Sitting on the sofa in front of the picture of the turbulent sea and the immobile cliff, Leo smoked a light-tobacco cigarette, breaking his New Year's resolution: to give up all secondary vices. He allowed the spirals to add a transparent, fleeting coat to the painting. Why was the sea turbulent if the cliff did not move? Why was the physical world so capricious? In Leo's desire, on that night everything had to be transformed, crossed, multiplied. The sea would become calm. The coast would rise up murmuring, trembling, to culminate in a vast barren

plain populated with unknown bodies that would advance naked but wrapped in transparent black veils, like the figures of Manuel Rodríguez Lozano in the main room of the apartment on Calle de Schiller.

He did not identify those two bodies. They were not familiar. He noticed that he did not recognize the colors offered him by the world of the painting. They were too new, perhaps happy, in any case, frighteningly pure. The colors were pure and bold. The figures, on the other hand, seemed impure and uncertain.

Leo shook his head. He looked directly at the painting. It was pure glass. It was transparent. It was the perfect work of art. Each person put in it what he or she wanted to see. Nothing more. And nothing less. That was the miracle of the Japanese painting. It was a virtual work. It was pure emptiness as liquid as the air, as aerial as the ocean. It was an invisible mirror. It was an eternally renewed story . . .

10. When he went into the bathroom, he found the mirror smeared with toothpaste and the tube, used up, tossed carelessly into the wastebasket.

Leo shrugged. He did not want to calculate which of the two had used this bathroom.

Chorus of the Savage Families

they come from the north
they occupy the city of nuestra señora de la porciúncula de
los ángeles on the border with mexico
they come from the south
they occupy the city of tapatatapachula south of chiapas on the
    border
with guatemala
they divide up the city of los ángeles
the mexican mafia are the southsiders
the salvadoran mara sansalvatrucha are in control from thirteenth
    street
to central venice
the mestizos from venice thirteen to south central
the mexican wetbacks wherever night finds them
they invade the city of tapachula
they cross the coatán river
they vandalize silversmiths goldsmiths as they please
they steal orange saddles still redolent of
sacrificed cattle
they take off their pants to feel the down on the saddle
mix with the hair of their sex
the clicas confront the gangas of los ángeles
the salvadoran marassansalvatruchas against the
mexican mafia
the confrontation
each crew sends its big guys in front
its giant headbreaking fighters
the clash takes place at the devil's corner calle

666 and eighteen
the raza endures
the maras break your head stomp on you fuck you up
but the mexican babes reward you with kisses after the brawl
the maras announce their attacks in tapachula
they close the schools
but nobody can run away
the maras come down whistling from the volcanoes
they walk like spiders with spiders
they pull out sawed-off shotguns and daggers that they saw off
they control the train run from chiapas to tabasco
they tie their victims to the train track
the train cuts off their legs
the gang members disappear in the forest
they reappear in los ángeles
they specialize in drive-by shootings
firing at random from their cars
at their mexican rivals
they pretend to be mexicans their accent gives them away
captain bobby of the LAPD the los ángeles police
force is capturing them one by one
they come from the wars of ronaldanger ronaldranger
ronaldanger in central america
sons of
grandsons of
exiles who identify themselves with a tattoo on the arm and they
give themselves away with a false mexican accent
they hate mexico
the captain smiles he knows
send them back to salvador captain bobby?
no way
fly them back home?
no way
they say they are mexicans? send them back through mexico

let mexico deal with them
from the south
from soconusco
from the north
from california
they advance toward the center mexicocity
greattenochtitlán
baptismal water of the nahuas from sacramento to nicaragua
an interminable pilgrimage
from south to north from north to south
the mara salvatrucha gang and the mara dieciocho gang
rivals united by death
a hundred thousand members on the two borders
a hundred thousand gangs in mexico city
between pensil norte and los indios verdes
they announce themselves with graffiti in all the urban centers
black spray paint stylized letters
they dress like hoods heads shaved and tattooed
they have their hole in lost cities
lairs in iztapalapa
refuges in gustavo madero
they attack kill extort rape murder
leave mutilated bodies in the streets
their leaders are called commanders of the clica
their head is called "the sinister one"
they wait for christmas for their great slaughter
twenty-eight people murdered on the D.F. subway
twenty-one wounded
six children
they want the land burned from border to border
"let them be afraid of us"
they murder to frighten
they free to tell about it
they have dry skin and foaming mouths

they are the army of silence
they never speak
they communicate by signs

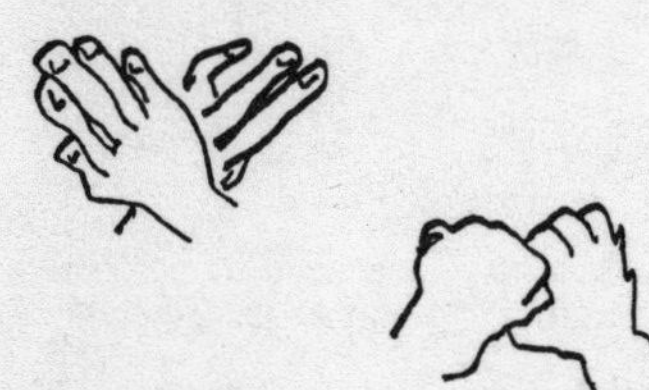

CALLE 8
CALLE 18
FLY AWAY,
BIRDS

Eternal Father

1. Each anniversary the father made an appointment with them in this old place next to the sunken park. The sunken park was not its official name, but Parque Luis G. Urbina, in honor of a poet of the last century. The popular name has survived the fame of the poet, and everybody gives as a direction "Take me to the sunken park," which is a cool, shaded urban depression in the midst of countless avenues and mute skyscrapers. Not a fierce oasis but a shadowy refuge. A green roof for lovers greener still. Even when you climb up from the park, you have the feeling that you're climbing down. The park is sinking, and the city is sinking along with it.

The three sisters—Julia, Genara, and Augusta—respond to their father's call on the day of the anniversary. For the rest of the year, they don't see or speak to one another. Genara makes pottery. Julia plays the violin. Augusta manages a bank, but she compensates for this lack of modesty with social work in working-class neighborhoods. Even though they don't search one another out, they are joined by the fact that they are daughters of the same father, and they do what they do in order to show their father that they don't need the inheritance. They refuse to receive a fatal inheritance because of the fact that they are their father's daughters. The three work as if they are not going to receive anything. Or perhaps as if they deserve to inherit only if they demonstrate from now on that with or without an inheritance, they can earn a living. Besides—except for Augusta—they do it with a humility calculated to offend or at least disconcert their father. Except for Augusta.

Is an inheritance won or lost? Augusta smiles at the thought. Do the sisters know which their father prefers? To offer the inheritance, although the three of them are perfect idlers? Or to save it until he finds out that the three of them are not waiting for the comfort of a promised bequest but are earning their livings without worrying about their father's desire? Or would their father be irritated if the sisters, instead of waiting idly for the testamentary period to be over, find occupations?

Their father is very severe. He would tell his daughters that the richer the family, the more ungrateful the descendants.

"You don't know how to value things. You didn't work your way up, like me. You feel like destiny's pampered darlings. Bah! Keep guessing whether you'll inherit or will be disinherited. And if you inherit, try to imagine how much I'll leave you."

He said that when children know how much they're going to inherit, they become ungrateful and stop calling.

"But you can revoke the inheritance at any moment, Papa."

Their father's gestures were somewhat truculent. "Who says I didn't do that already? You just keep sucking up to me if you don't want to starve."

"Let them wait," the father murmured before he went into the bathroom each morning. "What do you think? You should never hand over your money before you die. Have faith! Have hope! Be patient. Wait until I die."

He would say this and cackle before going in for his daily sauna. Augusta imagined him dissolving in sour vapors until he was changed into pure spirit.

"He was the regularity in our lives," Augusta said to Julia and Genara.

Julia had always thought her vocation was music. With or without the approval of her father, God willing, she would devote her life to playing the violin, indifferent to the famous inheritance. Genara says she prefers making pottery to the inheritance. A sum of money or owning real estate can't compare to the joy of creating a useful and beautiful object from essential clay: earth. And Augusta, the most disobedient, does not want to concede the game to humility or pride. She presides over a successful banking enterprise but pays her tribute to what she considers the ambiguous paternal inheritance with the rebellion of doing social work in proletarian districts.

Each sister knows what the other two have done. Only on the night of the anniversary, however, do the three see one another's faces, calculate how much they have aged, imagine what has happened to them during the past year, predict what the new one will bring: change, permanence, going backward, moving forward, kilos, wrinkles, hair color, contact lenses, fleeting styles . . .

On the anniversary, the three show up dressed in black. The three meet, at the new year, around a coffin.

2. The house in the sunken park scarcely deserves the name "house." It is an old bare garage with a sliding metal door and an improvised toilet on one side. The kitchen is part of the garage. An electric stove and a disconnected refrigerator. The adobe walls show weariness and a wounded color. The door clangs and sounds like prison bars. The sisters, familiar with the ritual, have each brought a seat. Julia a revolving piano stool. Genara a complicated beach chair with faded cloth strips. Augusta an easily transported folding chair.

They know they are going to spend many hours here without moving.

This was the testamentary decision of their father. For the ten years following my death, you will hold a wake for me on each anniversary of my birth in the same humble place where I was born: an old garage next to the sunken park.

This is my last will and testament. I want you to remember where the fortune comes from that you will inherit. From down below. Thanks to my effort. In virtue of—if you'll permit the irony—the vices you attribute to me. At the end of the decade, each one will receive her corresponding portion. I have no other condition but this one: to hold a respectful wake for me on each day of my birth. I don't care what you do for the rest of the year. Earn your living, not to oppose me but for your own good. I tell you this: There is no greater satisfaction than earning your bread by the etcetera. I could have left you the estate when I died. I would have condemned you to the idleness that is mother of all the etceteras. Now you are going to feel that inheriting is something more than a privilege. It is a reward. Not alms. In short, do what you want. Don't please me by doing what I would have wanted or not wanted you to do. In short, you know my condition: Do what you want, but don't get married. I don't want some loafer in trousers to enjoy my money and enslave you in the hope of filling his pockets. And don't have children. I'm a frustrated mathematician, and my calculations concern only three people. You, Augusta, Julia, and Genara. I don't need barnacles on my ship. I want to reach the final port unencumbered: I and my three adored daughters, sole possessors of all my affection, the love I give them, the love they give me, incomparable, incompatible.

3. Tonight the ten years prescribed as a condition of their father's will are over, and the three daughters prepare for the outcome. They arrived punctually (at nightfall), though Julia came early to light a long candle at each corner of the coffin. They arrive and give one another light, rapid, purely ceremonial kisses on the cheek. Each one knows she doesn't love the other two. No matter how Julia dissimulates with sweet gestures of affection. Genara disguises displeasure—real—as

well as love—nonexistent. Only Augusta appears with a sour face and crosses her arms.

The sisters don't speak to one another for a long time. Julia fusses over making certain the candles are lit. That they don't go out in spite of being very long. Augusta looks at her nails and doesn't say a word. Genara observes the ceiling of the garage as if it were the starry sky on a cold, clear winter night. Augusta, who knows her very well, murmurs quietly, "Tropics, we're in the tropics, fool."

Augusta doesn't hide the fact that her sisters bore her. Though her father bored her even more. The severe daughter corrects herself immediately. Saying "bored me" is a cheap way to debase her father. The truth is, he enervated her, made her uncomfortable. It has always been Augusta's opinion that their father was like flies. He had so many eyes he could see everything and wouldn't let himself be flattened by a slap. She would like to believe that recollection is all that remains of her father. He took care not to be simply a pious memory. This annual ceremony keeps him alive. Above all because of the unsettling question—more like a threat—that at the end of ten years, something will happen. And it won't be anything good, about that Augusta feels certain.

On the other hand, thinks the guileless Genara, after ten years the inheritance will be established. This doesn't concern her. She knows that the condition, which suspends for only a certain period of time the execution of the will, does not stop the daughters from acquiring a right to the inheritance. She looks at Augusta and understands that the oldest sister can read her thoughts. She considers her naive. To think that today, tonight, their father is going to resolve the enigma of his will is not to know the man.

Augusta would like to say to her sisters:

"Papa is deceiving us. He always deceived us. Deceit is his profession. He's like a smiling cardsharp." (There's a reason Genara always crossed herself when she saw her father.) (Genara avoids the piercing eyes of her older sister.) (Genara is superstitious.)

(Genara believes in the stars, lucky dates, black cats.) Augusta knows this and makes fun of her in secret. Their father also knows the power of superstition. He counts on it to keep the daughters unsettled year after year.

"Don't be superstitious," Augusta suddenly springs on Genara.

"What? What did you say?"

"Nothing."

"That's too bad," Julia gently intervenes.

"What?" Genara repeats.

"I said that's too bad. We ought to talk to one another. At least once a year."

"Do you know why we don't talk to one another?" Augusta interrupts inconsiderately.

Julia shakes her blond head.

"So Papa won't catch us."

Julia and Genara don't understand Augusta, and Augusta doesn't deign to clarify her words. She keeps her reasons to herself. The sisters exhaust her. They believe their father eventually will grow tired, and today, after a decade, he will free them of mourning so he himself can rest in peace.

This is a thought that, in a very different way, Julia and Genara share. Julia out of simple charity. That everything will conclude and everyone will be at peace. Be able to wear spring flower prints again. A pretty cream-colored dress with an asparagus print. A tailored dress with orchids on the lapel. Leave behind the mourning imposed by their father.

Julia believes more, much more, in the kindnesses of memory that her sisters, for different reasons, reject or malign. Julia selects the best moments from her recollection and puts them together in nosegays of happiness. Games, affections, roses. Her father's arms lifting her high. Her father's lap receiving the curled-up little girl. The father's hands . . .

"I was my father's little bird." The young woman smiles. "I was always at his side. In silence. I never contradicted him. I never was disrespectful. I never raised my voice to him."

Julia curbs her recollections as if her sisters can hear what she is thinking. She imagines that each of them at these moments does one of two things: She remembers or eliminates memories. Genara struggles against the memory of their father. She even makes the mistake of humming some tune from her childhood, revealing in this way what she does not wish to show.

Their father would accuse her: "You're a full-fledged lazy thing."

No, she wasn't lazy. She was indolent, which isn't the same thing. It isn't that she wouldn't or couldn't do things. She believed that in the end everything would work out, more or less, with no need for her to act. Perhaps she was a contented girl who, since she did not know how to lie, thought it better to be quiet. How could she call her father "daddy dear," like that hypocrite Julia, if she didn't believe it? No, she wasn't lazy. She avoided contradicting her father or fulfilling his expectations with regard to the affection he deserved. Perhaps Genara was simply walled inside her own childhood, distrustful of growing up in a world determined by the will of her father. What was wrong with that?

Only Augusta has sealed off her memory, carrying in her head a ridiculous mnemonic: the numbers of her bank accounts. But it is she, unexpectedly, who breaks the round of their silences by placing a hand on the coffin.

"He spent his life putting us to the test. How good that this is over."

The sisters look at her with disbelief, amazement, and grievance.

"It's true," wails Genara. "It's true. He's dead."

"He died," Julia insists without wanting to. "What a shame."

"Died, yes," Augusta concludes. She insists, "Do you remember? Do you remember that list of prohibitions he wrote out by hand and tacked at the entrance to the bathroom?"

"You don't remember that," Julia said with easy tolerance.

"I remember, and so do you, Julia," Augusta continued with the air of a gardener who cuts the overgrown grass and can't interrupt the work without changing the rhythm or destroying a bed of roses by mistake. "Don't touch yourself, don't look at yourself. Avoid mirrors. Get dressed in the dark. Bathe in your shift. Don't touch yourself. Don't look at yourself. Don't look at a man. Don't let anyone touch you. Don't go out alone. Sit in the first row at the movies even if it makes you cross-eyed. Don't let yourself be looked at. Put a fig leaf on the art prints at school. Better yet: Don't go to school anymore. I'll be your school. Come, Augusta, sit on my lap so I can teach you. Go on, Genara, let me dress and undress you while you close your eyes and imagine I'm the sweetheart I forbid you to have. Lie down, Julia, I'll sing you to sleep. You girls don't have a mother. I'll be father and mother both, I'll—"

"I'd say that a father can be a perverse mother." Augusta twisted her lips.

Julia touched Augusta's hand. "There were only good intentions."

"Then why do I remember them as perversions?"

"Because the perverse one is you," Genara dared to say, and Augusta slapped her, a heavy blow of square, metallic Caesarian rings.

Julia stopped Augusta's hand and looked incredulously at the signs of authority that adorned her sister's long, curved fingers.

"What, haven't you ever worn rings?" the oldest sister said haughtily.

Julia bowed her head artfully. "The one I wanted Papa denied me. He forbade the three of us. But you know that."

Genara bit a finger and thought of everything she and perhaps Augusta and certainly Julia had not done in their lives out of fear of their father while their father was alive. And now, now that he had been dead for ten years . . .

". . . why don't we have the courage to do everything he prohibited while he was alive?"

"Out of respect," Julia said sweetly, though with a lost, disoriented look, as if she had been left hanging on the last word said before this one.

"Out of greed," Augusta stated brusquely. "Because we don't want to lose the inheritance. Be honest with the devil. Because we're afraid to disobey him even though he's dead."

"Because you're afraid of him," Julia said almost inaudibly, "the way you were when he was alive?"

"Papa and his damn time periods. All of you wait. I'm coming. You'll find out. Have faith, have faith, have faith!"

Augusta's voice was lost in its own echo. Julia and Genara knew that echo. It was what Augusta emitted in order not to cry or shout. The two sisters approached to embrace her, caressing her head with its short, bristly, masculine hair. Genara, without meaning to, pulled off one of Augusta's earrings.

"Oh! You're always so clumsy."

Julia and Genara withdrew their hands from Augusta's head as if they had profaned an authority that competed only with that of the father. She was the oldest sister, though her authority always remained beneath that of their father, feeding a sense of inferiority in her that only increased her throbbing pride.

"Don't deceive yourselves," Augusta said to her sisters. "Don't forget his disdainful, pitying, triumphant face. 'Don't upset yourself, my girl. Don't deceive yourself. Don't lower your eyes when I come in. Without us you aren't . . .' "

"What is she saying?" said Julia.

"What are you saying?" asked Genara.

"Nothing." Augusta blew her nose with the cambric handkerchief she always had tucked in the long sleeve of her dress.

That "nothing" was the most certain reflection of the belief Augusta had been cultivating since their father had disappeared and she suddenly realized that now authority fell to the oldest sister. She felt overwhelmed by the suspicion that the fact of his death made the authority fall to her and was the inheritance that Augusta at one time rejected and longed for in a conflict with no way out that only her sisters, if they understood it, would dare to resolve for her. But Augusta not only did not want to explain to Julia and Genara what she herself could not really understand, she also wanted to admit that she, Augusta, felt uncomfortable with their father's moral inheritance.

"Do you remember Mama?" Julia interrupted Augusta's clouded thoughts in a melancholy way.

"Yes and no."

"What do you mean?"

"That it wasn't necessary to invent her. She was *there*. We came out of her and never really stopped living in her belly."

"How awful. Not even when she died?"

Genara listened with languid patience to this exchange between Augusta and Julia. Rocking back and forth on her heels, she valued being the patient sister, the one who counted up the longest times. She knew her sisters did not recognize that virtue—or any others—in her. They did not offend her, Julia with her goodness, Augusta with her arrogance. They simply ignored her. Julia because she was good, so good she could not admit comparable goodness in another sister. It was enough for Genara to know this to also know that Julia, despite her sweetness, was condemned to the flames of a hell where simulation is not admitted. Julia was good because it suited her, because she wanted to go to heaven, when in reality, good people are the largest population in hell. Being good may deceive God but not the devil.

Did Genara engage in this mental construct in order to acquit Augusta of an unhappy fate? She glanced at the oldest sister, and behind the hard facade, she guessed at a weakness disguised by the abrupt way Augusta had of distancing herself from emotion. Which was why it surprised and moved Genara when her sister emitted the echo of a sob. What do we expect of the unexpected? Are these actions sincere or calculated? Genara reflected: Augusta didn't allow herself to be carried away because of emotion or love for their father but because of absence of faith. Have faith, have faith. It was the chorus of a single voice. If Julia's modesty was pure hypocrisy, then Augusta's bitter will was a weak comedy put on to defy the father and, paradoxically, refuse to assume the authority that was hers as firstborn. An excuse. An evasion. Telling the father that at least one of his daughters was rebellious, obstinate, and wicked. As if the father didn't know how to see through filial farces and humiliate Augusta with the punishment of pity.

That is why Genara is languid and patient. That is why she persists in dressing in an old-fashioned way, with her hair rolled high like a dark tower and makeup typical of Joan Crawford in the 1940s.

Mouth very wide and very red. Eyes very open. Brows somewhat skeptical. And an expression very etcetera, as their father would say. She would say "imposed," because it was true. Genara felt like a caricature of another time and knew it was because her fiction had become her reality. Joan Crawford in the 1940s. *Mildred Pierce*. Despite the modesty of its owner, her black silk one-piece dress turned out to be provocative, striking. Genara wanted to provoke only sorrow and consolation.

It's true: In the annual reunions, there was a latent desire for consolation. Let the three, so different among themselves, remember that in the end, they were sisters. Perhaps they were brought together, with dissimilar masks, by the unconfessed pride of being daughters of a man so original and so involved in their origins, their powerful and eternal father. They were proud. The proof was in their reluctance to offer consolation to one another. That was why Genara was patient. In the depths of her soul, she believed that at some point mercy would flower, the three would embrace—as in that fleeting instant when Augusta, so unlike herself, made an echo of her sorrow.

"Save us from all responsibility," murmured Genara.

"What did you say?" Augusta was tense.

"Nothing, sister. It just occurred to me that since he isn't with us, in reality we can do whatever we want."

"You know very well why we can't do what we want."

"Why?"

"You know very well. It's in the will. It's our duty."

"It's greed."

"Or risk." Julia intervened for the first time. "Do you realize our lives would be at risk if we disobey? I mean, we don't know the cost of disobedience—"

"That doesn't matter anymore," Genara interrupted. "We've done our duty for nine years."

"That's why it would be foolish to avoid it now without knowing what would have happened if—"

Augusta interrupted in a tone comparable to Julia's: "Don't be stupid. We've done what we had to do. Let's not speculate on what would have happened if we had disobeyed Papa."

"We still can disobey him," Genara said slyly.

"Be quiet," Augusta continued. "It no longer makes sense, since we did obey him. We've come to the point he asked us to reach."

"And if we disobey him?" Genara insisted with childish perversity. "Just once?"

Julia did not hide her horror. She did not have to say anything to indicate the fear caused in her by the idea of having done their duty for nine years of obedience only to stop at the finish line, violate the promise, and be left forever without knowing the truth. She would have liked to scratch Genara, knock down her soaring hairdo of a film noir diva. Since that didn't correspond to her personality—a personality constructed so meticulously—Julia cried instead, her head leaning against the coffin. Mercy was safer than the passivity of the modest Genara or the authoritarian hardness of the proud Augusta, both pale imitations of their father. Perhaps similar to what their mother was in life. She didn't know. She hadn't known Mama.

Still, when she thought this, Julia felt she was better than her sisters. Superior to them. And along with pride, there beat in Julia a kind of loss or personal mourning for having been condemned, when Papa died, to always wear mourning, unnecessary for those people—members of the orchestra, the conductor, the stagehands—who did not know who the violinist's father was and what obligations he had imposed on her. Julia had auditioned for the orchestra under a false name. Only she knew the rule imposed by Papa, which was why she could have worn her youthful clothes, the springtime prints, the low necklines, the daring two-piece bathing suits when she was invited to Agua Azul to swim.

And she didn't. Why? Did she want to create mystery? Her colleagues in the orchestra did not dare to ask "Why do you always wear black?" and since black eventually became fashionable for women during those nine years and stopped being only a sign of mourning, no one said anything, and Julia let it be known that for her, even morning rehearsals were gala occasions. But she soon realized that her orchestra colleagues knew nothing about the existence of Julia's papa, that she could be named Julia without attracting anyone's attention.

Julia smiled sweetly at her sisters. "I've never doubted. Have you?"

Genara and Augusta observed her with indifference. Julia did not back down.

"Do you know something? I have faith. I'm not referring to the circumstances that bring us together today. Do you know what faith is? It's believing without condition, independent of circumstances. Faith is understanding that facts don't change the world. Faith moves everything. Faith is true even if it's absurd."

"Do you need to believe to live?" said Genara, suddenly enthralled by the primitive beauty, straight blond hair, blue eyes, bows on her head, clean hands, of the youngest sister. How well she trimmed her nails. How well she repeated the catechism. She seemed to be a saint.

"We can't be good if we don't believe," replied Julia. "Without faith, we'd be cynics."

"Faith can become blindness," Augusta scoffed in all seriousness. "Cynicism is better."

"No, no," Julia pleaded. "It's better for us to be credulous than cynical." And resting her hand on Augusta's shoulder: "Don't be afraid."

Augusta looked at her sister with contempt.

Genara looked at them with involuntary complicity.

"Don't you think that Papa was basically a simple man and that we're the complicated ones? Because if you think about it, Papa was something as simple as his smell of cologne."

"He smelled of incense," said an insolent Augusta.

"Tobacco," Julia said with a smile.

"Sweat," Augusta insisted. "He smelled of sour sweat."

"He was a courteous, ceremonious man." Julia blinked.

"Rigid, pretentious." Augusta grimaced.

"Very hardworking?" Julia inquired.

"He made other people work and took advantage of them," said a disagreeable Augusta.

"Just like you." Genara simulated a joking little smile.

"Genara, don't accuse your sister. It isn't nice," Julia intervened.

"Don't worry." Genara rested a hand on Julia's shoulder, like a comrade. Julia moved away from Genara.

"What's wrong?"

"I don't like—"

"You don't like what?"

"Nothing. Forget it. What were you going to say?"

"It doesn't matter."

"No, tell me, everything matters."

"Don't worry. I accept my limitations. It's my rule."

Augusta remained silent during this exchange. Looking at Julia, she thought that the innocent only complicate life for others. Evil, envy, malice, the great defects, the whole treasury of transgressions, when they appear, have the virtue of uprooting moral hypocrisy, false appearances, deceptive piety. In any event, Augusta was bored by her sisters. She was bored *with* her sisters. She laughed to herself. What could she do to liven up the vigil? It was not a question of making anyone indignant. And she did not want to give in to the provocation programmed ahead of time by their absent father. How many times had she confirmed that he did not want to talk about his daughters, he wanted his daughters to talk about him. That was why Augusta tended to remain silent while the sisters argued over who would speak first: You tell, no: you first . . . Augusta feared that the secret silence she knew how to maintain would be transformed, through the good works of her clumsy sisters, into a simple exchange of confidences. Didn't Augusta know, because she was the oldest and the one who first knew the father, that each time she wanted to keep something to herself, her desire was violated by their severe, vengeful, brutal father?

"What secret are you hiding, Augusta?"

"Nothing, Papa. You're imagining things."

"Of course I am. I imagine nothing less than the truth. Why do you keep your secrets from me? Are you ashamed? Or do you like to make me angry?"

"No, Papa. You're wrong."

"One of two things, my girl. You're acting this way out of the shame pleasure gives you or because of the pleasure shame gives you. There's not much to think about. You don't fool me, etcetera."

The young Augusta (she was forty-three now) blushed, and Papa looked at her with an air of understanding and forgiveness.

"The miserable bully." Augusta struggled to open the coffin. The sisters screamed and stopped her. Augusta only wanted to liven up the vigil. The younger sisters returned to their quibbling.

"What is it you don't . . . ?"

"Nothing. What were you going to—?"

"It doesn't mat—"

"No, tell me."

"That his motives were doubtful," murmured Augusta. "Doubtful, if not disagreeable."

She realized that Julia and Genara were paying attention to her. Had that been their father's triumph: to demand attention when they didn't give it to him? For a second, the oldest sister saw herself in the dead man's coffin, shut in, without the sisters coming to save her from silent asphyxiation. And she realized that at this moment, being in a coffin meant occupying their father's position.

This idea shamed and disturbed Augusta. She reproached herself for the temptation to supplant their father, even in death. She gave herself over to a kind of extremely personal prayer. Authority is authoritarian. Be careful, Augusta, try to give your sisters the grace that Papa denied them, try to make them content with the rhythms of life now that this long period of mourning is coming to an end, make them look outside, make them feel things like the temperature, the seasons, the neglected birds, the barking of dogs, the silence of butterflies, how the grass grows, everything Papa denied us because even a dragonfly could compete for the attention he deserved.

Augusta realized she wasn't saying what went through her mind because she was sure that when she tried to speak, she would have no voice. Was that their father's original theft: to make her mute? Did their father know that Augusta wouldn't dare ask Julia and Genara what they feared and desired when the time period imposed by him was concluded: Now we're going to live together at last, come, sisters, the time of wandering the world looking for other pleasures and other companions is over, I'm afraid that after tonight we'll all go mad, mad in our solitude, tied to calendars of fire, led to the very brink of old age . . . Together. Here in the sunken park. Together and finally free.

It was enough to listen to them.

"He never told us 'Don't leave, come live with me . . .' "

"We were all grown up, Julia, we had no reason to continue at his side."

"Despicable, despicable, that's what he called us."

"Well, now you see, he ground us down, he left us free."

"To do what? To die?"

"No, to go on living."

"Despicable."

"What freedom? Let me tell you. The freedom to come here every year to obey him as if he were alive."

"But if we didn't—"

"Say it, Julia, but if we didn't—"

"We'd be left without the inheritance."

"What an injustice! Isn't it?"

"But I thought when he was gone . . ."

"That we'd do what we wanted?"

"Why can't we see him?"

"He died."

"Do you think so? Maybe he just can't be seen, that's all."

"No. He died. This is just a ceremony. An empty ritual. Wake up. Realize what's happening."

"How hard you can be behind that cherub's face."

Augusta heard them without saying a word. She told herself she accepted fears because by now she was used to them. Now what would she have to accustom herself to when the custom of the annual ceremony around their father's coffin was ended? What would become of their lives? Would they change? Or was custom now too strong?

She imagined, with a mixture of revulsion and humor, that the three of them, Genara and Julia and, why not, she herself, Augusta, would continue returning year after year to the garage in the sunken park, celebrating this action that none of the three could classify as commitment, ceremony, duty, habit, caprice, because by dint of repetition, it had become a part of their lives. Would they dare to end the custom? Or would it become the customary obligation in a hollow formula, an empty ritual? How to maintain the sensation of menace in the duty their father had awarded them? Was that feeling his real inheritance: keep me alive, daughters, live on the alert, questioning, dissatisfied? Why do you think I've imposed these time periods on you? Out of love, my pretty babies, out of love and nothing but! To avoid your falling into the softness of girls with good inheritances pursued by a legion of lecherous upstarts, starving good-for-nothings who don't love you, cannot adore you as I do.

4. "Do you remember that we put on shifts and blindfolds when we bathed?"

"To avoid sin."

"That's what he said."

"Do you realize, Julia, that we ourselves never saw him naked, in the bathroom, shaving?"

"Didn't he let us see him?"

"Or didn't he let us see ourselves?"

As the hours passed, Augusta thought their father had told her that he didn't want his daughters to see him age. That he wanted to be forever young for them. An attractive father, in short.

"Do you know Papa's age when he died?" Augusta asked them.

Genara and Julia looked at each other. "I don't know . . . seventy, eighty? A hundred?"

"Do you remember him as an old man?"

"What?"

"Yes, old."

"No, young, always young. He ate the years."

Genara laughed a great deal. "It isn't the only thing he ate."

"We remember him young."

"But we never saw him young."

"Because we only have photographs of the young Papa."

"Isn't there a single photo of the old Papa?"

"What's the difference between what used to be and what was?"

"The difference between conscience and memory," Augusta pronounced, and the sisters laughed because they didn't understand.

Instead, they asked themselves: Why wasn't an obituary published in the papers? Wasn't that your obligation, Augusta? No, you said you'd do it, Genara. Don't look at me, said Julia.

5. Later, Augusta wondered if there was a difference between conscience and memory. She thought there was. Memory happens today. We remember today. Conscience is always repentance buried in the past. We prefer to forget.

She didn't say this because then she feels guilty for saying what she shouldn't only because her words dictate themselves and demand to be spoken even though Augusta does not know how to and cannot measure the reach of speaking. At times she felt that someone was speaking through her, someone who did understand the difference between conscience and memory, not her, the simple vehicle of a mysterious voice that demanded to be heard.

Whose voice was it?

Was it she herself at another stage of her life, a past or future time when Augusta could understand why her recollections of the past all occurred today but her conscious present always happened in another time, never in the present?

"His demands were excessive," murmured Genara. "He made the

three of us face all the temptations and asked us to beg him for the power to resist them."

"Speak clearly," said Julia. "Who was going to resist the temptation, he or us?"

"Who knows? He was very capricious." Genara shook her head.

"He was a tyrant," Julia said abruptly, and Genara looked at her in astonishment, Augusta with anticipatory resignation.

Julia had been the pampered little girl and then the defender of their father's image. This abrupt change was inexplicable unless, Augusta thought, Julia is trying to tell us that her devotion to Papa wasn't foolishness but an act of conscious will that still led to faith. Augusta took advantage of the moment.

"Did you ever see Papa naked?"

Julia became embarrassed. Then she assented. "And you?" she said to Augusta.

"I don't know if I saw him." The older sister smiled maliciously. "I have the impression that I smelled him. He smelled of dirt, of crusted shit, of sweaty armpits, of crotch, of—"

"That's not true." Julia covered her sister's mouth with her hand. "His body smelled of Yardley cologne, his hair of Barry's Tricopherous—"

"He smelled of urine," Augusta said with a smile, pleased by Julia's reaction, her instantaneous fall into the cult to their father, her weakness. "He was a disgusting, miserly, tyrannical old man."

"Generous, sweet, loving." Julia sobbed with a fictitious air of repentance.

"A miser," Augusta continued with repressed ferocity. "He was buried with his gold. He forbade us the comfort that was our right. He was like a wicked king. He would have liked to be buried with his servants and his cattle. And look how he achieved it. He saw our faces. He buried the three of us in his pyramid, like vile concubines. You're right, Julia, he was a tyrant."

"A good tyrant, a humane tyrant." Julia lowered her eyes.

"An authoritarian father," added Genara. "Isn't that what we wanted? A strong man who would tell us 'Do this, don't do that . . .' Without him, we would have been lost in the world."

"And he knew it." Augusta's response was biting. "That's why he abused his authority. What did he imagine? That if we were independent, we would steal his power? Why didn't he understand that our being free would make him stronger?" She looked at Julia scornfully. "He knew that you, Julia, had a vocation for slavery."

"And you didn't?" Julia moaned. "You did, too. That's why you're here, that's why the three of us are still here . . . because we're *slaves*."

"Don't be dense. You still haven't learned that being a tyrant is a courtesy that frees us from freedom."

Augusta kept the next thought to herself: Being a tyrant is also being a pedant. And a teacher: A pedant is before anything else the one who educates little boys. And girls. A pedagogue.

This was a pedantic pedagogical prelude to what obsessed Augusta. The fear that they had been the ones who created the tyrant, though he hadn't wanted it. He'd simply walked by naked. They were the ones who had dressed him. Because they themselves needed power but were afraid of exercising it. They preferred to give it to a poor passerby who was dumbfounded when the crown and ermine cape fell on him. They breathed a sigh of relief. They were rid of the burden.

Power is cowardice, it is our cowardice, Augusta wanted to say aloud and did not dare because she was assailed by the conviction that her sisters would not understand her words. And did not *deserve* them. Power is cowardice because we do not dare to be powerful. Power is the hot potato we have to pass to a poor, defenseless, naked, mediocre, unimaginative, spiritually disconsolate individual, a stupid creature whom we anoint with the crown and cover with the ermine that we ourselves do not have the courage to wear. The emperor is the distorted reflection of our impotence. The trouble is that once we hand him the scepter, the chosen one believes himself to be truly powerful. He does not know his strength is borrowed. He assumes it without responsibility because we are the responsible ones. We can no longer replace the chief. Only by killing him. Hanging him by the feet in a public square. Cornering him like a rat in a gloomy courtyard. Condemning him to oblivion in the most forsaken part of a prison filled with chronic ailments and deprived of words.

Then a great laugh sounds in Augusta's hollow skull. You're wrong, you innocent. I'll end my days on the Riviera. I'll occupy an entire floor of a New York hotel. I'll sail around the Caribbean on my yacht. A Roman legion of tough guys will protect me. I won't need more than twenty dollars in my pocket. My credit will be unlimited. Just like my laugh. Etcetera.

It made no sense to explain this to her sisters. Why disillusion them? Why deprive them of the illusion of an autonomous, powerful father capable of performing miracles, above all, the miracle of loving his daughters with infinite tenderness and compassion? Why drive them away from their annual visit around the paternal coffin? Why, as a matter of fact, bring them happiness?

Augusta shrugged discreetly. Let us continue to believe that when we gave all our power to our father, we would be exempt not only from responsibility. We would be exempt from blame.

How to explain this to her sisters when Genara was saying foolishness?

"I asked him to say I was all white inside. And he saw me black."

"Did he tell you that?"

"His eyes said it all. 'You have a black soul, Genara. Try to redeem yourself. Confess your sins.' "

"Which ones?" an irritated Augusta intervened.

"His," Genara continued. "When I knelt to make my confession, what came out of my mouth was an inventory of Papa's sins, old conservative, aristocratic, tiresome, you're not a decadent noble, as you imagine, you're shameless and arrogant, you're the worst kind of tyrant, you're the plebeian climber who doesn't know how to enjoy the goods of the world because he reverts to his low origins and isn't accustomed to controlling from above. He staggers. He stumbles. And he reacts by punishing. He abuses his impunity. Doesn't recognize his errors. Punishes others because he can't punish himself."

Genara dissolved into something resembling a gentle spring rain, though her weeping was acute, repeating "Errors, errors," until she had stripped the word of meaning.

"Which errors, Genara?" Julia looked at her sister, but it was Augusta who spoke, fearing too lifeless a response from Genara, the potter unaccustomed to giving free rein to her feelings beyond a certain limit, as if the world were a large clay vase that could become misshapen with one turn too many of the wheel. The truth is, she felt challenged, displaced by the unexpected vigor of Genara's words.

"Resentment," Augusta continued. "The worst sin. Suffering because of other people's happiness. Envying other people's luck. Looking out for other people's faults while you hide your own."

She stopped because once again her thoughts were faster than her words and her doubt that she'd be understood even greater. The fact is that Augusta wanted to take on, as much as possible, the faults of their father. Promising happiness in the future, never today. Defer. Defer. Defer everything. Replace necessity with hope and hope with ceremony. Talk about what we don't know and neither does he. Make us feel ignorant. Foment mistaken ideas about and within each of his daughters. Concede things too early or too late. Nothing at the opportune moment, Papa, do you realize that? Nothing at the right time, everything deferred until tomorrow, or console yourselves because you already have it and don't know it. Always leaving us in uncertainty. Do we threaten him or does he threaten us? Can we make him disappear in a cloud of smoke? Or can he make us disappear? Does he accept each plea as the homage he deserves, the gift that is requested of him, or the illusion that is fulfilled when we ask him for it? When we dare to doubt his wisdom, he escapes from us, transforming his ignorance into shrewdness.

Did her sisters realize the number of things they didn't do because they feared Papa? Did they realize that with this story about the day of the anniversary, they continued to defer their lives like old cars in a parking lot without a meter?

"Just count the demands he made on us from the time we were little girls. Didn't it give us a mischievous joy to do the opposite of what he asked? Isn't that what he expected of us, the pleasure of disobedience followed by redemptive penance? He condemned us. We condemned him. He treated us like simple things in his greenhouse, like little seeds subject to the temperature of his glance, the ice of his disapproval. He kept us in a larval state."

"He has us," Genara interrupted. "I mean in a larval state."

Augusta stopped speaking. She withdrew into herself again. She did not know if her silence was hers alone or had joined the clamor of everything not said by the sisters who had gathered tonight, for the last time, in the garage in the sunken park where Papa had been born.

6. Augusta looked with judicious cruelty at Julia. She thought the innocence of the youngest sister was—or could become—only the mask of a profound malice. She had her doubts. Did Julia get what she wanted? Had she used the restrictions of the inheritance to do the only thing she was interested in doing: playing the violin? Augusta did not want to believe in Julia's virginal appearance. She was always surrounded by men, in every orchestra. Perhaps she did not give the men her name. Perhaps she did not give her real name: Julia. Perhaps she went to bed with the clarinetist, let herself be fingered by the cellist, strummed with the guitarist, pulled out the stops with the man who played saxophone, blew with the piccolo player, all in a vast, harmonic, anonymous concupiscence. Julia had arranged things so her true life would be impenetrable.

Genara, on the other hand, was transparent. If she were to insinuate love affairs—something she had never done—her lies would have more weight than any truth. Possibly she had temptations. What she did not have were opportunities. All day at the wheel, with muddied hands and a stained brown apron. A woman with her sleeves rolled up and her hair pulled back. A strand falling over her forehead. Her legs spread as if she were giving birth to clay.

She once said about their father: "He watched over us as if we were his dolls." This passivity of a toy was the nature, not second but first and who knows if original, of the sister who was a potter. Waiting for the anniversary was by now part of her customary life. What would she do without this expectation? Genara was not a woman capable of living without the routine of her calendar. In her heart, she wanted this situation to go on until the end of time. Not doing anything but ceramics. Being the potter to a vast world of clay by rescuing the clay and giving it the shape of human work. Was each worker a rival of God?

Genara would never accept this reasoning. She did not want to do anything that might contradict Papa's wishes, though the contradiction in those wishes was that whatever she did, she would be both good and evil. Good if she obeyed instead of rebelling but evil because she disobeyed Papa. Genara wondered if this was the father's policy—leave his daughters in permanent suspense, condemn them if they acted and also if they did not act? Genara felt very sad about having this conflict. Julia at least deceived others. Genara deceived herself. She continued to be a doll sitting on their father's quilted bed, surrounded by flickering candles beneath a crucifix without nails where the figure of Our Lord seemed to be flying toward heaven.

Then their father came out of the bathroom, freshly shaved, smelling of Yardley lavender, of Barry's Tricopherous, of Mum deodorant, with his colorless eyes and his hair of a yearning albino, to say: "I'm going to show you something you've never seen before."

He always says it and disappears into the remains of the steam in the sauna.

None of them dares enter the sauna. Not even their father's bathroom.

All the cosmetics and lavenders cannot lubricate the dry skin of the father who disappears walking backward, at a turtle's pace, into the mists of his daily grooming routine.

A ceremonious man.

A rigid man.

The regularity of our lives.

A man who simultaneously represents the fantasy and the business of the world. Etcetera.

"Give us peace," Genara says in a frightened voice.

"That depends on us, not on him," interjects Augusta. "We shouldn't give him a minute's peace. We have to criticize him, question him, unmask him, pull the rabbits out of the hat, take the deck of cards out of his hands. Look, our father is a carnival magician, a theatrical wizard, a sorcerer at a fair. He is an illusion. A phantom. A sheet blown by the wind."

Julia again collapsed into tears, her arms around the coffin. Like a *Pietà* among sisters, the group composed itself when Genara and Augusta embraced Julia, dissolved when they separated, somewhat confused about their own attitudes, and embraced again as if a decisive warning—night falling, a period of time about to conclude, the end of the plot—obliged them to defend themselves, united, against their father's terrorist wishes, whatever they might be.

Augusta looked at them with a measure of scorn. The ten years would be over tonight. They had obeyed Papa's posthumous decision. And then what? Would they never meet again? Would they consider the test decade concluded, the time in which each one had done as she wished knowing that this was what their father wanted, for them to do what he didn't want them to do only in order to blame them and in this way oblige them to continue, as they had for the past ten years, this ceremony determined by him, almost as an act of contrition?

Is this what their father wanted? To have daughters who were free but poor (Genara), free but modest (Julia), prosperous but in the end obedient (Augusta)? And what were the three sisters looking for? To prove to their father that they could live without the inheritance even though they lived waiting for the inheritance? Because otherwise, why would they come to the annual appointment in the sunken park? Had none of them thought about rebelling against the command of their damn paterfamilias? Excluding herself from the ceremony? Telling him to go to hell?

"Did you ever think about disobeying Papa? Did one of you ever say to yourself: 'Enough, I've had it up to here. That's it. We don't know if this is a game or a punishment? In any case, it's tyranny.' Did you ever think that?" Augusta spoke in a moderate way. She looked at her sisters without emotion. "Let's see who is capable, right now, of leaving here," she continued.

"And be left not knowing the secret?" Julia said again.

"Never finding out how it all ended?" Genara supported her again. "Nobody leaves a movie without finding out how it all turned out. We can't even stand for somebody to tell us about it later."

"No matter the consequences?" Julia asked with the timidity of a novice.

Augusta did not reply. It was better, she thought, to leave the answer in the air. Or in the heart of each sister. She made a calculation. Genara could go. Julia and Augusta would remain. Julia and Genara could go. Augusta would remain alone.

The mere idea broke her impassivity. She felt real terror. Terror of absence. Knowing herself absent. Alone. Absent: stripped of inspiration or speculation. Incapable of even commemorating her own death.

How was she going to flee their father? Didn't she know that ten years after his death, as soon as the secret of the inheritance was revealed, their father would impose a new time period? And what new surprise was waiting for them when they completed this one, and the next, and the next? Didn't he once say before he went in for his daily sauna, "If I begin something, I don't stop"?

The twelve strokes of midnight sounded in San José Insurgentes.

7. Six in the morning had sounded. Genara stretched. She had fallen asleep against her will. The beach chair was comfortable.

Poor Julia, sitting all night on a piano stool. She wasn't there. Genara looked for her. Julia was putting on makeup, looking at herself in a pocket mirror. Pink powder. Purple lipstick. Eyeliner. Mascara. All arranged on top of the coffin.

Julia fluffed out her hair. She adjusted her bra. "Well, the next appointment is with the notary. We'll see one another then. This business of a conditional will is so annoying! Well, we've fulfilled the condition. Now we'll execute the will. Though we never lost our rights . . . did we?"

"Unless we're disinherited," Augusta said from the shadows in the garage.

"What are you talking about!" Julia laughed. "It's obvious you two didn't know Papa. He's a saint."

Julia pushed the clanking metal door. Light from the sunken park came in. Birds were chirping. Julia went out. A Mustang convertible was parked in front of the garage. A boy in a short-sleeved shirt with the collar open whistled at Julia and opened the door for her. He didn't have the courtesy to get out of the car. This didn't seem to bother Julia. She got in, sat down beside the handsome young man, and gave him a peck on the cheek.

Julia looked young and agile, as if she had shed a gigantic bearskin.

She did not look back. The car took off. She had forgotten the revolving stool.

Genara smoothed her skirt and arranged her blouse. She looked at Augusta, wanting to ask her questions. She felt a hunger to understand. Julia would not explain anything to her. Julia's world was resolved, free of problems. She was sure about inheriting. She had left.

Would Augusta explain things to her?

Genara took her handbag, a Gucci copy, and went toward the metal door. She insisted on looking at Augusta. The oldest sister did not return her look. Disorientation was etched on Genara's features. She knew she could not expect anything of Augusta. She armed herself with patience. She was prepared to continue living her life decorously. In solitude. In front of the wheel. And then in front of the television set. With a cold supper on a tray.

"The three of us will see one another with the notary, won't we?"

She put a foot outside the garage.

The foot stopped in midair.

8. Augusta did not see the actions of her sisters. Let them leave. Let them feel free. Let them run from their father. As if they could get away from him. As if the executors weren't loyal to their father. What an idea.

Augusta will remain beside the father's coffin. She will fulfill the funeral ritual until she herself occupies the father's coffin.

She is the heir.

Choruscodaconrad

the violence, the violence

A NOTE ON THE TYPE

This book is set in Fournier, a typeface named for Pierre Simon Fournier, the youngest son of a French printing family. He started out engraving woodblocks and large capitals, then moved on to fonts of type. In 1736 he began his own foundry and made several important contributions in the field of type design; he is said to have cut 147 alphabets of his own creation. Fournier is probably best remembered as the designer of St. Augustine Ordinaire, a face that served as the model for Monotype's Fournier, which was released in 1925.

ALSO AVAILABLE BY CARLOS FUENTES

DIANA:
THE GODDESS WHO HUNTS ALONE

They met for the first time at a New Year's Eve Party in Mexico, just as the sixties gave way to the seventies: the blonde movie actress Diana Soren, and the internationally renowned writer. For two months they lived together on location. While passions burned Diana became a slave to irrational manias and nocturnal frights. The story becomes one of paranoia and the FBI, of sexual jealousy and the Black Panthers.

*

'A writer with things to say and beauties worth expressing ... his prose lifts off and really flies'
TIMES LITERARY SUPPLEMENT

*

ISBN 9 780 7475 2541 7 · PAPERBACK · £5.99

THE CRYSTAL FRONTIER

Young José Francisco, Mexican and headstrong, grows up in Texas, determined to write about the border world – the immigrants and illegals, Mexican poverty and Yankee prosperity – stories to break the stand-off of silence with a victory shout, to shatter at last the crystal frontier.

*

'Exotic, beautifully written and powerfully convincing'
MAIL ON SUNDAY

*

ISBN 9 780 7475 4394 7 · PAPERBACK · £6.99

THE YEARS WITH LAURA DIAZ

Like Fuentes's masterpiece *The Death of Artemio Cruz*, the action in this novel begins in the state of Veracruz and moves to Mexico City. Now the principal figure Fuentes's first female protagonist, the extraordinary Laura Díaz. From 1905 to 1978 Fuentes traces Laura Díaz; a life filled with a multitude of witty, heartbreaking scenes and the sounds and colours, tastes and scents of Mexico. Laura grows into a politically committed artist who is also a wife and mother, a lover of great men, and a complicated and alluring heroine whose bravery prevails despite her losing a brother, son, and grandson to the darkest forces of Mexico's turbulent, often corrupt politics. Hers is a life which has helped to affect the course of history, and it is the story of a woman who has loved and understood with unflinching honesty.

*

'An admirable novel'
THE TIMES

'In this portrait of men and women swept along by great events, and determined to be on the side of the angels, Fuentes has invested the often colourless world of politics with romantic ardour'
SUNDAY TELEGRAPH

*

ISBN 9 780 7475 5766 1 · PAPERBACK · £7.99

B L O O M S B U R Y

INEZ

In this magical story of love and art, life and death, Carlos Fuentes entwines two narratives: one tells of the passion of orchestra conductor Gabriel Atlan-Ferrara for red-haired Mexican diva, Inez Prada; the other of the first encounter in human history between a man and a woman. Berlioz's music for *The Damnation of Faust* brings Atlan-Ferrara and Inez together, and continues to resound on every page of this haunting work. At the same time, the emergent love of neh-el and ah-nel – the original lovers – reminds us of the Faustian pact of love and death.

The link between these two stories is a beautiful crystal seal that belongs to Atlan-Ferrara, who is obsessed by its meaning. Maybe this ancient and seductive object gives its bearer the ability to read unknown languages and hear music of impossible beauty…

*

'A complex, focused novel suffused with death… Strange spirits and the impetus of Atlan-Ferrara's inevitable end haunt the book, yet music is the great symbol of hope and transcendence.'
THE TIMES

'Dazzling . . . The translation by Margaret Sayers Paden is elegant'
NEW YORK TIMES BOOK REVIEW

'Passionate ... a paean to music and musical genius, to romantic love and the mysterious sources of language and creativity'
NEWSDAY

*

ISBN 9 780 7475 6816 2 · PAPERBACK · £6.99

BLOOMSBURY